MW00769740

MISCHIEF MAKER

BRUCE NESMITH

CRAIG MARTELLE, INC.

First Edition

Cover art © Vivid Covers | www.VividCovers.com
Editing by Jean Rabe

Published by
Craig Martelle, Inc.
https://craigmartelle.com
PO Box 10235, Fairbanks, AK 99710
United States of America

For more information on this and other books by Bruce Nesmith, you can find him at his Amazon Author Page - https://www.amazon.com/Bruce-Nesmith/e/B08YKG3DM4/
Or on Facebook - https://www.facebook.com/Bruce-Nesmith-Author-103769655138160

To my wife and love of my life, Laurie, for all her support.
To those who support any author by buying and reading their
books, I salute you. I couldn't keep telling these stories if it weren't
for you and for the support team surrounding me. No one works
alone in this business.

STAGE SHOW

N ow, who would like to shoot me in the face?"

Uncomfortable laughter rippled through the high school auditorium. The Kiwanis Club had rented it for this summer fundraiser. It was an older building, which was pretty common for this Chicago suburb, and the raised, wooden stage had a classic red curtain behind it that I appreciated.

I admit it, I love being on stage. Having the audience in the proverbial palm of my hand, manipulating their emotions, is a natural high. I looked out over the faces staring up at me; a good mixture of young and old filled the seats. A few stood in the back. Usually, the crowd tended toward the older side because magicians are not as popular with the young, which also meant fewer smartphones recording my act.

I knew what they saw on the stage. Tall and fair-skinned, with long, slicked back blonde hair, the Magnificent Keystone cut a somewhat dashing figure, attractive but falling just short of handsome. A narrow, curved nose like a hawk's beak punctuated my somewhat narrow face. The daring twinkle in my blue eyes and the confident, knowing smile suggested everything would be all right. The Magnificent Keystone could be trusted to entertain and thrill them with amazing feats of magic. From a distance my tuxedo was impeccable, I hoped. Up close, the faintly worn patches on the elbows and the slightly frayed cuffs were more noticeable.

"Surely someone here is brave enough to help me? How about you, ma'am?" I added a sly grin as I pointed to a rather wide older woman.

She turned red and vigorously shook her head. But the man next to her, likely her husband, stood and marched his way up to the stage. Oh, great. A military man. You can always tell by their gait. Soldiers always made this particular trick a bit more difficult.

"Would someone be a gentleman and help the lovely lady up on the stage?" I quipped, eliciting laughter from the audience. The old man laughed good-naturedly too.

"And what is your name?" I asked, holding a microphone in front of him.

"Winston," he replied, his mouth too close causing feedback.

"Have you ever fired a gun before?"

"Yes, sir. In the army."

"World War I or II?"

That got another laugh.

"Vietnam."

"My mistake," I said with an exaggerated bow. "A round of applause for Winston and all our other brave servicemen. Your country owes you a debt."

"Esmeralda?" I said after the brief applause died down.

My assistant sauntered to the front of the stage, showing off the over-sized Smith & Wesson Magnum revolver to the audience by holding it high over her head. All good female magician's assistants saunter. The high cut, red sequined outfit was snug on her body. Great legs are also a must; anything to distract the audience.

A more famous magician would have a young, pretty, tall, blonde assistant with a dazzling smile. Esme was a short, curvy Latina and clearly younger than me. Her black hair was pulled back tight, emphasizing her round face and bright smile. Esmeralda was her idea for a stage name.

"Now, Winston, I have here a single bullet."

I began to pat all my pockets as if I was unable to find what I was looking for. The audience laughed again generously. Humor and stagecraft are two of the best tools for any performer.

Esmeralda strolled over behind me and thrust her hand firmly into my back pocket. I jumped wide-eyed, as if I had been goosed or pinched. More scattered laughter. With an overly dramatic roll of her eyes, she handed me a single bullet retrieved from that pocket.

"Thank you, dear," I said sheepishly, acting like I was trying to preserve my dignity.

"Now, Winston, here is a stylus. I'd like you to scratch a symbol, maybe a letter of the alphabet, into the soft lead of this bullet."

"Anything?" the old man asked.

"Any symbol you want," I reassured him.

He labored for a moment with the metal stylus. I held my breath; more than one older person had slipped and jabbed themselves at this point. Nothing stops a magic act quicker than a real injury, no matter how mild. Fortunately, he had a steady hand.

"Thank you," I said, refusing to accept the proffered bullet. I let Esme take it.

"Now, if you would be so good as to tell the audience what you inscribed on the bullet."

"The letter R. For Raske. That's me. Winston Raske."

"Esmeralda, would you please verify that? Winston here looks a bit shady," I said, pantomiming a squinty-eyed once over of the harmless old man. That drew a few chuckles from the audience.

"It kind of looks like an R," she said, turning the bullet different ways. "But you know men have horrible hand-writing."

"That's right!" shouted his wife from the audience. More laughter.

"Esmeralda, it's time to load the gun," I said loudly and dramatically. "Unfortunately Winston, the insurance company won't let us have you do that."

That would have been true, assuming that the insurance company even knew about this trick. Insurance for any trick involving guns was hideously expensive. Of course, a few hundred years ago I wouldn't have needed sleight of hand to do this trick.

Esmeralda loaded the bullet into the revolver, taking great pains to show Winston the back of the loaded bullet and the other empty chambers. He nodded in satisfaction.

"Notice I have not touched the gun or the bullet at any time," I said, moving to one end of the stage to take my mark.

Esme directed Winston to the other side, setting the gun on a small table next to him. He began to reach for it and she slapped his hand, eliciting snickers. She shook her finger at him dramatically. Esme took two steps forward, then spun and looked at him with narrow, distrustful eyes. Winston held his hands up with a grin.

She walked over to me and with a flourish produced a blindfold. My eyes grew wide and I shook my head vigor-ously. She stamped her foot and gave me her best 'mom' look. I sheepishly took the blindfold and put it on.

Esme returned to Winston, and I surreptitiously lifted the

blindfold an inch so I could see under it. I put my finger to my lips and pantomimed a shushing face to the audience, which *ooohed* on cue. Now Esme put the gun in Winston's hand, raised it, and pointed it in my general direction. His hand quivered under the weight and she clamped down on it while the audience twittered. Releasing it again, it quivered again and she clamped down again.

Looking exasperated, she dragged the table over to him and levered it up to about chin height with the telescoping stanchion. She set the pistol and his hand on the table with a satisfied pose. The audience liked that. Moving behind him, she looked down the barrel and shook her head in dismay. More laughter.

She took two colorful wooden blocks used in a previous trick and put them on either side of the pistol, to direct the aim, causing more chuckles. She looked at Winston dubiously, then pulled some duct tape out of a box of props and began taping the whole assembly. The audience really laughed at that.

Finally satisfied, she looked over at me and stamped her foot sharply. I lifted my shoulders sheepishly and let go of the blindfold. She strode quickly over to me and roughly adjusted the cloth. I could hear the people in the crowd whispering. At the same time, she deftly slipped the real bullet that she had palmed when loading the gun, into my mouth.

Though I was blind, I knew what was happening now from endless practice and many previous shows. She walked back to Winston and counted to three with her fingers, hand held high so the audience could see it. Winston probably strained, but nothing happened.

"Oops!" I heard her say loudly. "The safety."

Now I just had to wait. A few moments later there was a loud bang. Not as loud as a real gunshot, but loud enough. I launched myself backward, jerking my head. The fall would hurt. It always hurt, but such is the price of the show. The audience gasped, I heard several cries. I heard Esmeralda's footsteps racing to me. Winston was probably struggling with the duct taped assembly, conveniently unable to rush to my assistance.

I ripped the mask from my face and waved her off as I staggered drunkenly to my feet. Baring my teeth, I showed the audience the bullet between them. Esmeralda, now back with Winston, cut the duct tape, freeing his hands. I strode confidently to him. Esmeralda whispered in his ear and he held out his hands. I spit the bullet into them. I could see the crude R inscribed on it. A quick chill shivered down my spine.

"Is that the bullet you marked?" I asked loudly, suppressing my sudden case of nerves.

"Yes." Amazement tinged his voice. The audience applauded wildly.

P acking up went rather smoothly. I had a few people that wanted to chat after the show, which is pretty common. Esme had a guy trying to get her number, which is also par for the course, but they were all gone now. Only the janitor remained somewhere in the building, waiting for us to leave so he could lock up.

The parking lot was poorly lit by tall pole lights. My van was parked near the door for obvious reasons. It was mostly loaded. It also had a large raven perched on it. Like really big, like those ravens at the Tower of London if you've ever seen them. I tossed him a bit of jerky from my pocket; I always keep some there for him. Manny caught it deftly and swallowed it whole.

"I'll never understand why you take that bird everywhere," Esme said, giving Manny a sour glance. "You don't even use him in the act. I bet you could train him."

"Yeah, yeah. You keep saying that. And I keep telling you—"

"—he's too big and intimidating—" she sing-songed in time with me.

"—for an act."

Manny has been with me for ages, more a companion than a pet. I don't cage him. Sometimes I'm not sure if he belongs to me or it is the other way around.

With a single flap, Manny glided onto my shoulder. He is lighter than he looks, which is true of all birds, but he likes to dig in his claws. I've learned not to wince and to put extra pads in the shoulders of my coats. He hasn't soiled them for a while now.

"Well I think he's got great stage presence," she said, holding out a piece of jerky for him. I wasn't the only one who made sure to have snacks for Manny. He took it gently with a sharp, black beak that was as long as one of her fingers.

"I think we've got everything." I closed the wheeled aluminum packing crate. "See if you can find the janitor to lock up while I load this."

Esme went back inside and I pushed the crate to the van.

"Hey, Keystone. I gotta question for ya," I heard as a shadow detached itself from the wall. I recognized him from the audience. He had been standing in the back, a middle-aged man with dark hair, a noticeable potbelly, and about four days of unshaven beard growth. I had taken him for a party crasher just there to snag some free food.

"I always have time for my fans, but can you make it quick? I'd like to get home."

"Sure thing," he said, walking quickly toward me. "I was just wondering how ya dodged that bullet."

Manny lifted off my shoulder with a loud screech. He may be a grumpy old bird, but I've learned to trust certain reactions from him. I ducked behind the storage crate as the man lifted his hand and pointed at me. I didn't get a good look, but I thought he had a gun. I'd love to say this is the first time someone wanted to shoot me.

I gave the wheeled storage crate a hard shove in his direction, and I heard it hit him as I scrambled to hide behind the van. There was a gunshot. The movies underplay how loud a real gunshot is, especially up close. Yet even with my ears ringing I heard Manny screech again, followed by a deep-throated scream.

Most people have never tangled with a ferocious attack raven. Too bad I didn't have one. Instead, I have Manny, but he was doing just fine. Of course, my bird would never admit to doing anything to intentionally defend me; it would be all about the man's glasses or some other shiny bauble around his face.

"Fucking bird! Get it off me!"

Being a true idiot, I peeked around the back of the van. Clutching his scalp, the man turned and hustled toward a dark-colored sedan. The door slammed and the car peeled out. I tried to see the license plate, but it looked like he had it deliberately covered with mud.

"What happened?" I heard Esme say from the door.

"Get back inside!" I shouted.

"What? Why!"

"I just got shot at."

"Where? Who was it?" She stepped farther out. The irony of her standing there looking for my assailant while I cowered behind a crate was not lost on me.

The Arlington Heights police arrived quickly enough. But that was the only thing that was fast. I had to go to the station to talk to a detective and fill out endless pages of paperwork. It was almost dawn before I was done.

"A dark-colored sedan? An average height white guy? Is that the best you can do Mr. Keystone?" Detective Ananda asked. Even after all these hours we still weren't on a first-name basis. Maybe it was because I let him fill out some of the paperwork with my stage name before giving him my real one.

"In that parking lot? Under those lights? You're lucky I got that much," I lied. I got a pretty good look at his face, and though it wasn't anyone I knew, I'd rather the police not dig into my life any deeper than necessary. If it needed to be taken care of, I would do it myself. I could feel a slow burn building inside me.

He gave me a sour look and typed away on his computer using only two fingers. How did I get the one cop who couldn't type?

I have a penchant for practical jokes, and this guy was irritating me. I had slowly been working his metal in/out basket toward the edge of the desk. Who has one of those anymore? Detective Ananda, that's who. The back two legs were just barely on the edge of the desk now. The slightest bump would send the whole thing tumbling.

"We recovered the bullet and some blood. Maybe the labs will turn up something. There's a backlog, so it might take a few weeks."

"Let me guess, no injuries, no rush."

He just gave me that sour look again.

"Can I go now?"

"I suppose," he grunted.

"Thanks for coming in and making a report," he said, clearly not meaning it.

"You've been an absolute peach, Detective Ananda. A real paragon of law enforcement efficiency."

I hustled out of the squad room before he could look up what 'paragon' meant. Esme was waiting in the lobby, still in her costume, but with a coat over it. Behind me, I heard the metal basket crash and Detective Ananda curse. Served him right.

"It's about time Lowell," Esme said crossly. "So are they going to catch the guy? And why did someone shoot at you in the first place? Are you in trouble again?"

"Whoa, slow down. No, I really doubt they will catch the guy. They don't have a lot to work on."

"And whose god damn fault is that?" Her face darkened in anger.

"Hey, it was dark!"

"Someone fucking shoots at me, I remember what they look like."

"I didn't get a good look at him. Next time I'll tell him to shoot at you instead."

"Really, no clue why he was shooting at you?"

"How should I know?"

"You were playing cards again, weren't you?"

"What? No! I told you. I'm done with that," I said defensively. "The other players don't appreciate it when they find out what I do for a living."

I reached out and pulled an ace of hearts from her hair with a grin. She smacked my hand. Well, I'm mostly done with that. I'm too good at poker to not play every now and then. It helps pay the bills. But I didn't owe anyone money at the moment, and I hadn't pissed anyone off lately, so it probably wasn't related. I hoped.

"Liar. I bet you got caught cheating again. And now the mob is after you."

"The mob? What is this, the sixties'?"

"Whatever. It's still your fault," she sulked.

"Esme," I said, taking her hands. "I'm okay. I'm going to be okay. You're okay. This isn't about some poker game. I really don't know why it happened."

She sighed deeply. I could see tears, anger, and fear warring with each other in her face.

"That's not really better, Lowell. Not knowing is worse than knowing. What are we going to do?"

"Change our names, run away to Mexico and become tattoo artists."

She laughed, short and bitter while wiping a tear.

"If you fucking get killed, I swear I'll have you buried in the city dump. Face down."

"So that's a no to Mexico?"

2

MOON KIN

The sun was coming up when Esme finally dropped me back off at my houseboat. The *Voluspa* is a single story forty-three footer, just shy of an eyesore, but it's in good shape underneath the faded paint and rusty railings. I don't stay in one place for long, so it suits me better than a house or an apartment. Not that I could afford a house.

For the past few years I've used a berth on Fox Lake, one of the farther out suburbs of Chicago. Glen Garrison let me park my boat there in exchange for doing odd jobs on his property. During the winter he let me dry dock it there too, a great arrangement for a perennially broke stage magician.

I was tired and cranky, but I need to eat first. Manny normally flies off to do his thing when I get to the boat, but tonight he flew in with me. Contrary to appearances, I don't own him. He sticks with me because he wants to, even when I change cities, and frequently flies off for days at a time. I'm not really sure why he keeps coming back, but I appreciate the company. I sat to eat and Manny hopped onto the table.

"What do you have there?" I asked, seeing something shiny in his beak.

He dropped a bullet on the table. I picked it up and saw it was the bullet I used in the show, the one that Raske has scratched his mark into. I could have sworn I had left it in my pocket. I spun it around and looked at the crude 'R.' The curved top was a pair of angled straight lines, as you would expect. The joint at the bottom of the curve didn't meet the straight edge on the left, leaving a gap.

It was a raido, an old Norse rune. Old Norse writings were a hobby of mine. Raido represented a journey, usually an unexpected one. I hate omens. They make the scars on my chest itch. The scars on my chest were itching now.

"Yeah, I saw that. You trying to tell me we have to move again, Manny?"

He cawed his displeasure and turned his back on me. He doesn't like being called Manny, which is perhaps why I do it.

"So it's the silent treatment then? Fine. I'm too tired to argue.'"

I'm not stupid. I don't ignore omens, and I don't ignore Manny—at least not for long. I spent the next day preparing the houseboat. It's not as much work as it sounds because I normally keep it rigged for unwelcome visitors. I was pretty sure I was going to have uninvited company soon.

As an extra precaution, I dug out my Sig Sauer P229 and cleaned it. I'm not a gun nut, but the internet told me it's small, light, and reliable, and the internet wouldn't lie to me. I have a conceal carry permit, but I hate taking advantage of it unless I have a really good reason. Right now I believed I had a really good reason.

I was too tired to stay awake any longer, so I locked up and crawled into my unmade bed. The gun went under my pillow. I don't know where Manny went, but I hoped he would keep watch for me.

Despite my precautions, it was an uneventful week. Each night I sat on the top deck sipping my favorite pale ale, and on Friday at midnight I reverently brought out the box. Intricately carved with Viking-style figures and old Norse runes, it did not appear to have a lid.

I worked the hidden latch and opened it. Inside were nine velvet-lined cavities, six of which were empty. Two contained fruits the size of large apples but shaped more like pomegranates, pale yellow with darker yellow stripes. The last cavity held a quarter wedge of that same fruit. There was no sign of browning or decay.

Retrieving a knife with an antler horn handle, I carefully sliced a narrow sliver. It was so thin I could hold it up to the sky and see the moon through it. I reverently laid the slice on my tongue and let it rest there.

The taste, like a cross between a pear and an apple, but better, brought back memories of old times and better days. I let it dissolve as slowly as I could, trying not to cry. Then I carefully resealed and stowed the box.

I spent the rest of that night on the deck, under the stars and moon, remembering the night sky of my home. A place I was exiled from.

Esme was due at the *Voluspa* soon. We were going to have a late Sunday dinner and go over the program for our next series of shows. I try to change up the tricks to fit the crowd. It also helps keep us sharp.

Looking out the window and down the length of the pier, I saw them. Two men, thin and not particularly tall, wearing long coats. Who wears long coats in the summer? If they wanted to blend in, they were failing.

They didn't walk down the pier so much as glide. Their hands appeared empty, but who knew what was under those coats. I had a bad feeling. There isn't anywhere to run on a boat, or I would have fled. There wasn't enough time to cast off and sail out on the lake either. I thought about jumping overboard, but I doubted I could swim away fast enough if they intended harm.

I eased the safety off the Sig Sauer and made sure it was loose in the holster. I took down the boat's fire ax and set it where I could reach it. Then I turned off the lights and waited for them in the dark. The two intruders stepped onto my boat without hesitating. They opened the flimsy door and simultaneously drew short, gleaming swords from under their coats. Swords that glowed like moonlight.

The men were nearly twins with nearly flawless, pale faces and delicate features that would make any male runway model jealous. The long hair of the one on the right was silvery blond and fine as spider silk. The one on the left's hair was equally fine, but a few shades darker. Their hair moved in the still night as if a breeze was blowing—but there was no wind. I saw the short points of their ears peeking out between the moving strands. Alfar. Most people would have called them elves. Most people would be right.

"You can't hide from us in the dark," said the one on the right.

"It is well known that the alfar can see in the dark. I strive to be a hospitable host to my guests," I answered. I shifted a bit to the left and hefted my ax.

"Then you know why we are here," he replied, shifting to match me.

"I'm afraid I only made dinner for two. You'll have to share."

"Go ahead. Make jokes," said the silvery blond. It won't change what is going to happen."

"Then indulge me. Who sent you?"

"I'll whisper the name in your ear as you're dying."

"You know, it's a dangerous thing to threaten a magician."

"You have no real magic. No seidr. No galdr."

"Let's test that," I said with a smirk. I thrust my hand forward and intoned, "Andask reyna!"

I had him all lined up, so I tapped the release cord with my foot. The spear gun bolt lodged in his stomach and he went down, twitching. In this dim light I was hoping it looked like magic. The other alfr flowed across the room like a rushing river. I tried to pull the Sig Sauer, but with a flick of his wrist he cut my hand and the gun dropped to the floor from my numb fingers. Damn, he was fast.

I straightened, stood tall and took a deep breath. I've been ready to die for a long time. If today was that day I would meet it face on, not as a coward. The alfr stood equally calm with his blade pointed at my chest. I could see he wanted me to flinch or show fear; he would have to learn to live with disappointment.

His free hand was a blur striking me in the stomach and doubling me over. So much for meeting my fate on my feet. The pommel of the sword struck my left shoulder, dropping me to my knees. His free hand gripped my hair and tipped my face up to look at him while I gasped for air.

"On your knees, where you belong," he said with a smile. The alfar have a way of smiling that looks benign, but if you know them like I do, it's full of menace.

"I've been meaning to get a trim for a while. Keep it long in back, will you?"

"More jokes. How typical."

"Speaking of typical, why have the alfar stooped to being assassins?"

"Allegiances have shifted while you've been away." He placed the edge of the glowing blade against my throat.

"Whose bidding do you do? Whose puppet are you?" I demanded with a snarl.

"Unlike my brother, I made no bargain with you. The price of his death will be to die in ignorance."

The gunshot was deafeningly loud in the small cabin. The alfr's look of surprise as the bullet ripped through his throat from left to right was short-lived. Blood splattered all over my face and hair. The assassin feebly tried to slice me, then fell to the deck dead. His partner was finally still and hopefully just as dead.

Esme stood in the doorway holding a gun in both hands. Her hands began to shake and her knees started to buckle. I rushed to catch her with my good arm. Her gun clattered to the deck. It looked like one of the cheaper Taurus pistols, but it had been effective. I lowered her to the deck and collapsed next to her.

"Is he—?"

"Yes. Don't look. It's better if you don't look."

"Oh god, you're bleeding!"

"I'm not hurt." I said gently. Sadly, my Black Sabbath t-shirt was probably ruined though.

"He... he was going to kill you, wasn't he?" she asked uncertainly.

"Yes, I believe he was."

A flicker of relief crossed her face. It's one thing to kill to protect, it's another to kill an innocent.

"Thank god. I saw you... I saw him... that knife... so big—"

"It was a sword, actually."

"He really was going to—"

"Yes. You saved me by shooting the man that was going to kill me. You are my knight in shining armor."

"The police—"

"We will, but not just yet."

"The other one... did you—?"

"Yes. It was self-defense. They were both here to hurt me."

Esme buried her face in my chest. Great sobs wracked her body as she clung to me. I cradled her silently. What could I say? After a little while, she recovered and stood shakily. Esme is strong. A little shock and trauma weren't going to keep her down for long.

Manny chose that moment to land on the deck rail, silently for once. I gave him a stern look. He hopped over to the alfr with the spear in his belly. I really hoped he wasn't in a scavenger mood. He could be a very messy eater.

"Sure," I said quietly to him. "Now you show up. What good is having a ferocious attack raven if he's never around?"

"Are you hurt?" Esme asked, ignoring my bird.

"My shoulder is a bit sore, but I'll recover." I kept my sliced hand out of sight; I didn't need her worrying even more about me.

"I'll call the police," she said, digging her phone out of her pocket.

"Why don't you let me take care of that." I gently pushed her hand down before she could begin dialing. "Manny, could you—"

"Manny?" Esme asked, confused. "Why—"

The raven turned from the alfr he was pecking at and flapped over to land on the table next to Esme. She stared at him. He ever so gently touched her temple with his beak. The puzzlement in her face faded, replaced by a blank stare as if hypnotized. Manny has this thing he can do with memories. Very handy.

I hated doing this to her, but I really couldn't afford to get caught up in a murder investigation. Not that there was any real danger of either of us going to jail, but these investigations could drag on for months or even years and that would cramp my style.

I whispered a new story into her ear. Two men were menacing me. She pulled out her gun and frightened them away. They were just looking for money. No need to call the police. While I was doing that, I took off her shoes and put them back on the wrong feet; I couldn't help myself.

I had a few more minutes before she would wake. I wrestled the bodies into a cabinet. Out of sight, out of mind. I kicked the swords into the corner and tossed a cloth over them, conveniently covering the blood stains. Without knowing what kind of enchantment lay on them, I didn't dare touch the blades.

"They're gone?" Esme asked foggily as I turned back to her. She stood again.

"Ran like rabbits. You gave them quite a scare with that gun."

"I guess I did, didn't I?"

"Since when do you carry a gun?"

"Since you got shot at," she said. She was recovering quickly.

"Well, I'm glad you did."

"I suppose you're going to tell me they weren't here collecting a gambling debt."

"No! Honest."

"Right. Because honesty is your middle name."

I hate it when she gets sarcastic. Usually, it's because she's right, and I hate being wrong.

"If you're not going to be straight with me, you can plan the next show yourself."

"Esme—"

"Don't 'Esme' me. I'm going home. There's a bottle of wine there with my name on it."

I didn't bother to stop her. She can be quite stubborn.

Plus, I had a couple of bodies I needed to get rid of. She'd make me pay for this later with a verbal blistering, but as long as she was still able to talk, I would gladly take it.

As she took a step, her foot landed awkwardly and I suppressed a giggle. She took another ungainly step, then looked down at her feet.

"Lowell! How the hell did you do that?"

"What?" I asked innocently.

"You are fucking incorrigible," she muttered, sitting back down and switching her shoes. She let the door slam behind her on the way out.

With Esme gone, I uncovered the blades. I examined them carefully without touching them. On a hunch, I nudged one into the moonlight streaming through the window. The blade shimmered and became translucent. Manibrandr. Moon blades. Son of a bitch. They were moon kin.

I went to check on the alfr stuffed in the cabinet, the one with the harpoon in his belly. Unconscious, but still breathing—barely. Putting my foot on his chest, I pulled the spear gun harpoon out. He gurgled briefly. That stopped when I thrust it into his chest.

At least the blades would be easy to dispose of. All I had to do was leave them out in the sun and they would fade away. Only the wrappings from the handles would remain. If only I could do the same with the bodies. I'd have to weight them and drop them overboard in the middle of the lake. None of the lakes in the chain were deep, but there was a less shallow spot in Lake Pistakee that would have to do.

Manny kept me company out and back. He stayed quiet, letting me think. I could feel another slow burn building. I don't like it when people try to kill me. Had they arrived minutes later, Esme might have been killed too. I tried not to think about Esme getting hurt.

I couldn't let this continue.

It was late when I got back, but I had decided on a plan. There were two options, run or fight. I was tired of running, tired of fleeing my friends and having to make new ones, but I didn't see another option. I went to the box and cut another paper-thin slice of the fruit. Then I went to bed and slept like a baby. Killing has never bothered me, and anyway, right after an assassination attempt is the safest time. Nobody would be coming for me tonight. Plus, they'd have to get past my bird. Like that would be hard.

3

MEXICO

exico? You're leaving for Mexico?"

"I have to, Esme," I entreated.

We were standing on the deck of the *Voluspa*, 'discussing' what to do about multiple attempts on my life. She wore sneakers, jeans, and a lime green shirt which failed to properly accent the fiery scowl she directed at me. I'm more of a boots guy. My Led Zeppelin t-shirt didn't accent the pleading look I gave her back.

"It must be bad if you're fleeing the country," she said.

"I don't know when I'll be back. Or if I'll be back."

"So these guys that keep trying to hurt you, it's that serious, huh?"

"Yeah, it's serious," I said with a heavy sigh.

"But you won't go to the police?" she said angrily.

"It wouldn't do any good. But I didn't ask you to come here to discuss my options. I came here to ask you to take care of the *Voluspa*."

"Holy shit. You're serious."

"And the props too. Take those. Use them if you want to. If I'm not back in a year, you can sell them."

22

"A year? I suppose I have to take Manny too."

"No, he's coming with me."

"You're taking the bird?"

"Here's the keys to the boat and a storage locker. The deed and all the other paperwork are in this envelope."

"You're leaving, probably for good, and you won't even tell me why?" Anger was turning to dismay.

"It's not for good. At least I hope not. Esme, I don't want you to get hurt. It was probably a bad idea for me to even tell you where I'm going."

"Have you ever been to Mexico? Do you speak Spanish?"

"I was in Mexico once a long time ago. And you know I don't speak Spanish."

That was when she dressed me down in rapid-fire Spanish. It went on for a while, loud and with lots of angry gestures. I tried to get a word in, but she just got louder and angrier. Finally, she wound down and stopped, arms crossed and glaring at me.

"I won't have any trouble getting where I need to go," I said defensively.

"No, you won't. Because I'm going with you."

"No! Absolutely not." I stood suddenly, fists clenched.

"Mexico is not safe these days. If you die down there because you say the wrong thing, or look at the wrong people, or wander into the wrong place... well, that's not going to happen, because I'm going to be with you."

"You'll lose your job."

"I'll put in for vacation time. Someone else can enter the doctor's notes for a while. I haven't taken any vacation time yet this year, so I have plenty."

"This trip is dangerous. People are trying to kill me."

"If you don't take me with you, I'll publish every magic trick you know."

Hard to argue with logic like that. I've known Esme for

years. The stubborn look on her face and tense posture told me I wasn't going to change her mind. I hate that I like strong women. Manny landed on the roof of the car with a loud caw.

"All right, all right!" I said throwing my hands in the air. "Be here by eight tomorrow morning, and if you are even one minute late I'm leaving without you."

———

I was ready to go by six the next morning. If Esme wouldn't see reason, I'd just leave without her. She'd be pissed off, but she'd be alive and safe. I didn't know who exactly was trying to kill me, as there are a lot of possibilities there. But I knew how far they would go, and hurting Esme to get to me wouldn't bother them in the least. I grabbed my single duffel bag and stepped off the boat. Esme was leaning up against the car, arms folded.

"I was going to bring you coffee, but for some ungodly reason you don't drink it," she said calmly.

"Esme—"

"You're taking the first shift behind the wheel. I'll take over after lunch. You'll just fall asleep then anyway."

I know when I'm beaten. Deep down I was secretly pleased to have her along. I would just have to do everything in my power to keep her safe.

"So where in Mexico are we going?" she asked once the Chevy was moving.

"Oaxaca."

"That's pretty far from the border. Who are you meeting there? Family or friend?"

"Enough with the questions. You forced yourself into going with me. You'll just have to wait. Besides, you wouldn't believe me if I told you."

Manny settled in on the back seat.

The border crossing went easier with her along, as did our stops in Mexico. She pestered me relentlessly, but I refused to give her any details about why I wanted to get to Oaxaca.

"Santa Maria?" Esme asked, confused. "I thought we were going to Oaxaca City?"

It was evening and we were just pulling into Santa Maria del Tule. The night was warm and cloudless. Strike that. It was hot and cloudless. My well-worn jeans and equally well-worn black and white Led Zeppelin t-shirt were sticking to me. Southern Mexico in July is not fit for us gringos. I should have brought shorts.

"I said Oaxaca. You assumed it was the city. Santa Maria is in Oaxaca. And the full name is Santa Maria del Tule."

"I can read," she said sharply. "So why are we here? Are we meeting someone? Do you have some special hideout here? An old girlfriend? If you just needed to get out of the States, we could have stopped a few hundred miles ago."

"Do you ever just ask one question at a time?"

"Only if you ever give me a straight answer to a question."

Manny cawed from where he was perched on the back seat. That damn bird was laughing at me. I gave him a dirty look as we pulled into a parking spot in front of a restaurant that looked out on the mighty Tule tree.

"Fine. We are here for the tree."

"Arbor del Tule? Seriously? We came here for a tourist attraction?"

"The Tule tree is one of the largest and oldest trees in the world. It's a magnificent cypress growing in the middle—"

"Enough with the tour guide talk," she snapped. "I was

bored and looked up most of that on my phone when we entered the city limits. Why do you care about a tree, regardless of how big or how old it is? And what does it have to do with escaping from the people trying to kill you?"

I was silent for a while, debating how much to tell her.

"I can't run from these people. No matter where I go, they will find me. I've run from them for most of my life. This time I need to take more... drastic measures to put them off my trail."

"What the hell are you talking about? This isn't about gambling debts?"

"I told you it wasn't. You just didn't believe me. You should know me well enough to realize I never lie about important things."

"Drastic measures? Are you thinking of killing them?" she asked, scared and wide-eyed.

"I doubt I would be able to. But seeing as they are trying to kill me, if I got the chance I just might."

"You're scaring me Lowell. This isn't like you."

"How many years have you known me? Seven? Eight? All of this is ancient history from long before you and I met. There are many things you don't know about me."

"Yeah, but that's supposed to be things like your family, who you never talk about, or those scars on your chest, or why you don't have a day job. It's not supposed to be things like 'I'm being chased by killers and I just might kill them too.'"

"I don't *want* to kill anyone. I just want to lose them long enough to be able to hide again. Maybe lead a normal life for a while. Hopefully a long while."

"And how the hell is this tree going to do that?"

I took a deep breath. "The tree's magic will take me to a place where they can't find me so easily."

"Tree's magic? What are you talking about?"

"The Tule tree is magic. I can use that magic to escape."

"Wait. You're talking real magic? Not a trick?" she said, shocked. "Lowell, magic doesn't exist. You've told hundreds of people that what you do is just tricks, not real."

"And that's true. What I do with you isn't magic. It is just tricks. But this is *real* magic. Old magic. As old as that tree, maybe older."

"Lowell, that's crazy! Magic? Look, I know a doctor who helps people. He's back in the States, but he can do something about your delusions. And we can get you police protection. Maybe even witness protection. You'll be safe."

"I didn't expect you to believe me. But I have to do this."

"What are you going to do?" she said, panicking.

"I'm not going to hurt anybody. I'm not going to hurt myself. I'm not even going to hurt the tree."

"Okay—" she said, not convinced.

"I tell you what. If what I do doesn't work, I'll go back to the States with you. I'll see a doctor. I'll go to the police. I'll do all of it. But please, Esme, don't interfere with this."

"You'll really go back and get help?"

"On my honor."

It was her turn to take a deep breath. "If you go back on your word—'"

I got out and grabbed my duffel. I poked my head back into the passenger window for one last look at Esme, and some last-minute instructions. I wondered how long it would take for her to find the 'palmada a mi asno' sign I had stuck to her back. Hopefully, the kids that I got to write it out in Spanish didn't pull a fast one on me.

"Remember, if I'm not back in a year, everything I own is yours. But today, if this works, sell the Blazer and use the money to get a plane ticket back to Illinois."

"Lowell," she said, as I was turning away. "Be careful. And come back. I don't want your crappy houseboat."

I grinned but kept moving away from the car, Manny perched on my shoulder. Ahead of me was the huge Tule cypress tree. It was more than thirty feet in diameter, which is every bit as thick as the largest California redwood. It looked like it was a dozen or more trees grown together, but lots of scientific testing had shown it was a single tree. I have an interest in unusual trees, so I keep up on these things.

It is not much taller than it is wide, giving it the appearance of an enormous bush. The crown is full and thick with healthy, green leaves. Despite its great age it didn't have many dead branches. It's one of the most impressive trees in the world.

The Tule tree is also known for the shapes and faces that seem to naturally grow out of its trunk. Most are just optical illusions pawned off on gullible tourists, but some were more important. More important to me that is.

The small-town block dedicated to the tree was surrounded by a tall metal fence. It wouldn't be easy to hop over it, but there was only one policeman strolling through the crowd. Still, I would have to be quick. I waited for the cop to get on the opposite side and then tossed my duffel bag over the fence. The people near me muttered in surprise, but I ignored them.

I hoisted myself up and over, grateful that I was still in decent shape. Grabbing the duffel, I ran to the tree, Manny following. The wolf was the closest face growing out of the tree. I slapped it with my palm and started trotting counter-clockwise around it. The crowd was getting loud, calling for the cop and shouting Spanish obscenities at me.

Jaguar... elephant... There it was. The bear. I slapped it and kept moving. I heard a police whistle and a man shouting at me from closer than I liked. Glancing behind me, I saw the cop in lukewarm pursuit. He wasn't going to set any land speed records. There must have been a gate on the far side that let him in. I started moving faster. I had to make at least one full circuit. I saw the caribou. I slapped the face and sprinted. Back home I was known for being fast. I could easily outrace this cop. Manny landed on my shoulder again and dug his claws in to hold on.

As I closed in on where I started, I spotted a gap in the bole of the tree widen. I skidded to a stop right in front of it. The cop was still lumbering toward me, huffing and puffing. I bowed to him in a flourish and stepped back through the gap as a familiar disorientation seized me.

My vision blurred briefly and then cleared. I stood once more on the trunk of mighty Yggdrasil.

4

YGGDRASIL

At first glance, it looked like I was standing on the side of a gigantic toppled tree. The rough bark stretched under a night sky filled with stars that provided plenty of light to see by.

Yggdrasil. The tree of life.

The tree did not grow up and down, but rather forward and back. Actually, that's not true. Up and down are relative here. The tree grew, straight and strong, connecting the Nine Worlds. Those of us who walked on her stood on branches or the main bole. Down was always toward the center of whatever part we stood on. Up was always away from it. If I walked around the branch, I would be upside-down relative to where I was now, but it would feel normal. There was no way to fall off.

I stood on a branch at least a hundred yards in diameter. Looking behind me, I could see it tapering off into what seemed like an infinite distance. More branches grew at wild angles from the one I was on. Ahead were only a few thick branches. A dozen miles or so away was the main trunk, I think. If so, I had gotten lucky to arrive so close to it.

Clusters of small branches and twigs were tipped with cypress leaves. The tree was gnarled and covered in cypress bark, evoking the Tule tree. Elsewhere Yggdrasil would look like other trees, replicating their leaves and bark, and even their flowers. More accurately, the trees in the Nine Worlds imitated Yggdrasil.

Yggdrasil connected to every tree everywhere in the Nine Worlds, from the tiniest sapling to the mighty Tule. Once, it was easy to use any substantial tree in one of the worlds to access Yggdrasil. Times change. I've changed. In my current condition, I needed a tree like the Tule to make the connection to Yggdrasil.

The stars were the same ones I would see from Earth. It looked like Yggdrasil was growing in outer space, but that was just an illusion. I had to remind myself to think of Earth as Midgard now. An unseen source of light filtered through the miles-distant branches to my right, toward the top of the world tree. I've always assumed it was the sun, but I've never traveled high enough to make sure.

"I hope you know what you're doing," cawed Manny, still on my shoulder. I had gotten so used to his silence in Midgard, it started me for a second.

"Are you doubting me?" I said, mockingly.

"Ow!" I cried as he pecked the side of my head. He's a big bird with a powerful beak. It hurt.

"That's not my name," he cawed. "You will use my rightful name."

"Muninn, okay? Muninn."

"It's a noble name, full of meaning."

"Okay, okay. I got it."

He glared at me while I rubbed my head.

"You know, Esme likes the name Manny."

"She does?" he cawed.

"She says it sounds noble. She thinks it fits you."

31

He gave a short screech, but I could tell he was flattered.

"Of course, she thinks it's short for Emmanuel."

"Emmanuel means God is with us," he cawed, preening himself. "Well, if Esme likes it—"

That made me laugh. As I turned my attention back to what was around me, I sensed something.

"I can feel the Tree's power," I said, more to myself than to him.

Yggdrasil connected the physical and the spiritual. It bound the Nine Worlds together. It is possible to tap into that connection, that energy, and do things that are otherwise impossible. In past times this spirit energy was called frodleikr. Call it magic if you will, but it's just a part of nature that is not well understood by most people on Midgard. I'm not most people.

"You lived too long in Midgard," Muninn cawed with a hint of disdain. "You don't remember what the touch of Yggdrasil feels like. What it can do."

"I remember," I said wistfully. "It's just been so long."

Contact with the Tree is like putting a sponge in water. If you are like me, it soaks into you, filling you up. And I was empty, so empty. I could actually feel the frodleikr, the spirit energy, filling the void inside me, a void I had almost forgotten.

Each of the Nine Worlds has a different relationship with the Tree of Life. Some, like Jotunheim and Alfheim are close to the Tree both physically and spiritually. Magic replenishes more quickly there. Not nearly as fast as on Yggdrasil itself, but faster than in the other worlds.

Midgard was always weak in spirit energy. In the important ways, Midgard is the most distant of the Nine Worlds from the Tree. And it was moving farther away every year. When I was first exiled, I could still feel Yggdrasil on Midgard. Frodleikr replenished, but much more slowly than in Asgard. It had been a couple centuries since I had last felt it at all. Even at the Tule tree, it had been thin and diluted.

Muninn interrupted my reverie, "Before we left I told Esme, just like you asked. I still think it was a mistake."

"She deserves to know. Maybe she'll even believe it."

"See for yourself," he cawed, pecking me sharply on the head again. It hurt. A lot.

Suddenly I was in Muninn's memory. Or more accurately he had pushed his memory into my head. It's one of his tricks. Of course, he only needed to touch me, not poke a hole in my temple.

I was inside Manny's head, perched on the passenger side door window. The two hundred and seventy-degree field of view was a bit disorienting.

"Esme," I heard Manny caw.

"Did you just say something, Manny?" she asked, surprised.

"Yes. I don't have much time, so just listen."

"Wait... you can talk?"

"It's about the man you know as Lowell," I cawed.

"You're like one of those parrots. He trained you to repeat this, didn't he? Another one of his tricks."

"No, I'm not 'trained.' Will you just shut up and listen. The man you know as Lowell is son of Farbauti and Laufey, brother of Helblindi and Byleistr, ward of Odin. He is Loki, the God of Mischief."

"Oh, Lowell," Esme said, shaking her head sadly. "I'm going to make him pay for this. God of Mischief, eh?"

"When he makes a full circuit of the sacred Tule tree, he will leave Midgard, or Earth as you know it, and return to his true home."

"I really need to get Lowell to a hospital."

I t was equally disorienting to suddenly be back in my own body. My head hurt like a son of a bitch where Manny had drilled me twice.

"You laid it on a little thick, didn't you? God of Mischief? Really?" I complained.

"To the men of Midgard you are a god," Manny cawed haughtily.

"No. That was Odin's conceit. It was never mine," I said sharply. "If anyone was a god of mischief, it was him. He fooled men into believing his godhood crap."

Manny stayed quiet, refusing to rise to the bait. He had served Odin faithfully for close to a millennium. Gods know, it might have been more. I wasn't around when they met.

"We should get going. It's a long way to Alfheim."

"Alfhiem?" Manny cawed. "I thought you would be going to Asgard or maybe Jotunheim."

"Those two moon kin were alfar. I want answers before going to either of those places."

"All Manibrandr are alfar," Manny cawed. It's hard to tell when a raven is being sarcastic, but I've had a lot of practice.

Ignoring the not so subtle dig, I hoisted the duffel bag and walked down the branch. It took more than three hours to get to the central trunk. The trunk looked to be half a mile wide here. I stood still and waited to feel the hugr vindr, the spirit wind. When it came I felt it on my skin, although it didn't ruffle my hair or Manny's feathers. I was able to 'smell' the scents carried by the wind. There was ice and snow, sunlight, gold and magic. Sunlight led to Alfheim. I turned upwind.

"Alfheim is this way."

"Of course it is," Manny cawed. "I've traveled Yggdrasil a thousand times. I know the way to each of the Nine Worlds."

"You can't memorize the way," I snorted. "Yggdrasil doesn't work that way."

It's easy to assume that the Nine Worlds were laid out in order along the trunk of Yggdrasil. The truth is far more complicated. They exist within and beside each other, like horribly complicated multi-dimensional puzzle pieces. Yggdrasil grows in the gaps, connecting and binding them. Or more accurately they grow around it. Or both. Every world touches all the other worlds in many places through the tree. It is our small minds that insist on seeing them stacked from top to bottom. If I repeated my transport from Midgard to Yggdrasil a year from now, Alfheim might be in a different direction.

"Hah!" Manny cawed. "You think yours is the only way to navigate the World Tree? I know nine different ways to travel its branches."

We traveled in silence for a while after that. I hate smart ass birds.

"Something's coming," Manny cawed after a while.

I turned to look behind us. In the distance, I saw a small, dark dot on the surface of the trunk. It seemed to be moving. There really isn't anywhere to hide on the main trunk. However, there are also a limited number of beings with the ability to travel the World Tree. Unfortunately, most of them would not be friendly to me.

We kept walking. During the next hour, the dot behind us got larger. I could tell it was a reddish-brown and seemed to be bouncing. If it was who I suspected, it wasn't an enemy.

"Ratatoskr!" I hailed when it came close enough to hear me.

The giant red squirrel headed toward us in bounding leaps. Its back was perhaps the height of an African elephant.

Of course, it was much longer from nose to hindquarters than an elephant. It's rapidly flicking, bushy tail doubled that.

"Loki? Is that you?" the high, chittering voice asked. "And Muninn? Or is that Huginn? What an odd pair."

"Muninn. And not so odd. I see that you are looking quite fine, Ratatoskr, even after the many centuries since I last saw you."

"Centuries? I'm not sure. I know it has been 4,937 round trips."

"You are headed to the crown. I presume you are carrying a message from Nidhoggr to his dear friend Vedrfolnir."

"Oh, ho! Yes," he squeaked, with a few rapid flicks of his bushy, over-sized tail. "I carry a devastating insult about the lay of the fourth feather in the second row of his right wing. Vedrfolnir will screech for days when he hears it."

"So the old serpent came up with a great zinger then?" I laughed. "I'm sure the great eagle will have an equally creative retort. Maybe something about Nidhoggr's second claw on his back right foot."

"Pfft. That was one hundred and four round trips ago. Vedrfolnir is insulting the scales on Nidhoggr's tail now."

"Well, neither of them could find anything bad to say about your magnificent tail."

"My tail *is* quite handsome," Ratatoskr admitted, preening.

"The color is like a sunset on the ocean. The fur is soft and resplendent."

"My tail *is* the envy of all other animals," Ratatoskr conceded.

"Yet it pales in comparison to your ears."

"You think so?"

"Definitely. They are so much taller and perkier than the ears on other squirrels."

"I suppose they are."

"And the tufts, oh those tufts."

"What about my ear tufts?"

"They turn your extraordinary ears into incomparable works of art."

"I do rather like them."

"It's too bad I don't have more time to admire your stunning beauty."

"What? Where are you going? Are you leaving so soon?"

"I have to get to Alfheim. I'm afraid it's a long journey and I can't dally here any longer."

Ratatoskr sat silently on his haunches, tail flickering like mad. I could almost see the gears turning in his little rodent brain.

"So long Ratatoskr. Give my regards to Vedrfolnir," I said turning away and continuing my trek down the tree.

"Wait! Loki, wait. What if I carried you? You would get there so much sooner. Alfheim is almost on the way to Vedrfolnir. And you could tell me all about how wonderful I am on the way."

"Huh," I said, turning back and looking surprised. "I hadn't thought of that. I really do have many more observations of your beauty. But no, I couldn't put you out, as tempting as the offer might be."

"But I insist," he said, bounding right up to me.

"Well, I really shouldn't, but since you are so determined, I'd hate to disappoint you."

I grabbed a fistful of fur and pulled myself up the giant squirrel's side. I could feel him wince as I yanked on his delicate hairs. Once up behind his neck, I was able to hold on without causing as much discomfort. Manny gripped my shoulder. I kept the duffel bag in front of me, trapped under my arms. Ratatoskr bounded forward in great leaps and I began to regale him with shameless compliments.

"You haven't lost your silver tongue, Loki," Manny cawed quietly.

<hr />

My voice was beginning to get hoarse when we arrived at a large branch. We had turned off the main trunk a couple of hours before.

"This burl leads to Alfheim," Ratatoskr said, somewhat sadly. "Are you sure you don't want to keep me company to the top of the tree? I could have you back here by autumn."

"My heart is breaking at the thought of being denied your company, Ratatoskr. But I have matters of great urgency to attend to. If you hear weeping as you race off to deliver your urgent message, don't look back. I couldn't stand the thought that I might delay you further."

"Well. I suppose. If you insist."

"I do."

"Then I guess I'd best be on my way."

"You should."

"I'll be leaving now."

"Farewell."

"Maybe we'll meet again when I'm on my way back to Nidhoggr."

"I'll count the moments."

"Goodbye," Ratatoskr said, finally turning and bounding off.

"What an amazingly stupid and vain creature," Manny cawed when Ratatoskr was safely out of earshot.

"And yet I rather enjoyed my time with him."

"You just love the sound of your own voice."

"So true."

"And manipulating gullible creatures."

"Have I told you the story of how I convinced a flea-infested crow to be my companion?"

"I've never had fleas! And if you'll recall, I offered to travel with you."

"If you say so."

5

ALFHEIM

Alfheim is a land of perpetual sunshine and eternal spring. Not that the sun never sets, it does, but it never rains and the weather is always fair. It is also a place of unending green. Tall grasses, trees, shrubs, and flowers are everywhere. You are rarely far from streams or small ponds, but there are no oceans or large lakes. It looks like the Christian Garden of Eden. Or Ireland.

Indeed, this is what I saw upon entering Alfheim. It was early morning, warm and with a light breeze. After the other-worldliness of Yggdrasil, it was a relief. I stood for several long minutes just soaking in the environment.

"I think it might be time to spread your wings," Manny cawed.

"I'm not sure I have the power."

"Your time in Midgard did drain you of frodleikr, but Yggdrasil should have replenished it sufficiently. And Alfheim will sustain you as well."

"I suppose it's worth trying," I said reluctantly.

I had been performing as a stage magician for almost one

hundred and fifty years under various stage names. Now I suddenly had performance anxiety for the real thing. I wished Esme was here, which made no sense at all.

I started the galdr spell, the magic of the self, by forming the image of a crane in my mind. Next to it I envisioned myself. In my mind I bound the two with a braided cord, making sure to superimpose the crane over the man. You would think it would be painful and slow to transform into another creature, but it isn't. It's disorienting though, especially if the new form is a lot different. Like a bird. Fortunately, I had a talent for shape-shifting.

I was standing much closer to the ground in this new form, tangled in my clothes. Like an idiot, I had forgotten a key part of the process. It took a while to untangle myself. Manny thought it was hysterical. Finally free, I took inventory. Everything appeared to be normal. Crane normal that is. Well, at least I got that part right.

"I'll just walk," I said, after turning back and dressing.

"Better to work out the kinks now," Manny cawed.

"I was weak before. There's no way I can do it a second time."

"You underestimate yourself, Loki."

"Fine," I groused. "I'll rest for an hour and try again. But if it doesn't work, I'm walking."

There are two types of magic. At least that's what I was taught. There is galdr, the magic of the self, and seidr, the magic of things outside the self. I needed to use both. I chanted a focusing rhyme for the seidr spell, binding my possessions to myself. I could sense it take effect. That done, I tried the galdr spell to change my own shape and felt it sucking the last of my reserves as my body shifted. I stretched my wings and felt the wind filling them like sails. With a screech, I flapped hard and launched into the air.

"I told you so," Manny cawed.

If I could have flipped him off I would have.

Flying is one of my greatest pleasures. It had been centuries since I indulged myself. The land beneath me was a gorgeous rolling green. Numerous streams and ponds dotted the landscape. Manny darted ahead and veered to the left. I followed.

In the distance, I saw Vidrheim, the city of the alfar court. A ring of mighty oaks intertwined with numerous smaller trees, which in turn were intertwined with brambles. They formed a tall wall and inside the ring were dozens of clearings, small and large, separated by lines of shrubs. Huge cypress, cedars and yew trees formed enclaves, like arboreal versions of tall buildings on Midgard. It looked both artificial and natural at the same time.

I set down outside the wall, letting my shape return to normal. Manny landed on my shoulder and I wove through the trees until I could see the oak and bramble wall. A bog-like moat, half mud, half water, was in my way. However, a bridge of living ash tree bent over it. I knew that the lord of Alfheim could command those trees to rise should the Court ever be attacked.

"Manny, has the Court ever been attacked by an army?"

"I have no memory of that."

When Manny says he has no memory of something, it probably didn't happen.

"Have they ever raised the ash bridge?" I asked, casually picking a nearby wildflower.

"Seventeen times the ash bridge has been raised. But never to shut out an army. Nine times were for ceremonies, such as the crowning of a new king or queen. Seven times to prevent unwelcome guests. And one time that the alfar do not talk of."

"Since it's down, I'm going to assume that we are welcome," I said with a grin.

"Of course you do," he cawed.

Two alfar guarded the gate on the far side of the ash bridge. They wore green tunics with a sun symbol emblazoned on them. Golden saffron leggings ended in soft brown sandals. Definitely not war gear. However, each carried a solspjot, a spear whose tip glowed softly. In battle, it would be too bright to look at directly and burn like fire. Definitely not a weapon to be messed with. They thoroughly ignored us, as Manny and I tentatively walked between them.

The vaulted oak archway was thirty feet deep. The courtyard beyond was a large forest clearing covered in ankle-high grass. A crystal blue pond, perfectly circular, sat in the center. A scattering of alfar bustled about on unknown errands. If you ignored the fact that they were decidedly thin with pointed ears, you could mistake them for Midgard humans. Several wore the sunburst tunic. Greens and yellows dominated the garb of the rest.

"You must be disappointed," Manny cawed. "No fanfare for the entrance of the mighty God of Mischief."

"Don't call me that," I muttered.

"So where to now, oh lowly stage magician?"

"I'm not really sure. We need to find out who sent the Manibrandr to kill me."

"Really? I think it's pretty obvious," Manny cawed. "As the most hated man in the Nine Worlds, you have a wealth of enemies, but one stands out above all others."

"It's not Thor's style. If he wanted me dead, he'd do it himself. And it wouldn't be subtle, either. And why would he wait this long?"

"That's a thin thread to hang your life upon."

"Well, if it is Thor, all I can do is hide again. If it isn't, there might be something else that can be done. So let's see where the trail leads."

"Which brings me back to, what now?"

"I suppose I should present myself first. Don't want anyone thinking I'm sneaking around. Then we'll find a local skald. Rumors and gossip are their stock in trade."

"You should know," Manny replied.

Ignoring the openings between the hedges on either side, I marched across the courtyard clearing toward the large opening directly opposite the gate. It was framed by two willow trees. Another pair of alfar guards with sun spears stood on either side. They paid just as much attention to me as the other set when I entered the... castle? Palace? I wasn't sure what to call it, but clearly, the alfar ruler lived there.

A tall alfr dressed in a long, golden yellow robe stood opposite me in the glade that lay beyond. Behind him, I saw the crown of a massive oak tree rising above the tall hedge that served as walls in this place. I was going to have trouble getting used to the lack of roofs. He strode toward me purposefully. Closer, I could see detailed golden embroidery on the hems and neckline. A motif of golden suns around his waist almost faded into the background of the robe.

"Lord Loki," he said with a bow. "I am Einar, steward to her highness Queen Alfhildr. On her behalf, we welcome you to Alfheim and to the city of Vidrheim."

"A gracious greeting Einar. Please convey to her highness my most humble thanks."

"Noble raven, I am embarrassed to ask, but are you Huginn or Muninn?"

"I am Muninn, master of memory, prince among ravens."

"And egotistical blowhard," I muttered just loud enough for Manny to hear. He gave me a sharp look, which is better than a sharp poke with his beak.

"I'm sure you would like to make yourself more

presentable before greeting the queen," Einar suggested. "We have guest quarters ready. I've set your appointment with her highness for noon."

I guess jeans and a Zeppelin t-shirt aren't appropriate for royalty. I almost jumped when two guards with those damn spears stepped up on either side of me. Manny did, cawing loudly and flapping his wings.

"These wardens will show you to your room."

I bowed with a wry smile. I was being treated with cautious respect. I had hoped for open arms, a fatted calf, and maybe a beer, but I guess they knew my reputation. Like anyone in the Nine Worlds didn't.

They were polite but silent, pointing the way instead of speaking. They led me down several hedge halls ending up at a wooden door, clouds and blue sky overhead the whole time. The door was a slightly curved wooden slab fallen from a large tree. No axe or saw had ever touched it, yet it fit perfectly between two living aspens.

I stood melodramatically at attention and saluted the two wardens. They spun on their heels, expressionless, and marched away. Maybe my reception wasn't as cold as it seemed. There was nothing to stop me from wandering wherever I wanted. So of course, I went into my room.

"Lord Loki," said the woman in my room with a stiff bow.

"And who might you be?"

"I am Huld. I will be your handmaiden while you are here."

Huld was old. The mere fact it showed meant she must be very old. The alfar live for many centuries, possibly even millennia, but don't show it. For her to look old meant she must indeed be ancient.

She was straight-backed and held her head at a haughty angle, although the top of it only came up to my collar. She seemed active and capable despite her age. Her gray hair was tied in a simple ponytail with a green vine of some sort, which accentuated her pointed ears. Her shift was dark green and thin, blue wave patterns formed horizontal stripes of sorts.

"A flower for the beauteous Huld," I said with a bow, making a wildflower seemingly appear in my hand.

"Save your tricks," she snorted. Obviously, she didn't like pink. I'd have to try yellow next time.

"So I'm led to believe my rags need to be swapped out for alfar finery," I said. "Oh, and I think I'm supposed to take a bath as well."

"You do smell like a wild animal." Huld wrinkled her nose. "I suppose that is to be expected."

"Squirrel or crane?"

Manny laughed. Ravens shouldn't laugh. It sounds creepy.

"Pardon?" She asked, puzzled.

"Nevermind."

"The bath is through there." She pointed to a gap in the hedge wall.

I hadn't really looked around the room yet. It was of modest size. In the center, a round bed of moss was, well, the bed. A pair of stunted birch trees cleverly made a long bench. The trunks started at opposite ends, grew to knee height, then grew sideways for a good six feet before bending sharply up again. An extra kink near the base of each provided a support for the far end of the other.

A similar set of trees grew to form a countertop against one wall. My new clothes were folded neatly on it. A couple of tree chairs along the other wall finished the furniture. I was convinced the alfar could grow anything a carpenter could make.

"Vidrheim is an unusual city," I commented. "Quite impressive what you can do with nature."

"Do not judge all of Alfheim by the queen's city. Most of

my people live in the forest, closer to nature. Vidrheim is one of the few places where we build as the other races do."

Huld looked at me expectantly, then glanced pointedly at the bath.

"Are you going to undress me for my bath?" I asked with an exaggerated waggle of my eyebrows. Older women usually like it when I flirt with them.

"Disrobe in the bathing room," she said with a disdainful frown. "Put your soiled garments by the doorway. I'll collect them after you're in the water."

"I never took the alfar for prudes," I laughed.

"We are not as free with our bodies as the aesir of Asgard," she said with evident disgust.

The aesir are a randy lot. Fidelity was publicly touted and privately flouted. Through the centuries I had learned to adapt to whatever the local social norm was, so I would try to be on my best behavior here. I much preferred the sixties in America, though.

It was obvious Huld wasn't going to loosen up and banter with me. In fact, I'm pretty sure she really didn't like me.

The bath was a small stone-lined pond. A variety of barks and mosses were arrayed on the edge, which I assumed were to be used to scrub with. I tossed my jeans, t-shirt, and underwear in a heap by the door. I wondered briefly what Huld would think of modern clothing. The water was a bit chilly, but refreshing. The sun on my shoulders was warm.

I wondered what Esme was doing now. She had to be so confused. Hopefully she'd listened and went back to Chicago. Somehow I doubted that.

"Lord Muninn, is there anything I can do for you?" I heard Huld ask from the other room. I heard him cawing softly, but couldn't make out any words.

Huld had laid out a towel that felt like cotton, but softer. Smelling far less offensive, I returned to the bedroom with the towel wrapped around me. Huld was still there, standing silently by the door. Her eyes briefly went wide when she saw the mass of scars on my chest. It's not a pretty sight. Silently she pointed at the clothes on the shelf and turned her back to the room. Taking the hint, I got dressed.

The green tunic was surprisingly comfortable, as were the breeches. Intricate yellow and gold abstract patterns were woven into it with threads as fine as hairs. The supple boots were more comfortable than anything I had worn on Midgard, certainly better than the sneakers. The whole outfit did indeed make me look like Lord Loki instead of humble Lowell Keystone.

I didn't see Manny. He was probably flying over the city, taking advantage of its open-air architecture. I rarely questioned when he left. He is his own bird. Someday I'll learn why he hangs around with me.

"Sit and I will manage your hair," Huld said. I had almost forgotten about her.

I sat sideways on one of the chair trees and let her go to work with a wooden comb. I'm pretty sure she pulled harder on the knots than was necessary. Surprisingly hard for an old woman. My shoulder-length hair ended up being expertly plaited and braided, although some of it was left to fall naturally. Aloes and lotions were rubbed into my skin.

"I believe the queen is waiting," Huld said when there was nothing left to fix on me.

"Don't lose my Led Zeppelin shirt. It would be hard to replace."

"Led Zeppelin?"

"Nevermind. It would take too long to explain."

A single warden waited outside the door. He guided me through the hedge hallways back to the entrance hall I had first seen. A set of vines were pulled to the side on the far wall, leaving a wide doorway to an even larger room. Einar stood to one side.

"You look quite presentable, my lord."

"I suppose I do."

The throne room was a vast clearing with a great, old oak at its center. The trunk soared forty or fifty feet before the canopy spread over us. The base of the oak jutted out from the main trunk, forming a natural seat complete with armrests. On it sat an alfr woman of indeterminate age. Dark brown hair hung down to her waist, framing a tanned face with small, delicate features. Her dark brown eyes were sharp and knowing. On her head was a laurel crown, and her deep green gown was woven so finely the patterns seemed to swim.

"Gracious Queen Alfhildr," I said with a sweeping bow. "I am humbled by your presence and the magnificence of your court."

"Alfhildr is honored by your visit and your kind words," said an alfr standing near her. There were maybe a dozen other alfar in the room, all clearly members of the ruling elite. I was really regretting not learning more about the alfar and Alfheim before my exile.

"I'll speak for myself," Alfhildr wheezed. Clearly, the queen wasn't well.

"But we agreed—"

"Bah. You agreed. I just didn't disagree," she said, suppressing a cough. "Loki, why have you never visited the alfar court before?"

"Oh most, glorious queen, I was afraid I would be envious of your magnificence."

49

"Cut the crap. I get enough of that from these fools."

"All right... uh, I wasn't really free to travel on my own when I was among the aesir. Neither Odin nor Thor visited Alfhiem while I was in their company."

"Yes, a ward of Odin, weren't you? A hostage from Jotunheim, meant to ensure peace. That didn't work out, did it?"

"Uh, no," I said, confused. This isn't how I imagined this conversation going. I made a conscious effort to switch gears.

"A thousand pardons, but were you queen while I was still with the aesir?"

"No. My grandmother was queen when you broke the Bifrost Bridge and laid waste to Asgard. She died shortly after. My mother took the throne for a few centuries until she grew frustrated with the rigors of ruling. Now I sit on the Oak Throne."

"I would have liked to have met your grandmother."

"No, you wouldn't. She was a real bitch. Like me. But she was a good queen. Also like me."

Alfhildr was seized by a coughing fit that lasted a while.

"Your highness," said one of the alfar courtiers, stepping closer to Alfhildr. "Are you sure you are up to this?"

"Shut up Fritjof."

The chastened courtier retreated.

"I've been away from Asgard for a long time," I said, changing topics. "Could you perhaps tell me who rules in Asgard now?

"Thor sits on Hladskjalf," Alfhildr said with distaste. "Rumor has it he is unable to master the high seat to spy upon the Nine Worlds. And neither will Mimir speak to him."

"Thor? He lives? Last I heard Vili took on the throne after Odin's death." I already knew Thor lived, but I was fishing for more information.

"Odin's brother had no desire to rule. After a century or so he abdicated to Vidarr. Once Thor recovered from his battle with Jormangundr, he deposed Vidarr. As the older son of Odin, that was his right."

"Thor was ever the bully."

"Enough of aesir politics. I'm dying, Loki. Don't look sad. It's been happening for a while. It's going to take a while longer. But these fools think they can run things for me."

The courtiers shifted uncomfortably and cast sideways glances at each other.

"I'm sure they only have your best interests at heart."

Alfhildr laughed, flinging herself back in her throne. It quickly turned into another coughing fit. The alfar court looked indignant, which only confirmed her opinion of them.

"What is it you came here for, God of Mischief?" she said when she had regained her breath.

"I don't answer to that title, highness," I said seriously. "Odin tried to convince the Nine Worlds that the aesir were gods, especially to the humans of Midgard, because some of them had special gifts. Odin would fondly call me his God of Mischief because I was always getting into trouble. It stuck with the Norsemen. Then Thor turned it into an insult."

"Hah! Good answer. If any of the races could be thought of as gods, it would be one of the older races, like the vanir or the jotnar, not the upstart aesir. Odin was a sneaky bastard. My grandmother never trusted him."

I would never have considered the giant of Jotunheim as candidate for godhood. They call themselves jotnar. Jotunn if it's just one. The vanir were the old gods that predated the aesir. Or at least that's what Odin taught me.

"Far be it for me to disagree with your highness."

"Enough with the pleasantries, Loki. I tire easily these days. What is it you came here for?"

"A pair of alfar tried to kill me recently. Manibrandr. I would know more about them and about why they did this."

"Manibrandr are stories to frighten alfar children."

"Their moon blades were certainly real enough."

"For the sake of argument, let's assume the Manibrandr do exist," she said with a smile and a glint in her eye. "Since you stand here, I assume they are dead."

I smiled in return. I carefully watched the alfar court out of the corner of my eye, but none of them reacted in a way that would cast suspicion. That would have been too easy.

"I thought so. I certainly didn't order any assassination attempt. I would much rather you live and be a thorn in the side of the aesir."

"Thank you, your highness. I try my best."

"But it troubles me that Manibrandr, or any of the alfar, would attack an aesir noble. I will look into the matter."

So much for the Manibrandr being children's stories. She had gone from denying them to accepting responsibility for them awfully fast.

"I hardly think I qualify as a noble anymore. I've been an outcast for more than nine hundred years."

"Even so, it shouldn't happen without my permission," she said dryly. "Now, I have a gift for you as a symbol of your status as an honored guest."

She stood, slowly and unsteadily. I wasn't sure what I was supposed to do, so I remained motionless. Einar handed her what looked like a necklace. I've never been fond of jewelry, but this wasn't a time to object.

"Turn around so I can put this on you," Alfhildr said, gliding toward me. Even sick she was graceful. I did as she asked. I felt her shaky hands draping the bauble around my neck and fumbling with the clasp. Looking down I could see the silver chain, braided like thorny vines.

"Wear this while you are in Alfhiem, not that you'll have much choice," she said. There was a strange note in her voice.

I turned and found two wardens between me and the queen. Where the heck had they come from? She was strolling back to her throne.

"I don't understand, your highness."

"My daughter died a century or so ago," Alfhildr wheezed, finally regaining her seat. "My granddaughter Lidveig has been a 'ward' of the aesir for far longer than that. It kept the peace between our domains."

"I was in a similar position," I said coldly. I didn't like where this was going. "Odin sent his son Meili to Jotunheim, to live with the jotnar, and they sent me to Asgard. I was but a child. Unfortunately, it did little to keep the peace."

"The jotnar were fools to trust the aesir. I'm no fool. What I am, is without an heir. You, Lord Loki, will do the alfar a great service. We will trade you for Lidveig. I will regain my granddaughter, my heir, and the aesir will gain their most hated enemy."

"I came here freely and in peace!" I shouted. "Is this how you treat guests in your home?"

"A good monarch does what is necessary, even if it breaks the laws or social rules. Odin knew that. He did many things for the good of his people that disgusted or angered them. My people will get over this."

"And you think you can keep me here?" I growled. "I may not be a god, but I still have a few tricks up my sleeve."

"Go ahead. Change into a bird or whatever. That necklace you wear, it will shrink and strangle you if you leave my court, no matter what form you take."

I formed the image of an osprey in my mind. I pulled open my tunic. I felt my flesh shift and I launched myself into the air with a screech. These fools can't hold me. I am Loki!

Oft times the mental outlook of the creatures I become affect my own attitude. Ospreys are proud and fierce.

I rose swiftly. I expected to be shot at with bows. The alfar are famous for their archery. But none came. As I flew over the tops of the tallest trees of the court, I felt the necklace tighten. I tried to dive quickly and get back below the tree line, but I passed out before that happened.

6

FISH OUT OF WATER

I woke in my room on the moss bed under a cover of
woven leaves. It was surprisingly comfortable, but the
coughing fit that wracked me was not. A quarter moon
shone high in the night sky. I felt hands helping me sit up
and turned to see Huld.

"Looks like being stupid didn't kill you," cawed Manny.
"This time."

He was perched on a branch in a tree in front of me. A
wooden bowl of water was presented to my mouth and I
drank deeply. That seems to help the coughing fit.

"I'm surprised I'm not in a dungeon cell," I said when I
could talk again.

"A cell? For our honored guest?" Huld's voice dripped
with sarcasm.

"You hate me that much, eh?"

"It's not just you. I hate all the aesir."

"Then your hatred is largely misplaced." I laughed bitterly.
"My father was a jotunn and my mother was half jotunn. She
would never talk about the rest of her heritage, but if it was
aesir she never said. At best I'm only a quarter aesir."

55

"Most of the aesir are half-breeds," she said with disdain. "Even Odin was a half-blood. And here you stand, not a giant like a real jotunn, and no taller than a typical man. You are more aesir than jotnar."

"Size is a matter of... perspective among the jotnar," I said. "At times they are no taller than you or I. In the right or wrong moods, they are bigger. Just because I am not twelve feet tall doesn't mean I'm not jotnar."

"Still, you still lived and fought with the aesir. You're one in name if not in blood."

"Do you know the story of how I came to live with the aesir?" I asked

"Why would I bother to learn that?" she replied dismissively.

"If you are going to condemn someone, you should understand them. I was born and raised in Jotunheim. My father was Farbauti, chieftain of the Vedrfell clan and brother of Skyrmir. My mother was Laufey, whose mother was a jotunn." I stepped closer.

"All through my childhood Jotunheim and Asgard waged war. The jotnar are physically strong, far stronger than the aesir. But we are clannish and independent. We don't work well together."

"Obviously."

"The aesir raided our villages and killed our people, but never marched against us as an army. So when the calls for help would go out, few would answer. It wasn't enough of a threat to stir all of Jotunheim or even a significant number of clans."

I paused and she nodded for me to continue.

"Yet Skrymir saw and understood what was happening. Thrym may have been king in Jotunheim, but Skrymir was the wisest of his advisers. He knew that Odin and the aesir would chip away at the jotnar until we were weak enough to conquer. Skrymir took a large party of warriors drawn from several clans to Asgard to parlay with Odin. Skrymir showed the aesir that his troupe was made of multiple clans and that he would be able to raise all of Jotunheim to go to war with Asgard."

"To war," Manny cawed. "To war. To war."

I scowled at the bird. "Odin believed the bluff and agreed to negotiate a peace. Skrymir knew he couldn't stop all of the aesir raids. Both of their people were too independent and warlike to honor a true peace. So the terms were that no group of aesir larger than a hand would be allowed to travel in Jotunheim. If six or more were found together in his lands, Skrymir would bring the hosts of Jotunheim to the gates of Asgard. And no group of jotnar numbering more than three could raid in Asgard."

"And how did they manage that?" she asked.

"With vigilance and an agreement that ensured each side had incentive to keep to it. Odin sent his son Meili, brother to Thor and Baldr, to live with Skrymir as his ward. Since Skrymir had no children, my father offered me to Odin. I was considered a half-breed, and I didn't share their flexibility with size. So I became an unwilling ward of Asgard."

I worked a kink out of my neck and she gestured that I finish my tale.

"Meili and I were of similar ages, having just come into puberty. Meili cried piteously as they took him. His mother, Frigg, turned her face, unable to watch. To my eyes, Odin did not seem to care. I know now that he hid how deeply it hurt him. I also know that he denied all memory of Meili and never spoke of him again. No soul in Asgard did, not even Thor. I clung to my father, but I refused to cry like Meili. He swore to me that he would never forget me and that I would always be his son. And so I walked over to Odin, who put his hand on my shoulder. I never saw my father again.

"It was difficult learning the ways of Asgard. Thor hated me for replacing his brother. But Odin commanded Thor to watch over me and threatened grave punishments should harm ever come to me. Still, Thor never forgave me. He taunted and tormented me in a thousand ways, the least of which was spreading the tale of me as the god of mischief and making sure I was blamed for many things I had no hand in."

Huld was quiet for several moments. I couldn't tell if my tale had affected her. My own feelings were roiling with memories of past transgressions.

"There is food for you over there," she said coldly. "You should get some rest. I'll be back in the morning."

Huld was silent the next morning. She tried to help me get dressed and fashion my hair, but I shrugged her off. She threw her hands up and stormed off in a huff, or as close to storming as a woman her age could manage. I finished making myself ready and dug through my duffel for my weapons. Gone. The bitch queen had taken my axe, my knife, and the Sig Sauer.

"What did you expect?" Manny cawed.

"I expected them not to touch my damn stuff!"

"And leave you armed?" Manny laughed. I'll never get used to how creepy his laugh sounds.

Mustering up as much dignity as I could, which is quite a lot thank you very much, I marched out the door alone, planning to see how far Alfhildr's 'hospitality' extended. I knew how to get to the entrance hall, so I went there. On a lark, I tried to enter the throne room, but the wardens blocked my way with their spears. However, the wardens at the main entrance let me leave the queen's court. So I guess I had free run of the city.

I headed for the Ash bridge. I might as well test the limits of my confinement. It didn't take long to get there, and I stood in front of the archway for a moment before strolling slowly through it. The wardens ignored me. Midway through the arch, I felt the necklace around my throat tighten. I quickly backed out.

"Almost dying once wasn't enough for you?" cawed Manny from a low hanging branch.

"Where have you been?"

"Exploring. Learning the streets of Vidrheim."

"Excellent work, Munnin. Tell me, is there a major waterway that winds through the city?"

"I did happen to see one," he cawed.

"Show me where it goes under the wall and leaves Vidrheim."

Manny led me to a narrow river, maybe thirty feet across and flowing into the massive roots of the trees that formed the wall. The current was swifter than I would like. Fortunately, it was somewhat isolated. With no obvious prying eyes around, I set about examining my gift from Alfhildr. I pulled and tugged at it, but it stayed snug on my neck. I felt for a clasp, but my fingers couldn't find one.

"Manny, can you find a clasp?"

"No." He said, peering around both sides of my neck from his perch on my shoulder. "It appears to be one continuous piece."

"What is it made of? It looks like metal in the water's reflection."

"It's silver, braided to look like thorny vines."

Never doubt a raven when it comes to shiny metal things.

"Dvergar work I bet. The alfar don't work in metal."

"Maybe if I pecked at it hard it would break."

"What? No! Keep your beak to yourself."

Manny laughed. I winced.

"Well, let's try a few tricks, shall we?"

Shucking my clothes, I held the shape of a salmon in my mind. I put an image of myself next to it, then tied them together with a braided cord until they merged. My shape twisted and shrank. I quickly flung myself into a shallow side pool away from the current. The world grew larger as I grew smaller. It always takes a few moments to get used to breathing water.

Salmon have no necks. I was hoping to slide the necklace off by scraping it against a rock. I was able to get it to catch, but it wouldn't come loose. I had figured as much, but it was worth a try. Steeling myself, I swam out into the current.

I let the current carry me to the tree roots. Continuing with the theme of salmon have no necks, I hoped that when the band shrank it would just slide off the front of my fish face. As I entered the shadows of the roots, I felt the band constrict. The damn thing wasn't sliding at all.

I hurriedly turned and swam upstream. I made headway at first, such that the damn necklace stopped squeezing. But I quickly tired and began to lose ground to the current. I needed a few feet more before I could change back. If I changed here I would be trapped in the roots and drown. I tried moving sideways to get closer to the shore where the current was weaker.

Suddenly I was gripped tightly. Claws dug into my sides and I was lifted out of the water. Fish vision is quite bad out of the water. I was hoping this was Manny rescuing me and not a hungry fish hawk. The claws let go and I fell to the ground, my gills working desperately.

I quickly changed back, gasping and choking. I was soaking wet and blood ran down my side from a puncture there.

"I have a hole in my side," I complained as soon as I could breathe.

"You're welcome," Manny cawed.

———

I got back to my rooms around sunset and eased myself into the bath pond. The wound in my side was painful, but shallow. After soaking for several minutes I heard Huld in the other room. I waited, not really wanting to deal with her.

When I came out of the bathing room wrapped in the alfar equivalent of a towel, she was standing stiffly by a plate of food. I turned away from her and dropped the towel. She would just have to deal with it. My jeans and t-shirt were set neatly on the shelf next to my boots, but I pulled on a fresh alfar tunic and breeches before turning back. She hadn't moved.

"Your evening meal is getting cold, Lord Loki."

"I'm certain I don't need help eating it. Or are you just here to gloat at the captive Asgardian?" I asked bitterly.

"You are an honored guest until the full moon. And I'm here to clear the meal when you are done."

"Are all honored guests collared like a temperamental hound?"

"No. Only you," she said with a satisfied grin.

"So what happens on the full moon?"

She shrugged. "The queen is no longer obliged to provide for you. In your case, you are free to leave."

"Interesting. So this necklace loses it's enchantment then?"

"I suppose. But it doesn't matter," she said grimly. "You'll be on your way to Asgard long before then."

"Ah, yes. The prisoner exchange."

We were silent for a moment. Each contemplating the future, albeit with very different feelings.

"You knew Frey, did you not?" Huld asked, changing topics.

"Yngvi? Of course. All of Asgard knew Frigg's twin brother."

"We knew him here as Frey, or Lord," she said stonily. "His sister we called Freyja, or Lady."

"Odin gifted him Alfheim," I noted, wondering where she was going with this.

"Alfheim was not Odin's to give," she hissed. Obviously, this was a sensitive issue.

"You know Yngvi was pureblood vanir, not aesir?"

"No," she said, taken aback for a moment. "But it doesn't matter. He was from Asgard. He was aesir in spirit if not in blood."

I was curious why she was getting so worked up over Yngvi. He died almost a thousand years ago at Ragnarokkr.

"True. He embraced Asgard, as did Frigg."

"So you admired him?" she asked cautiously.

"Yngvi?" I laughed. "He was a mighty warrior, but an arrogant, womanizing bastard. In other words, a typical Asgardian."

Manny cawed in agreement.

"But you're an Asgardian," she said, clearly surprised at my answer.

"That's debatable after Ragnarokkr. I led the armies of Jotunheim across the Bifrost Bridge and laid waste to Asgard. Somehow I think they may hold that against me, what's left of them."

"I... I suppose that's true."

I had finished eating while telling my story. Huld took the wooden dishes and left, deep in thought. I heard her trip and fall just outside the door followed by some impressive cursing. Manny squawked and gave me a hard look.

"What?" I asked with exaggerated innocence.

7

MERRIMENT

T oday we are looking for Manibrandr," I said to Manny once we got out of the Court.

"It's morning," he cawed. "Don't you think night would be the time to search?"

"Then we'll identify places to search when night falls." I hate it when he's right.

By noon I had identified two taverns with the appropriate amount of disrepute, the Rook's Eye and the Burning Burl. Of course, the alfar definition of tavern was not what I was used to. Both were small glades overshadowed by old oaks and walled in by thorny bramble. But ultimately a tavern is a tavern. It serves intoxicating beverages and trades in gossip and rowdy behavior. It was no different here in Vidrheim.

I found a shop selling lyres easily enough.

"How much for this one?" I asked the alfar shopkeeper. He was a small man with unusually large ears and a balding pate. He wore a simple brown shift that left his knobby knees and wide, flat bare feet exposed.

"What do you have to trade?"

"Just what you see before you," I answered ruefully. I had

already gleaned that the alfar had a barter economy. The rest of the Nine Worlds used gold, but the alfar disdained the value of anything dug out of the ground, especially metal.

"What can you shape?"

"I am not an alfr. I don't have the talent to shape wood."

"Sadly it sounds like you have nothing to trade for my lyre," The shopkeeper said, shaking his head.

I picked up the lyre and plucked at the strings. It was in good tune. I softly sang a few lines of a sea shanty that had been forgotten on Midgard long before Ragnarokkr.

"You have a fine voice," the shopkeeper observed. "And a good touch on the strings. I tell you what. You play out front of my shop until sunset and you can have that lyre."

"Done," I said a little too quickly. Too many decades in America and I had lost the talent for haggling. Fortunately, the shopkeeper didn't take advantage of me by changing the deal.

I was rusty at first but soon found my voice. Back in the day, I had been one of the finest skalds in Asgard and Midgard. I had bested Bragi Boddason in a contest and composed for Eyvindr Finnsson. I sang the Ragnarsdrapa in honor of Bragi and Hakonamal for Evyindr.

The shopkeeper seemed pleased that my playing brought customers into his shop. In Midgard, I would have put out a hat and collected tips. Here I collected compliments.

Sunset came quickly as I lost myself in the poems and the music. I found myself chanting the Husdrapa as the sun found its bed. The scenes of Baldr's funeral brought tears to my eyes, but my voice and fingers were steady. I set the lyre down and cried shamelessly while alfar hands brushed my shoulders and back in sympathy.

The shopkeeper, whose name I had never gotten, silently handed me the lyre with a smile. I wiped my eyes and gave him a brief hug. As I made my way to the Rook's

Eye, I put away all those stinging memories and steeled myself.

All societies have their seedy sides. There are always people who don't agree with society's rules ... or any rules whatsoever. Yet they have to live with them, so they cheat and steal on the sly, and make trouble just for the joy of it. And many of them apparently like to drink at the Rook's Eye.

I entered boldly with Manny on my shoulder. What better way to call attention to myself than with a rook on my shoulder. Okay, he's not exactly a rook, but he's closely related. Not that I pointed it out to him. I didn't need another hole in my temple.

There were less than a dozen alfar in the tavern, mostly men. It would be kind to call the patrons unkempt and half drunk. The tavern keeper was pouring ale for a man at the counter.

"Kind sir, would you allow me to play and sing a few songs for the odd coin?" I asked, hefting my lyre.

He gave me a long look before jerking his head in the direction of the back of the place. Most taverns like skalds to play. Patrons stay longer and drink more if there is entertainment. I was betting that my being aesir made him nervous though.

I started out with something simple, "I Dreamt a Dream Last Night." It wasn't exactly a rousing song, but I had a plan to get their attention.

> *Droymde mik ein draum i nott*
>> *um silk ok aerlig pell,*
>> *um haegindi sva djupt ok mjott,*

um rosemd med engan skell.

The first stanza is all about dreaming of sleeping peacefully in a soft bed. I don't have the skill of Bragi, but I am a damn fine skald. I had their attention. The rhyme goes on to describe setting aside all cares and worries. Instead, I sang about the mystery sleeper being joined by a lover. A few grins and guffaws broke out. The song turned bawdier, drawing out a few coarse cheers and some foot-stomping. I concluded with the sleeper waking suddenly to find the lover was just a dog. That got some big laughs.

The tavern keeper handed me a wooden mug of ale. "That was a fine song."

"A grand thank you kind sir," I answered with a deep bow.

I sang two more songs, one about Thor where he ended up pulling his own chariot while his goats held the reins and wielded the whip. Another about a pair of jotnar who fell in love with each other's wives, only to discover the wives had left them for a pair of alfar. I got a second mug of ale from someone in the audience for that one.

I switched to sleight-of-hand tricks, pulling flowers from behind ears and making mugs disappear. As I entertained, I watched each of them, looking for a clue as to who might know about the more dangerous parts of alfar society, such as the moon kin. I spotted one such man in the back toying with a chert dagger. No self-respecting alfr would have a stone weapon.

"A break, I beg of you," I shouted over the din of cat-calls and cheers. "I'll sing some ballads after I've rested my throat."

I plopped myself down at the small table with my dagger wielding friend.

"Mind if I sit for a spell?" I asked, my ass already firmly in the seat. He grudgingly nodded.

"I noticed your knife," I said. "Fine chert from the look of it."

He slid the knife inside his tunic, clearly not happy that I had noticed it.

"What of it?"

"Oh, it's no skin off my back if you carry a stone weapon," I said with a broad smile. "I hope you haven't had much cause to use it in self-defense."

He leered at me, not so subtly telling me it had indeed tasted blood. Watching him toy with it earlier, I was convinced he had little or no talent with blades, but it doesn't take a lot of talent to stick a man.

"You look like a man whose skill with the blade would be a match even for the Manibrandr."

"Nah. I ain't that good. Manibrandr, they move like the fog and strike like a wasp."

"Surely they can't be all that," I said, feigning disbelief.

"I tell ya, they be true killers of the night. By the time a man sees them, he's already been dead for nine heartbeats."

"Since your heart is still beating, you've not met one yourself," I challenged. "So how do you know?"

"I just do," he said, suddenly cagey. Jackpot.

"A man of knowledge I see. I am Ulfr."

"Knutr," he said proudly, as if that would mean something to me.

I bought drinks for us both with coin I had pickpocketed from audience members. I worked Knutr for a while, wheedling and flattering and cajoling. He wanted to say something. He wanted to brag and put me in my place while affirming his superiority. So I left him and went back to performing.

I sang ballads of Odin and spun tales of Loki. I wonder what they would have thought had they known who I was. For all I knew they did. Word gets around in a city like

Vidrheim. I did more magic tricks using things I had planted elsewhere in the tavern before I returned to sing again. Finally, I begged off for another break and returned to my odd friend's table with a pair of drinks donated by a couple of new fans.

"I've met Manibrandr," he gloated abruptly.

"We've already established that your heart still beats, Knutr, so I strongly doubt that," I said, shaking my head sadly.

"It's true," he said fervently. "My brother's wife's nephew left to join them."

"Just up and left? One day just decided to become an alfr assassin of the night?"

"It's true, I tell you," he said obstinately. He was drunk and getting belligerent.

"So does she ever see him now? Do they have family supper at the Manibrandr manse?"

"You mock me, but I swear it's true you aesir whore!"

Our conversation went downhill from there. I did manage to weasel his brother's wife's name out of him before mugs went flying. I would hunt her down tomorrow. I did well for myself in the ensuing brawl. It seems a lot of the patrons had grudges against one another, which left me to pick and choose my targets. Of course, Knutr lay unconscious under his table with a mug shaped welt in his skull.

It was past midnight when I returned to my room. Huld was there, of course. I scowled at her and she ignored me and laid out the dishes for my supper.

"I've already eaten," I growled.

"By your smell, you've been drinking too," she said sourly.

"Better to loosen the tongues of the alfar."

"And what did you hope to learn from drunks?"

"If you must know, I'm looking for the moon kin. I figured the less reputable parts of town were the best place to ask around."

"Manibrandr? They are myths, stories told to frighten alfar children. Why would you look for them?"

"If you must know, someone sent two of them to kill me on Midgard. I'd like to know who."

"What?"

"Oh, and they are real. Odin told me tales of them. I even tried to persuade them to join me at Ragnarokkr. So I've been face to face with them before."

"They are real? Is it true about their moon blades?"

"Yes. The blade cuts your spirit as well as your body. If a moon blade kills you, there is no spirit to go to Hel. Or Valhalla, or Folkvangr, or anywhere else. Odin told me the moon kin absorb their enemy's spirit through the blade, but it seemed like he didn't believe that."

"I... I need to go."

I watched quietly as she gathered my dishes and hurried out.

"Is it wise to tell her so much?" Manny cawed.

"Probably not, but I'm a little bit drunk. Sometimes I do stupid things when I drink too much."

"And sometimes when you don't," he cackled.

8

THE VISITOR

"Y ou have a visitor," Huld told me as she cleared my breakfast dishes the next day. "I'm to see you to the throne room."

"A visitor? But nobody knows I'm here. Wait... she sent word to Asgard. It's an Asgardian, isn't it?"

"I don't know, Lord Loki. I haven't seen him. But I assume so."

"Well, this should be interesting. Let's go see who's come to collect me."

The last dish Huld grabbed slipped from her fingers. As she tried to catch it, the rest teetered before also slipping away. I shook my head in mock disapproval. I suppose it really wasn't fair of me to smear hair oil all around the edge. And who still puts oil in hair anymore? It's way too old fashioned for a modern man like myself. But it was fun to listen to her curse.

I made sure to dress in my best alfar duds. I strode past Einar into the throne room like I owned the place. Haughty and strutting, I was the epitome of an Asgardian Lord.

Alfhildr was on her throne, surrounded by the same set of simpering alfar.

"Queen Alfhildr," I said, bowing low and overly dramatically. I've found it never hurts to overdo it with royalty.

"Lord Loki," she said, voice quavering. She sounded weaker than at our first audience. "So good of you to join us."

"It is always my pleasure to attend to your highness."

She laughed but ended up coughing. A man stepped out from behind the crowd of alfar lords.

"Skirnir, old friend! So good to see you. It's wonderful to see another Asgardian face here. When her highness is through with us, I'll have to show you around the city."

"I'm not here to sight-see or carouse," Skirnir said grimly. He looked older but still energetic, with collar-length steel gray hair and a full gray beard. Quite frankly I was surprised he was alive. I hadn't figured Thor to be that generous with Idunn's fruit.

His pale blue eyes flickered to Manny, who sat on my shoulder, then locked again with mine. He wore a leather hauberk that looked more ceremonial than battle-tested. A sword hung at one side, and a coil of thin, silvery chain hung on the other. Despite his obvious age, he looked fit and competent.

"Then you must be here to take over Frey's estate," I said conspiratorially. "After all, you were his manservant. I'm certain the alfar have kept it in tip-top shape for the last thousand years."

"No aesir will ever take possession of that place," Alfhildr said, all but spitting the words. The entire room grew tense.

"Loki," Skirnir said calmly. "Do not seek to open old wounds between Asgard and Alfheim. I know your ways of old, God of Mischief. Queen Alfhildr knows we do not seek dominion over Alfheim."

Alfhildr relaxed in her tree throne. The rest of the courtiers did likewise. It had been worth a try.

"God?" I laughed. "None of them are gods, Skirnir. Not you and especially not me."

"You would rank us with the jotnar? Or the midgardians? We are as far above them as they are above their sheep."

"And where would you rank the alfar? Or the dvergar? Are they sheep too?"

The room got still. Aesir arrogance was a sore point with all the races of the Nine Worlds. The Skirnir I knew of old looked down on all of them.

"You twist my words, mischief maker. The alfar are loyal allies of Asgard."

"Your words twist themselves. Come now. Are the alfar the equals of the aesir, or are they just loyal like a good hunting dog?"

"Queen Alfhildr," Skirnir said, ignoring me and pulling out the thin, silvery chain. "By your leave, I'll take charge of your prisoner now."

"Have you come for me with Gleipnir? Are you here to chain me like you did my son," I asked softly but menacingly.

"He was an animal," Skirnir said coldly. "And he took his pound of flesh."

"He was just a boy! My boy. My son!" I shouted. Even after a thousand years, the pain of that betrayal stung.

"Enough. Loki is not your prisoner, he is an honored guest," Alfhildr said with a scowl. "And you do not yet have my leave."

Interesting.

"There is the matter of my granddaughter," she continued.

"That was not part of the deal," Skirnir said, looking cautiously frustrated.

"I think it may be time to renegotiate that deal," she said firmly.

"I don't think Thor will take kindly to that," I said sweetly.

"He will if he wants you," Alfhildr snapped. "And if he doesn't, there are others who would pay for you."

"So who am I to be sold to, Skirnir?" I interrupted again. "Or will it be an auction to the highest bidder?"

"That's enough, Loki," Alfhildr said. "Leave us."

A pair of wardens appeared next to me. Sneaky bastards. Skirnir's look told me I wasn't going to get an answer. They marched me out while Alfhildr and Skirnir stared coldly at each other. Well, at least I had caused a little mischief. Finding who sent the Manibrandr after me was suddenly not as urgent. Skirnir and Thor were far more pressing problems.

Back in my room, I paced, furiously trying to come up with a plan. There must be a way to get rid of this damned necklace. If we were closer to the full moon, I might try to delay Skirnir's negotiations until time ran out, but it was too far away.

9

FREEDOM

"ood morrow, Lord Loki," Huld said as I groggily raised my head from the moss bed. The sun was just peeking over the hedge walls. She began picking up my cast-off clothes, shaking her head in mild disgust.

"Manny! You let me sleep all day and night!"

"I doubt I could have woken you had I wanted to," Manny cawed.

"I'm surprised I'm not trussed on the back of a horse behind Skirnir on my way to Asgard," I said grumpily.

"He still negotiates with Alfhildr," Huld said.

As she picked up the under tunic, a small bird burst from under it, flying into her face. Huld stumbled back and fell onto her skinny ass. A short laugh escaped my lips before I could stop it. I quickly donned my well-practiced "'who, me?'" face. It only takes a small seidr to charm a bird into thinking a garment is her nest.

"I suppose you think that was funny." Huld regained her feet.

I just grinned.

"I thought Alfhildr had already made a deal with Asgard," I said, changing the subject.

"No. The queen told you what she wants. Asgard only promised goodwill in exchange for you."

"And Skirnir can make new bargains? I'm surprised Thor allows that."

"I'm not privy to details of their discussions, but that is what I was told."

"So I have some time then," I mused. Then I had a thought. "Huld, have any other Asgardians visited Vidrheim in the past year or so?"

"Vidarr paid his respects to the queen half a dozen moons ago."

"Vidarr? Vengeance. The fox told me it would be vengeance. Odin used to call him the avenger. Vidarr avenged Odin's death at Ragnarokkr. Do you know what Vidarr wanted?"

"Court rumor held that he only asked to travel in Alfheim."

"It could be that he searched for the Manibrandr," Manny cawed.

"It could also be that he had to admit that to Alfhildr," I said. "If so, that is who she would send a message to once I was her 'guest of honor.'" I paused, "Vidarr has no love for me, nor I for him."

"Did he wrong you?" Huld asked. I wasn't sure, but it looked like she might like the idea that someone had wronged me.

"He killed my son, Fenrir," I said coldly. "And if I ever have him under my power... well, let's just say it won't be pretty."

I wandered Vidrheim fruitlessly, watching the sun creep overhead. Time was passing and I was no closer to escaping. Alfhildr and Skirnir would eventually make a bargain, and it would certainly include sending me to Asgard. As good as a death sentence.

I got back to Alfhildr's court well after sundown. I had contemplated hiding somewhere in the city, but ultimately decided that would only buy me a day at most. Better to face them and try to bargain for myself.

Huld was pacing my room when I arrived. "Loki! Where have you been?"

"Out."

"Alfhildr and Skirnir have made their bargain. In the morning he will take you to Asgard. In chains."

"And why would you care about that? You've made it clear you have no love for aesir or Asgardians."

"You... you are not what I thought you would be," she said uncomfortably. "You are different."

"At least I persuaded someone I'm not an evil bastard," I said with a sigh. "Not that it matters."

"I know a way out of Virdheim. A way out that won't end up with you choked to death by that necklace."

"Now why would you help me escape?" I asked suspiciously. "You hate all Asgardians, and you would be betraying your own queen."

"What would you do if you had Skirnir in your power?"

"Kill him," I said instantly. What did that have to do with anything?

"That's why," she said vehemently.

"What did Skirnir ever do to you?"

"He was a vassal of Frey," she said, taking a deep breath. "I hated Frey. My only regret is that he died at Ragnarokkr and not by my hand."

"I watched Surtur slay him," I said softly. "Only ash was left."

"Frey ruled Alfheim, or at least kept an estate here and did whatever he pleased. That you know. What you don't know is that he had his way with many of his alfar serving girls. Many he would seduce. Those he couldn't he forced himself on."

"Yngvi did have a way with women."

"I was very young, just coming into my womanhood when Frey began to pay attention to me. I was flattered. He was so handsome and so charming. My mother tried to warn me about him, but I wouldn't listen. Then one day he stopped. He ignored me completely no matter how outrageously I flirted with him. I discovered my mother was giving herself to him, and in exchange, he was leaving me alone. She would come back to our home bruised and hurting. He acted out some of his darker urges on her because she wouldn't complain."

I moved closer and met her gaze. She continued.

"I saw him differently then. He held no attraction for me after that. Nevertheless I tried to make the same bargain for her that she had for me. I would let him take me if he would leave my mother alone. He just laughed and told me that it was only a matter of time before my mother would break and then he would have me anyway. When I told my mother this, she secreted me out of his estate. The next day she was dead. She killed herself rather than let him touch her again. Skirnir delivered the news to me. He gleefully whispered to me that my mother had whored herself out to him in exchange for my freedom."

"A dark tale," I admitted.

"So you ask me why would I help you? Because there is the smallest chance that if you go free you'll kill Skirnir."

"I cannot make you any promises, Huld," I said. "But I

hold no love for Yngvi or his vassals. If I get the chance, I will avenge my son and your mother."

I put my old jeans and t-shirt back on. Huld led me out of the room and down some unfamiliar halls. We finally stopped at an unremarkable hedge wall. Overhead the three-quarter waxing moon lit the space around us. Manny rode my shoulder.

"The throne room is on the other side of this wall," Huld whispered. "You'll need to climb to the top and wait for me to distract the guards."

"And how do you expect me to climb a bush?" I asked. I knew how, but I was curious how much she really knew about me.

"Change into some sort of animal, you fool."

Okay, so she knew me well enough.

"Alfhildr's throne is a gateway to Yggdrasil," she continued. "I don't know how to use it. You'll have to figure it out yourself."

"I don't see how that helps. So I'll be dead on Yggdrasil."

"Every curse has a weakness, a way to break it. It's one of the rules of enchanting. The necklace's enchantment only works in Alfheim."

"So the exception is to leave both Vidrheim and Alfheim at the same time, which seems impossible, but it isn't," I said, nodding my approval. "Clever."

"Kill him slowly if you get the chance."

And with that, she strode away. Alone in the passage, I stripped off my clothes. Next, I called up an image of a pine marten. I've become weasels and ferrets like the pine marten before, but it's hard. Smaller is more difficult, and this is about as small as I could get at the moment. The hedge was no match for my tiny claws and superb balance, even dragging my bundled clothes. I was soon atop the leafy wall and looking down into the grassy glade of the throne room.

Manny took flight and silently glided to a perch in the old oak tree of the throne. I noticed he approached high and into the moonlight to avoid casting a shadow. He ain't no dummy.

I didn't have long to wait. Huld came in with a wooden plate laden with food. The wardens relaxed and strolled over to sample it. While their backs were turned I scampered down the hedge and behind the oak before changing back.

This close to the tree I could feel the connection. I kicked myself mentally for not noticing it before. I slunk widdershins around the large trunk, waiting for the spirit wind to show me the portal. Three times turned out to be the magic number. I eased my naked self onto the throne, duffel bag modestly in my lap. Manny glided down and perched on my shoulder again. I draped myself on the seat in an insolent pose.

"Oh boys," I called out, overly loud. "I really don't know how Alfhid sits on this uncomfortable stump."

The wardens turned with a cry, spears at the ready. Seeing me seated on the throne like I was the king of all Alfheim must have enraged them. They charged me with those bright tipped spears aimed right at my chest.

"Don't miss me when I'm gone," I said, blowing them a kiss and falling into the tree and out onto Yggdrasil.

10

SAGA

I steadied myself and clawed at that damnable necklace. My fingers shredded it easily and I breathed a sigh of relief.

"So Huld was telling the truth," Manny cawed.

"You thought she might me lying?" I shouted. "And you didn't say anything."

"I thought she might be wrong," he replied. "There's a difference. And if there had been any other options, I would have warned you."

"Next time warn me anyway," I fired back. "Even if there aren't any other options."

"Where's the fun in that?" Manny laughed.

"I'm stumbling around in the dark here. I need answers."

"The Norns then?" Manny cawed.

"No! By Odin's beard I'm not going to see those three witches. Their price is too high."

"Who then?"

"An old friend back on Midgard."

"Are you sure she's up to it?"

"No, but she's my best option."

I've visited the Morton Arboretum a few times during the years. I've visited all the arboretums in the Chicago area more than once. The big old oak was not the largest or oldest oak in the state, but it was a respectable specimen, resplendent with fall colors.

A little bump and lift at the nearby Walmart and I had what I needed to get into the city. I wanted to check on Esme, but first I was going to visit an old drinking buddy.

"Saga," I said, kneeling to look the nearly passed out, drunken woman in the eye.

"Whut?" she asked belligerently.

"Let's get you sober."

She looked awful and smelled worse. It was hard to see what time had done to the once great beauty with crystal blue eyes and cascading blonde locks. Saga looked like one of the long-suffering homeless addicts of Chicago, because she was one. I hauled her up, trying not to gasp as I got a strong whiff. The stale booze almost drowned out the more pungent odors. Almost.

I dragged her to a shelter not too far away. I always made sure to know where a nearby shelter was when I visited her. Shower and some coffee were definitely called for.

"Is it time already, Loki?" she asked, sitting down with me at a dilapidated table.

She was still drunk, but now she was clean and wearing the cheap, gray sweatpants and sweatshirt I had brought. A large cup of bad coffee was waiting for her. She cleaned up well. Long blonde hair, tangled and uncombed, framed a classic Nordic face. Saga was neither young nor old.

"Lowell. No. Not yet."

"Then what'r you here for?"

"I need your help."

She spit her first mouthful of coffee out on the floor. "God, that's awful. You ain't got somethin' stronger do ya?"

"No. You know how this goes. Coffee first. Then we talk. Then you can have some fruit."

"This ain't coffee. It's mud and dog shit in water."

"It's what they have here, and it's not that bad."

It was that bad. But I took a sip of my own to encourage her. An hour later she was relatively sober. Saga always did have a high tolerance for alcohol. It took a lot to get her drunk and more to keep her that way. Yet somehow she managed to stay sloshed all the time. Go figure.

"You didn't have to sober me just to get an apple," Saga said. 'Apple' was how we referred to Idunn's fruit in public.

"That's not why I'm here. I'm not out of them just yet."

"I thought it was too soon. So go away and let me get drunk again."

"Can't do that." I shook my head. I felt like an ass for what I was about to do.

"Don't ask me," she said, beginning to tremble.

"I need to."

"No, please," she begged quietly.

"I have to. You owe me."

"Bastard," she hissed, crossing her arms and looking away. I saw a tear rolling down one cheek.

"Lady Saga, I call upon you to honor your debt to me, Loki, by using your foresight to read my possible futures."

"You really are a cold-hearted bastard."

"Yeah, I know," I said miserably.

"Not here. Let's go somewhere else."

The vacant lot was well hidden from the road. Empty buildings loomed over it on either side. The rundown tenement behind it had a couple of dim lights on since the sun was just setting. The October air was chilly.

"Sit there." Saga pointed, wrapping her arms around herself.

"There? That's a mud puddle."

"I know."

Manny laughed his creepy crow laugh. I wanted to argue, but I was the one being an asshole here. She was allowed to be one back. So I sat. Cold and wet instantly seeped into my pants. Saga smiled, pulling out a cord from her hair. I swear it hadn't been there before.

"I'll call the vaettir, but you ask the questions."

I nodded. She chanted softly in old Norse, retelling the story of Gullveig, who taught seidr to the Aesir. A good story for the task. I joined her and we chanted together while she slowly braided the cord. The rhyming stanzas came easily.

That man hon fokvig,
   fyrst I heimi,
   er gullveigu,
   geirum studdu,
   ok I holl Hars,
   hana brenndu,
   thrisvar brenndu,
   thrisvar borna,
   oft, osjaldan,
   tho hon enn lifir.

The spirit wind took shape. The material world faded, but didn't vanish. I saw through the shrubs and trash piles and brick walls. I spotted the glowing blobs of the spirits of the people around us, devoid of shape in our altered state. Only Manny and Saga were solid and real. Even with Saga directing, it took an effort of will to balance myself between the spirit wind and the real world. More than one seidrmenn had lost his spirit to the wind and drifted away.

All around me fog-like tendrils carried small sparks on the spirit wind, which always flowed toward Yggdrasil. That wind would flow to the roots of the mighty Tree of Life, nourishing it with sparks, which were the spirits of small animals and even insects that had died.

Saga and I watched for a larger spark, a vaettir. It took a while, but she spotted one first. The vaettir don't like big cities. Saga focused her chanting, speaking directly to the approaching vaettir. I let my spirit drift nearer, cutting across the wind, but not against it. I could sense the essence of a fox. Out of the corner of my eye I saw a snake vaettir slither to Saga. It was always a snake for her.

The vaettir are ancient spirits of nature. They sometimes like to play in the spirit wind, carried along with the dead, but never straying too far from the places they've chosen to claim.

"Brother fox," I whispered in my mind, still focusing on the vaettir. Continuing to chant with my mouth and thinking a completely different thing to the fox is one of the hardest parts of the seid.

"Brother jotunn," it pulsed, its ears swiveling toward me.

"What see you of the times behind me?" I asked. It was the first of the three ritual questions.

"You drifted. Then you ran like the rabbit, first from the uncle, then the brother. Then you drifted, and ran, over and over for as long as I can see."

"What see you of the times around me?"

"The snare wound tight around your neck. It sits with

another snare and another. Should you escape one, you are in danger of stepping in the next."

"What see you of the times ahead of me?"

"On the left paw, vengeance takes you and skins you. On the right paw, the child releases you and you hunt the waning moon. On the tail, you follow the spirit wind."

With that, the vaettir floated away, carried by the spirit wind. I knew trying to ask more was futile. They are capricious and once they've answered the three required questions it's difficult to make them stay. The Saga of old could cajole one into talking with her for many long minutes, but not now.

The story of Gullveig was ending. Saga's trembling hands finished braiding the cord. As we chanted the last stanza, they became solid and Saga collapsed on the trash strewn ground.

"Back with the living?" Manny cawed.

"Shut up," I said, scrambling over to tend to Saga.

"No, no, no," she was weeping.

"It's okay," I said softy, pulling her to me. "It's over. It's over."

"Let me die," she cried, clinging to me. "Just let me die."

"What did you see?"

"What she always sees," Manny cawed.

"Which is what?"

"It's not for you to know."

Saga pushed away and scrambled over the ground searching for something. I stood up and followed her. She grabbed an empty glass bottle and quickly smashed it on a piece of rubble. I grabbed her hand as she tried to jam it into her neck.

"Just let me die," she sobbed. "Let it be over."

Half an hour later, I eased Saga back into her spot in the alley, a half empty bottle of gin in her hand. As much as I'd love to keep her sober, drinking was the only thing that stopped her from harming herself after her visions. Better drunk and alive than sober and dead.

"I spoke with a fox vaettir," I said to Manny.

"A fox? Luck was with you."

"Maybe. He only spoke in riddles, describing three possible futures."

"Riddles are better than most get."

"The spirits speak almost plainly to Frigg," I griped.

"Her mastery of seidr is unsurpassed," Manny cawed. "Only Odin ever came close to her skill."

"Hey, I was considered a master of seidr when I lived in Asgard."

"You were the unsurpassed master of galdr, but not seidr. Among the Aesir you were outmatched by at least four others. Among the Vanir from which Frigg hails, you would have been of middling skill at best."

"It mentioned vengeance."

"Vengeance?" Manny cawed.

"Vidarr."

"The God of Vengeance."

"God? Hardly," I snorted. "If it is Vidarr, I'm guessing he isn't doing Thor's bidding. Skirnir certainly wasn't. Unless Vidarr suddenly became a schemer in the past nine hundred years, he's doing someone else's bidding. I say we go ask him."

"The lion's den it is," Manny cawed.

"First a nap. I'm exhausted."

"And Esme?"

"After the nap."

E sme wasn't home. In fact, she wasn't anywhere. Her friend Corinne hadn't seen her in more than a week.

Reluctantly I went back to the *Voluspa*. Manny scouted it out from the air and gave it the all clear. None of Alfhildr's goons were waiting for me. I retrieved my phone and called Esme. Finally!

"Lowell? Is that you?"

"Yes. I just wanted to call and let you know I'm okay."

"Where are you? I'll come get you."

"I'm not in Mexico," I said, flinching. There was silence on the other end. Then a torrent of Spanish erupted from the speaker.

"Esme... Esme!"

"You piece of shit! I've spent the last week looking for you and you're not even in Mexico."

"I'd told you to fly home."

"Well, I didn't. I looked for you."

"You can come home now."

"Oh, I can?" she said, her voice dripping sarcasm. "How generous of you Lowell. You go and fucking disappear for a week, leaving me on my own in Mexico and now you give me permission to come home."

"I'm sorry, Esme," I said, wincing. "I wish I could explain, but I can't. I'm sorry."

"Oh, you'll explain all right. When I get back I'm going to cut your balls off and you'll get them back when I know what the fuck is going on."

"This is why I didn't want you coming with me."

I knew as soon as I said it, that it was a mistake.

"You what? You didn't just give me an 'I told you so.'"

"Esme—"

"Lowell," she said, her voice breaking. "I know you're in trouble. I can help you. Just tell me what is going on."

"You wouldn't believe me if I told you," I said miserably. "Just come home."

"What? And then we'll—"

"I won't be here, so don't look for me."

"What do you mean you won't be there?"

"I have to go. Keep the car. It's yours for all the trouble I've caused."

I hung up on the rapid-fire Spanish, feeling like a turd. This happens to me a lot when I get close to people. I hurt them because I'm not like them. And when my other life rears its ugly head, they suffer along with me. Wiping the tears from my face, I left the *Voluspa* in search of a gateway tree to Yggdrasil.

TO ASGARD

Walking Yggdrasil is mostly boring. I was soon wishing we had Thor's chariot or Odin's mighty horse Sleipnir. Either would have made the trip much faster. I still missed Sleipnir. The only true dangers on the Tree are the other travelers. Fortunately, we didn't meet any of them. I was wishing I had thought to grab some food though.

We arrived in a shallow gully in sparse woods. I had no idea where we were, but I could feel the familiarity of it. Asgard. My prison and home for many centuries. I had so many conflicting feelings. Everything is over-sized in Asgard. The trees around me were large, even the saplings. The colors were richer than a Midgard forest. It was beautiful.

I also remembered what it looked like after Ragnarokkr as I walked the battlefield, the sour taste of victory in my mouth, the sun coming out from behind the moon. Smoke and fire obscured even that pale light. The smell of death assaulting my nose.

I shook my head to clear my thoughts. There was no point in revisiting that past. It was done. History. I couldn't undo it if I wanted to, not that I did.

"Painful memories?" Manny asked.

"You should know. You were there, on Odin's shoulder."

"I do. I remember it all. I remember everything. Every detail, sight, smell, and sound."

"Why did you come to me afterward? I was responsible for Odin's death."

"Memory does not belong to just one man. While I served Odin, he needed me most. Now you do."

"You need a new line. I still don't understand. Why do I need you?"

"It is important for you to remember Ragnarokkr. If it comes again, *when* it comes again, you need to remember the heavy toll it takes. You need to remember the price of victory. Of destruction."

"So you want me to stop the next Ragnarokkr?" I asked incredulously. "You are memory, not fate nor future. You cannot know that it will happen again."

"History repeats itself. That's what memory knows."

"Asgard was broken. I broke it. Odin is dead. Many of the old powers on both sides are dead. Even if they all still lived, Thor is no Odin. He is not a danger to the Nine Worlds."

"So you fought on the fields of Vigrid because Odin was a threat to the Nine Worlds?"

"Fly away you heartless raven," I said, remembering why I had done it. "Do something useful and figure out where we are."

I hate arguing with Manny. Someday I hope to win. Just once. Instead, I stomped away. The trees where hard to see through the tears welling in my eyes, trying to forget certain memories.

Manny spotted the city from the air a few leagues away. It wasn't a total surprise. Compared to Midgard, the rest of the Nine Worlds are small, including Asgard.

The world of Asgard is beautiful but rugged. I didn't recognize this patch of forest even though I likely roamed it when I lived with the aesir. A few centuries will make a place unrecognizable. Aspen, rowan, and alder trees surrounded me. Birds and small animals abounded. I passed through gentle glades of soft grasses and wildflowers.

It was late in the day by the time I saw Asgard's walls. It hadn't changed at all since I left. When I first came to Asgard massive log timbers, as big as California redwoods, stood upright in a thick stone base taller than a tall man. The timbers were chinked with clay. The aesir are not skilled builders, having brought human engineers from Midgard to design those walls.

It was only later that Odin struck a deal with a jotnar mason to build better walls. A deal that I paid for dearly when I helped cheat him out of his payment. Since then the walls of Asgard were made of large, white, rectangular granite blocks six feet wide and three feet high. They were fit together so well that a sheet of paper could not be fit between them. The high walls were broken by fat, round towers every so often. Bright blue-tiled conical roofs topped the towers with waving yellow pendants. To an unknowing visitor, it might look more like Camelot. A heavily fortified Camelot.

The walls encircled a town and the several estates of the aesir lords. I was on the west side of Asgard. The main gate lay to the east. I could have just flown over the walls and into the city, but because I valued my life I just watched for a while. Just before full dark, I saw a bird shot out of the sky by arrows. I guess they still guarded against me.

I waited until several hours after full dark. Lanterns were lit along the wall. It was easier to see the sentinels now. Although every tower seemed to be manned, the walls were walked only occasionally. It was hard to tell from this distance, but they looked to be unarmored men bearing bows. I'm sure they also carried some sort of axe or sword, but I couldn't make it out.

"See you on the other side," I said cheerfully to Manny. He just cawed in a way that I've learned is the crow equivalent of an eye roll.

"I'm not going into the city with you," Manny cawed.

"What? Why not?"

"I have my reasons."

"Stop trying to be mysterious."

"Asgard was my home for centuries," Manny said. "Returning there now would bring back many memories that I'd rather not face."

"You're lying. You are the master of memory. There must be some other reason."

"Actually, I'm the Steward of Memory."

"Stop changing the subject. Why are you lying to me and why won't you go into the city."

"'I'm not telling you the whole truth, but I can't say any more," Manny cawed. "But no matter what you say or do, I'm not going in there with you. You're on your own."

"Fine," I said, peeved. "I can do this on my own."

"I'll find you when you leave."

I waited for the timing to be right and then changed into an owl. Between the great night vision and the silent wing flaps it was an obvious choice.

With a hoot, I launched myself into the air. Manny also took wing but headed back toward the trees. I kept low to avoid my silhouette from showing against the sky. I made for the center of the wall, between two lanterns. Luck was with me. No arrows came whizzing out of the night as I flew just over the crenellations, across the wall, and down the other side.

I circled, looking for a good prospect and struggled to get my bearings. Everything within the inner wall should have been familiar to me. I had roamed Asgard at will for centuries before being exiled.

I landed on the sill of an open window on the upper story of a house. Best as I could remember this should have been the tallow maker's abode. But I didn't detect any of the usual smells. I guess after nine hundred years they finally moved on from tallow candles to oil lanterns. I'm also certain that the old man I once knew lived here had passed long ago. Aesir are long-lived, but without Idunn's fruit, a century or two is all they can expect. Predictably only the noble class got access to her bounty.

I didn't worry about Manny. He'd either find me or he wouldn't. I hopped inside. Once on the floor I changed back. No point in tempting fate if the owner had a cat or dog. I really hoped they didn't have a dog.

I was in a bedroom. No pets that I could see. A heavily breathing lump under the covers of the bed was certainly the home's owner. There was a large wooden wardrobe against the far wall. I quietly opened it and picked a hooded cloak, breeches and a pair of boots. The cloak had deep pockets lining the inside.

I saw a second pair of breeches and couldn't resist. I frayed the cord. His breeches would likely fall off at a most inopportune time. Thinking about that made me smile.

I tossed my purloined clothes out the window and then eased myself through the narrow opening. It was a bit of a drop to the ground, which rattled my teeth, but I didn't twist or strain anything. I put on the clothes and presto, I looked like a local. I hoped.

12

IDUNN'S ORCHARD

I strode through the streets like a man with a purpose. I knew where I was going, and as long as I acted normal I wouldn't provoke suspicions. The upper city of Asgard held the estates of the rich and powerful. They lined the long, broad Avenue of Heroes where I walked now. The road was paved with large, flat stones.

In the distance was Valhalla, dwarfing all the other aesir halls. Huge timbers formed the walls. Mighty Glasir stood in front of it, a tree unlike any other in the Nine Worlds. Its red-gold leaves never turned in winter or greened in spring. The trunk was so thick around that it took nine men to encircle it. It stood well more than a hundred feet tall, yet the beaten silver roof of Valhalla was easily visible over it.

I passed my former home, placed far from Valhalla, without looking at it. I had no desire to run into Sigyn. Were it not for my innocent wife, I'm sure they would have burned it down. I owed her a debt I could never repay. But I did the best I could by removing myself from her life.

Farther down I could see Breidablik. I quickly turned my eye from it. I fought back the tears as I remembered Baldr and the many hours we spent together there. Gods, I missed him.

I could see Fensalir and Bilkirnir halls much farther down the avenue, right next to Valhalla itself. Frigg's Fensalir hall was one of the most beautiful estates in Asgard. Bilkirnir, on the other hand, was a massive, severe hall that reflected the personality of its owner, Thor.

I turned off the avenue well before I got to either of them. I had two purposes in Asgard tonight. Only one of those was to question Vidarr.

Behind the massive halls of the rulers of Asgard were rows of homes belonging to important servants and craftsmen. At the far end of this street was the House of Glass. I passed a few people hurrying on errands or other unknown purposes. None paid me any attention.

The House of Glass was almost as large as one of the ruling halls on the Avenue of Heroes. The walls were made of huge panes of glass more than two dozen feet high joined with silver. The peaked roof above that was also glass. Although its contents were the most precious in all of Asgard, there were no guards. The gardener refused to have them, much to Odin's consternation.

I carefully opened the tall glass door and eased inside. I knew from experience that it would shut with a loud click if it wasn't eased closed. The inside was warm, humid, and smelled of strange flowers. It was the size of a football field filled with several rows of blue leaved trees. Idunn's garden. The trees weren't particularly large. Their leaves were small and spade-shaped with short, strange dangling silver threads. The trunk was dark brown with patches of white. Clear tubes breached the ground and punctured the trunk of each tree. Pulsing blue and purple fluid slowly oozed into the trees from some unknown source underground. Each tree grew a few dozen of the strange fruit I kept in my box.

I touched one of the tubes. Smooth and hard, the feel was unmistakable. Plastic! The damn tubes were made of plastic, or something very much like it. How in the Nine Worlds did Idunn have plastic more than a thousand years before it was invented? That would be a question for another time, a question I was definitely going to ask.

I quickly slipped deeper into the rows, looking for ripe fruit. Three rows in, I found some. I carefully plucked the fruit and filled the pockets that lined my cape. Then I heard the telltale click of the door. Someone else was in the garden with me. Who would be here at this hour? I crouched behind the bole of the nearest tree, even though I knew it was too narrow to hide me.

"I harvested some fruit for you," I heard Idunn say. When had she entered? Had she seen me?

"Thank you, Idunn," a woman's voice replied. I knew that voice. The blood drained from me and I felt momentarily faint.

"You are most welcome, Sigyn. Maybe someday you will be able to visit me during the day."

"I've given up on that," Sigyn said sadly. "If they haven't forgiven me for my husband's sins by now, I doubt they ever will."

"Maybe. But then maybe your husband can help. Loki? Why don't you join us?"

Oh shit.

"Idunn," Sigyn said with a sob. "Don't. That's cruel. You've never been cruel."

Taking a deep breath, I walked through the trees toward them.

"Loki? Loki! But you're dead?" Sigyn's eyes were wide with disbelief, and her slender form shook.

"He's been stealing my fruit. Not often, but often enough to keep him alive for... what is it now? A thousand years?"

"Not quite," I said with a catch in my throat. "But who's counting?"

Idunn was neither beautiful nor plain, young nor old. Her straight blonde hair hung just past her shoulders, parted in the center. She wore a simple white gown. I'd never seen her wear anything else. I knew without looking that her amazingly agile fingers each had an extra joint. And that if you looked closely at her eyes, the irises were violet. Even for an aesir, she was strange.

Despite all of that, I only gave Idunn a glance. My eyes fixed on Sigyn, her face was filled with shock, horror, and hope. I stood a few steps away, shame and regret were likely obvious in my own visage.

Sigyn was young and ethereally beautiful; she hadn't changed a bit. Long blonde hair hung in gentle waves down to the middle of her back. Her elfin face with it's pointed chin and upturned nose was stunning. Pale blue eyes brimmed with tears beneath the golden circlet on her brow. She was small, not much more than five feet, and she wore a snug baby blue gown belted and trimmed in silver.

"My Loki!" She flung herself into my arms.

She was everything a man could wish for, gorgeous, adoring, loyal, and steadfast. And I didn't love her. I did once, but not anymore.

"Sigyn," I said gently, pushing her just far enough away so I could see her face. Relief and joy were written all over it. She still wore her heart on her sleeve.

"Have you come back?" she asked breathlessly. "For me? You can't stay here. We can't stay here. They'll kill you. Or worse. We could go to—"

"Sigyn—"

"We need to leave. Tonight. Flee Asgard."

"Sigyn—"

99

"You pluck enough fruit for the both of us. I'll go get some things. But first—"

And then she was back in my arms, kissing me. Old habits and old desires die hard, and I kissed her back for a moment. It was sweet and haunting at the same time. I felt my desire stirring.

"No," I said, pulling away. "Sigyn... no."

"Loki... please. Don't—"

"I can't, Sigyn. I can't run away with you."

She had no words. She just started sobbing again. Her knees buckled and I sank to the ground with her, holding her while she clung desperately to me.

"We.... Our lives have gone separate ways."

"But I love you," she cried. "I've always loved you."

"It wasn't right between us, even long before... before I was exiled. You had to know that."

"You mean Angrboda?" she whispered. "I forgave you for taking a lover a long time ago. I even forgave you for the children she bore you. Do you think I would have stayed by you when you were chained if I had not?"

"It's not that simple."

"I know you've had other lovers. I forgive you for all of them," she cried with a hint of desperation.

"All of them?" I asked, momentarily distracted from what I needed to say.

"Yes," she said quietly, burying her face in my cloak. "All of them."

"You give me forgiveness like you gave me your heart, freely and unconditionally," I said with a catch in my voice. "But I cannot forgive myself one thing. Falling out of love with you. I don't love you, not like you love me."

"No!" She clutched tightly at my cloak. I clung to her, sobbing just as loudly.

"I'm sorry," I said when I could talk again. "I should have

told you long before now. It was cruel of me not to. You do mean the world to me and I hate myself for hurting you. But love—" I shook my head.

"There must be something I can do. I can change! I can be who you want me to be."

"No. No, you can't," I said, my own tears soaking her dress. "It took me many lifetimes to learn, but you can't force someone's heart. And it's not you who should change. The problem is, I haven't."

Sigyn pushed me away and collapsed on the ground, still crying. I reached for her and she batted my hand away. I just sat watching her, tears continuing to stream down my face.

Finally, she wiped her face and stood, her hands clenched in tiny fists, her face reddened and tear-streaked.

"It was better when I thought you were dead," she said tonelessly.

"Sigyn—"

"I grieved for you for almost a millennium. Take the fruit you came for and leave. Leave like the thief you are."

"Sigyn!" I cried, as she turned and stumbled toward the door. She ignored me and fled into the night.

I cried for a while longer. I had never wanted to hurt her. Faithless men and women rarely do. But they do it anyway. My tears were selfish. They were about *my* pain, not hers. I hadn't earned the right to cry. It took a few more moments to regain control of myself. I took some solace in seeing her strength. She had always had an inner iron strength.

"Well, that didn't go well," Idunn said from nearby.

I quickly stood and wiped my face. She stared back dispassionately. Idunn had always been a bit of a cold fish.

"I'm sorry you had to witness that."

"Oh, I didn't," she replied. "I went into the house to give you some privacy. I didn't come back out until I heard the door. You can tell a lot from the sound of a door slamming."

Idunn's home was attached to the House of Glass. It was neither large nor palatial like the other halls on the hill.

"Then I'm sorry... I don't know. I guess I'm just sorry about everything."

"You came here to steal fruit from my orchard. Do you have enough?"

"I think so. You knew I'd been back before to take some?"

"Of course. Nothing happens in my orchard without me knowing about it."

"So you let me take them?"

"Why not?" She shrugged. "You deserved them as much as any other Asgardian lord."

"I don't understand you," I said, shaking my head.

"I would be surprised if you did," she answered with a wry smile.

"Maybe you would be inclined to help me just a little bit more?"

"Possibly."

"Where can I find Vidarr?"

She was quiet for a long moment.

"He is most likely in Bilkirnir."

"Thor's hall?" I was confused.

"Thor hasn't set foot inside it for centuries now. He lives in Valhalla, sitting on the Alfodr's High Seat, eating at the Alfodr's table, and sleeping in Alfodr's bed."

"From what I heard, he is now the Alfodr. So I suppose it is only fitting."

"He may rule Asgard, but he will never be the Alfodr. Odin was the true Alfodr."

Obviously, this was a sore point with her. "I humbly thank you, Idunn. Both for the gift of your fruit and for your assistance."

"Go on, thief. You have things to do."

13

VIDARR

I sat outside Bilkirnir on a stone bench eating one of Idunn's fruit. A whole fruit. I hadn't eaten a whole fruit in one sitting in more than nine hundred years. Fortunately, there were no guards in this part of the city. All of its residents were more than capable of taking care of themselves. So I ate alone under the stars in the middle of the night.

Bilkirnir is a fortress of a house. Built of large stone blocks like those that formed the city walls, it has two stories —each nearly twenty feet high. Thick Onyx trimmed the windows, the front doors made from a massive single piece of oak six feet wide, fifteen feet high, and a foot thick. They were barred from the inside, so I wasn't getting in that way.

All the windows were shuttered with heavy white ash planks. I had to hand it to Thor. The place was really ugly but almost impossible to break into. Almost. I had a set of lock picks, but they were far too small and delicate for the over-sized lock on the door.

I licked my fingers clean of the sticky, sweet juice. I felt better than I had since the French Revolution. I easily shifted to spider monkey, and dragged the duffel with my clothes behind me.

The wall was harder to scale than I had anticipated, but I made it up to the roof. Thick, over-sized wood shingles plated the roof like armor. I made my way to the chimney where thin wisps of smoke wafted up into the chilly night air. I pushed my duffle in and quickly scrambled into the smoky chimney.

It wasn't lined in ceramic like a modern Midgard chimney. Thank goodness for Thor's insistence on the old ways. Large stones joined with cement formed the square shaft. My paws found easy purchase.

I had to hold my breath and keep my eyes shut, feeling my way down. I scampered out of the shaft as soon as I felt the hearth lip. Only coals remained of the fire in the hearth at the bottom. I had hoped for such when I gauged the smoke from the ground.

I changed back quickly, muffling a coughing fit with my hand. I stank of soot and smoke. Dressing quickly, I saw I was in some sort of parlor with high vaulted ceilings, dimly lit by the remnants of the fire in the fireplace. A couple of animal heads hung on the walls, a testament to Thor's decorating talents. They looked like stags or antlered creatures of some sort. A polar bear skin lay on the floor, like a bad cliché.

Given the hour, Vidarr was most likely in bed. He could be in any of the guest rooms. I knew Bilkirnir of old. I hadn't been a frequent guest, but I had been here often enough to know the layout. I looked around the parlor, spotting the inevitable set of weapons mounted above the fireplace.

It doesn't take much skill to wield a hand axe, so I chose that. Compared to most Midgard humans I was pretty handy with an axe. Compared to anyone in Asgard I was a clumsy oaf. I tested the blade with my thumb. Sharp. Trust Thor to keep his weapons in fighting shape.

I skulked through the empty hall, going from guest room to guest room. I ignored the bunk rooms. Vidarr would be in one of the honored guest rooms. But he wasn't. Puzzled, I carefully checked the bunk rooms. Empty.

I went through the parlors and game halls and trophy rooms, and still no Viddar. There was only one place I had not looked. I stood before Thor and Sif's rooms. A faint flickering light came from under the door. Did I dare enter? Thor was not likely to be here, so it would just be Sif. Or would it?

I carefully eased open the door and peered inside. A massive bed dominated the space beyond. Animal furs were heaped on a side bench. A single figure lay under a cloth bed sheet. Definitely male. I crept closer. In the flickering firelight, I could easily make out Vidarr's face, softly snoring in Sif's bed. I wondered if Thor knew his wife was sleeping with his half-brother.

I climbed onto the bed slowly and scooted over to Vidarr's sleeping form. His long red braid draped beside him on the pillow. A thick red mustache continued down his face and just past his stubbled chin. Bushy red eyebrows sheltered the eyes that I knew were deep blue. Raising my axe, I said in a sweet falsetto, "Oh Vidarr! Take me, you rogue."

Vidarr's eyes flew open and I took a firm grip on his braid with my free hand. My upraised axe was aimed squarely at his neck.

"Loki!" Vidarr gasped.

"In the flesh, old friend," I spat maliciously.

"You've finally come to kill me!"

"I think it's only fitting. After all, you killed my son. And I have it on good authority that you sent Skirnir to come collect me to be executed."

"Fenrir may have been your son, but he was also a

monster." Vidarr's voice dripped with venom. "He killed Odin at Ragnarokkr. Swallowed him whole. I only avenged the death of my father."

"He was a troubled boy, I'll give you that. But it is a father's duty to avenge his son's death."

"As it is a son's to avenge his father's. And I am the God of Vengeance!"

"Touché. But I'm the one with the axe. And you're no god. None of you are."

"So what are you waiting for coward? Do it already."

"All in good time. Who told you I was in Alfheim? You're no mastermind. Who suddenly decided it was so important for me to die?"

"Thor has had a bounty on your head for almost a millennium."

"True, but he wouldn't send a lackey. He would come himself with Mjolnir and smite me. So I ask you again, who is behind all this?"

I was unprepared for the kick. In hindsight, he had been wriggling a bit under that bedsheet. His sheet-covered knee struck my forearm and the axe flew out of my nerveless fingers. Vidarr clamped his hand atop mine that gripped his braid. With a quick roll, pain shot through my wrist as it was bent at an unnatural angle. I let go.

Vidarr finished his roll off the side of the bed. Anger flared inside me and I quickly chanted a galdr spell. A massive polar bear swallowed my shape, ripping my clothes at the seams. I stood on all fours on the bed; the rags of my breeches still caught around one leg. I roared at Vidarr as he stood naked, gripping the axe. He was big for a man but small next to a bear. Heavily muscled with many battle scars peeking out from his chest hair.

"Can't face me as a man, Loki? Have to hide behind that bear skin?" Vidarr taunted.

I tried to charge him, but a mattress is a poor surface for a fifteen-hundred-pound bear. I floundered off the bed onto the floor, shedding the last of the shredded pants that tangled my legs. Anger and hatred burned hot and sharp inside me. Vidarr circled behind a heavy wooden chair. My charge was much more successful this time. I swatted the heavy chair to the side and it careened across the room. Vidarr swung the axe, scoring my left foreleg.

"First blood!" Vidarr shouted. "Even as a great northern bear, you are a fumbling fighter."

Bright pain flared, but it was only a shallow cut. With another roar, I moved to cut him off from the door. It was hard to keep the bear's instincts from overwhelming my human tactical sense, particularly in the heat of combat.

"I will deliver your head to Sif, human or bear."

Well, at least I knew who directed him now. I didn't think there would be a chance to ask him why though. Vidarr danced out to the middle of the room by the bed, left foot slightly in front of the right, axe gripped in his right hand.

His foot was as dangerous as the axe. As a child, Vidarr lost that foot in a jotnar attack. Odin commissioned the dvergar to make a bronze foot for him. It magically attached itself and grew as he did. Frigg objected to the noise he made clanking around Asgard, so he covered it with scraps of cast-off leather. At Ragnarokkr, Vidarr jammed his foot into Fenrir's mouth, shattering his jaw and pinning it to the ground.

I kept a wary eye on both that foot and his axe as I padded carefully toward him. Vidarr was a seasoned warrior, and almost as strong as Thor. Underestimating him would get me more than a cut on my leg.

"You were right not to suspect Thor," Vidarr taunted. "He doesn't have the wit for these games. Soon I will take the high seat with Sif by my side."

I lunged, swiping at his left side with a massive clawed paw. He rolled back onto the bed, but I felt my claws catch on flesh. I bounded around the foot of the bed, refusing to be drawn back onto the mattress. Vidarr's left arm was bleeding and hung limp.

"Curse your damnable shape-shifting!"

My left paw swung wildly, missing him as he bounced back onto the mattress, but catching the post at the foot of the bed, snapping it in two. Vidarr flipped the bedsheet over my head, and for a moment I was blinded.

I lunged to my right blindly, guessing where he was going, while shredding the bedsheet. Vidarr had indeed leaped off the foot of the bed to try and make it to the door. With a roar I swatted a nearby chair, sending it flying into his back. He turned his fall into a roll and was out the door, slamming it behind him.

I charged the door, rearing up and coming down with both of my front paws. It shook and cracked, but held. With a roar, I slammed my shoulder into it and it shattered. I lumbered through.

I could smell him. Sweat and adrenaline, but no fear. That way. I padded down the hall toward his scent. I paused at the top of the stairs, scanning the broad hall below. Vidarr stepped out of a doorway and hurled a spear at me. I flung myself against the railing, but not quickly enough. The short spear stuck in my shoulder. The railing never stood a chance and I fell headlong onto the floor below.

"I've hunted hundreds of snow bears, Loki," Vidarr called from the darkened opening. "I'll lay your skin by my hearth."

The fall was worse than the shallow spear wound. I lurched to all fours and loped through the doorway. Vidarr was at the far end with another spear. He launched it, but this time I batted it out of the air. He fled deeper into the building.

"Maybe I'll take Sigyn on your pelt," he taunted, his voice echoing through the halls. "Whether she wants me or not."

Over my dead body. I charged after him with a ground-shaking roar. As I rounded the corner into a short hallway, he jumped onto my back from the rafters, screaming "For Baldr!"

Pain blossomed between my shoulders as his bronze foot slammed between them, driving me to the floor despite my size. Furious, I shambled to my feet as his axe bit into my back. I managed to rise up on my hind legs with an agonizing roar and slammed my back against the wall. I heard something snap, but it wasn't me. I tried to spin and pin him but the hall was too narrow and I felt a sharp pain in my back when I tried to turn.

Vidarr rolled under my swinging paw, which dug a deep furrow in the wall, and ran down the hall. I could see he was still favoring his left arm. I loped after him, the pain in my back brutal.

I burst into the next room, shattering the door. Vidarr stood in the center of it. He gripped my axe in his right hand. His left arm hung limp. There were no other exits.

"Come, Loki," Vidarr said, grinning. "Let's fight like true warriors. There is no honor in hunting you like a simple animal."

I padded slowly toward him. At the last minute, I charged hoping to take him by surprise, but Vidarr saw it coming. He swung at me, grazing my arm, and deftly rolled over a table landing on his feet on the other side. I spun painfully and flipped the table. He grunted as it hit his legs, but he still managed to skip back out of the way.

I tried to leap the overturned table, but that's not something a massive bear does well. I stumbled onto the floor and felt the bite of his axe on my wounded arm. Blinding pain nearly made me pass out. I clawed at his leg with my good arm, figuring he had to have stepped in close. I felt my claws stick deep in flesh. I pulled hard.

Hoisting myself up, I found that my claws had sunk in his calf. Vidarr wriggled like a fish on a hook. He spun onto his back as I reared with my right paw.

"For Odin!" he screamed.

He buried the axe deep in my rib cage as I clamped my jaws on his skull. Brain, blood, and bone sprayed across the floor and wall. I roared in pain. Bending my neck low, I bit the axe handle and ripped it free of my side. My own blood spurted onto the floor mingling with Vidarr's. Red rage filled my bear brain as I mauled his corpse.

As my temper cooled, I let go of the red ruin of Vidarr's body and sat on my haunches to lick my wounds. The deep wound in my chest bled freely. My arm hung limp and useless. I could see the bone in the deep cut. With an effort, I focused through the pain and returned to human form. I lay on the floor naked, bleeding, and probably dying, my magic drained for the moment.

Metal shod feet kicked the pieces of the splintered door aside. I only had the energy to turn my head and look. A pair of Valkyries with loaded crossbows stepped into the room, followed by another identical pair. All wore gleaming ring mail, sealskin breeches, and helmets with stylized wings on each side. Flowing white capes hung down past their knees. I knew without seeing it that each would have a round, steel shield strapped to her back. All four kept their weapons trained on me. Behind them stood Sif and a handmaiden holding a lantern. The room looked worse in the light.

Sif wore all white. Ironically the fur cape was polar bear. Gold necklaces, rings, and bracelets hung from her neck and hands. Golden hair hung straight all the way to her waist. Not blonde or yellow, but actual gold hair, like the precious metal. Her skin was pale and flawless, like ice.

The Valkyries were tall women, none less than six feet. Their long blonde hair hung in braids down their backs. Strong golden armor covered them from ankle to wrist. Even under the armor, their heavy muscles were obvious.

"So Havardr was right," Sif said, looking down at me. "He swore he saw Loki himself change into an animal and climb into this house."

Sif spotted Vidarr's mauled corpse on the far side of the room. She strode purposefully toward it, ignoring the blood and gore underfoot. The handmaiden struggled to pick her way through the mess. Sif stood over the body, her hands slowly knotting into fists.

I sat up, propping my back against the side of the bed. This made several of the soldiers nervous, but I didn't care. I was pretty sure a crossbow bolt to the chest would be kinder than my other options.

"He killed my son," I said weakly.

"Fenrir was a monster." She kept her back to me.

"He was a boy. My boy."

"He was simple, Loki. He had the mind of a young child in the body of a man," she said coldly. "A man who turned into a giant wolf whenever he got upset, and he got upset a lot."

She slowly turned toward me, her face impassive. Were it not for her clenched fists I would have thought she felt nothing at all.

"Oh, and he tried to have me killed," I added, inclining my head toward Vidarr's mangled corpse. "I almost forgot that part."

"How did you do that? He was the God of Vengeance. He cannot be defeated by anyone who has wronged him."

"I guess that was the problem," I said, stopping briefly to spit blood. "I hadn't wrong him, but he had wronged me."

"I was fond of Vidarr," she mused.

"Fond? He was planning on usurping Thor and making you his queen."

"Aesir men," she said, shaking her head. "You always underestimate your women. I already rule Asgard in all but name. Thor does whatever I ask. But it amused me to let Vidarr have his dreams."

"Good thing I'm not aesir."

"Not wholly. Most of you is jotunn," she said, as if being jotunn was a disease.

The pain was overwhelming me, but I was going to force out the words. She needed to listen. "I remember a time when you did whatever Thor asked out of fear. I remember how he treated you then. I remember the bruises. I remember you running to me when he hacked off all your beautiful hair, and half your scalp with it."

Her hand went to her hair before she even thought about it. That gorgeous hair that was literally spun out of gold by a dvergr smith. I paid a hefty price for that golden hairpiece, and not in coin. Sif owed me and I was calling in the marker.

"What changed?" I asked, trying not to cough.

"Ragnarokkr, you fool," she said her eyes darkening. "Ragnarokkr changed him. He went to war totally convinced of his own prowess and invulnerability, confident in his ability to defeat anyone or anything. Jormungand almost killed him. Another of your monster children. When he finally recovered, he was changed. He was uncertain and even fearful. He turned to me for advice and counsel."

"So you finally got the upper hand on your husband. Why come after me?"

"Bind him," Sif ordered, ignoring my question. "Take him to Valhalla's dungeon and see to his wounds. He's not to die —yet. Too many have seen him here in Asgard. So we'll present him to Thor in the morning. And for Odin's sake, put some clothes on him."

"And you," she said, turning to the handmaiden. "Get this cleaned up. Save the bone and gore. Spread it in Vidarr's hall with his corpse."

So much for markers and debts owed.

14

THOR

They'd saved my old cell for me. If I hadn't been gagged, I would have been all misty-eyed over the thoughtfulness. It turns out gags are a cheap and easy way to stop someone like me from casting galdr or seidr. That and the heavy wooden yoke around my wrists and neck. My side hurt like a son of a bitch, and it was still seeping blood.

The cell hadn't changed much in nine hundred years. Made of rough-hewn, well-fitted stone, it was small and damp. The small window grate in the thick iron door was the only source of light. There hadn't been a way out before, and I'm sure that hadn't changed since.

I wasn't in it for long. A pair of Valkyries came in, grabbed me by the yoke, and dragged me out. Several narrow halls, a set of painful stairs, and a not so narrow hallway, and I was tossed on the floor of the grand hall of Valhalla.

The vast space defied architectural laws. The roof was held up by soaring columns of bundled spears, lances, and swords tied together. The distant ceiling was layered in shields, like shingles, held together by a barely discernable crosshatch of spears. The floor was polished marble inlaid with a map of Asgard. The space was occupied by a small group of Asgardian nobles, an ancient wooden throne, and the man who sat in it.

"Ungag him," I heard Thor say.

I looked up at my arch-nemesis of more than a thousand years. He was a big man, standing taller than seven feet. His shaggy mane of bright red hair surrounded his face like a corona. His full, red beard streaked with gray almost hid his mouth. Last time I had seen him on that fateful day on the plains of Vigrid he had been in his prime and glory, heavily muscled and full of vigor. Now he looked gaunt.

I wasn't fooled though. He still wore Megingjoro around his waist, the massive belt which gives him twice the strength he ought to have. Mjolnir was at his feet, head down, the stunted handle upright. In his left hand, he held the unbreakable iron staff he won from the jotunn Gridr. Aside from all that magical gear, he was dressed in an intricately woven leather tunic and sealskin breeches, a polar bear cape pulled around his shoulders, complemented Sif's all-white attire.

Thor sat on Hlidskjalf, the high seat. Carved from a single piece of rich, golden wood, it was centered on a dais of gold. Odin had once told me the high seat was not of the Nine Worlds, whatever that meant. My personal theory is that it was carved from a piece of Yggdrasil.

The chair was large enough to make even Thor look small in it. Two normal men could sit side by side comfortably. The back rose six feet from the seat to an arch with a rising sun carved into it. Lower down, hidden by Thor at the moment, were all the phases of the moon. On the back were representations of all the Nine Worlds. The two posts for the seat back were carved to look like thick spears, the two posts for the front legs looked like swords, points down.

Sif stood to Thor's left, her hand resting lightly on his

arm and looking every bit the ice queen. Their son Magni was next to her. Odin's widow, Frigg, was on Thor's other side. She was achingly beautiful in a too perfect to be true manner, looking young enough to be Thor's daughter. She fashioned herself a goddess of love, beauty, sex, fertility, etc. She was also the vainest woman I had ever met. It was an open secret that she used magic to keep her beauty.

At least a dozen other aesir were gathered around. Some I knew. All were young and fit from a steady diet of Idunn's fruit. I saw Skirnir staring at me to my left. I caught a glimpse of Sigyn behind Ullr. I felt the loathing coming off of them in waves.

"Gee," I said, ignoring the pain in my side. "All this pomp and circumstance just for little ol' me?"

"You are here to pay for your crimes," Sif said frostily. "Odin took you in and treated you like a son, despite your filthy jotnar blood. The aesir treated you with kindness and respect. And you repaid us with bloodshed at Ragnarokkr. You led a jotnar army into Asgard. Many of the aesir fell that day, including Odin."

"Loki," Thor said, his voice still carrying a bit of thunder. "I'm going to enjoy killing you."

Sif put a hand on Thor's shoulder and he subsided with a scowl. Interesting.

"I was treated kindly by many and with respect by some," I replied to Sif before turning my gaze to Thor. "But not by you Thor. You tormented me for all my childhood and all the years I spent in Asgard."

"So you admit that the aesir gave you no cause," Sif interjected.

"No cause?" I cried out angrily. "What about Baldr? Is his murder cause enough for you?"

"Do not speak the name of my son with that treacherous

mouth," Frigg hissed. A low mutter rolled through the other aesir.

"You know I didn't kill Baldr," I growled. "I could never have killed him."

Thor shifted uncomfortably on the high seat. His eyes burned with hate, and something else. With a start, I realized it was fear and uncertainty, two emotions alien to the Thor I had known.

"I loved Baldr. I would sooner cut out my own heart than kill him. The day he died, a piece of me died with him."

"Liar!" screamed Frigg, her unearthly beauty marred by her rage.

The muttering rose among the small crowd. I heard a gasp and sob that was surely Sigyn. My own face was red and tear-streaked as I remembered that awful day.

"That's right, we were lovers. And you all knew it, you just refused to admit it because Baldr was everyone's favorite."

"Enough!" Thor thundered. Lightning struck the roof of Valhalla, making everyone in the hall flinch and reminding them of his power. "You'll not defame the memory of Baldr any further."

Thor began to stand, but stopped when Sif put her hand on his shoulder again.

"Okay, then let's talk about Odin," I hissed. "Baldr's own father couldn't handle having a son with a man for a lover. Gods forbid his son was argr."

"No," Frigg said, teeth clenched in denial. "My son was beloved by all. He was not argr! Not Baldr."

"It's true, Frigg," I spat. "He was loved by all. He had more lovers, women *and* men, than anyone in Asgard. Half of you in this room warmed his bed. Nobody could resist him. I certainly couldn't."

"Enough of this," Sif said, cutting us off. "Let's execute him now."

"No," Thor said with a spiteful grin. I could see Sif's hand tighten on his arm.

"But my love," Sif pleaded with false deference. "He has been your mortal enemy for a thousand years."

"Technically it's closer to nine hundred," I interrupted. Sometimes I just don't know when to shut up.

"His son killed your own father," Sif continued, ignoring me. "His brethren killed your brothers. His other son left you crippled—"

"Enough!" Thor bellowed. Lightning flashed outside followed by a roll of thunder. I could see that Sif had gone too far mentioning Thor's health. The uncertainty was gone from his eyes.

"Did you know that Sif sent Manibrandr assassins to kill me in Midgard?" I asked. Let's see if I can give her a little shove while she is on the defensive.

"Is this true, wife?" Thor turned a baleful eye on her. "You knew where he was and didn't tell me?"

"My husband, it wasn't me," she said, looking genuinely surprised. "It must have been Vidarr. He was misguided and thought he was doing me a favor."

Cute. Blame the one person who can't be questioned. I saw Thor waver.

"Why would he have thought my death a favor to you instead of Thor?" I asked innocently.

"It was a favor for both of us," Sif said icily, trying to stare daggers into my skull.

"And how would this have been a favor for me?" Thor asked, with just a hint of emphasis on 'me.'

"It's a prophecy," Frigg interjected. "I cast the divination myself and saw it."

"So my mother and my wife are keeping secrets from me

now?" Thor asked, thunderheads growing on his eyebrows, lightning crackling again outside. He looked for a moment like a cornered animal, beset on all sides by enemies.

"I did not wish to concern you, milord," Frigg said smoothly. "The divination merely said that Loki could thwart our plans. But you've had a bounty on his head for a thousand years now."

"Technically nine hundred," I added. I couldn't help it. Honest. "And what plans?"

Thor looked at me for a long moment.

"Bring him," Thor said, standing with an effort and shrugging off Sif's grip. He leveraged himself up using Gridarvolr, the iron staff. He picked up Mjolnir with a grunt. Apparently, my son Jormungandr had left a lasting impression.

It was a long walk behind the high seat to the nearest set of gigantic doors. Or a long drag in my case. Thor strode with a purpose despite his apparent weakness, making the others scurry to keep up with his uneven gait. A pair of Valkyries at the huge doors pulled them open as we neared.

Immediately the cacophony of swords clashing and men shouting and swearing burst over us. Thor strode through the doors, followed by the other aesir. I was dragged by my Valkyrie handlers and set on my feet.

The new hall made the one we left look cozy. It stretched off into the distance for what I'm guessing was a mile or so. It was filled with men fighting, drinking, eating, and singing. The einherjar. The spirits of men fallen in battle made into flesh again by the Valkyries. Only the most savage fighters are given this honor. Dozens of Valkyries walked among them serving food and drink and giving them tips on combat.

I saw every medieval era weapon known to man represented. Every nation and culture was here. Strangely, there was not a woman to be seen other than the Valkyries, and the most advanced weapon I spotted was a crossbow. No guns anywhere.

"Gods!" I whispered. "How many of them are there?"

"My Valkyries tell me more than a hundred thousand," Thor answered proudly. Out of the corner of my eye, I saw Frigg smile knowingly.

"Odin only had ten thousand at Ragnarokkr," he continued. "Since then Midgard has grown. More wars. More dead. More heroes for the Valkyries to pluck from the battlefields."

"Odin didn't take heroes," I said. "He took the most savage and bloodthirsty of those that died."

"I do the same," Thor said, looking at me with a feral grin. "That's what makes them heroes. Frigg takes her pick of the rest."

"And Hel takes those that neither of you want," I said. "I know how this works. Why do you need so many? Ragnarokkr is done."

"Aye. And we lost," Thor said, his face dark with anger. "We lost because you betrayed us. You and your miscreant offspring. And the jotnar. Let's not forget the giants. And now they will pay. They will all pay."

"Gods!" I breathed. "You mean to march on Jotunheim."

"Yes!" Thor cried, his face alight with the joy of the coming battles. Thunder boomed overhead. "We will rid the Nine Worlds once and for all of the scourge of the jotnar."

"That's genocide!"

"Bah. A Midgard word. The jotnar do not deserve to live. They are an abomination. The Nine Worlds needs to be rid of them."

"And when they are gone? Then what?"

"Then nothing." He shrugged. "The Nine Worlds will be at peace."

"So that's just it? You kill them all and go home?"

"You know the jotnar are monsters, Loki. They need to be

exterminated. The rest of the Nine Worlds will thank me when they are gone."

"You're batshit crazy," I said, shaking my head. "I know you've always hated the jotnar, but you realize you are part jotnar, and half vanir? Most of the aesir here have jotnar blood."

I didn't even see him move. The blow to my head knocked me back a dozen feet. Damn that belt of his.

"Liar! You are still the God of Mischief who tells falsehoods to cause trouble and divides loyalties. We are the aesir. Our blood runs true."

I had a pithy rejoinder, but my jaw wasn't working too well. Thor was mad with his hatred of the jotnar. Sif looked on like the cat that ate the canary. He would wipe them from the Nine Worlds given a chance. That army could do it easily. My people. Gone. And I didn't believe he would stop with them. Likely the alfar would be next, or the dvergar.

Thor interrupted my thoughts, "I've made my decision. Loki will be bound to the rock. The serpent will spill venom on him to remind him of Jormungand's treachery and death will be by my hand. It was Odin's own decree. I am only reinstating his will."

Sif looked startled. "But—"

"I have passed judgment."

That shut everyone up, like kids when their mother starts counting to three. Sif was visibly upset. Frigg didn't look too happy either. Only Sigyn seemed relieved. The gag was summarily stuffed back in my mouth. As they dragged me away, Thor's seething eyes never left mine. Sif was urgently whispering to him.

15

PRISON CELL

I was dumped in my cell and the door slammed shut. The yoke hurt like hell, but I knew it was nothing compared to the serpent that awaited me. I had vowed I would kill myself rather than be bound to that rock again, but somehow I didn't think I'd get the opportunity.

Don't ask me how I fell asleep, but I was woken by the sound of the key of the lock. A pair of Valkyries entered, with Sigyn behind them.

"The gag," Sigyn ordered. "And the yoke."

With a shrug, one of the Valkyrie approached me and yanked the gag out of my mouth while the other stood by the door with an unsheathed sword. Keys rattled in the yoke and it fell free. I gasped with relief. If I had been stronger I would have stood, but instead, I just sat there. The two Valkyries left, locking the door behind them and leaving Sigyn in the cell with me. My feet were still shackled.

I stared at her, not knowing what to say. I had already said it all. She walked over to me.

"Lie back," she said calmly. I did as I was told. She pulled my shirt up sharply, ripping the wound underneath open. I said a few choice words after I stopped screaming.

She spent a while tending to my wound in silence. I cried like a baby when she stitched it, but I kept still so she could work. Salves and a poultice were bound into place. When all that was done, she pulled one of Idunn's fruit from her bag and handed it to me.

"This is from Thor. He wants you to be strong enough to suffer," Sigyn said, looking away from me. "And Frigg bade me tell you that those leg shackles have been enchanted to prevent seidr or galdr."

"Why?" I asked. "Why are you helping me?"

"You are my husband."

"That's it? After everything I've done? All the lies and betrayals?"

"Yes."

I couldn't think of anything to say to that, so I just sat there and ate the fruit. Sigyn watched me, her face expressionless.

"You know, since I've admitted to being argr, you now have grounds to divorce me."

"No," she said, a little too quickly. "I've shared a bed with you. You are not only argr. You are my husband, now and always."

"I loved you once, I truly did," I said sadly. "You should move on with your life."

"I know," she said quietly. "Let's not talk about that. Tell me about Baldr's death instead. Finish the tale you started."

"Baldr? Are you sure?"

"Please. He was important to you, so he's important to me."

I took a deep breath. "Odin caught us together one day. Until that moment, I think he denied what he knew in his heart, just like the rest of Asgard. I think he couldn't stand the idea of Baldr being argr. He would rather have no son than one who had men as well as women for lovers.

"He sent me on an errand to deliver a message to Heimdall at his hall by the Bifrost Bridge. When I came back, Baldr was dead."

"But Hodr says you were the one that gave him the spear," she said, confused.

"Over the years I've pieced together what I think happened. Odin told me himself that he arranged Baldr's death, so I know it was him. But he didn't give me details."

She leaned closer to catch my words.

"Not long after Odin saw me with Baldr, Frigg had prophetic dreams of Baldr's death. She cast a mighty seidr on him, protecting him from everything in the Nine Worlds. It almost killed her. She lay comatose for a year and a day. No object or substance could harm Baldr. Every aesir knows this tale. Many aesir played at trying to hurt Baldr with all manner of weapons. The blows would strangely miss, or the weapon would fall apart or mysteriously drop out of the attacker's hand. The aesir made sport out of trying to hurt him."

"I hadn't known," she whispered.

"Hodr the Blind heard me offer to help him play at this game. I think that was Odin mimicking my voice. Hodr threw the spear that Odin gave him, Gungnir, Odin's spear that never misses. It was enchanted to look like a flimsy mistletoe shaft. Odin's magic spear versus Frigg's protective seidr. The spear was able to pierce her seidr and Baldr's heart. He rid himself of an embarrassing son and a troublesome ward all with one stroke. A very neat plan, wouldn't you say?"

"That is a hard tale to believe," Sigyn admitted.

"I have no proof. Heimdall might have been able to vouch

for me, but he rarely left Himinbjorg at the foot of the Bifrost Bridge. And of course, now he's dead."

"A hard tale to believe, but I do believe you," she said after a long pause. "I know your moods. Your grief and shock at his death were real. You had no cause to kill Baldr."

"Ha!" I laughed. "Odin and Thor claimed it was just pure mischief that motivated me."

"You are the God of Mischief," Sigyn said. "But you are not foolish. Only a fool would have blatantly killed Baldr and risk the ire of all the gods."

"I'm no god," I said bitterly. "None of the aesir are gods. We are just men and women."

"You're wrong, Loki," she said matter-of-factly. "We are men and women who are also gods. Being one does not negate the other."

"I won't argue with you," I said wearily. "I need to sleep, Sigyn. You can stay or go."

I closed my eyes and slept, not waiting for her answer. An unknown amount of time later I woke with my head in her lap. She looked down on me with loving eyes. Not young love, but the deep calm of patient, abiding love. I had to look away.

16

SIGYN'S MERCY

The door clanged open, startling me awake. My head was still in Sigyn's lap. Four Valkyries entered, two with crossbows.

"It's time, Loki."

I stood and took a step toward the Valkyries, a wave of dizziness overcame me and I stumbled into one of their arms. The Valkyrie roughly pushed me away and I swayed, trying to keep on my feet. Sigyn was instantly beside me, helping me stand straight. I leaned heavily on her.

"After you," I said weakly.

The two unarmed Valkyries each took an arm, pushing Sigyn out of the way. I was dragged unceremoniously out of the cell. I attempted to mutter a galdr of transformation, but the Valkyrie was ready and struck my mouth.

My stone slabs are under Valhalla. Directly under the high seat actually. It's in a natural cave that was expanded and carved to be my cell. I know every bump and chisel mark of that hated place. It looked exactly the same.

The rocks, *my* rocks, are three large, flat stones set on their edges. One holds my head and shoulders up off the ground. The second my chest and hips. The third my legs. Very painful. The chains pass through holes drilled in the stones and are made of a strange, deep red metal. Tears welled up in my eyes as I saw them. They were all that was left of my son Nari.

After I was tried and convicted of Baldr's murder, Odin himself transformed my son Narfi into a wolf. Narfi was kept in a cage for nine days without food until he was mad with hunger. Nari was tossed into the cage and Narfi devoured him. They made me watch. Even with my eyes closed, I could hear my son screaming for mercy.

Odin's son Vali took Nari's entrails and transformed them into unbreakable chains, immune to any chisel or the magic of any seidr. Anyone bound in those chains cannot use magic either. They bound me to the rocks with my own son's entrails. The aesir have a poetic sense of justice.

All those vile memories flooded my mind as I was dragged to the rocks again. I struggled and swore at the Valkyries, but it did no good. Sigyn watched as they stripped me naked and chained me to the rocks. They left without glancing back, leaving me alone with her.

I looked up and saw the serpent. It was a stone carved to look like the head of a snake. The mouth was open and the stony forked tongue hung out between the fangs. A drop of greenish liquid was forming on the end of that tongue.

"Sigyn!" I cried, desperate. "Get the bowl. Quick. Catch the poison."

"I have no bowl," she said calmly. "I'll go get one."

"No! No, don't leave me. Don't let it fall on me. Please, I beg you."

"You are my husband. I am faithful to you. I will bring you a bowl as you ask."

She turned and walked solemnly out of the cave. I watched in horror as the drop grew larger and larger until it was too large to stay hanging on the stone tongue and fell. The world seemed to slow as that drop fell. I writhed on the rocks to no avail. The drop splashed on my chest, wetting the scars that drops just like it had burned into my flesh centuries ago. I screamed.

I'm not sure how long it was before Sigyn returned. I know that fifty-seven drops had splashed on my chest. The pain was excruciating.

"Thank the gods you're back," I said weakly. "Quickly, hold the bowl under the serpent."

She moved carefully and purposefully, extending the bowl just as another drop fell. I gasped with relief.

"Thank you, Sigyn," I gasped. "Thank you."

"It is my duty."

"Sigyn, put your hand in your pocket."

Looking at me quizzically, she did and pulled out an iron key, the old fashioned skeleton type key.

"It's the key to the chains. I lifted it from the Valkyrie. Quickly, unchain me."

"But husband," she said with a beatific smile. "You need me. If I unchain you, then you won't need me anymore. You'll leave and leave me behind. Again."

"No! Sigyn, we'll go together. Tonight. We'll flee Asgard. For the love of all that is right and true, free me."

"I think this is better," she said solemnly. "I can take care of you. We will be together forever."

Sigyn had snapped. That was the only explanation. She was crazy.

"What kind of life is this? I'm chained to this rock being tortured while you watch. If you still love me, if you have even the slightest shred of feelings left in your heart for me, for gods' sake set me free."

She just smiled and dabbed at the fresh burns on my chest

with a cloth. Her other hand held the bowl up high. I began to weep.

I don't know how many hours it took for the bowl to fill. Sigyn sang to me while we waited. I lay silent except for the occasional whimper. Her arm never shook. The bowl stayed level and rock steady. It was an amazing feat of strength and endurance.

"No! Just a little longer. A few more drops. Please!"

"Husband, it's full. It needs to be emptied."

"Then just fling it in the corner! Quickly, between drops."

"That would be messy and unseemly," she said shaking her head sadly. "I'll go empty it outside."

"No!"

I screamed again when the fresh drops began to fall on my chest. Having a respite was almost worse. She was gone for twelve long drops.

"You're back! Thank the gods. The bowl! Put the bowl back under the serpent."

And so the time passed. Every day Sigyn would feed me one of Idunn's fruit. I assumed it was once a day. That's what Sigyn claimed. She would catch poison drops until the bowl was almost overflowing. Then she would leave to empty it and I would scream. And scream. And scream.

I could see her fondling the key in her pocket from time to time. Occasionally, she would flinch when the first drops of venom struck my chest after the bowl was full. Otherwise we talked while the bowl filled. I tried everything to persuade her to free me. I made false promises that she saw through. I flattered her shamelessly. I threatened her. I begged her. All to no avail.

On the ninety-ninth day, or at least the ninety-ninth fruit, she broke down and began to cry while feeding me.

"I can't do it anymore, Loki."

"What? Do what?" I asked around a mouthful of fruit.

"I can't watch you suffer like this. I thought I could do it. Sif reassured me I could do it. I could have you here to myself, forever."

"Sif? I should have guessed."

"All I wanted, all I've ever wanted, was to be with you, to love you and have you love me." Her tears flowed freely.

"I do love you, but not as a husband loves a wife. But as a man loves his dear friend. I'm sorry. That is the best I can do. No amount of torture from this damnable serpent will change that."

"I know, I know," she sobbed. "But what am I to do? I still love you, despite your treachery and unfaithfulness and deceit."

"You need to let me go," I said quietly. "I don't mean from the rocks, although that would be wonderful, but in your heart."

"I don't know if I can do that," she said wiping away the tears.

"It is a selfish love that clings and clutches its lover to its breast. A selfless love takes what is given freely and gives without consideration of return."

She sat there crying for a while longer, holding the bowl aloft. Her arm was rock steady and the bowl never quivered. Never underestimate the strength of a woman's love.

"If I free you, you need to make me a promise."

"Anything."

"Never seek me out. Do not let my eyes catch sight of you. I don't think I can bear the sight of you and not have you in my life."

"I promise. I will not seek you out or let you catch sight of me if I can help it."

"You always took me for granted, Loki. You will have to pay a price for that."

She turned the bowl over, dumping the serpent's poison

all over my chest. It splashed up under my chin and ran down my hips and thighs and over my groin. I screamed and writhed in pain before passing out.

I woke slowly, my body throbbing with pain, my skin on fire. I heard the drip of a falling drop. I screamed in anticipation, but nothing happened. My eyes didn't want to work, but I forced them to open. I was lying on the cave floor. The grotesque manacles lay open on the rocks. Sigyn was nowhere to be seen.

My front burned painfully. Looking down at my naked body, it was a red ruin of burns and dissolved skin and flesh. I wept as I tried to stand and failed. I tried again, getting onto my shaking hands and knees. I screamed when I collapsed and the rock floor scraped my chest and stomach.

I saw a large satchel on the other side of the small cave. I crawled toward it and forced myself not to cry out or scream. Tears stung my raw cheeks. I grunted through clenched teeth with each excruciating lurch.

Finally, I was within reach of the satchel. My clothes were folded neatly on top. The bottom was filled with Idunn's fruit. A couple dozen at least. I plucked one and greedily devoured it. The juices ran down my chin, but I didn't care.

I don't know how long I lay there. I slept and woke. I lay contemplating my future and making useless plots of revenge. I held off eating the next fruit for as long as I could. I was able to crawl painfully around the cave when I finally gave in to the hunger.

I ate the fourth fruit while sitting on the edge of the stones that had bound me. The venom dripped slowly and steadily behind me, seeping into a crack between the stones and going gods knew where. I was healed except for the old scars on my chest. No amount of fruit would fix those. A new network of fine scar lines covered my thighs, groin, stomach and upper arms. Because they were fresh, a steady diet of Idunn's fruit would eventually remove them. Unfortunately, I was pretty sure the fruit in this satchel was all I would get for a long time.

Thor and Sif had to be stopped. The jotnar have never been a numerous people. His army was actually large enough to wipe out my people. I needed to warn them. Maybe an alliance could be made with the other races of the Nine Worlds. But first, I needed a plan. They wouldn't listen to me without one. It was time to consult the foremost authority on war that I knew.

Escaping my cell was almost trivial. Frigg herself had warded it against seidr and galdr, so no shapeshifting or magic would work. However, there were no guards or locked doors. It was unthinkable that anyone would free me, and anyone who wanted to watch my agony or put me out of it was welcome to do so. So I just walked out.

I was free.

The cave entrance was on the north side of Valhalla's hall. I heard the noise of tens of thousands of rowdy men above and behind me. In front of me was a grove of trees. In the distance was the city wall. A moment later the great black cormorant that flew over it was joined by a large raven.

17

ROAD TO HEL

They say the road to Hell is paved in good intentions. The road to the Norse Hel isn't paved at all, but it is long and arduous. Still, I had good intentions and the moral of that modern-day Midgard saying was not one to ignore lightly. On the long trip, I fretted about my motivations and whether what I was doing was truly necessary. No matter how I turned it around in my head, Thor and Sif had to be stopped. I thought about Esme back on Midgard and hoped my absence was keeping her safe. I thought about the great loves of my old life, Sigyn, Baldr, and certainly not least, Angrboda. In other words, it was a depressing journey.

The spirit wind blew at my back, guiding me along Yggdrasil's mighty trunk. I chose to travel as a stallion, my spirit energy constantly replenished by the Tree, my pack hanging on a strap around my thick neck. Manny flew next to me or rode on my back. We did not talk, even when I resumed my normal shape. I think he knew where we were going without my speaking it.

Although Yggdrasil is not truly straight like a traditional

tree, it appears straight to any who travel it. The top of the Tree is near Muspelheim, the realm of fire. Its roots grow down toward Niflheim, the realm of darkness and cold. That's where I was headed.

"We have company," Manny cawed, interrupting my reveries.

"I don't see anything," I said, looking up and down the tree.

"Not yet. Valkyries. Two of them."

"Shit. I was hoping it would take longer for them to discover I had escaped."

"You can't outrun them. Or outfly them."

"A Danish king once told me 'when you can't run, it's time to fight.'"

"Are you serious? Two Valkyries?"

"Of course not. Only a fool would fight a Valkyrie let alone two of them. We're going to hide. That Danish king was an idiot."

There wasn't much time. I cast a spell of concealment. As long as we didn't move much or make any noise, their eyes would skip right over us. We weren't so much invisible as unnoticeable.

It wasn't long before I spotted them. They rode hardy ponies, one black and one brown, although 'rode' is a misnomer. Flew would be more accurate. The ponies raced across the sky, hooves flying as if there was an elevated road that only they could see. The Valkyries' white cloaks streamed behind them. Each had a spear and shield.

Odin had a thing for flying animals. I never learned how he did it. Odin's own horse, Sleipnr could ride the skies, as could Thor's goats. Long before I was sent to Asgard, the Vanir gifted Odin and his Valkyries a pair of special horses that could fly. Over the centuries the Valkyries bred them and jealously guarded them. Each horse would only bond with one rider, making theft pointless. I found that out the hard way as a youth.

The two Valkyries flew by without seeing us. Manny and I waited until even he couldn't see them anymore. Once it was safe, we resumed our journey, again in silence.

I don't know how long I traveled, but it was a long trip. There is no clear boundary where Yggdrasil's roots begin and the trunk ends. But as the light grew dimmer and the trunk became more gnarled, I had to concede we were somewhere in that zone. I could feel the spirit wind at my back, still blowing strongly. I shifted back to human.

"Manny," I said softly. "I need you to guide me from here."

"Where should I guide you?" he cawed.

"Do I really need to spell it out?"

He just looked at me.

"Take me to my daughter. My only daughter. Take me to Hel. No living being can travel Helvegr, the road to Hel, without a guide. So either you help me or we might as well go back to the Chicago suburbs."

"If I do this boon for you, you shall owe me a boon in return."

"What do you want, old crow?" I asked, both irritated and surprised.

"Besides more respect from you? A favor to be collected later. When I ask for it, you must give it to me even if your heart screams no. Even if it betrays everything you desire."

"That sounds awfully dramatic and ominous."

"I want to make sure you understand how serious I am."

"The aesir call me a trickster. How do you know I'll keep my word?"

"I've traveled with you for more than nine hundred years. In all that time you have never gone back on your word. Plus, I intend you to seal it with seidr."

"Will you use this boon to stop me from halting Thor's and Sif's plan?"

Manny just looked at me.

"You might as well answer. I'm only going down there to find a way to stop them. If you're just going to use my promise against me to prevent that, there isn't any point in going.

"No. My boon will not be used for that."

"Okay then. Let's do this."

I opened myself up to the full weight of the spirit wind. The dead of all the Nine Worlds on their way to Hel blew here. The roots of Yggdrasil fairly pulsed with power.

"I, Loki, son of Farbauti and Laufey, swear to grant Muninn, servant of Odin, a boon to be collected in times to come."

The seidr spell folded around me like a billowing cloak. Manny hopped closer to me.

"I, Muninn, eldest of the Thegnratad, servant of Odin, swear to guide Loki, son of Farbauti and Laufey, to the gates of Hel."

A matching seidr cloak billowed around the raven. Its edges met mine and bonded, enclosing us in a sphere of seidr.

"I seal my oath to Loki's oath," Manny cawed at the same time as I intoned, "I seal my oath to Muninn's oath."

The sphere collapsed, passing through us. All that was left behind was a faint thread binding Manny's heart to mine. After a moment, that faded from view.

"So, you can cast seidr," I said after a long moment.

"What of it?" the raven asked, turning his back on me.

"I can think of many times since we've traveled together when that would have been useful."

He was silent.

"And Thegnratad? What is that? Roving servant?"

"Servant of the Rovers. And it's none of your business."

"How is that none of my business? We've been together for almost a thousand years."

Manny launched himself into the air. Gods be damned he is a stubborn bird.

M anny flew and I trotted. My hooves made dull muffled clops as I headed down into the dim valley. The road was barely discernible from the landscape. Nothing lived here. Gray rocks on darker gray soil surrounded by enormous tangles of tree roots that were also gray in this poor light. The spirit wind blew at my back. It smelled of death and decay.

Manny led me through nine valleys, each darker and drearier than the one before. The roots grew smaller, but the tangles thicker. Always the road found a way through them. There was no sun or moon or stars. I don't know where the diffuse light came from, but there was less of it the farther we traveled.

I wanted to stop and lie down many times. The few times I did, Manny pecked me in the head until I was moving again. Each step became more difficult. I went from tired to exhausted. Hunger and thirst dogged me. These lands were never meant for the living. Yggdrasil fed on the spirits of the dead; stay here too long and it would suck the spirit out of the living too.

"Wake up," Manny cawed, landing on my shoulder.

I looked up and whinnied softly. My dulled senses took several seconds to make sense of what I saw. The river Gjoll. Aesir stories said that its dark waters were half a mile wide here. Only a fool would seek to swim it. They told stories of the waters being filled with the weapons used by murderers.

Even if that fanciful tale was wrong, I didn't want to find out what lurked beneath its gray surface.

I shifted back to human with an effort. Spirit energy was in short supply here. I could feel the stream of spirits flowing thick all around me. Some seventy thousand souls passed onto Yggdrasil every day and most of them came this way. But this close to Hel, they were much harder to tap.

"Which way to the bridge?" I croaked. My throat was dry and I had an unhealthy urge to drink deeply from the river. I was desperately hungry.

"Downstream. It's not far."

I tried to cast my galdr to shift back to a horse, but it failed. Defeated, I trudged downstream, looking longingly at the water. I fell into a sort of trance, putting one foot in front of the other. At one point Manny woke me by pecking my hand bloody. I was crawling toward the river. Had I reached it I would certainly have drunk from it.

"Almost there, Loki," Manny cawed.

I saw the bridge less than a hundred yards away, dimly lit in this dark land. With an effort, I dragged myself to my feet and shuffled forward. It seemed to take forever before I could put my hand on its stone support.

I collapsed, unable to hold myself up any longer. I rummaged around in my pack and drew out one of Idunn's fruits. I meant to eat it slowly and savor every last bite. But as soon as those replenishing juices hit my tongue, I tore into it. I ate the whole thing, even the seeds. I dressed in a change of clothes that had been stuffed in the bottom of the pack.

I felt alive again. I stood and brushed myself off. Although I could barely pierce the darkness around me to see the landscape, a dim light illuminated the rough stone bridge behind me. With nothing better to do, I crossed the bridge.

The ancient bridge was wide and waist-high stone walls lined each side. Thick candles burned in shallow alcoves embedded in the walls. The march of dim lights faded off into the blackness. I walked down the center of the bridge with Manny on my shoulder.

"I thought Gjallarbru was made out of gold."

"Midgard myths," Manny cawed. "The yellow candlelight is the closest thing to gold about this bridge."

Somewhere in the middle, I found a skeleton. It was a rather large skeleton, maybe twice my height. The rusted remains of some sort of mail armor draped over the chest. A broken and badly rusted axe lay to the side. I would have had to wield it with both hands. I was betting this jotunn could wield it with only one.

"Midgudr," Manny cawed.

"What?"

"Midgudr. That was her name. It means 'furious battle.'"

"I know what it means. Who was she?"

"It was her duty to guard this bridge from the living."

"That was an actual problem? Living people trying to get across? It just about killed me to get this far."

"Hence Hel never replaced her."

"Or maybe she doesn't even know her guardian is dead."

"When it comes to death, Hel knows."

I didn't know what to say to that. Manny is always good at getting the last word. We crossed the rest of the bridge in silence. The world grew brighter toward the far end. By the time we set foot on the far side, it was bright as a Midgard day.

Overhead was a black sky with more stars than a clear West Virginia night. There was grass, actual green grass, and no more giant tree roots. I couldn't find any source for the light that lit the landscape. Looking down, I noticed I had no shadow. The whole place felt very otherworldly. Maybe a hundred yards away was a dilapidated stone wall about a dozen feet high with an iron bar gate. The wall stretched out of sight in either direction.

"You can't go through the gate," Manny cawed.

"Why not?"

"The gate is for the dead. The living cannot pass. Your spirit will be allowed through, but your body will remain here."

I gave a low whistle. "So it's over the wall I guess."

Shapeshifting has many advantages, but I wanted to conserve my energy. So I looked for a place to climb. Fortunately, the wall looked ancient with missing stones and vines growing over it. With some effort, I was up and over. Manny flew of course, landing in front of me. He began to preen his feathers.

"Show off," I muttered.

18

REUNION

We were surrounded by small farms, no two alike. The closest farmhouse was rough timbers and a thatch roof. The next looked for all the world like an Amish-style log cabin. Beyond that was one made of crude brick. Each seemed to have a small field that was fallow, some plowed, but most just filled with weeds. People were tilling the soil and pulling the weeds. They were moving slowly, not in any hurry to finish. They took no notice of me as I walked the trails between the farmsteads.

In the distance I spotted the Midnight Palace, Grimasalr. I'd never been to visit my daughter here. I only knew of it from tales told to me by Odin. I couldn't make out the materials from here, but whatever they were, they were jet black.

It took more than an hour to reach the palace. As I got closer I could see it was made of granite with wood trim, both a dull black. Tall, narrow, open slots served as windows, all well above my reach. A pair of ivory doors were open but unwelcoming. I entered with some trepidation. Manny stayed outside, the coward.

White marble floors sharply contrasted the black wood walls. At least my black and white Led Zeppelin shirt matched the décor. My boots echoed as I walked down the hall and into a large chamber with black granite pillars holding up a high ceiling. A girl of likely ten years sat on a black onyx throne, an enormous wolfhound lay curled at her feet.

"Daddy!" the young girl screamed as she launched herself at me.

I stared at her as she leaped into my arms and gave me a tight hug. The wolfhound sat up on its haunches and watched. I was unprepared. My daughter, Hel, was more than a thousand years old, and last I saw her she had been a full-grown woman.

"I sensed when you came over the wall." She disentangled herself from me. "At first I was all like 'who dares do that,' but then I could tell it wasn't just some person it was someone *special*, and I thought maybe it was family like Odin, but he's dead so it wasn't him, and I never thought it would be you after all these years. But then I saw you and knew it was you come to visit me. I had little time to prepare, and—"

"Whoa!" I interrupted. "Slow down"

"Sorry." Hel took my hand. "It's just been so long since someone living came to visit ... and you never visited me before. I knew you really couldn't because it's really hard to get here and—"

"Hel." I laughed. "Let me get a word in edgewise."

"Okay," she said with a big grin and gave me another hug.

"You're so young." I held her at arm's length. "When I saw you last you were a grown woman."

"That was so long ago," she chided.

"So how are you so young now?"

"You know who make great teachers, Daddy? Dead

people. They don't have anything else to do, so they teach me."

"Wait, dead people taught you how to become younger?"

"No, silly. Dead people taught me how to control all of me. Well, mostly one dead person."

"I don't understand."

She stepped back and concentrated for a moment. The shift was quick. Hel stood before me looking like the woman I had last seen. Thin and waif-like with stringy, straight black hair and that same pale complexion.

"Would you prefer me to look like this, father?"

"Uh—"

She shifted again and became an old woman, bent and gnarled. I could see hints of Hel's looks in her face.

"Maybe you want me to look my age," she said with a quavering voice.

"But I thought you'd like me best like this," she said. "My best memories of you are when I was like this." She returned to her child form.

"How do you do that? Is... is that galdr magic?"

"Of course, silly."

"I always thought I was the best shapeshifter in the Nine Worlds."

"I can't do animals, just people. Turn into a puppy for me again, daddy!" she said, clapping her hands.

"I used to do that for you when you were a child," I said, fondly. "But I don't remember you ever being able to use magic."

"Odin taught me," she said simply. "It took forever, but I finally got it. He said any child of yours should be able to shapeshift if she really wanted to."

"I'm glad you and Odin are friends. Is he around? Can I talk to him?"

"I told him you were coming," she said, taking my hand. "He's waiting for us."

I hate being predictable, but in this case, it sure made things easier. Hel led me out of Grimasalr and down a different road than I took to get here. Manny landed on my shoulder as we exited. The hound followed us to the door, but stayed in the building.

"Munnin!" Hel exclaimed, clapping her hands.

"See, nothing to be afraid of here Manny," I said.

"Manny?" she said with a smile. "I like that name. Munnin is kind of stuffy."

"Hello, Hel," he said.

"Oh, so it's okay for her to call you Manny?" I griped.

"It's growing on me."

"Are you going with us to see Odin?" Hel asked. "Daddy wants to talk to him."

"It would be unseemly of me to come this far and not see him of all people."

"Good. This is going to be so much fun."

We walked for quite a while with Hel chattering aimlessly like she was really a child and not a thousand-year-old aesir lord. The people we passed rarely acknowledged us. Some gave us a simple glance, but most just continued with whatever menial chore they were involved in.

"These are all spirits of the dead?" I asked.

"Of course," she giggled. "Who else do you think they would be?"

"Why do you reanimate them?"

"They aren't reanimated. I gave them new bodies is all. Odin says I must have Valkyrie blood in me."

"Why do you give them new bodies?"

"So I can play with them."

She let go of my hand and approached a man who was

clearing stones out of a small field. She touched his hand and he seemed to instantly become more alive.

"Hello Hel," he said with a genuine smile. "Would you like to play?"

"Hello, Barry. That's my daddy over there. He's going to play with me today."

"How do you do, sir," Barry said, nodding toward me.

"We're on our way to see Odin right now. Bye, Barry."

She let go of his hand and his personality faded almost instantly. He went back to slowly picking up rocks and putting them on the low stone wall.

"You always did have a way with spirits," I said. "The spirit wind would swirl around you, and you would talk to them. I was sad when Odin sent you down here."

"Then why did you let him?"

"I didn't have a choice. He was our king."

"But there were lots of times you didn't do what he told you to."

"You're right, but your mother and I also thought it was best for you. You weren't doing well among people. I think you would have been unhappy if we made you stay with us."

"Oh. Sometimes I'm unhappy here."

"Barry is a modern name," I said, thinking about the man we had spoken to. "How long ago did he die?"

She looked back at Barry, squinted, and said, "Forty-three years, two months, nineteen days, and four minutes ago. He probably won't be here much longer."

"That's pretty precise sweetheart."

"I know," she said with a broad grin.

"So everyone who ever dies in Midgard comes here? You must have billions of spirits. Exactly how big is this place?"

"Ygg wouldn't like it if I kept them all. She gets awfully hungry. So we made a deal. I only keep them until nobody living remembers who they were. Then I send them on to her."

"You talk to Yggdrasil?" I asked in amazement.

"I've been here a long time, daddy," she said giggling. "I've learned all kinds of tricks. It's not really talking. It's more like feeling ideas."

I knew Yggdrasil consumed the spirits from the spirit wind. Or at least that's what Frigg had always told me. But to think that Yggdrasil was sentient or semi-sentient or whatever 'feeling ideas' implied was new.

"Even so, there still must be a lot of people here."

"It keeps changing, so I can't tell you exactly how many right now," she said with a cute little frown. "Fifty-three million is close though. I keep all my favorites, like Barry, nearby."

"You... you have that kind of power? To keep them here?" I asked incredulously.

"Of course. What did you think I do down here?" Her face never changed, but suddenly she no longer looked like a child. An ancient intelligence filled those eyes and stared back at me. I shuddered and looked away.

"We're here!" she said gleefully, suddenly childish again. "Odin! Daddy's here!"

It was a small log cabin, one that would look at home in the American west of a hundred and fifty years ago. Seated in a rocking chair on the porch was an old man in a wide-brimmed, gray hat. A long staff stood propped against the wall next to him. He was talking quietly to an old woman. He turned to look at us with his one good eye. Except for the eye patch, he looked more like Gandalf than the king of the Norse gods.

"Thank you so much for the stories, Fadilah," he said to the old woman.

As she doddered off, he turned his full attention to us.

"Hel!" he said with a friendly but commanding voice. "Have you come to chat with me again? I do so like our chats."

"Not this time, Alfodr. I've brought someone to see you."

"Oh, I know. I saw him lurking behind you. Come, Loki. You traveled a long way to speak to me. And Muninn, old friend!"

"My lord Odin," Manny cawed.

"You can have two hours with him, but no more," Hel said with childlike seriousness.

"Thank you."

"Oh, I didn't do this for you," she said with a twinkle in her eye.

"What do you mean?"

"That would be telling, Daddy," she said before skipping away.

"Loki, let's talk," Odin said from behind me.

I turned and saw Manny sitting on his shoulder. It brought back memories of Odin sitting on the High Seat with Munnin and Huggin on his shoulders, whispering into his ears. I suppressed a twinge of jealousy that Manny would choose Odin over me so readily.

"Almighty Alfodr, king of gods, I've come to ask a boon of you," I said with a sweeping bow.

"That's laying it on a bit thick, even for you, Loki," he grunted.

"Okay." I grinned. "I need your help, old man."

"First get me some mead or ale. Whatever I have in the house. These are the only times I can enjoy having a drink. And get something for Muninn, too."

I found the drinks and put a large mug of mead in front of him and kept another for myself. I found some strips of dried meat for Manny, who was still perched on Odin's

147

shoulder when I walked back outside. Taking a chair on the porch with him, we sipped in silence for a moment.

"I have a problem, Alfodr. Thor is going to war and I need to stop him."

"I know."

"You do?"

"I am the God of Knowledge. Of course I know."

"You are no god," I said scornfully. "None of the aesir are. Especially now. You're just a dead man. A spirit waiting to feed Yggdrasil."

"I will never go to the tree." Odin laughed. "Hel only sends those who are not remembered. I will be remembered for all of time."

"All hail Lord Odin," Manny piped up. I'm pretty sure he was serious. Divided loyalties and all.

"That's a bit of a stretch, isn't it?"

"I suppose." He chuckled. "I was always drawn to grand proclamations. But you have to admit I'm not going anywhere for a long time. I'm still remembered throughout the Nine Worlds, and likely will be for another thousand years."

"So you know all about Thor's plans?"

"I know what Hel tells me, and the occasional aesir who passes through" he admitted. "There isn't much you can hide from someone who can talk to spirits."

"See, you are no god. You're just an old gossip."

"What makes a man a god, Loki?"

"We don't have time for theology, Alfodr. I need to know how to stop Thor."

"The aesir are going to war, and you don't think it's important to understand what makes them gods?"

"It doesn't matter what they *think* they are."

"So humor me. What is a god?"

I sighed. "I'll play your game. Midgard humans would say

it's the force that created everything. But in our case, they would probably say a person or spirit that can control some aspect of the natural world."

"Those same Midgard humans are becoming masters of their world right now. They send people to the moon, tame lightning, and control the very forces that power the sun. Are they gods?"

"I suppose you want me to say it's someone with the gift, an affinity. Someone able to do those things without machines."

"I've heard tell of an eel in a distant part of Midgard that can harness the power of lightning. Is it a god?"

"Of course not."

"So, what is a god?"

I sighed. I wasn't a fan of these games. "If you want to get metaphysical, I suppose a god also needs worshipers. There are Midgard storytellers who write tales about gods having more power when they have more worshipers."

"The Chinese and Japanese emperors had more worshipers than any aesir ever did. That was within the past century or two. Were they gods?"

"Obviously not."

"Yet they were venerated and worshiped. So why aren't they gods?"

After a long pause, I said, "I don't think there is one definition of a god. It means different things to different people."

"That's the best answer you've given so far," he said with a grunt. "So what is a god to the aesir?"

"A story we told stupid humans," I said crossly. "A story you told gullible people because you were more powerful because of your affinities. You got them to worship you because they thought you could answer their prayers."

"Ha! They are stupid and gullible and I was more powerful, but it wasn't just a story."

"So you tell me then," I said holding back my irritation. "What makes an aesir a god?"

"We are the embodiment of a principle and ideal. You were partially right when you said we can control nature. In some cases, we can. But just as often, nature controls us. I was the God of Battles, among other things. I drove men to fight and die in my name, but just as often the battle lust consumed me."

"So Thor is thunder and thunder is Thor?"

"Not thunder, the storm. He is the God of Storms. He can bring the storm, but just as often he is the storm. His nature is like that of the storm, wild, dangerous, and unpredictable."

"That's certainly the Thor I grew up with."

"It's the gift and the curse of the aesir lords. Each of us is drawn to something of the world. We embody it and it changes and reflects us."

"Assuming I believe all this, how does this help me?" I asked crossly.

"Tell me, what does this war have to do with storms?"

"Storms? Nothing. I don't see any connection."

"Exactly."

"I don't get it." I frowned. This was getting frustrating.

"When you do, you might just be able to stop my favorite son from waging war across the Nine Worlds."

"I'm not sure that will be enough to stop a hundred thousand warriors."

"The einherjar were never meant to be a conquering force. They were only meant to defend Asgard."

"Just tell me," I pleaded, standing. "If you don't, he'll succeed."

"I have. You aren't listening."

"Argh!" I shouted, grinding my teeth and standing in front of him with clenched fists.

"You must understand, Loki. My loyalties are divided

here. On the one hand, I have my favorite son who could end up ruling everything, and on the other is the fate of all the races of the Nine Worlds. It's hard to choose."

Manny laughed his creepy raven laugh.

I flung myself back into the chair and took a deep drink of my mead. Getting mad at Odin's ghost wasn't going to help. I needed to calm myself and think more clearly.

"So, you say you are the God of Battles and the God of Knowledge. Teach me how to beat Thor on the battlefield."

"Well done, Loki. Appealing to two of my natures," he said, nodding. "How can I resist?"

"I'm hoping you can't."

"It will be a glorious battle." His ghost-eyes shone. "Many will die fighting furiously."

"How about a way to win that will minimize the bloodshed. Or better yet, a way to stop it from happening in the first place."

"War is inevitable. Always has been, always will be. As for winning it, I lived for the joy of the battle, not the joy of victory. I can tell you how to kill many of your enemies. It's up to you to make a victory out of that. It's really too bad I'm dead. I would love to see the second Ragnarokkr. It's shaping up to be a glorious battle."

"You bastard," I hissed. "That's why you'll only give me half-answers. Even dead you still want to make the biggest, bloodiest battle you can."

Odin smiled at me. I sat fuming and sipping my mead for a while as Odin talked about Viking battlefield tactics. I was talking to the wrong aesir. I needed Tyr, God of War, not Odin. While I was at it, I could stop by and see all the aesir who died at Ragnarokkr, I thought bitterly. I was personally responsible for most of their deaths. I'm sure they would be eager to help.

"You've accused me of being an impostor," Odin said, changing the topic.

"You are," I said gloomily. "You convinced humans to worship you and pay you tribute just because you have gifts that they don't. It was a very slick con, but it was still a con."

"So you deny your own godhood?"

"Mine? I'm no god."

"You are ageless and eternal. You can use seidr and galdr magic. Loki, you are the God of Mischief, whether you choose to believe it or not. You may think you don't cause it, but it is part of your nature. You can't help yourself."

"I'm mostly jotnar," I said defensively. "And anyone who eats Idunn's fruit is ageless."

"But you are part aesir too," Odin said with a shrug. "I have a lot of jotunn blood as well. But aesir blood runs true and deep."

"My mother would never talk about her father."

"He was aesir."

"Who was he?" I asked leaning forward.

"It no longer matters. What matters is that you are part aesir and that you accept your true nature as the God of Mischief."

"The God of Mischief is just an insulting name you gave me as a child. It doesn't mean anything. I don't have an affinity. Believe me, I'd love to be able to control the wind or make trees grow or something."

"I gave you that name because it is you. I spent many hours with Mimir confirming your true nature."

I snorted my derision. Odin was trying to make me out to be some sort of walking Murphy's Law, and I wasn't buying it.

"Muninn," Odin said, looking over at my bird. "Show him."

I flinched as Muninn flapped over to land on my shoulder.

"Show me what?" I tipped my head away from Manny. His damn beak hurts.

This touch was gentle, like a mother's caress. The world fell away and I was standing in front of a younger Odin seated on Hlidskajf. He held the severed head of Mimir to his ear. Muninn and Huginn perched on the back of the throne. Odin's eyes had that faraway look he got when he was using Hlidskajf to see things that were not here.

"You asked for me, milord?"

"Mimir and I have been discussing you, Loki," Odin said without looking at me. Mimir's head was disturbing.

"Yes, milord," I said, not knowing how else to respond to that.

"You have aesir blood, yet you have not demonstrated any affinity."

"I'm sorry, milord."

"It's not something to apologize for. Many aesir don't have affinities. Only certain bloodlines carry that gift."

"I'm sure my aesir grandfather was nobody special. Either that or my aesir blood is too thin."

I had learned the hard way to always be modest and never show pride in myself or my family.

"I'm not so sure. I hear you're learning to cast spells. Frigg tells me you have a natural talent."

"I study hard, milord," I said carefully. "Milady is a good teacher."

I wished he would look at me.

"Mimir thinks he may know your affinity. He thinks you have an affinity for mischief."

"I... They're just pranks, milord. Harmless pranks," I said, beginning to panic. No child likes to be caught.

"Some are less harmless than others."

"Milord, I swear I'll never pull another prank. I'll be good, I promise," I begged. Punishments in Asgard were harsh. I was terrified of what Odin might do.

"I don't think that will be necessary. I called you here to see more deeply inside your heart. To see the real you with the aid of Mimir and Hlidskajf. I see now that this was a mistake, that knowing your true nature will make things happen sooner. I want to put that off for as long as possible."

"What do you mean?" I asked.

"Muninn, if you would."

I stumbled back and Muninn launched himself at me. I tried to shield myself to no avail. I felt his beak touch my head.

I was back on that porch. I shot out of my chair, causing Manny to take flight and seek the shelter of the railing. I was breathing heavily, trying to control my emotions. Odin had fucked with my memories. No, Manny had fucked with my memories.

"Was that the only time?" I asked heatedly.

Odin was silent for long seconds. "No."

"I want them back," I shouted. "All of them."

"No."

"What do you mean, no? Those are my memories."

"Are you going to return all the memories you've had Muninn steal?"

It was my turn to be silent for too long. "No."

"You have good reasons for keeping them. So do I."

"Gods!" I shouted to nobody in particular. I paced.

After letting me stomp around a bit, Odin asked, "Why are you here?"

"I told you. I need to stop Thor."

"So just kill him."

"Easier said than done. And even if I did, Sif would just take over. It's her plan Thor is following."

"Interesting. You didn't mention Sif before."

"She's leading Thor around by the nose," I said with a snort. "You'd hardly recognize her. She's colder and crueler."

"My favorite son is like a bull with a nose ring. Most times you can lead him where you want, but sometimes the bull gets a mind of its own."

"Ha!" I laughed. "Either way, I have to stop both of them."

"Why would Sif care about the jotnar?" Odin mused.

"You've been dead a long time, Alfodr. People change. Sif has changed a lot."

"The right forge can turn a plowshare into a sword, but it doesn't change itself."

"What does that mean?"

"Why?" Odin asked, clearly changing the topic. "Why do you care about the jotnar at all?"

"The jotnar are my people. They'll wipe them out."

"So if Thor left Jotunheim alone and only conquered the rest of the Nine Worlds, you wouldn't be bothered?"

"No," I said slowly. "I think I'd try to stop him anyway."

"Why?"

"I don't know," I said, frustration building again. "What he's doing is wrong. Somebody should stop him."

"And how did you get mixed up in all of this? You were living a simple life in Midgard, yet here you are trying to save the Nine Worlds."

"Hey, that's not my fault," I said defensively. "They sent manibrandr assassins to kill me."

"And yet they didn't succeed. Their plan went awry. What horrible bad luck."

"You're trying to say that I made that happen?"

"And why did they even bother to try and kill you?" Odin

continued, ignoring my question. "They could have started their war and you would have been none the wiser."

"I don't know. Sif mentioned something about a prophecy."

"So they tried to change a prophecy and instead triggered it. Such bad luck again. It seems like your enemies just keep running into bad luck. Almost like someone is causing mischief, whether they mean to or not."

"Very clever, you old ghost."

"You are mischief and mischief is you. It is your Gift. It will seek you out and you will seek it out. Just accept it."

"Daddy."

I turned and saw Hel standing just off the porch.

"It's time," she said. "Can't you see how tired he is?"

Odin looked more frail and distant than just a few minutes ago. He seemed to lose interest in us without being directly addressed. Manny was still perched on his shoulder. I almost felt sorry for smearing bitterroot in the bottom of a couple of his mugs.

"But I didn't get what I came for. How can I stop Thor and Sif?"

"You've gotten less than you deserved, but more than you needed," Hel said cryptically.

"I guess it was too much to expect him to just tell me the answers."

"See, you get smarter all the time."

"I guess it's time to go, Manny."

"I'll be along shortly," Manny cawed.

"Maybe you can play with me now, Daddy. We'll have a tea party."

"What happened to him?" I asked as we walked away.

I watched as Manny gently touched his beak to Odin's temple. There was no way to tell if he was giving or taking memories. Either way left me feeling uncomfortable.

"The spirits here are just echoes of their living selves. The essence of their being, but without the body to support it. The bodies I give them are just shells that hold the spirit. It isn't truly connected. If I turn my attention to them, they can become more like they were in life. I can make that connection stronger for a while."

"But he wasn't that way when we first got here."

"Odin is special. He's... well, he's Odin. For a short time, he can be more like his old self without my attention. He usually spends an hour or two a day talking to newcomers to catch up on the comings and goings of the Nine Worlds. After that though, he fades."

"Can I talk to some of the others?"

"No," she said with a sad face. "You're only allowed to talk to one spirit. Those are the rules, Daddy."

"You make the rules," I pointed out.

"So you understand then."

"Not really," I said with a frown.

"Come on, Daddy. Let's go have a tea party."

So Hel and I walked back to her palace and had a tea party. It was quite lovely and surreal at the same time. Manny joined us in the middle of it, drinking tea and eating cookies. After we had drunk our fill of tea and eaten all the cookies, it was time to go. I don't think I ever had such a good time with my daughter, even while she still lived in Asgard.

W here to now, oh great one," Manny cawed mockingly.

"Shut your pie hole."

"I prefer cookies to pie."

We were back on Yggdrasil, heading toward the crown of

that mighty tree. The trip out of Hel had been exhausting but uneventful. It had taken a full day of rest to feel like myself again.

"Jotunheim," I answered. "I have to warn them. If nothing else, they need to know what is coming so they can prepare."

"Prepare? Prepare to be slaughtered you mean. The Einherjar outnumber the jotnar ten to one."

"I know that," I snapped. "But I can't do nothing."

He didn't have a retort, so we set off down the tree. Or up the tree I suppose. I stuffed my clothes in the pack, changed into a horse to make the trip easier, and slung the pack around my neck. Manny rode on my back. Damn bird was too lazy to even fly.

19

HUNTED

There is something following us," Manny cawed.

We had been traveling for a couple of days now. I peered behind us but didn't see anything. Of course, a horse's eyesight isn't the best for long distances.

"It's just a black spot on the horizon, but it's moving, keeping pace with us."

The horizon along the trunk of Yggdrasil is quite distant. Much farther than on Midgard because there's no curvature. I picked up my pace. After a few hours, I was forced to slow to a walk.

"It's back again," Manny said an hour later.

I tried to put on a burst of speed, but it didn't last long. So rather than exhaust myself further, I turned back to human, dressed, and just walked. If whatever it was got too close I wanted to have enough in the tank to sprint for a while.

"It's a man," Manny said after a while longer. "Or maybe a woman. Hard to tell."

I took his word for it and kept plodding forward. There was a chance he—or she—wasn't after me. I angled my path so that I would go around the tree.

"He's turning too."

"Can you fly back there and see who or what that is?"

He took flight. I kept trudging forward. It was a while before Manny returned.

"Well?"

"It's Ullr," Manny cawed. "And he shot at me."

"And he missed? Ullr never misses."

"I suspect he was just trying scare to me off."

"Or he's not after you. He's after me. Sif must have discovered I escaped from my rock in Asgard."

For the next several hours, I tried to shake my follower. No matter what I did, he was slowly gaining. I wasn't surprised. Ullr could track a snow hare in a blizzard, and he could run down a caribou until it died from exhaustion. I needed a different plan.

"Manny," I puffed, out of breath. "Fly ahead. See if we are lucky enough that Ratatoskr is on his way back down."

I took off walking at a brisk pace, trying to ignore the stitch in my side. Looking back I could see a tiny stick figure loping along.

"I didn't see Ratatoskr," Manny said when he returned. "Only the four stags."

"The stags?" I said with some interest. "Are they close enough we can reach them before Ullr catches us?"

"Definitely, but they won't help you. The stags never talk to anyone. I'm not sure they even can."

"That's okay. I have an idea."

The stags weren't as close as I had hoped, but we got to them well ahead of our pursuer. The four watched me casually as I approached. I stopped a good hundred yards away and put my hands on my knees trying to catch my breath.

The four stags were the only other creatures to live on Yggdrasil's trunk besides Ratatoskr. They were considered sacred to the aesir. Killing them was unthinkable. Imitating them was not.

It wasn't long before Ullr came within range. He stopped far closer to the stags than I had. Ullr was tall and handsome, with long wheat-hued hair held back with a woven headband, and a heavy bearskin cloak draped over his back; he looked like he had stepped right out of a history book. He was never without his bow.

"Five stags," Ullr said, not nearly as out of breath as I had been. "There are only supposed to be four, Dainn, Dvalinn, Duneyrr and Durathror I know. The fifth must be Loki. Very clever. I'm only here to talk."

Five stags looked back at him with disinterest. Manny circled us high above. Talk my ass. Ullr is Sif's son. There is no way he was only here to talk.

"Now what shall we do?" he said, putting his hand to his chin. "I could try waiting you out. You can't stay a stag forever."

I craned my neck and nibbled on a low hanging leaf.

"If I watch long enough, you might give yourself away. I bet I know more about how deer behave than you do."

I let the deer part of my brain chew the leaf and shifted my weight from one hoof to another.

"But there might be a faster way. Loki is a coward. If I start shooting deer, I bet you are the first to flee."

One of the stags, gods knows which one, bolted. Quick as a flash Ullr knocked a bow and fired, just barely missing. Obviously a warning shot to get me to stop. Too bad that wasn't me. Another stag took off in another direction. So I did what any good coward will do. I fled, too. All five of us ran in different directions. Ullr followed the first stag. Manny flew off, staying over the first stag as we had agreed.

I ran until the stag shape was exhausted. They are built for bursts of speed, not endurance runs, so it wasn't as far as

I would have liked. Back in human form, this time without my bag so I was forced to remain naked, I plodded on while I caught my breath.

I had avoided what seemed like an obvious solution. With a deep sigh, I took on the form of a swan. I took off gliding easily enough. However, once I was in the air I began to get lightheaded. I was able to last a little over an hour before vertigo forced me to land. Hopefully, that put enough miles between me and Ullr to shake him for a while. Something about Yggdrasil made it very difficult for me to fly as a bird. Maybe there wasn't as much air up off the surface. I don't know how Manny does it so easily.

20

JOTUNHEIM

Manny rejoined me shortly before I stepped into Jotunheim. Ullr would eventually catch up to me again. There was no shaking him once he had your trail. Hopefully, I could reach my refuge before him.

Jotunheim is a rough, mountainous land. Craggy, snow-covered peaks towered over the rock-strewn valleys. Massive pines clustered together in patches as we made our way toward Utgard, the only real city in Jotunheim, if you could call it that.

Manny and I gave wide berth to the occasional jotnar farm, save one where clothes were drying on a line and I found a shirt I could use as a tunic. I wasn't sure what kind of reception I would get at the farmsteads. Heck, I wasn't sure what kind of reception I would get at Utgard, but I had to risk it.

The city of Utgard bore a striking resemblance to Asgard, at least from the outside. Small wonder since jotnar masons had built both. Soaring white granite walls almost looked like they were made from a single stone. Massive battlements, far too large for a normal person, ran the lengths. Thick, round towers were set at intervals. The open gate before me would let a Macy's Thanksgiving Day parade balloon pass through unhindered.

I didn't see anyone on the walls and nobody was manning the gate. Throwing my shoulders back, I marched through like I was a returning king. A rather small returning king, but showing confidence was important.

There weren't many people on the street. And by people, I mean jotnar of all sizes. Those that were out and about glanced at me and then kept walking. Manny laughed. I hate his laugh.

"Lord Loki," he cawed. "Should I announce you to the waiting throng?"

"Shut up," I muttered.

Of the handful of jotnar in the streets, the shortest was at least a head taller than me. The tallest was twice that. Taking my pride in my hands, I approached the nearest person. He was working on an over-sized hide stretched on a frame.

"Excuse me, kind sir, but could you direct me to the king's castle?"

"Just follow the main road," he grunted without stopping his work.

He didn't seem inclined to expound upon that, so I set off on what appeared to be the main road. The other jotnar in the streets glanced at me curiously but otherwise ignored me. They were slightly thicker bodied than the typical aesir, with fuller facial features like wider lips and noses and a heavier brow ridge. Not enough to look alien, but enough to set them apart. The men had beards and women had long braids. They wore clothing that looked for all the world like Greek or Roman togas. I wasn't as out of place as I had feared.

The buildings were made of natural stone in a variety of

colors. The doorways varied as well, from half again as tall as me to three times my height. It gave a strange mismatched look to the place. I had been here once before, a long time ago, traveling with Thor. The layout was completely different, but the look of the place was the same.

It didn't take long to get to the enormous castle, far bigger than any Midgard castle. Although to be fair, all the features were three to four times normal size. So for a jotunn, it probably didn't seem that big.

As I approached, I could hear the deep bass roar of a crowd. No guard was posted at the castle door, which stood open. So far I wasn't impressed by their military readiness. The hall inside was far taller than any of the jotnar I had seen on the street and obviously was meant to impress visitors. The stone carvings and reliefs that ran up the walls and columns were amazingly detailed and life-like.

I followed the sound of the crowd, and I came up behind a broad balcony with half a dozen giant jotnar clustered around a huge stone seat, the back of which was to me. The jotnar were cheering and catcalling.

"My lords and ladies," I shouted, trying to make myself heard over the din. "I have come seeking an audience with the king of Jotunheim."

One of the giantesses turned and saw me. "Are you here for the sport?" she asked.

"No. I'm here for an audience with the king."

"And who might you be?"

"He is Loki, son of Farbauti of clan Vedrfell. Victor of Ragnarokkr and prince of Asgard," Manny chimed in. I gave him a dirty look.

"Clan Vedrfell? Never heard of it. But every jotunn alive knows about the great hero Loki."

"Well, that's me," I said with a bow and a flourish.

"You're a bit small, aren't you?"

"Never judge a man by his size."

"Why not? Seems like the best way to do it."

"Let's set that aside for now," I said, irked. "I'd like an audience with the king."

"He's busy right now. Why don't you watch with us? When it's done you can have your audience and he'll decide what to do with you."

She opened a path for me to get to the front of the small crowd. Obviously, I wasn't considered much of a threat. I was standing with two elderly jotnar, a hulking jotnar man who looked to be in the prime of his life, the woman I had been speaking with, a smaller jotunn no taller than me who had been hidden near what was apparently a throne, and a giant of a jotunn sitting in the throne. Each of them glanced at me and then went back to screaming at whatever sport was on the other side of the stone railing.

I approached the carved stone railing that surrounded the balcony and put my head between a pair of carved bears. The balcony looked down upon a rather large arena, but since it was filled with a couple hundred giant jotnar, it seemed small. The central pit was substantial as well. A pair of naked, grease-covered jotnar men wrestled in it.

As I watched, I could tell the two of them were skilled and well-matched. Their sizes kept fluctuating, which they used to help them execute various holds and throws. Finally, one of the men got a chokehold on the other and the match was over just like that. The crowd cheered and jeered, showing their favor to one or the other of the wrestlers. The huge jotunn on the throne, whom I assumed was the king, stood and held up his hands.

"The victor is Thjori!" he boomed. The crowd cheered louder. The unconscious jotunn was dragged out of the ring by the victor.

"Did I hear you say that you are the fabled Loki?" the king asked, looking down at me. I barely came up to his kneecap.

"Yes, your highness," I said, bowing low. "Please pardon my ignorance, but I've been away so long I no longer know who sits on the throne in Jotunheim."

"I am Ymyd," he said, thumping his chest. "This is my wife, Sydro, my son, Hrengr, and my grandson, Uglr. These two ancient wrecks are my advisors, Hrim and Solufn."

"I am honored to be in your presence."

Hrengr just glared at me, and then at the giantess that had let me squeeze to the front. Hrim and Solufn remained aloof.

"Can I play with him?" Ulgr asked.

"No," Hrengr said, pulling his son back. "Loki may look like a child, but he is full-grown man of his kind. And very dangerous."

"Ah, mom!" the boy pouted.

"Nonsense, Hrengr," Ymyd said, cheerfully. "Loki is a legendary hero, breaker of the Bifrost Bridge, war chief of Ragnarokkr, and plunderer of Asgard."

"Don't forget kinslayer," Hrengr added.

"Oh, I haven't," Ymyd said, still cheerfully. "With Thor by his side, he's slain many a jotunn. And since he lived for so long with aesir, let us not forget how many of those adopted kin died at Ragnarokkr. What say you Loki?"

"Truly I must own all of those titles," I said wryly. "Even the dishonorable ones."

"How do you know he's truly Loki," Sydro asked.

"He's Loki," Hrim said somberly. "And the raven is either Huginn or Muninn."

"Of course he is." Ymyd laughed. "I never doubted it for a moment."

"Your highness," I said. "I have an urgent matter to discuss with you."

"I'm sure you do, Loki. Solufn predicted as much."

"She predicted I would come here?"

"No, she predicted trouble would find its way to my doorstep. And if ever there was a harbinger of trouble, it's Loki, God of Mischief."

"I'm not... nevermind. So can we talk? Somewhere quieter?"

"There is one more match to watch. The last of the day. I think we should watch it first. Then we will talk."

"I don't think—"

Ymyd turned and thundered out at the audience, "For our final match, we will relive the day of victory. The day we defeated our enemies! We will relive a battle from Ragnarokkr!"

He sounded like a carnival barker. I returned to watching through the railing as two people emerged from opposite ends of the arena. I did a double-take as I saw Thor on the far side. But no, not quite Thor. Close enough though. Tall and brawny with thick red hair and a full red beard. He was dressed like Thor in a chainmail hauberk and carrying a short-handled hammer. On the close side was a man just as big and burly, but clearly a jotunn. He wore a bearskin tunic and dragged a club behind him that was taller than he was.

Skrymir was probably rolling over in his grave at this depiction of him from Ragnarokkr. Thor was reasonably accurate, but the real Skrymir had worn a leather shirt with a large steel plate sewn to it. He had carried an enchanted spear made for him by the dvergar.

The actor playing Thor chanted in a sing-song voice, stomping his feet and shaking his fist. I recognized the galdr of the berserkers immediately. He was working himself into a battle frenzy. On the other side 'Skrymir' was doing his own chanting and beginning to grow taller.

For the jotnar, size is a matter of perspective and attitude. The more attitude, the larger they became, the better their perspective. They literally talk themselves into growing. Those who can grow the largest and control it the easiest gained the most respect in jotnar society. For Ymyd to be so large so easily said something.

Thor's chanting grew louder and he grabbed his mail shirt in one hand and tore it off. At first, I assumed it had been a stage prop, but as metal links flew everywhere, I realized he had really just ripped a chainmail shirt in half. I looked closely at his face. There was a resemblance to Thor, but it clearly wasn't him. But I could also see that he wasn't a jotunn. He was aesir or possible Vanir.

"Hardly seems like a fair fight," Manny commented.

The Skrymir warrior was well over twice the height of Thor by now. The crowd was stomping its feet in time with his chant, feeding into his power. With an animal howl, Thor charged the giant. The pretend Skrymir swung the club at Thor who ducked under it. Head down, Thor charged into the giant's legs, but Skrymir sidestepped and Thor went racing past. The crowd roared. He swung his hammer to the side and connected with Skrymir's leg, sending the jotnar giant hobbling. Cheers changed to boos.

Thor spun and ran at the limping jotunn, hammer raised high. Skrymir swept his club around and connected with the hammer, sending it flying across the arena while the crowd cheered. Thor didn't even slow his charge, but plowed into Skrymir's leg, striking it with a double-handed, overhead blow.

The giant buckled but was already in the middle of a backswing that connected solidly with Thor. Skrymir went down with a howl, but Thor went flying across the arena and slammed into the wall with an audible crunch. I expected that to be the end of the fight, short and sweet, but Thor bounced up from the dirt floor and howled in fury. He pulled great chunks out of his hair, which I could now see was a wig, and beat his chest.

Skrymir climbed to his feet and readied the club. Thor ignored the hammer that was maybe two steps away and charged again. Skrymir set up for an uppercut golf swing with the club. Thor met it head-on, clasping the giant's club in both hands.

Instead of going flying again like he should have, he stopped it cold and wrestled the club from Skyrmir. Holding it in both hands, Thor snapped it in two. The crowd howled in anger. How the heck strong was this guy?

Skrymir snatched at Thor, picking him up in one meaty hand. Lifting him high overhead, he made to fling him to the ground. Instead, Thor took hold of his opponent's over-sized thumb and bent it back. Skrymir howled and dropped his captive.

Clutching at his hand Skrymir kicked at Thor, connecting solidly and sending Thor sailing across the arena again. The crack as he hit the wall for a second time was even audible over the roar of the crowd. Thor fell to the ground on his face and didn't move.

Holding his injured hand to his chest, Skrymir raised his other fist in victory. The crowd began to chant "Skrymir, Skrymir." They didn't concern themselves as Thor rose to his hands and knees.

Skrymir basked in the adulation of the throng.

Behind him, Thor stood, swaying. It took me a minute to realize it, but the sway was not the stagger of a woozy combatant. It was the rhythmic sway of a chant. I recognized the galdr spell.

Thor's body changed, growing taller, thicker and hairier. What clothes he had on ripped away. It only took a few seconds until a huge brown bear stood in his place. I shifted uncomfortably remembering my recent time as a polar bear.

Skrymir turned as the crowd's cheers turned to gasps. The bear hit him square on, bowling him over. Then the mauling began.

Two large jotnar below the viewing stand where I was watching vaulted into the arena. Each wore heavy leather armor with thick forearm and neck protectors. It was immediately obvious that they had been waiting to separate the combatants if something went wrong. They each grabbed a rear leg and pulled the giant bear off the bleeding giant.

Another jotnar rushed to get in front of the bear while one circled behind. Each had a chain noose. The bear regained his feet quickly, broke free, and charged.

The jotunn was ready, but it didn't matter. He went down under a ton of raging claws and teeth. The thick forearm and neck protectors proved their usefulness as the bear clawed and bit at them.

The downed jotunn wouldn't last long. His companion tried to get the bear's attention by waving and hollering, but to no effect. Cursing inwardly, I shucked my oversized shirt off.

"Mom, why is the new man taking his clothes off?" Ulgr asked.

I shifted into a large gray wolf, one of the easiest forms for me. Leaping over the stone wall, I landed heavily on the packed dirt floor of the arena. The leather protectors on the downed giant were shredded now, and the other giant was failing to toss the chain loop over the bear's head.

With a snarl I charged the bear, biting at its ankle hard and then running off without waiting to see what effect it had. It's a common wolf tactic to run in and out, biting at vulnerable spots. The bear reared up with a roar, its victim forgotten. I circled back, drawing its attention away from the two giants. I saw a couple more scrambling over the walls to help.

The bear charged me, the swipe of a great paw missing me as I juked to the side. I was far more nimble than any bear. However, this bear was quicker than it had a right to be. On its next charge it anticipated my dodge, and only narrowly missed me. Unfortunately, now I was backed up against the wall.

The bear was preparing for another assault, one that would be almost impossible for me to avoid. What I wouldn't give for him to slip and fall right now. I knew I wouldn't escape this time. The bear launched itself at me with a roar, but misjudged and landed short. I raced around the beast as it rose back up.

A pair of steel nooses quickly slipped over its head. The beast roared and stood to its full ten-foot height and shook. The four jotnar, two on each side holding the chains taut, were nearly pulled off their feet. I watched as giant muscles bulged and chains tightened. The bear grew weaker as it choked. It clawed at the chains futilely before eventually passing out. The four jotnar stood sweating and puffing as the bear transformed back into a man, still unconscious. Another pair of jotnar ran out to tend to the bleeding and groaning Skrymir.

I shifted back to human. I was able to snatch a scrap of torn breeches from the arena floor to protect my modesty. The Thor actor was carried out of the arena.

A thick wooden door opened Ymyd strolled through with his retinue.

"Well, wasn't that interesting," Ymyd boomed with a laugh. A servant twice my height handed me a cloak to wrap in. Several feet of it dragged in the dirt behind me.

"I've never been a fan of blood sport," I said.

"And yet you acquitted yourself quite well." He guided me out of the arena with a giant hand on my back. "I have to confess that didn't go quite as planned."

"The jotunn was supposed to beat the aesir to a pulp I presume."

"On the contrary," Ymyd said frowning. "It was supposed to be a staged match. It's a celebration of Skrymir's triumph over Asgard at Ragnarokkr. But it should have ended in a traditional wrestling match."

"So what went wrong?"

"I'm told that Umgre and Meili went drinking last night. Words were exchanged. They entered the arena with chips on their shoulders."

"You knew this and still let them fight?"

"The crowd loves a good brawl," Ymyd said with a shrug. "But I did make sure a few of my best were on hand to stop anyone from getting too seriously hurt. They were almost too late for Umgre."

"Meili is an aesir name. I didn't know any of the aesir lived in Jotunheim."

"That's Thor's brother. The one Odin sent to live in Jotunheim when you were sent to Asgard."

"Wait, he's that Meili?"

"Oh yes," Ymyd said with a huge grin. "We've kept him around just in case the aesir decide to do something stupid. After Ragnarokkr he decided to stay with us on his own."

"And he can shape change?"

"Only into a bear. If he works himself up into a frenzy the change just happens."

"So he's a true berserker then," I said thoughtfully.

"A bear shirt warrior," Manny cawed.

"I thought the berserkers were all gone."

"He may be the last," Manny cawed.

"He's certainly one of a kind," Ymyd said.

21

MAKING MISCHIEF

My meeting with Ymyd was delayed further when he dragged me to a feast. Although they had a chair specially designed for my size, I still felt like a child at the grownups table. I could not complain about the food though, and certainly not about the portions.

Huge roasted boars were set on the tables. Steamed vegetables and baked fruit lined the platters. Loaves of bread the size of my leg were stacked in piles. Gigantic mugs of wine and mead were served. I found myself sharing a boar with Thjori, the victor in the wrestling match I had caught the end of. The mood was buoyant and celebratory and everyone was eating and drinking with gusto. Manny hopped around grabbing juicy morsels from everyone's plates.

"It is an honor to share a meal with Loki," Thjori said, ripping the haunch off the boar like it was a leg off of a turkey.

"I am the one who is honored. That was quite a match you won."

"The luck was with me," Thjori said with a wink. "He was a bit hungover. In a fair match, he would have beaten me."

"Better to be lucky than good." I grinned. "That's what I always say."

"I'll drink to that." He laughed, downing his entire mug.

Ymyd stood, casting a large shadow. He pounded his mug, which was the size of my chest, on the table three times. The room grew quiet as everyone faced him. I spied Meili slinking into the giant hall and taking a seat in the back. An idea was beginning to take root within me.

"This is an auspicious day," Ymyd thundered. "As we celebrate the victory of Jotunheim over Asgard, Lord Loki himself came to watch, and even participated."

The Jotnar began pounding their mugs on the tables rhythmically while chanting my name louder and louder. Ymyd held up his arms and the raucous cheer died down.

"As befitting a noble guest, we invite him to speak."

I was caught a little by surprise. I turned to Thjori and whispered, "What am I supposed to do?"

"Give a speech, sing a song, tell a tale, whatever you wish."

"There are those who doubt you are truly Loki," Ymyd said from my other side. "Prove yourself to them. Prove yourself to me. Be Loki."

I climbed onto the table. Eyes the size of saucers all turned to stare at me.

"Hvars thu bol kannt

"kved thu the bolvi at

"ok get-at thinum fjandum frid."

Which loosely translates to "where you recognize evil, speak out against it, and give no truces to your enemies." It drew some uplifted mugs and mutters of agreement. After a suitable pause, I launched into the poetic version of the tale of Ragnarokkr. It seemed fitting.

The assembly got into it, in no small part because of the

drink. I love a good crowd, which got me into it too. I stalked the table acting out the charge of Fenrir. I dropped to my knees in grief at the death of Thrym, king of Jotunheim. And, of course, I portrayed myself as the wronged prince of Asgard seeking vengeance upon the gods that spurned him. Every good story needs a half-truth.

———

O h, my head," I groaned as I woke.

I didn't remember being put to bed, but that's where I was. It was a very large bed. Manny watched me from a high window. Then I noticed the very large redheaded woman in the bed with me. She smiled and gave me a peck on the cheek.

"Aslaug?" I asked, still fuzzy and a bit hungover.

"Ylva," She said with a forgiving smile

"Nice to meet you."

"We did far more than meet, Loki." She laughed.

I had vague memories of warm kisses and sweaty embraces. Hopefully, I didn't embarrass myself. I hate not remembering things like that. Takes all the fun out of it.

"I have to go," she said climbing out of the bed naked. "But I wanted to wait for you to wake first."

Right. She just wanted to make sure I remembered her. She was tall and full-figured and a natural redhead. I wouldn't be forgetting her soon. She pulled on a simple shift and headed for the door. Just before leaving, she turned and blew me a kiss.

"I had a wonderful time," I said lamely. "Thank you."

"I doubt you remember a thing, but I do." She smiled, and then she was gone.

"How bad did it get last night? Before Ylva that is," I asked Manny.

"You stood on the table and sang," he cawed.

"Ouch."

"Then you tried to do magic tricks. Emphasis on 'tried.'"

"Double ouch."

"Fortunately for you, all the other guests were drunk. They thought you were hilarious, especially when you snuck a fish into Ymyd's ale."

"Well, let's go find the king," I said. "He owes me a conversation and I owe him an apology."

"For bedding his granddaughter? I doubt it," he asked. "For putting a fish in his drink? Probably. For coming here to warn them? Never."

"Granddaughter? Gods be damned."

Manny just laughed. So I threw a shoe at him.

The only thing worse than being hungover is being lectured by a smart ass raven while being hungover. Someone set a step ladder by the annoyingly high bed, which was both kind and a bit humiliating. Once I was presentable and more clear-headed, Manny and I found our way to what passed for a throne room in Ymyd's palace.

"Good morrow, Lord Loki," Ymyd bellowed as I walked into the giant marble hall. I wished he'd lower his voice.

He was seated on an iron throne gilded in gold and suitably sized for his enormous frame. A couple of jotnar guards stood to either side. A man with a long blonde braid and dressed in furs was kneeling before Ymyd. He stood and turned. I almost stumbled when I saw Ullr in his trademark bearskin cloak looking every bit the Viking lord. Had I stepped into another hostage situation?

Ullr is an imposing man, tall and lean with piercing blue eyes. Maidens in Asgard often referred to him as handsome but brooding. I've never known a better archer or skier in my long life. He spent far more time hunting in the deep woods than he did in the city or courts of Asgard. He never seemed comfortable in social situations.

"Lord Loki," Ullr said with a deep bow. "I've been searching for you."

"Oh dear," I said mockingly. Ullr had the good graces to smile wryly at the pun. "You've found me. Now is it your turn to hide?"

Ymyd laughed loudly. It echoed like thunder in the enormous chamber. Manny flew from my shoulder and took up a roost on the carvings of a high column.

"This is no children's game, Loki."

"So now what? You buy me off of Ymyd and return me to Asgard? I'm not sure I can survive another face to face with Thor. Or Sif for that matter. And I'm certain the jotnar won't survive him."

"You think I would sell you?" Ymyd said, looking truly offended. "To Asgard? I'm insulted."

"My apologies, your highness. It's already happened to me once. I should have known better."

"And don't be so sure the jotnar would be easily overrun," Ymyd said with a dark smile. "We were here before the aesir, and we plan to be here long after them."

"Your highness." Ullr turned to Ymyd with a bow. "May we dispense with the threats and boasts? Loki, I'm not here to take you back as a prisoner."

"You aren't?" Ymyd said, surprised. "And here I was hoping to get a better price than Alfhildr."

Ymyd winked at me. He might look and act like a jolly giant, but Ymyd was no dummy. He obviously had his own sources of information too.

"So what's your game, Ullr?" I asked.

"The same as yours. Thor must be stopped. I was just telling Ymyd about his plans to invade Jotunheim and slaughter every jotunn he can find."

"You are Sif's firstborn. Why should I trust you?"

"I am proud to call Sif my mother. But you know Thor is not my father."

"Sif sides with her husband, but her son doesn't side with his own mother?"

Ymyd watched this exchange, his head swiveling like the chair umpire in a tennis match.

"I have no love of Thor. You of all people know the terrors he's inflicted on her."

"I do," I said softly. "But you still haven't told me why I should trust you. Why do you care what happens to the jotnar?"

"I don't," Ullr said. He glanced quickly back at Ymyd.

Ymyd wore a serious frown, but said nothing.

"I want Thor dead. He has stolen my mother from me. Sif was once happy and kind. Now she is cold and distant. The mother I knew is gone, and he is to blame."

"So why not just kill him yourself?"

"I tried once. Bragi found me with an arrow knocked, aimed at his heart, and stopped me. He promised not to say anything if I promised not to try again. I had to swear an oath on my mother's life."

"But if Thor's plans are ruined, or gods forbid, he dies by someone else's hand, you've kept your oath."

"Odin always said you were a clever one. If I help you, we both get what we want."

"And what makes you think I'm going to do something about this war? Why should I care about what happens between Asgard and Jotunheim?"

"You came back," he said pointedly. "You came back to Asgard after a thousand years in exile."

"Actually, just over nine hundred."

"You could have stayed away, but you didn't. And then

there is Frigg's vision. Something about you stopping Thor. At the very least I was going to hunt you down and ask."

"Let's say I believe you—"

"Enough questions, Loki," Ymyd rumbled. "I believe him."

Truthfully, I did too, but Ullr and I had never been close. I knew he was loyal to Sif and had hard feelings for Thor, but a lot can change in nine hundred years. It can, but apparently, it hadn't.

"I will accept your judgment, your majesty," I said with a deep bow.

"So how do we stop Thor?" Ullr asked, looking at me.

"I have no idea" I admitted.

"So much for prophecies and visions." Ullr snorted.

Ymyd's laughter boomed in the huge open hall.

"If we can find out where they will come out on Yggdrasil, we'd only have to fight them a few at a time. Like in the movie 300."

"Like what?" asked Ymyd and Ullr simultaneously.

"Nevermind. What's important is that we can fight them a few at a time instead of all at once."

"I wish that were true," Ullr said gravely. "Thor has commissioned the dvergar to build him a new bridge to connect the Nine Worlds."

"Oh, shit." I breathed.

The Bifrost had been a crowning achievement of dvergar craftsmanship. It had connected most of the Nine Worlds like a highway. A traveler didn't need to know how to navigate Yggdrasil, he could just walk the Bifrost Bridge. It was wide enough for nine jotnar to walk abreast. If Thor built a bridge even half as broad, an army the size of Thor's could cross it in a day or two.

"Have they started yet?" I asked.

"Started? They are nearly finished. Just a few more months, maybe less."

"Will it connect to all the worlds or just Jotunheim?"

"The same worlds the Bifrost Bridge led to, Jotunheim, Vanaheim, Nidavellir, Alfheim, and Midgard."

"Midgard? Oh gods, no, not Midgard," I begged.

"Why are you worried about Midgard?" Ymyd asked. "They are the least of our problems."

"No, Ymyd," I said. "They are the greatest threat to you and to the rest of the Nine Worlds."

"One jotunn is worth ten men of Midgard," Ymyd boasted. "Even an aesir is worth three of them."

"Maybe a thousand years ago that was true, but Midgard has changed. They are more numerous than midges in summer. They can bring a hundred or even a thousand men for every jotunn. Even the einherjar that Thor has assembled would be outnumbered ten to one if Midgard came in force. And every one of those soldiers would have weapons far more powerful than anything your warriors wield. Weapons that can kill dozens at a great distance."

"Thor believes Midgard to be the least of the Nine Worlds," Ullr said somberly. "If what you say is true, they are the most dangerous."

"One threat at a time," Ymyd growled. "First we stop Thor from wiping out the jotnar. Where will this new bridge open into Jotunheim?"

"I don't know," Ullr admitted.

"I'll tell my scouts to watch for it," Ymyd said. "In the meantime, what actions can we take right now?"

"What about Vanaheim?" I asked. "Do you think the vanir would ally with us?"

"You've been away too long, Loki" Ymyd said. "After Ragnarokkr, Vanaheim sealed itself away from the Nine Worlds."

"Yggdrasil doesn't connect to them anymore?" I asked incredulously. "How can that be?"

"Nobody knows," Ullr said. "The spirit wind still blows from Vanaheim, although weakly, so they are still in there. But you can't travel Yggdrasil to get there."

"I have to return to Asgard," Ullr said. "Not all the aesir agree with Thor. Hopefully, some of them are brave enough to oppose him."

I put my head in my hands and tried to think. Gods knew I didn't want another Ragnarokkr, but I was being forced into fighting one. If this was just Thor, we wouldn't have a problem. He has the strategic mind of a rabid dog. But with Sif and possibly others in Asgard calling the real shots...

"I have an idea for how to cause some mischief," I said, lifting my head out of my hands. "Let's send Meili home."

"What!" Ymyd leaned forward on his throne.

"Meili?" Ullr asked. "He still lives?"

"Hear me out, your highness. Meili is only in Jotunheim because of the peace treaty Thrym struck with Odin over a thousand years ago. I went to live in Asgard in exchange to seal the peace."

"That treaty died at Ragnarokkr," Ymyd said with a shrug, relaxing back on his throne.

"Why does Meili still live then?" Ullr asked.

"We broke the treaty at Ragnarokkr, not the Asgardians. And certainly not Meili. We won. There was no reason to slay an innocent man. He still has value as a hostage. But why should I send one of our best warriors to Asgard? Our loss would be their gain."

"From what I saw, Meili may be more trouble than he is worth."

"He's a challenge, that's true."

"So, you think he'll cause enough trouble in Asgard to derail Thor's plans?" Ullr asked skeptically.

"No, at least not the way you're thinking. I'm hoping Meili will return Thor to his truer nature."

"What in the Nine Worlds does that mean?" Ullr asked.

"That's what Odin said when I went to see him."

"You what?" Ullr shouted.

"It is not for mortals of any of the Nine Worlds to visit Hel," Ymyd cautioned.

"Well it's too late for that, isn't it? Besides, I have a special connection."

"So your daughter let you talk to Odin's shade," Ullr said.

"Yes. Odin said something that I didn't understand at first, but I think I do now. He told me that Thor is not acting like himself and that I should try to return him to his truer self."

"And Meili will do that?" Ymyd raised an eyebrow.

"Meili is Thor's brother. His *long lost* brother. If you were Thor and Meili returned after more than a thousand years, what would you do?"

"Thor will greet him with open arms and fete him generously," Ullr said.

"Exactly. Thor will keep Meili close to him at all times. How do you think Meili will affect Thor? Or Sif?"

"Meili is wild and hard to manage," Ymyd said thoughtfully. "Are you saying Thor will become more like Meili?"

"Maybe. Maybe he'll become more like the Thor of old and maybe he won't."

"You play a dangerous game here, Loki," Ullr warned. "It's true that since Thor recovered from Jormundgandr's venom, he hasn't been himself. But do you really want the old Thor back?"

"The Thor I met was different. He's letting Sif and others make decisions for him. The old Thor was impetuous and rash and never listened to anyone. I want to drive a wedge between him and his more reasonable advisors. Meili could be that wedge. Who do you want Thor paying heed to when he leads the einherjar into Jotunheim?"

"Meili," Ymyd said without hesitation. "He's like the Thor of old. He charges into battle without thinking. He makes mistakes."

"So let's send Meili back to Asgard. Let me talk to him."

So maybe Odin was right and I was the god of mischief after all. God with a little 'g' that is. It was a subtle plan, but if it worked, it could have a major impact. If it didn't, all we lost was one shape-shifting warrior capable of standing toe-to-toe with the best jotnar warrior. I really hoped it would work.

We spent the rest of the day making plans. I didn't have any more clever ideas, so we settled for more mundane war plans to defend Jotunheim. Ymyd was surprisingly good at it. Ullr would take Meili back to Asgard if he agreed to go. I would head to Nidavellir and talk to the dvergar. I was pretty certain they would not march on Asgard, but there were more interesting things there than armies.

22

MEILI

H ello Meili," I said, leaning casually against the doorjamb of his chambers.

"So you're Loki," he replied without looking up from his seat at a table. "I suppose I need to thank you for stopping me from killing Umgre."

He didn't sound very thankful. I couldn't be sure if it was because of his grudge against the jotunn, or his obvious disdain for me. Probably both.

Meili was a bear of a man, pun intended, brawny and hairy with a thick brown beard. My last memory of him was as a child during the hostage exchange. He was no child now. His neck was bandaged, presumably where the chains had choked him.

"We share a common history," I said. "We were both given away by our parents as hostages to secure the peace between Asgard and Jotunheim."

"A peace you broke at Ragnarokkr," Meili growled, finally looking up at me.

"I did that," I admitted. "If you want me to apologize, I can't do that."

"At the time I wanted to kill you. My father died there. I thought my brother, Thor, died, but we learned later he survived as a cripple."

"Very little good comes out of war. Ragnarokkr was no exception."

"So what do you want, Loki kinslayer?"

"Have you thought about returning to Asgard? Leaving Jotunheim?"

"I'm still a hostage," he said bitterly. "My life is forfeit if Asgard ever retaliates for Ragnarokkr."

"I don't see any chains or locked doors. You could leave at any time. I doubt Ymyd would even send out a search party."

"After a thousand years, this is my home," he said sullenly. "Besides, if they had wanted me back, they could have sent someone. Or bargained for me."

"Maybe they were waiting for you to want to go home. I've spoken to Ymyd and he thinks you should go."

"Ymyd doesn't want me here anymore?" he growled. I must have touched a nerve.

"He said you will always be welcome back in Jotunheim."

"There is nothing in Asgard for me. I've lived so long in Jotunheim, I feel like a jotunn."

"But you're not, are you? You don't belong here. At least I can pass for aesir. Everyone knows you aren't a jotunn just by looking at you."

I was intentionally poking what I saw as a sore spot. I knew how he felt. I was always an outsider in Asgard. Thor reminded me of it on a daily basis. Yet it was still home. I guess home is always home no matter how terrible it might be.

"So how is it you are still alive over a thousand years after leaving Asgard?" I asked, switching topics. He wasn't rising to my bait.

"Frigg sends Idunn's fruit to me now and then."

"Really? And Ymyd doesn't take them for himself?"

"A jotunn would never do that," he said proudly. "Ymyd would never do that. Besides, Idunn's fruit doesn't work very well on jotnar. Just ask Thjazi."

"That old thieving jotunn?" I said with a grin. "Yeah, he coerced me into stealing her fruit for him."

"And found out that they don't do anything if you don't have aesir blood."

"I was surprised myself when I found that out."

We were silent for a few moments. Meili drank from his mug, lost in thought.

"So why do you think she does it?" I asked. "Frigg. Why does she send you Idunn's fruit?"

"I don't know," he answered without looking up. "Guilt?"

"So for over a thousand years, she has sent you Idunn's fruit to keep you alive. She did it when Odin disowned you. When Thor refused to let anyone in Asgard say your name. She even did it after Ragnarokkr when your adopted people slew her husband, her twin brother, and almost slew her firstborn son."

I could see a complex mix of grief, guilt, and rage building in him.

"That doesn't sound like guilt to me," I pressed. "That sounds like love. A mother's love for a son that she was forced to give up. Love for a son that has never contacted her or visited her."

"She gave me up!" he raged, jumping to his feet. The chair and his drink went flying. His face was red with emotion.

"You gave up on her."

"She never wanted me," he screamed, veins standing out in his neck.

"She loved you so much that she went behind Odin's back to get you Idunn's fruit."

He fell to his knees, tears streaming down his face. His

fists were still clenched in rage as competing emotions warred within him. Sometimes a thousand years is not enough to heal a wounded heart.

"Get out," Meili growled. "Get out before I kill you."

I left. I had pushed him as far as I could. Any more and he might have turned berserker again and I don't think I could win that fight.

Ymyd gave Ullr and me horses and loaded us down with food and supplies. I worried that my horse would be unable to walk under the burden, even though it was as big as a Clydesdale. Ullr's horse was equally burdened. He had his huge longbow, Einngr, slung on his back. Ymyd and his queen, Sydro, came to see us off. None of the other jotnar in his court did though.

"Is Meili coming?" Ullr asked.

"He should be along shortly," Ymyd said. "What did you say to him, Loki? I was sure he would choose to stay here."

"We talked about family obligations and the true meaning of Christmas."

"Well, whatever Christmas is, it seemed to have done the trick." Ymyd chuckled, slapping me on the back hard enough to make me stumble. "I'll miss that little bastard."

"I just hope it wasn't a mistake," I said.

Meili came trudging out of the city. Compared to Ullr and me, he was traveling light with just a pack slung over his back.

"Safe travels, all of you," Sydro said, embracing me.

"You've been gracious hosts," Ullr said with a deep bow. "And we are grateful."

Ymyd wrapped Meili up in a big hug that Meili reluctantly returned. Sydro gave him a more motherly one that he returned with more comfort. Meili glared at me, daring me to say something. I put on my best innocent child face.

We led our overburdened horses a few dozen paces when we heard Sydro shriek. I guess even jotnar women don't like mice crawling out of their pockets. I grinned and tugged on my horse's reins. A steady walk was as fast as he could manage carrying Ymyd's gifts. Meili gave me a sour look, but he matched my pace. Ullr just shook his head.

We rode until the castle gate was out of sight. Ullr stopped his horse at a small farmstead. The house was the size of a Midgard barn, but small for jotnar. The jotunn owner watched suspiciously as Ullr sorted through his pack, dumping about two-thirds of it on the ground.

"We'll do better riding light," he said. "You should dump your pack too."

"It doesn't seem right to just throw it away."

"We aren't. We're donating it to this kind farmer who is staring at us with a giant club in his hand."

"Fvaldr," Meili said. "His name is Fvaldr."

I didn't like it, but Ullr had a point. I ended up leaving about half my stuff on the ground. Meili just watched us silently. The horses seemed grateful, at least until we climbed up into their saddles. As we rode off, the jotnar farmer edged closer to the pile, poking at it with his massive club. Well, at least it wouldn't go to waste.

The horses didn't freak out when we set foot on Yggdrasil. Ymyd continued to surprise me. Ullr set a steady pace and we rode in silence. Manny glided along above us while I brooded about Meili and whether I had done the right thing. I snuck sideways looks at him as he walked beside our mounts. He was going home. Or was he leaving home? Probably both. At various times, I had called Jotunheim, Asgard, and Midgard home. Each was special in its own way. Each has something to offer. That gave me an idea.

"Ullr," I called, bring my horse to a stop. Meili trudged ahead a few steps before stopping and turning to look at me.

"Change of plan," I said quietly when Ullr pulled his horse next to mine. "I'm going back to Midgard first."

He just raised an eyebrow and glanced over at Meili. I hoped he was out of earshot.

"I need to get a few things. It won't take long. Nidavellir and the dvergar can wait a day or two."

After a moment's silence, Ullr said, "Don't take too long."

23

MIDGARD

The oldest and largest Ohio buckeye tree in the U.S. is in Oak Brook Illinois. It's on the McDonald's Hamburger University campus, believe it or not. Although the Tule tree in Mexico eclipses it in both size and age, it's still special to Yggdrasil for being the largest of its kind. When I left Midgard in Mexico, I was starved for spirit energy. There were probably only a dozen trees in the world I could have used to travel to Yggdrasil then. Now I was full, fresh from walking the Tree herself, as I slid out of that Ohio Buckeye. I had reluctantly left the horse behind.

The tree is in a courtyard outside a small office building on the Hamburger U campus. It has a nice plaque telling you all about it. To the undiscerning passerby, it's otherwise unremarkable. I arrived at the evening rush hour, so the campus was emptying. People and cars hurried toward the exits and I joined them, trying not to stand out. Manny found a perch in the tree.

It's jarring to go from the medieval worlds of Asgard and Jotunheim to modern Midgard. After Ragnarokkr and the destruction of the Bifrost Bridge, Midgard became isolated. The other worlds withdrew into themselves to lick their wounds, especially Asgard. Aside from the dvergar, most of the races in the Nine Worlds are not very innovative. Instead, they've copied some of the new discoveries and technologies of Midgard. Closed off from it, they stagnated in the medieval period. You could think of it as a very long Dark Ages. A few things were adopted, brought in by the occasional traveler, but mostly they were content to live the way they had for centuries.

Out of habit, I found myself digging through my pockets for money. Of course, I didn't have any. I'd have to get back to my houseboat the hard way, by hitchhiking. Turns out it's hard to hitchhike in a dense suburban area. However, when a seidr spell makes you look like a young, innocent woman, it's somewhat easier.

A nice old gentleman in a Chevy picked me up as it was beginning to rain. He was more than willing to go out of his way and drive me all the way to Fox Lake while trying not to leer at me. When we got there, he forced his hand between my legs. His shock and dismay at what he found there made it easy to steal his wallet without him noticing. I'm sure he heard me laughing as he roared away, leaving me standing in the pouring rain.

Miraculously the houseboat was still there. Esme must have paid the docking fees because I sure hadn't. I didn't plan on staying on Midgard long, and I was hoping to avoid her. I really didn't feel like answering the nine thousand questions she was sure to have. That and I couldn't ensure anyone's safety around me right now.

I watched my boat for an hour in the cold, wet dark. Manny flew reconnaissance for me. After being satisfied that it was safe, I went in. An hour later I left. But now I was prepared for the modern world with a clean change of clothes, cash and a credit card in my pocket, a smartphone, a raincoat, and a dozen other necessities.

You would think an aesir god, with a lowercase 'g,' who had survived almost a millennium on Midgard would be rich as sin. I definitely had the sin part down, but not the riches. Through the centuries I had made and lost a dozen fortunes. Hoarding and building wealth was boring. Spending money on the other hand was not. I did have some rainy day funds set aside, though. It was literally and figuratively pouring right now.

I came back to Midgard for a reason. If I was going to war, I wanted the best gear available. Nobody does war like Midgard. More than nine hundred years of military advancements since Ragnarokkr meant the best gear was here.

I had lied to Ullr. It would take a week or so to get everything I wanted. Damn waiting periods. Then it would be right on to Nidavellir. I didn't trust the *Voluspa* to be safe for that long, so I needed a place to hang out while I did my business.

"Hello, Jerry," I said when he picked up the phone. "It's Lowell. Lowell Keystone."

"Lowell? Holy cow. What's it been, ten years?"

"Only nine, Jerry."

"Damn, buddy. I thought you had dropped off the face of the earth."

"Yeah, we kinda lost touch when you went out to Vegas. I hear you moved back to Chicago a couple years ago."

"Yep. It's hard to make a living as a stage magician in Vegas. Too much competition."

"I hear ya. That's why I stayed here."

"So I know you didn't just pick up the phone after all these years to catch up. What do you need?"

"I hate to ask this, but I need a place to crash for a week."

"Calling in that marker, eh?"

"I'd rather think of it as asking an old friend for a favor."

"I got a spare room you can use if you don't mind sharing it with my stage equipment."

"That will be fine, Jerry. And I really appreciate this."

"Well, I owe you one. But no stealing my tricks, you hear?"

"I figured out all your tricks a decade ago." I laughed.

"You wish." he laughed back.

I got his address and headed out. The first stop was the bank. Next, I took an Uber to a motorcycle dealership. Several hours later I left on the back of a Ducati Multistrada 1260 Enduro with all the storage accessories I could fit. The internet said it was the best off-road bike for my needs, lightweight but with a good carrying capacity. Who was I to argue? Before I roared off down the road, I cut up the credit card I used to buy the bike. It was maxed out now. I didn't worry about how the guy who tried to grope me would pay for it.

It had been a while since I had ridden a bike, but as they say, it's like riding a bicycle. Only with more horsepower. It wasn't long before I was at Jerry's place.

Jerry Kantor had taught me stage magic twenty years ago or more. Through the centuries I had dabbled in stage magic. But I was rusty then, and so many new tricks had been invented by the end of the 20th century.

"Jerry!" I said boisterously when he opened the door.

He looked older, no surprise. He had to be in his sixties now. His clothes were rumpled and his graying hair went in a few too many directions. He was a bit pudgier, but he still had that glint in his eye for making mischief that had made me hook up with him some twenty years ago.

"Lowell?" he said. "Damn you look good. You haven't aged a bit. If I didn't know better, I'd say you looked younger."

"Clean living."

"You never lived clean a moment in your life." he chuckled.

True for the decade or so that he had known me. Actually, true for most of my life. I've always admitted to having a flexible morality when it comes to petty crime, but I like to think down deep I'm an honest charlatan.

"Is that the same bird, or a new one?" he asked, nodding at Manny.

"New one. The old one got too annoying so I fed it to the lions at the zoo."

Manny cawed his dismay.

"Well, just make sure he doesn't shit on the furniture."

Manny glared at him.

"He'll be on his best behavior," I said, giving Manny a squinty-eyed stare. He flapped off to perch on a chair back.

"Never understood why you didn't include your bird in your act. Ravens are smart ones."

Manny preened.

"He's only smart when he wants to be. He's not reliable enough to put in the act."

Manny had threatened to peck out an eye if I put him in my act. He considers it demeaning. Since I didn't want to wear an eye patch, I didn't push it.

"You still performing?" Jerry asked. I knew he knew the answer.

"Small groups, events, that sort of thing."

"*Shtupping* your assistant?"

"Not this time. Esme is too good for me to make that mistake again. And nobody says *shtupping* anymore."

"I thought maybe she'd kicked you out."

"No, no. Nothing like that. I've got problems with the boat and need someplace to stay while they're sorted out."

"Heh. Bill collectors. The thieves always have their hands in your pockets."

"Something like that."

Having established a reasonable alibi for why I needed a place to stay, our conversation turned to old times and new magic tricks. I didn't comment on the slight tremor in his hands that probably lost him the gigs in Vegas, and he didn't pry into my business any further. Good friends respect boundaries.

I woke on a lumpy mattress surrounded by crates and boxes of stage props and memorabilia. I resigned myself to a week of living like this. Most of what I needed to do was online shopping. I just had to wait for the packages to be delivered. All hail the internet age.

The only tricky part was the body armor. It's illegal to sell it to private citizens. Ironically you can buy a gun that will penetrate it like a knit-sweater with just a twenty-four hour waiting period. But I had to go black market to get the armor. America. Go figure. Fortunately, I had a few less than legal contacts that would sell me the stuff for an arm and a leg.

Meanwhile, I just had to bide my time. Jerry and I would talk in the evenings. He was making ends meet by working as a stagehand at a theater. He was usually back late, but I didn't have anything else to do, so I waited up for him. I cooked for both of us and did my best to tidy up his place. It was the least I could do. I didn't see much of Manny. Apartment living didn't suit him.

Boredom sucks.

So I began to have some fun with Jerry. I put hot sauce in his dinner. I drew glasses on his face while he slept. He's a heavy sleeper. I sawed down two of the legs on his bed. He got pissed about that one, so I had to fix them. I slipped a love letter from him to his seventy-year-old neighbor under her door. I put cellophane over the toilet. I ordered him a transsexual prostitute for the evening. Jerry thought that was hilarious and left me with her to go to his local bar.

Finally, the last of the packages arrived. It was time to travel. I left a note for Jerry and made sure his fridge was well stocked. I'm sure by now Jerry would be glad to see me go. It took me a while to load up the bike. The specs said it could carry two hundred pounds of cargo, but that didn't mean it would all fit in the side panniers and my backpack. I ended up with some bulky stuff strapped awkwardly to my back and to the bike.

It was well past the evening rush hour. Against my better judgment, I swung by Esme's apartment building. Her lights were out, which didn't mean a damn thing. Still, I would have felt better if they had been on.

One last stop to make before leaving Midgard. I had left my Smith & Wesson on the *Voluspa*. I had replaced the Sig Sauer during one of my many purchases, but the Smith & Wesson's stopping power might be handy in the coming days. After watching my boat for half an hour or so, I decided it was safe to approach.

Inside, I meant to go right to the gun and leave. But what I saw on the wall stopped me dead in my tracks. Moonlight illuminated glowing old Norse runes painted on a wall, like something revealed by a blacklight. A few seconds later a cloud obscured the moon and they vanished. Moon runes. Gods damned alfar.

Queen Alfhildr was holding Esme in Alfheim and demanding I surrender myself to her. Of course, they didn't use her name. They referred to her as my maiden, but that's the only person it could be. In a foul mood I snatched up my pistols and stormed out of the houseboat. I gunned the Ducati and sped off. Just over the border in Wisconsin there was a large Burr Oak in a farm field waiting for me.

24

RESCUE

I opened up the bike on I94, hitting 120 mph in places. I dared a cop to pull me over. Manny was left far behind, unable to keep up with that kind of speed. He could find his own way. Before long I was at the farm after topping off the tank at a gas station a few miles back. Without pausing, I turned into the dirt field and headed for the tree. I'm sure I woke the farmer, but before he could do anything, I would be long gone.

I rode slowly around the trunk counter-clockwise, waiting for the portal. I saw the gaping black crack where one hadn't been before. I pushed the bike forward into it and stopped, the front wheel inside it. Gunning the engine and chanting a spell of travel and safe passage, I forced the bike through inch by inch. Yggdrasil didn't seem to want to let me through, but finally I made it. The bike nearly threw me as I suddenly accelerated wildly. I was a good hundred feet away before I got it under control.

Now I understood why Thor used the Bifrost Bridge when he traveled the Nine Worlds in his chariot. Odin had once told me that Yggdrasil was attuned to spirits, dead or alive, and had a limited tolerance for things that had never lived. I guess my bike pushed the limits.

Taking a moment to test the spirit wind, I headed up tree, goosing the Ducati as fast as I dared go. The bike has a range of about three hundred miles, which would take me ten days to walk. It only took a few hours to get to an Alfheim branch. Ullr was waiting for me.

"What in the Nine Worlds is that?" he asked from atop his horse. To the horse's credit, it wasn't shying at the loud metal beast I was riding. I probably looked strange too, dressed in a black leather jacket, jeans, boots, gloves, and a full riding helmet.

"It's called a motorcycle."

"Looks like something the dvergar would dream up."

"Midgard. They've come a long way, Ullr. Their machines rival or sometimes exceed what the dvergar can make."

"Is that Midgard armor?"

"Sort of. What are you doing here?"

"Tracking you."

"How can you track me to someplace I haven't been yet?"

"If a man's intentions are strong enough, I can track him to where he will be."

Odin's spear! He had always been known as the god of hunting, but since I didn't believe in divine power, I just assumed that meant he was really skillful and Odin was just pulling another con.

"You can really do that?"

"Of course. I'm the God of Hunting."

I guess I walked into that one.

"So how did your visit to Asgard go?" I asked, changing topics.

"Poorly. The other aesir are too afraid of Thor and have no desire to involve themselves."

"If you haven't got any other business, I could use your help."

"Anything to help stop Thor," he said, unslinging Einngr.

"This is more of a personal favor."

"Oh. What favor would you ask?"

"A friend of mine, Esme, has been taken captive by the alfar. By queen Alfhildr. If I submit to Alfhildr and let her trade me to Thor, she'll let Esme go."

"I suppose just leaving this Esme in Alfhildr's hands is out of the question?"

"Yes. If Alfhildr thinks Esme is no longer of use, she'll probably kill her."

"And she is just a friend, not a lover?"

"Just a friend. An important friend."

Actually, I had hit on her one night after too many beers. Let's just say it didn't go well. Since I don't speak Spanish, I'm not sure what she really said, but I got the gist of it. So did everyone else in the bar. She eventually forgave me or I would have had to find a new assistant.

"Okay," Ullr said with a weak grin. "I've always had a soft spot for saving princesses."

"Good. I brought you a new toy. This will give you a chance to try it out."

I swung the heavy gun case off my back. Laying it on the bark that serves as the ground here, I opened it to reveal an M82A1 Barrett .50 caliber rifle. It's one of the best sniper rifles in the world. I stood there proudly gesturing to it.

"What in the Nine Worlds is that?" Ullr said, confused.

"It's a rifle. It's used for hunting, among other things, on Midgard."

"Is it broken?"

"No," I said, getting irritated. "It's just disassembled. You have to put it together."

"Oh. How long does that take?"

"It's fast. Only thirty seconds or so," I said proudly. I had spent some time watching YouTube videos and practicing.

Ullr unslung his massive bow, bent it into a curve and hooked the drawstring. I wasn't sure I could string his bow at all.

"That's too slow," He said, deadpan.

"And how far away can you hit and kill a deer?"

Rather than answer, he turned, and drew his bow almost to the breaking point. Aiming high for maximum distance, he released. I'm no master archer, but I have more than a passing familiarity with the bow. That arrow arced and fell, striking a distant branch. On my best day I could only shoot half that far, and my best days were behind me.

"This gun is accurate up to a mile and can kill two elk, passing through the first to strike the second."

Now I had his attention. Of course, I had no idea if it could really kill two elk at that distance. Heck, I wasn't even sure exactly how far his arrows traveled. But I knew the rifle could kill a man in a bulletproof vest at that distance. The brochures told me so. Brochures wouldn't lie.

"Show me."

So I showed him how to assemble it and load and fire it. I explained that the higher velocity of the shell meant less wind effect to account for and less drop than an arrow. I showed him the reticle thingy and how to adjust for distance and wind. Then I disassembled it and made him put it back together. He shrugged, and seconds later was holding the assembled rifle. Much faster than my time. Show off.

He laid down on the ground with the gun supported by the tripod. Taking aim through the scope, he fired at a branch that was maybe half a mile away. The sound was deafening. I had totally forgotten to buy shooting earmuffs.

"Too high," Ullr grunted. "And too loud. That would spook all the deer in a whole valley."

He made a minor adjustment to the sights and fired again. He lifted his head from the scope and squinted at the target branch.

"That's better."

"You can see where you hit from here?"

"Of course. Among the aesir, only Heimdall had sharper eyes. But they are both drinking with Hel now, thanks to you."

That was a not so subtle reminder that we were allies of necessity, not loyalty. He stood and removed the scope and folded the tripod away. Facing the opposite direction, he stood in a shooter's stance and took aim at a branch that was way more than a mile away. Lowering the rifle, he handed me the detached scope.

"The small branch on the right. The lowest one that is hanging down."

It took me a minute to find it. It was hard to tell from here, but I was guessing it was about a foot in diameter. Just a twig for Yggdrasil. Two quick, deafening shots left my ears ringing. A small offshoot branch on the right side of the branch and another lower down on the left, each just a couple inches in diameter, exploded into splinters.

"You missed. One on each side."

"No I didn't," he said, squinting down range again. "Those were the ones I was aiming at."

I just looked at him. Words rarely fail me, but they did now. He just shrugged.

"It's good for long shots," Ullr said appreciatively, patting the rifle. "Einngr is better up close."

He disassembled the gun like he had been doing it for years. Picking up the case, he asked, "What's the plan?"

I left the bike and the gear I didn't need behind the branch near the portal. I doubted anyone would find it on Yggdrasil. We came through the portal much closer to Vedrfolnir than the first time I visited. We had to circle around for the proper vantage point. Once there, I changed into an orangutan and climbed up a particularly large, tall tree. I had to help Ullr, who did not have the advantage of shape-changing galdr magic.

I first saw monkeys in a zoo in Paris in the late 1800s. Given my special talent, I've toured many zoos around the world since then. For some reason though, the animals of Scandinavia are still easiest for me to assume. I guess it gets harder to learn new animals as I get older. Or maybe it's that the more animals I know, the harder it is to use new ones.

As we were setting up his rifle, Manny landed on a nearby branch.

"Noble Munnin," Ullr said with an acknowledging nod.

"Took you long enough," I said, trying to hide a grin.

"I've been in Alfheim for a while," he cawed. "It just took me some time to find you."

"You beat us here?"

"I told you I'm better at navigating Yggdrasil. And I don't have to travel as far to find a tree that can carry me."

I had never really thought about Manny traveling Yggdrasil on his own. I just assumed he could only travel with someone else.

"Well, I'm glad you're here."

"Who could resist watching the God of Mischief make a fool of himself," Manny said derisively. "Again."

"Oh ye of little faith."

Once Ullr's tree blind was complete, I changed to an eagle and flew down into Vedrfolnir. I circled a couple of times, looking for Esme. You'd think in a city that didn't believe in rooftops I'd be able to find her from the air. Frustratingly, there were many large trees whose canopies hid the grassy ground beneath them. Of course, why should Alfhildr make it easy on me?

I landed just out of sight of the front gate and quickly shifted to my true self. I strapped myself into the all-black body armor I had left there. It's the stuff prison guards use that is specially made to resist knives and shanks rather than bullets, and includes leg and arm guards and a helmet, which I had tucked under my arm. My free hand held a black matte tactical tomahawk axe like those used by the military. I had a few other knives strapped to me in convenient places, and the new Sig Sauer on my waist. I looked pretty badass if I do say so myself. The gate guards didn't react as I strolled into Vedrfolnir. I hate being predictable. Alfar scurried out of the way as I marched to the palace.

"Queen Alfhildr," I shouted in my best theater voice. "I am here to discuss the terms of Esme's release."

While I waited for a response, I softly chanted battle spells. I frequently use galdr magic to change my shape. But it can be used in many ways. It's the magic of the self, particularly of the body. Thor uses it to bolster his already formidable battle prowess. So do the Valkyries. I'm betting Ullr uses it as well.

It wasn't long before a couple dozen alfar guardsmen came pouring out of the palace door, half of them with arrows knocked and pointed at me, the other half leveled sun spears. Einar strode calmly out behind them, the epitome of the unflappable steward. I stuffed down the simmering anger that threatened to overwhelm me.

"Queen Alfhildr has been eagerly awaiting your arrival," Einar said calmly. "You can remove what I assume is your armor and leave all your weapons. The guards will take you into custody."

"Not so fast Jeeves," I said insolently. "First, I only negotiate with your bitch queen Alfhildr."

I could hear the bowstrings stretch tighter. Einar turned
pale. I was feeling jittery from the spells but controlled
myself well enough to speak evenly. Not my first rodeo.

"Second, I stay armed until Esme is safe and out of
Alfheim."

"Who or what is a Jeeves?" he said, aggravated.

"It's an insulting Midgard name for gutless royal
stewards."

To his credit, only his eyes betrayed his anger; his face
and posture remained composed.

"I will convey your terms to her highness."

He turned and left. I tried to look bored and I scanned the
sky for Manny. Nothing. It didn't mean he wasn't there, but I
couldn't spot him easily.

"You boys," I said nonchalantly to the nearest guards. "I
could get you some Foster Grants. Shades would make it a
lot easy to use those sun spears."

I didn't think it was possible for their grim faces to
become grimmer. That just made me smile.

"After today, those of you who survive will have a tale to
tell your grandchildren of the time Loki made a fool of the
alfar queen. I'm sure the wee ones will ask you to tell it over
and over."

I had a few more choice barbs ready, but Einar appeared
again.

"Her royal highness has deigned to grant you an audience," he said.

"Aw. That's awful swell of her, Jeeves," I said with a
saccharine grin. "Let's not keep the pointy-eared bitch
waiting."

Half the spear wielders proceeded us, and the other half
followed. I didn't see where the archers went, presumably to

find good vantage points. Einar walked within arm's reach of me, silently daring me to strike him. I took the opportunity to put on the helmet, leaving the visor up. I pulled out a second axe, holding both of them loosely at my sides.

Queen Alfhildr sat on her throne, slightly slouched. There was no sign of her court. I figured them for cowards. The spearmen arrayed themselves around the room, with four positioned between Alfhildr and me, leaving just a narrow human corridor so we could see each other. Einar stood by her side.

"Your highness," I said, bowing low.

"Ha!" she barked. "Now you talk sweet. Einar tells me you were not so generous in the courtyard."

"I do recall referring to you as a bitch queen," I said with false contrition. Alfhildr laughed loudly, which quickly turned into a coughing fit. Einar handed her a supple leaf to wipe the spittle from her face.

"I am a right bitch," she said with a wheeze. "Surrender now and I won't hurt your trollop."

"Kill Esme and your guardsman will not be able to protect you from my vengeance, though I may die exacting it."

Alfhildr looked at me shrewdly. I'm sure she didn't know what to make of my strange arms and armor. While not as obviously threatening as Thor or Odin, I was not an aesir to be underestimated.

"Hastening my death is not much of a bargaining chip," she said bitterly.

"No, but your death coupled with mine removes any reason for Asgard to return your granddaughter," I pointed out. "Thor would hold the rightful queen of Alfheim and your kingdom would have nothing to bargain for her return."

"So it would seem we have a stalemate," she said, failing to suppress a cough. "Fine, I'll consider your terms."

"First, let me see Esme. Unless she is unharmed, there will be no deal today."

Alfhildr waved her hand to Einar, who in turn nodded to a guardsman near the side door. While we waited, I whistled a merry tune, which seemed to irritate Alfhildr, which was the whole point. After a while, Esme was led into the room. She had been dressed in alfar garb and her hair done back in plaits.

"Esme," I said, keeping any urgency from my voice. "Are you unharmed?"

"Lowell?" she cried out. "Lowell!"

The guard grabbed her upper arm to stop her from rushing to me. She unleashed a short stream of Spanish that I was sure would blister the ears of anyone who understood her. One of these days I would have to learn that language.

"Lowell," Esme said, worry replacing anger. "Why are you dressed like that? What is going on here? Nobody will tell me what's going on."

"Release Esme," I said, returning my attention to Alfhildr. "When she is safely out of Alfheim, I'll surrender to you. You can turn me over to Asgard in exchange for your granddaughter."

"You would do this for that Midgard harlot?" Alfhildr asked with raised brows.

"Hey!" Esme shouted angrily. Apparently, she could understand old Norse. I hoped I'd get to hear that story from her later.

"Aye, she is worth that to me," I answered casually. Or at least doing my best to act casual. I don't think I fooled myself, let along Alfhildr. "However, don't think I'm going to let Thor execute me without a fight. When you turn me over to Skirnir, or whoever they send, you'll make sure I have the means to escape once I'm out of Alfheim."

"I should have known that Loki would have a trick prepared," she said.

"Loki?" Esme said, surprised. "You really are Loki? Lowell?"

"Fine," Alfhildr said weakly. "You have my word that we will give you weapons or enchantments to give you a chance to escape."

I knew she was lying. She knew I knew she was lying. Alfhildr was counting on me being willing to delude myself for Esme's sake. The only problem with that is I couldn't tell if Alfhildr was lying about ensuring Esme's safety. Not willing to take that chance, I flipped my visor down and let my anger off its leash.

A red flower blossomed in the chest of the alfar guard holding Esme. I moved. My spells boosted my speed considerably. With the axe in my right hand, I swept the spear point of the alfr just to the right of Esme, I heard the crack of the rifle shot arriving after the hypersonic bullet that struck the alfr. Stepping in, I swung at the spear-wielding guard's neck with my left hand. Blood spurted, coating my axe and my chest.

"Esme—"

I spun, leading with my right hand. The alfar were reacting in what seemed like slow motion, confusion and determination on their faces as they moved to close. Compared to the Vikings, I'm a badass warrior. Compared to the alfar guards, I was merely adequate. Fortunately, I was augmented to superhuman levels by my spells. I was going to show Alfhildr what kind of mischief a truly pissed off Loki can cause.

"—get—"

The spike on the back of the axe struck the upper arm of the alfr on that side. His grip on the spear loosened.

"—down."

Spears tips were blooming all around in slow motion like little miniature suns being turned on. The darkened visor helped some. One of the spells I had cast earlier took care of the rest. The spear points were still bright, but not blinding. I heard another shot, but none of the alfar was hit.

I swung the axe in my left hand around to hook around the neck of the alfr with the injured arm. An arrow whizzed by my face. A second bounced off the back armor plate. A gunshot was followed by a coarse shout. Ullr was taking out the archers. Pulling with my left hand, I brought the wounded alfr up against my chest. The closest guards hesitated to impale one of their own. If ever there was a time for my supposed godly powers to show up this was it. One of them shifted to the side, but lost his footing and went down on one knee. I threw the axe in my right hand into the face of the nearest standing guard. It stuck. I heard Esme scream.

I gripped the sun spear of my meat shield with my free hand and rammed his chest with my shoulder, sending him stumbling forward and leaving me holding the spear. An arrow grazed my calf where there wasn't any armor. Another bounced off my helmet uncomfortably close to my neck. A third stuck in the breastplate, apparently lodging in a crease. More gunshots. More shouts. More screams.

I was far faster than the alfar, but they had numbers on their side. I knew to stack them up so that I was fighting as few as possible at once. Sliding right, I threw the spear at a nearby alfr. He managed to deflect it from his chest to his thigh. Another gunshot. One of the guardsmen advanced, but tripped over the spear stuck in his friend's thigh.

Another step and I yanked the axe out of the downed alfr's face, letting a spear point pass above me. An arrow shot through the space where my chest had been a moment ago. With the other axe I swung at a nearby leg but missed. Another gunshot.

An arrow struck the back of my thigh where there wasn't any armor. I could feel the distant, dull ache shielded by one of my battle spells. On the move, I hacked at a nearby alfr, burying the axe in his side. Another step and I swung the other axe at an alfr's head, connecting but not penetrating his helmet. He crumpled anyway. I expected to hear another gunshot but didn't. Ullr was slowing down. The alfar archers had probably located him and were staying out of his line of sight.

A spear struck my back hard. I heard the sizzle of the armor melting. The blow was hard enough to send me stumbling forward. I tried to hit the ground in a roll, but only partially succeeded. I swung wildly at a set of legs nearby and was rewarded with the wet thunk of the edge penetrating. Another spear point struck my shin guard, burning a hole in it.

I wasn't sure how many alfar were left standing. I had lost track. My world was just a set of bright, shining spear points to be hacked at and grim faces behind them to be bloodied. I was struck twice more by spear points that burned at the plastic armor. No more arrows though, thank the gods.

Something grabbed my ankle and I went down. A near-dead alfr with a bloody face and a hole where my axe spike had ruined his eye was clutching my foot. I hacked at his hand and set myself free. Looking up I saw an alfr with an upraised spear beginning the two-handed downward plunge into my chest. My armor was unlikely to stop the blow.

Suddenly he lurched forward and on top of me. I was able to weakly push the spear point to the side as he fell. It struck my shoulder, but the burning light had been extinguished. Even unlit it would have hurt like anything if I hadn't blocked most of my ability to feel pain.

Pushing the dead alfr off of me, I lifted my head to see Esme still holding the spear she had thrust into his back.

Looking around, I saw the blood-soaked ground littered with bodies. None of Alfhildr's guards remained standing, and about half of the downed ones were dead. Alfhildr sat on her wooden throne as if nothing had happened. Esme fell to her knees, sobbing. The anger and bloodlust drained from me. I stood with effort and took the time to pull out the arrows I could reach. I think I had lost a significant amount of blood, but I wouldn't know for sure for a while.

"Alfhildr," I said, still trying to catch my breath. "I'm taking Esme and we're leaving now."

"I underestimated you, Loki," she said bitterly. "Go. Take your bed warmer."

"I'm going to stop Thor and Sif," I said. "If Alfheim remains uncommitted, and you don't get in my way, I'll do what I can to free your granddaughter and return her to Alfheim."

I paused to let the queen finish a fresh coughing fit. Manny took that moment to land on my shoulder. My trusty bodyguard.

"However," I continued. "If you side with them, I will kill her if I find her."

Manny cawed. I'm not sure what he was trying to say.

She didn't answer. I didn't need an answer. Her actions would tell me all I needed to know. I approached the queen and gently took her arm.

"Esme," I called. "Could you help me?"

Esme looked up at me like she had just noticed I was in the room. Slowly she climbed to her feet. Picking her way carefully between the bodies, she stood in front of the throne and queen Alfhildr.

"Would she really have killed me?" she asked.

"Or worse," I said softly. "I'm not sure there is anything she would not have done to get her granddaughter back."

"Family," Esme said, tonelessly. "I can understand that."

Then she slapped Alfhildr, hard. The queen took the rebuke stoically.

"I have family too," she said, a little heat creeping back into her voice.

Together we pulled Alfhildr off the throne and set her on the ground. I had done enough mischief for one day. I walked Esme counter-clockwise around the bole of the tree three times. She didn't resist or comment. Then I sat us on the wide seat with Manny still on my shoulder. A moment later we were on Yggdrasil.

25

ESME

"Are you okay?" I asked Esme, pulling off my helmet and easing her to the ground. "Did they hurt you?"

"No," she said, staring off into the void. "No."

Just to be sure I checked all the bloody spots on her. I was nudging her head to the right to check some blood on her neck when she pushed my hands away and looked right at me.

"So what should I call you?" She demanded. "Lowell? Loki? Your highness? What?"

"I like the sound of your highness," I said with a smile. "But let's stick with Loki. It's the name I was born with."

"Born?" she said a little incredulously. "You're a fucking Norse god. You weren't born."

"Actually—"

"Lowell was born. But there is no Lowell, is there?" she said angrily, scrambling to her feet.

"Esme—"

"I read up on Loki after that trick you pulled with Manny. Loki is the fucking god of evil."

"It's not—"

"You're basically Satan, El Diablo," she yelled.

"Now wait—"

"I've been working for the Devil for years! Has this all been part of some evil plot to corrupt my soul? Huh? Has it, 'Lowell'?"

"Can I say something?" I pleaded.

Esme stood a little away from me, hands balled in fists. I'd never seen her this angry and afraid. Well, maybe this angry, but she gets angry easily. Still, I recognized that her world had been turned upside down, and she blamed me. She had a point.

"I'm not the Devil, but I am Loki," I confessed. "Although it's debatable as to whether I'm a god. Personally... never-mind. We can discuss that later. But it is true I'm not quite human, and it's true I can do things normal people can't. That doesn't make me evil. And I'm not after your soul. That's a Christian thing and not a Norse thing."

"You can do things? Like magic?" she asked heatedly. "You can do real magic? Like walking into a tree and vanishing? Like moving really fast?"

"Yes," I said with a sigh. "Real magic. Like vanishing into a tree. And a few other tricks besides."

"Why didn't you use it in your act? Nothing in your act was real magic. Or was it? In fact, why were you pretending to be a magician at all?"

"I was hiding on Midgard. That's what we call Earth. The aesir, or the Norse gods as you think of them, don't have easy access to magic on Midgard. We can bring it in, but we can't replenish it once it's gone. Not anymore. Vanishing into the Tule tree in Mexico was more about the tree itself than about me."

"I hung around for over a week," Esme said. "I waited for you."

"I told you not to. And I called you as soon as I could."

"You left me!"

"I did the best I could," I pleaded. She just snorted derisively.

"So as I was saying," I said, trying to pick up where I left off. "I'm hiding on Midgard. I have been hiding for more than nine hundred years."

"*Dios mio!*" she said quietly. "Are you immortal? Of course, you're immortal. You're a fucking Norse god."

"I'm not a god. I'm kind of immortal, though. It's complicated. But I can be hurt and killed just like you or anyone on Midgard."

"Can you just call it Earth?"

"Okay. Earth. Other than living for too long, I've been just like anyone else on Earth for centuries now."

"Do you realize how ridiculous that sounds? 'I'm just like you except I'm a god and I live forever.' Do you get sick? I don't think I've ever seen you get sick."

"The same thing that keeps me alive also makes it really hard for me to get sick, but it's still possible. I was bedridden for a couple of days during the bubonic plague."

"Can we just skip the whole history lesson bullshit for now? What the fuck is happening, Lowell? I'm kidnapped by elves who bring me to some sort of giant, magical tree. And I just watched you kill a bunch of them while dressed up like some sort of demented biker."

"I'm really sorry, Esme. They were using you to get to me."

"So your answer was to kill them all?" she asked incredulously.

"It works in the movies," I said with a weak smile. I really wasn't feeling good. The battle spells were beginning wear off.

"This isn't the fucking movies!" she screamed.

"Whether you want to accept it or not," I said, trying hard

to keep my voice from shaking, "those people wanted to kill me. Or at least sell me to someone who would kill me. And there was a good chance they were going to kill you too."

Esme stormed off. She needed some time to adjust I told myself. I'd explain the rest when she cooled down. In the meantime, I was just going to sit down. The throbbing arrow wound in my leg was still leaking blood. I could feel a sharp pain in my back too. In fact, I think it might be better if I—

I slowly swam back to consciousness to see Esme kneeling beside me. A couple dozen feet past her Ullr was cleaning the M82. Manny hopped onto my chest. When had they gotten here? As ravens go, Manny is really damn big. Even bigger than the ones at the Tower of London. It was a little intimidating. He pecked my forehead.

"Ow!" I said, lifting a hand to rub my latest, albeit minor, wound.

"He's okay," Manny cawed, hopping down. It was noticeably easier to breathe without his weight.

"Lowell—" Esme started. "Loki. You were badly hurt in that fight. A lot worse than I realized. Why didn't you say something?"

"I used spells to protect me," I said weakly, struggling to sit up. "I wasn't actually feeling much pain until I passed out. Besides, you weren't exactly interested in how hurt I was."

"Magic? Real magic? I supposed I should be surprised."

"Ow. Don't make me laugh. Or smile. Ow."

"You are a stubborn pain in the ass," she said without any heat. "I should have said thank you. That's the first thing I should have said. I kinda freaked out. To be honest, I'm still kind of freaked out. And I'm not used to having anyone come rescue me. I hate being treated like a fucking damsel in distress."

"That's okay. I seem to have lost my white horse. And if I recall, you saved me in there again."

"Like I said, I'm not some fucking princess."

"Well, you certainly don't talk like one."

I shifted position to get more comfortable. A shooting pain lanced through my side, making me grimace. I could see my armor lying in a heap not far away. It had a lot of burns and holes in it. I had hoped to get more than one use out it. So much for that.

"Don't move," she warned. "Ullr says you were in bad shape. But he gave you something to help."

"Idunn's?" I asked him.

He just nodded and strolled closer.

"Always good for what ails you," I said. I was getting tired. Really tired.

"I didn't understand that," Esme said a little crossly. "But there's a lot I don't understand."

"By the way," I asked. "How are you able to understand old Norse?"

"One of those elves gave me an earring. When I put it on, everyone started speaking English. It took me a little while to realize they were still speaking the same language, but now I could understand it."

"Was the elf's name Huld?"

"Yes," Esme said, surprised.

"I thought so."

"Wait. You said I saved you again. What did you mean?"

Crap. Had I really said that? I thought back to my conversation with Odin. About how pissed off I was that he had stolen my memories. Now the shoe was on the other foot.

"Manny?" I asked.

"Are you sure?" he asked.

"Yeah."

"What?" Esme asked looking from one of us to the other. "What's going on?"

"Esme, there is something you need to know," I said. Manny hopped closer to her.

"There's a whole lot I need to fucking know."

Manny gently touched her with his beak. She rocked backward and ended up sitting on the ground. She shut her eyes tight, covering them with her hands. After a moment she uncovered them and looked at me.

"I... I shot a man?"

"You saved my life. That was the first time."

"Why am I only remembering this now?"

"You were in shock, traumatized by what you had done. So I asked Manny to take those memories. I replaced them with new ones."

Esme looked at Manny like he was something she had stepped in.

"You're welcome," he cawed.

"You fucking stole my memories?"

"I'm sorry. It seemed like a good idea at the time."

"You fuck with my head again and I'll... I'll... you'll be sorry."

"I swear we won't, will we Manny?"

"I don't think it will be necessary," he cawed. Not exactly a promise.

"I'm feeling kind of tired, Esme. I think I'm going to sleep for a bit."

I felt a lot better when I woke the next time. Almost like my old self. I stood carefully and found I was achy but mostly healed. Esme and Ullr were talking quietly a little ways away. Esme hurried over.

"Are you feeling better?" she asked. "Ullr said his weird fruit would heal you. I wouldn't have believed it if I hadn't seen it with my own eyes."

"Yeah, I'm better," I said.

"He and Manny have been telling me all about the Ashire and Igdrazil and the Nine Worlds."

"Aesir and Yggdrasil. And there's no way I've been out long enough for him to tell you everything. That would be a long telling."

"Don't make fun of my pronunciation," she said, feigning defensiveness. "I've had a tough week. And your Spanish is bad enough to make my ears bleed."

"Deal. I won't criticize your old Norse if you don't say anything about my Spanish."

"Has Manny always been able to talk?" she asked. "Not like a bird, but really talk? Like a person, like he's intelligent or something?"

"Or something," I muttered.

"I heard that," Manny said.

"Yes. His real name is Munnin," I answered without elaborating.

Esme thought on that for a moment.

"So Thor wants to kill you?" she asked, changing subjects. "And he's raising an army to kill all the giants?"

"That's about right."

"Why do you care about the giants? Aren't they the bad guys? They are in the Norse mythology stories I read."

"Jotnar. They call themselves jotnar. Jotunn if it's just one. And I care because they aren't the bad guys and they don't deserve to die."

Not a lie, but not the whole truth.

"In the stories I read, Loki is the bad guy and so are the giants... the jotnar," she said stubbornly.

"Real life is always more complicated than myths and legends," I said with a sigh. "Most of the stories you read are exaggerated to make them more interesting. The Norsemen of those times loved good stories and would make them wilder with each telling."

Manny laughed, which made Esme shudder. I guess I wasn't the only one that found it creepy.

"You don't like it when people lump all Latinos together," I said. "Calling them criminals or lazy or whatever. The same is true for the jotnar. There are good and bad jotnar, and there are good and bad aesir. Most of both groups are just trying to live their lives."

"And Loki? Those stories say some pretty bad things about him. About you. Are they true?"

"Some are," I reluctantly admitted. "And some are not."

"Like Ragnarokkr? Since the world is still here, I'm guessing that one is fake."

"Ragnarokkr. No, unfortunately, that one is real," I confessed. "I really did lead an army of jotnar into war against Odin and the aesir. But it was just a war. Lots of people died, but the world survived just fine.

She just looked at me like I had snakes growing out of my ears.

"I feel like I don't even know you." She looked confused and sad. "So you were just pretending to be someone you're not? For years?"

"Yes and no," I said, trying to be as honest as possible. "I'm still the person you've known for the past few years. You can't be someone you're not for that long. But I lied about my history, where I came from and things like that. Besides, you wouldn't have believed me if I had told you the truth."

"I guess not. But I'm not sure I trust you, Loki," she said, eyeing my warily. "God, it feels weird to call you that."

"Milady," Ullr said, gently interrupting us. "We have to go, Loki. We have things to do."

"The dvergar," Manny cawed.

"Dvergar?" Esme asked.

"In the old stories, they were sometimes known as dwarves, just like the alfar that were holding you prisoner were called elves."

"What about her?" Ullr asked, pointing at Esme.

"Yeah," she said, looking at me expectantly. "What about Esme? I don't just want to be some fucking princess that needs to be rescued."

"I don't know," I admitted, avoiding reminding her that I had indeed just rescued her. "It might be safe for you back on Midgard, but it might not. I don't think Alfhildr will do anything to you. But if Thor finds out about you, it could be very bad."

"What about Jotunheim?" Ullr asked.

"That's probably where you would be safest," I said to her. "What do you want to do?"

"You mean I have a say in this?" she asked sarcastically.

"Of course. It's your life. What do you want to do?"

Esme was quiet for a while. Ullr and I let her think.

"There's no way I can go back to Earth and pretend this never happened," she said, thinking out loud now. "What if I want to go with you, Loki?"

"No. Too dangerous."

"I thought it was my life?"

"It's also mine. I need to be able to do things without having to watch out for you."

"You mean kill people. More people."

"Possibly, although I hope not. And that's not what I was worried about."

"Ullr," she said, turning to him. "Are you going to stay with me, with the giants, the jotnar, if you take me there?"

"No, milady. I have things I must do elsewhere."

"Can you stay there with me for a week? If I don't like it, can you take me back to Earth?"

"I can give you three days," he said reluctantly.

"Okay," Esme said. "Take me to Jotunheim. If I decide I don't like it in three days, you'll take me back to Earth, right?"

Ullr looked helplessly at me. I nodded.

"Yes, I can do that," he said somewhat sourly. I don't think he appreciated being a babysitter.

"Here," I said, handing Esme the Sig Sauer. "Since you know how to shoot a pistol now, you might feel safer with this."

"Wait, you had a gun?" she asked surprised. "You had a gun and you didn't use it against those alfer elves?"

"Alfar. But if it's just one of them it's alfr. Confusing I—"

She cut me off. "You had a gun and you chose to use those axes?"

She was looking scared and angry at the same time again.

"Esme, I needed Alfhildr to be afraid of me, not the gun I was holding. She needed to see that I was more dangerous than the weapon I was using."

That was all true, but it wasn't the whole truth. A part of me wanted to use the axes instead of the gun. A part of me that I didn't particularly like. The part of me that rises up when people close to me are threatened or hurt.

"So you chose to hack those people to death rather than shoot them?" she asked. Fear was beginning to overtake anger.

"Dead is dead. It doesn't matter if it's done with an axe or a gun."

"You... just stay away from me."

"I know you're upset, but I did it for you. To rescue you."

"I'm not sure that makes it better."

"I understand. If it makes any difference, I'm glad you're going to Jotunheim. You'll be safe there."

"Oh, I'm not doing this for you," she said archly. "I'm doing this to try and understand this shit. And you. If you really are an evil asshole godlike in the stories, I'm already fucked, so it doesn't matter what I do. But if you're right about the giants, this way I'll know you're telling me the truth. Or at least enough of it to know if I can trust you."

26

NIDAVELLIR

It took a few hours to walk back to where I had left the bike. Yggdrasil isn't exactly built for straight-line travel. Manny flew ahead and was waiting for me there. I stored all the gear and roared off down the wide branch with Manny on my shoulder. He should have been blown off by the wind at this speed, but all it seemed to do was ruffle his feathers. I would have asked him about it, but between the wind and the helmet, talking was almost impossible.

Nidavellir, home of the dvergar, is a very different place from Asgard or Jotunheim or Alfheim. It had gotten worse since I was there last. I was sweating as I pushed the Ducati through the huge fig tree. Yggdrasil wasn't going to make it easy to use the motorcycle.

The fig tree's leaves didn't look healthy. Many of the scattered trees nearby were sickly. The air was tainted with industrial smells that wrinkled my nose. Although I arrived in mid-morning, the sun was red where it peeked out from the heavy clouds.

"This is worse than those factories in Gary," Manny cawed.

"It's a lot worse than the last time I was here. Esme should be glad she didn't come with me."

I kicked the bike into motion. The rough terrain and sporadic trees and brush didn't let me hit full speed, but I didn't mind. It wasn't long before I found a dirt road which let me open it up. I could see city-like smog to the south along the road, so I set off that way. The air got worse as we got closer, making me cough. I didn't meet anyone on the road, despite it joining a wider roadway. When we crested a small rise, we could see the city in the shallow valley before it.

Stalheim literally translates to steel home, and that's where my road ended. On the outskirts were odd metal shapes thrusting out of the dirt and rock. Some were clearly thick pipes. Others may once have been small buildings, now abandoned. They were made of streaked steel, rusty iron, green coated copper and other metals I didn't recognize. Many structures were just puzzling. In the center of the jumble, Stalheim itself was a giant conglomeration of metal cubes, pipes, and jutting shapes piled into a hill a hundred feet high and maybe half a mile across. Dozens of large smokestacks stuck out at odd angles before stretching straight up. Black and gray smoke poured from them.

"Much has changed in Nidavellir," Manny cawed.

"You said it," I added with a low whistle. "It looks so industrial."

"You are seeing the smoke of a thousand forges being worked by ten thousand dvergar."

"Really?" I gave him an appraising stare. "And how exactly would you know that? You've been with me for more than nine hundred years. When did you visit Stalheim?"

"I didn't," he complained.

"So how do you know that?" I pressed.

Manny hopped around for a minute before confessing, "I got it from the manibrandr that tried to kill you on your boat. He had been here recently on an 'assignment.'"

"You read his memories," I said, amazed. "What else did you get from him? Wait, did you know who hired the manibrandr from the beginning?"

"Not with certainty. He was given his task by another alfr. Who hired them is moot now."

"You knew and you didn't tell me?" I said, fuming. More lies from that damn bird. "You let me take a dangerous and meaningless trip to Alfheim?"

"It was for your own good. For the first time in centuries you were acting like yourself," he cawed. "You were the Loki of old, the God of Mischief. I didn't want to ruin that."

"You know what would have really ruined that? Being killed or taken back to Asgard in chains."

"You ended up in chains in Asgard anyway. I don't think I significantly altered your fate."

I spent the next half hour throwing rocks at my black-hearted raven and cursing him in nine languages. He flew around me, jeering and taunting and generally enjoying himself far too much. When my arm was too sore to throw more, and I couldn't find any more suitable stones nearby, I sat in a funk. Manny landed a dozen feet away.

"Did you get it all out of your system?" Manny cawed.

"I suppose," I said sullenly.

"So get up and move," he said. "You have things to get done."

Studiously ignoring him, I stood and looked down into the vale at Stalheim. It would have to wait for another day. My journey ended elsewhere. I turned west and goosed the bike down the road leading away from Stalheim.

Once I was over the hills and out of sight of Stalheim, the

breeze in my face kept the worst of the foul air away. I was actually enjoying the ride, to the point where I even considered forgiving Manny. He clung to my right shoulder, unfazed by the speed or the wind. Any other bird would have been flung off and left in the dust.

I gunned it up the next low rise, catching some air over the top just for the pure joy of it. That's when I saw them less than a mile off, flying low over the stunted treetops. Valkyries, three of them, astride horses. Between the noise of the bike and my little airborne stunt, there was no hiding from them. I brought the bike to a rough stop, the back wheel spinning.

"Thrudr," Manny said as I gunned the bike back the way we had come.

Thrudr is one of Thor and Sif's daughters. I had no doubt where her allegiance lay. She had joined the Valkyries young. By the time I had left Asgard for good, she led a host of Valkyries. For reasons best known only to Odin, there are always nine hosts of Valkyries, each with nine warriors.

The Ducati was definitely faster than the Valkyries on an open Midgard highway. On this dirt road, I had an advantage, but not by much. My best bet was to get to Stalheim. The Valkyries couldn't act with impunity in the dvergar city. If I couldn't get in, I'd have to leave Nidavellir altogether. Fighting just wasn't an option. Not against three of them.

Glancing over my shoulder, I saw all three of them still about half a mile behind me, hooves pounding invisibly on the air. The Valkyries' long blonde hair streaming behind them as they clung bareback to their horses, heads down close to the animal's necks. Their spears were leveled like lances, steel shields gleaming.

I bore down, opening the throttle wider. I needed to pull away from them, which wasn't happening. The bike had great shocks, but I was still getting my teeth and kidneys rattled with every big bump. Manny was positively serene, which pissed me off.

Up over the last hill into the valley where Stalheim nestled, I tried to control how much air I got, but I still went airborne. I saw another Valkyrie astride her horse standing in the roadway just a hundred yards away. Shit, shit, and double shit. I hit the ground with a bone-rattling bounce. Braking hard for the second time in this situation, the back wheel slung sideways and I almost lost control of the bike.

"Hold, Loki," she called. "I am not your enemy."

"That's funny," I shouted, revving the bike. "Your three sisters have been chasing me for a couple dozen miles."

"Nevertheless."

"What in the Nine Worlds is that supposed to mean?"

"I think you should trust her," Manny cawed.

"That's asking a lot."

We were maybe forty yards apart. I didn't recognize her, but that didn't mean much. There was no way I could get to Stalheim without going through her. I'd have to take a sharp right and go cross country and try and make it back to the fig tree. Except there was no way I could outrun them over the rougher terrain. Time to roll the dice.

I gunned the engine and charged right at her. She stood her ground calmly, spear in her right hand pointing to the heavens, shield in her left covering that side of her torso. Her horse pawed softly at the ground, also unimpressed by the onrushing motorcycle.

At the last second I swerved and cut a tight circle around her, braking to a stop on her right side. She didn't even look at me. Of course, that's probably because the other three Valkyries had crested the hill and were fanning out before us.

"You better be right about this," I hissed to Manny.

Thrudr urged her mount forward, landing maybe fifty feet from us. The other two did the same, trotting closer to her. Thrudr's face was sweat-stained and dusty. In fact, there was a layer of filth on her armor and her horse. I guess the bike kicked up more dust than I realized.

"Brynhildr," Thrudr called. "Thank you for detaining my prisoner."

"He's mine," Brynhildr said firmly.

"Nay," Thrudr said with some heat. "Thor, Lord of Asgard and ruler of all the aesir, has charged me and my host with hunting down the renegade and traitor Loki. So I'll thank you to turn him over."

"Thor, or Lady Sif?" Brynhildr asked, seemingly unimpressed with Thrudr's authority.

"Lady Sif speaks with Thor's authority."

"With, or for?"

"It matters not. What matters is that that treasonous snake is returned to his rock to suffer for his crimes."

"Never again!" I shouted. Brynhildr extended her spear in front of me like a toll gate.

"And that you are the one to take him there," Brynhildr stated. It wasn't a question.

"Aye," Thrudr said with a malicious smile.

"Then you'll get one more chance to beat me in combat," Brynhildr said, shifting her shield in front of her. "Only this time it won't be practice."

Thrudr's horse backed up. The other two Valkyries looked nervous. Brynhildr dismounted and struck a warrior's pose with spear extended and shield held before her.

"There are three of us against one of you," Thrudr said, not sounding at all confident.

"Only a coward would fear those odds."

Thrudr angrily dismounted. The other two followed suit, although they didn't look at all happy about it. In unison, all three took a single step forward.

Brynhildr flung her spear at the leftmost Valkyrie with startling power and speed. The Valkyrie lowered her shield to protect her left thigh. The spear deflected and drove into her right foot and at least a foot into the ground. To her credit, the Valkyrie did not cry out.

Thrudr and her remaining companion charged with spear points forward and shields covering their chests. Brynhildr drew her sword and waited for them. I pushed the bike several yards backward. Fair fights are not my thing. Even with the spells I had used to defeat the alfar guardsmen, I wouldn't be a match for a Valkyrie.

The three met with a clash and ringing of steel. Thrudr's spear seemed to dance with a mind of its own. Her companion's spear wove a complex pattern of jabs and sweeps that pushed Brynhildr back. Her sword and shield were everywhere, seeming to anticipate the other Valkyries' attacks and feints. Thrudr's spear went spinning into the air, so she drew her sword. I pushed the bike back even farther. If this went south, I was taking off.

I didn't see the blow, but the Valkyrie on the right suddenly dropped her spear. Blood streamed down her arm, which hung limp at her side. She retreated from the fight. The other Valkyrie was sitting on the ground working at the spear pinning her foot to the ground.

Thrudr and Brynhildr danced. Thrudr's swordplay was amazing. Her blade wove swiftly and gracefully in and out and around. Her shield seemed to be everywhere at once. But she used her sword as a sword and her shield as a shield. Brynhildr and her sword and shield were a single thing. She would attack or defend with the sword and attack or defend with the shield. She blocked with her forearm vambrace and kicked with her shin greaves.

With a cry of anger and shame, Thrudr fell backward.

Brynhildr's sword was pointed at her neck. Both were breathing hard.

"Yield," Brynhildr demanded.

"I yield," Thrudr said bitterly.

"The prisoner is mine. You may tell what tale you wish to your masters."

"Fine," Thrudr said, angrily. "He's yours. Take the credit. But don't expect me to toast you in Valhalla for this."

Brynhildr just smiled. Thrudr backed away and helped pull the spear from her companion's foot. Then the three of them mounted rode off in the general direction of my fig tree.

"So apparently I'm yours," I said, apprehensively. "What are you going to do with me?"

"Wrong question," she said, looking back at me. "What are you going to do with me?"

"Huh?"

"I have broken with my sisters and refused to follow Thor."

"I told you she could be trusted," Manny cawed.

"And how exactly did you know that?" I asked with a touch of irritation.

"Ullr and I talked about all the things he has seen and done in Asgard recently."

"And you didn't think to tell me?" I said, getting a little hot. "More secrets?"

"You were sleeping off your injuries," Manny cawed indifferently.

"And after that? What about afterward?"

"Just as you are Mischief, Loki, I am Memory. I keep many secrets. They are mine to share when I choose and with whom I choose."

"Loki," Brynhildr interrupted. "My host and I have decided to join with you. We are setting ourselves against the rightful lord of Asgard, breaking a tradition that is more than a thousand years old. Do you think we could finish talking about that? You can squabble with Munnin later."

"Fine," I said. "But we're not done, bird."

Manny just laughed. Both Brynhildr and I shuddered.

"Your whole host is with you?" I asked.

"Yes. I made it known they did not have to follow me into this folly, but they chose to anyway."

"What about the other hosts?"

"All are loyal to Thor."

"Are you okay to fight your sisters? To kill them if necessary? Are they?"

"We're Valkyries," she said, suddenly imperious.

"I'll take that as a yes. Take your host to Ymyd in Jotunheim. You may find Ullr there. Help them plan... help them plan whatever it is they are planning."

"Milord," she said with a bow of her head.

"One more thing. How did you know to be here? How did you know I would be in trouble?"

"Ullr told me you were going to Nidavellir. When I heard Thrudr was heading there too I thought you might need help."

"But you didn't bring your whole host?"

"I didn't need them, did I?" she asked with a satisfied smile.

I watched as she gave a war cry and launched her horse into the air. Show off. She headed north, probably to the same fig tree I used.

27

SURTR

It took the rest of the day to reach the cave. Nidavellir is riddled with caves. The dvergar feel about caves and the earth the way the alfar feel about trees and wildlife. A thousand years ago most of them lived in such caves, working their trade in isolation or with close family members. From what Manny told me, most of them now lived in Stalheim, but I was betting quite a few still followed the old ways in the caves. The particular dvergr I was looking for wouldn't have adapted to city life very well.

I still recognized this cave despite having passed half a hundred similar ones. It wound down into the darkness. I debated what to do and finally settled on changing into a raccoon. They have excellent night vision and are good climbers. I would need both to get through the cave.

"I don't like caves," Manny cawed. I shrugged my raccoon shoulders as best I could and pushed my duffle into the dark opening ahead of me. Manny cawed in frustration and followed me.

The cave was deeper than I remembered. At one point I had to climb high to fit through a hole just barely wide enough for a raccoon and a crow. I was able to hear the thrum of engines and the rhythmic pounding of machines now. My eyes strained, and I spotted a red glimmer around the next bend. As it grew brighter and I could see better, I reverted to human and dressed myself.

"I hate being underground," Manny cawed.

"Well, the dvergar like it."

"No sky," he complained. "No air."

"There's plenty of air. At least so long as you don't use it all up whining."

He was quiet after that.

Around another corner and we faced a giant iron door lit by glowing red panels. There was no visible handle, but the surface of the door was covered in glowing red runes. Nordic runes were the first written language I learned, but these runes were different. I recognized many of them, but dozens of strange runic symbols were amid them as well. There was even a word or two in old Norse that I could make out.

Frustrated, I pounded on the door with a rock. I felt the throbbing vibrations under my hands. "Svar! Open the damn door. It's Loki."

Five full minutes of pounding and shouting achieved nothing. I sat on the cave floor in disgust. I took another stab at reading the runes. I wasn't getting very far when the door opened. I scrambled out of the way. It stopped just wide enough to allow a person to slip past the two-foot thick metal door.

"Come on," a voice from inside snipped. "Do not waste my time."

I had to turn sideways to slide through. Manny hopped in behind me because it was too narrow for him to fly. The floor gleamed silver and the walls and ceiling were a ruddy metal, all lit by dim red light. The machine noises were louder in here, and I felt the vibrations rise up through my bare feet. This room was empty, but corridors led off in a couple of different directions. A tall thin black man had a hand on a large metal ring in the center of the door, like a bank vault wheel. As soon as we cleared the door frame he spun the wheel and the door slowly closed behind us with an ominous *thunk*.

After the age of Vikings, the dvergar and dwarves of Germanic literature started to blend together in the stories told by skalds and historians. The dvergar, or dwarves, were never short, stout, bearded men. However, they are kin to the alfar and share their pointed ears. Their skin is a shade of black with subtle hues of blue. The dvergr before me was taller than normal and had a darker shade of skin than most.

"Svar?" I asked tentatively. He kind of looked like the Svar of old, although that was a really long time ago. I didn't really know how long dvergar lived.

"Sviarr," he answered in a deep voice that seemed to cut through the pulsating machine sounds. "Ninth in the line of Svar. I was told Loki, God of Mischief, might come someday."

"How did you know it was me?"

Rather than answering, he just pointed at the door. The red panels I had seen from the other side were thick, red-tinted windows.

"Oh."

"For nine generations we have been told that if you ever came to one of us, we should give you whatever you ask for," Sviarr said stiffly.

"Really? Wow. That makes this easy."

"I don't always do what I'm told."

Of course not.

"I'm hoping you still have Surtr."

"Surtr was destroyed at Ragnarokkr."

"I was at Ragnarokkr. Surtr was not destroyed. Svar himself hauled it away. It took nine giant jotnar to pull the damn thing."

"Do you know what Svar said as he left?" he asked.

"Is this a test?" I asked, surprised. "This is a test. You're not sure I'm Loki."

"Only Loki knows what Svar said to him after Ragnarokkr. Loki and me."

I took a deep breath. "He said, 'I never did like the fucking aesir'"

"Close enough. The version I was told had more profanity. But you've proven you're truly Loki."

"Svar did have a way with words."

"Before I just give you the most dangerous thing in all the Nine Worlds, what do you intend to do with Surtr?" he asked. I didn't like the look in his eyes.

I told him about what I had seen in Valhalla and Thor's threats. I told him about my trip to Jotunheim. I left out Alfheim and Midgard, other than to say I had been hiding out there until assassins forced me to leave.

"Once the jotnar are gone, Thor isn't going to stop. One by one he's going to invade each of the Nine Worlds."

"All nine?" Sviarr said with a scoff. "Five at best if you don't count Asgard. Muspelheim and Niflheim aren't really worlds."

"What?"

"I suppose you were taught that Muspelheim is the land of fire where the Eldthursr and the Muspellmegr live."

"Odin himself taught me that."

"It figures," Sviarr said, making a sour face. "That ignorant aesir always did have problems with cosmology. He preferred mysticism to science."

Manny cawed indignantly.

"Have you ever seen an Eldtursr or a Muspellmegr?" he

continued. "No. Because they don't exist. They are just stories made up by Odin's grandfather Buri to explain things he didn't understand."

"Odin said Muspelheim was made of fire and impossible to visit."

"And Niflheim is ice and darkness and equally inhospitable."

"So there are only seven worlds?" I asked, struggling to keep up.

"Depends on what you count as a world. Yggdrasil connects directly to six, Midgard, Asgard, Jotunheim, Vanaheim, Alfheim, and Nidavellir."

"Yggdrasil doesn't connect to Muspelheim or Niflheim? Or Hel?"

"Hel didn't exist until your daughter created it. She named it after herself."

"She... she created a world?" I asked, stunned.

"That's up for debate. Not that she created it, but whether it's a world. For all the other worlds you translate to them from Yggdrasil. But you just walk into Hel, assuming you can survive the trip. Plus there is a mathematical contradiction if we consider Hel to be its own world."

"Mathematical contradiction?"

"Too many worlds. Not enough tree."

"Can we get back to Surtr?" I asked. This conversation was spinning wildly out of control and making my head hurt. Translate to them?

"Of course," Sviarr said somewhat eagerly. "You've seen Surtr in action. Would you call it a fiery giant with a flaming sword, as the old Norse stories on Midgard do?"

"No. It's a siege engine. Like a giant cannon that shoots fire."

"Natural flames, like in a fireplace?" he asked, still testing me, or at least my memory.

"No, it was much more than that. It's hard to describe."

"Surtr harnesses the same power that lights the sun. If there is a Muspelheim, it would be our own sun."

"That sounds dangerous."

"Gloriously so."

I didn't like the eager look on his face.

"I need to know that you are going to use Surtr in dangerous ways. That it will kill and destroy."

I was beginning to see why he was living as a hermit behind a heavy metal door. Sviarr was batshit crazy. Svar had been a little off his rocker, but not like this. It's scary how the truly mad seem fine at first until the crazy starts leaking out.

"I only want to use it to stop Thor. To defeat his army."

"That sounds perfect," he said, practically vibrating with excitement."

"So you really still have Surtr?" I asked, changing the subject. "Can I see it?"

He scurried down a corridor and I trotted to keep with him. Manny flew with us, staying well away from Sviarr. I didn't blame him.

The corridor emptied into a large cavern lit with brass lanterns that gave off the same red light that seemed to fill Sviarr's home. Half a dozen large oiled tarps were covering strange shapes which I presumed to be machines of some sort. The smallest was the size of a pony. The largest the size of a house. A modern suburban home, not a medieval hut. Sviarr scurried over to the largest one and turned a winch which in turn began to lift the gigantic tarp with ropes.

Slowly an enormous machine made of silver and copper was revealed. It was both strange and familiar to me. Nine hundred years ago it had reminded me of a metal toad that fired beams of fiery light that killed everything they touched. To my eyes now it resembled a gigantic tank, like some misshapen World War I monstrosity. I guess Svar had been ahead of his time by a few centuries.

Six huge, coal-black wheels, each ten feet tall and covered in hundreds of foot-long cleats, held it off the cave floor. There was a glass cab that I don't recall seeing before. But the whole thing was dominated by a coppery barrel forty feet long and half that in diameter. It looked short and stubby despite its size.

"Isn't it magnificent?" Sviarr crowed.

Manny cawed his dismay. I had forgotten how gods damned big Surtr was, although it had been more than nine hundred years since I had last seen it. Maybe it wasn't quite the same.

"This is the same machine that was at Ragnarokkr?"

"Yes," Sviarr said. "Well, mostly. Each generation has made small improvements. Sver, son of Svar, put the pressure-sensitive spikes on the wheels. My father, Svuar, enhanced the defensive enchantments."

"And what did you add?"

"I put in a motor so you can drive it like a Midgard tank instead of having to drag it everywhere."

"You know about tanks?"

"Many dvergar are fascinated by Midgard technology. The people of Midgard are primitive in so many ways, but in others, they are positively genius. No dvergr would ever have made a computer."

"I've never driven a tank. Can you teach me how to use it?"

"Teach you? Why would I need to teach you? Surtr is mine," he said emphatically. "I will bring it to the field of battle. I will man it. I will destroy everything before me."

Odin's spear. This was going sideways fast. His eyes had that far-off look that crazy people get when they see something you don't.

"We only want to defeat Thor's army. Once they surrender or retreat, you have to stop. No more killing or destroying after that. Okay?"

"Stop? I suppose so. But his army is really big, isn't it?" Sviarr asked. "It might take a long time to defeat it. A gloriously long time."

"Trust me, his army is huge."

"When do we leave?" he asked with big, shining eyes.

"How are you going to get it there?"

"I have ways."

"If you say so. I'll send word to you, Sviarr. I'll let you know when you can bring Surtr to the battlefield and where it is."

I would deal with Sviarr and Surtr if we won the day against Thor. I wasn't sure how, but I'd think of something. If we were defeated, well, he'd be Thor's problem and I'd either be dead or back on my rocks. Preferably dead though.

"I have one more favor to ask," I said cautiously.

"Favor? You are the one doing me a favor. Eight generations of my family haven't been able to see Surtr in action. I will be the first since Svar. It is a great honor."

"I need to find Laevateinn."

"What?" Manny cawed. I don't think he was happy.

"The weapon you wielded at Ragnarokkr? What makes you think I know where it is?"

"Maybe you don't, but I do know that Sigyn gave it to Svar after Ragnarokkr."

"Loki," Manny cawed. "This is a bad idea."

Many people died at Ragnarokkr. I was almost one of them. The battle was all but over when Heimdall found me on the battlefield. The duel did not last long. Heimdall was a far better swordsman than me. He slipped on a blood slick corpse and I dealt him a mortal blow with Laevateinn. With his dying breath, he pulled me down onto his sword.

I don't know how long I lay gasping out my life draped over Heimdall's corpse. A Valkyrie came for him and gave me a cold stare as it led his spirit away. Sigyn found me only moments before I would have expired. Although she is a novice with magic, she somehow stabilized me at death's door.

Lifting me bodily with a strength she shouldn't have possessed, she ran to where Svar was persuading the jotnar to haul away Surtr. She tossed Laevateinn to him, begging him to destroy it. When he said that was impossible, she begged him to hide it where no man or god would ever find it.

"So she did," Sviarr said, breaking me out of my reverie.

"So, where is it?"

"Svar gave it to Laegjarn. After all, it was he who made it for you."

"Okay," I said. "So where's Laegjarn? Wait, he's probably dead by now."

"He is. And his line is gone as well."

"So it's lost?"

"I never said that," he said with a shit-eating grin.

"Out with it Sviarr."

"Laegjarn sealed Laevateinn in a chest with nine locks. He then set Sinmoera to guard it."

"And—"

"In Eldrgap. Or in a cave at its base."

Eldrgap is a volcano in Nidavellir. Actually, it's the only volcano in Nidavellir. Interestingly the name is almost identical to the name of one in Iceland.

"Tell me how to find that cave."

"For a price," he said, eyes glowing again with desire. "My grandfather stole many of the notes from Laergjarn's workshop when the last of his line died out."

"I'm guessing your grandfather had something to do with that line dying. So what is your price?"

"Bring me back Sinmoera's body."

"What? Why would you want that?"

"None of your concern. But that is my price."

"All right," I grumbled. The sooner I could be rid of this ghoulish dvergr, the better.

"You'll regret this," Manny cawed.

28

SINMOERA

I set off to the east, a plume of dust rising behind me from the bike, Manny perched on my shoulder. Eldrgap is easy to find. It's on the eastern edge of Nidavellir. To the best of my knowledge, nobody had ventured farther. For all I knew there wasn't anything out there. All of the Nine Worlds, or six I guess, were much smaller than Midgard. I didn't understand how that could be, but it was. Of all the races, only the Midgardians had the exploration bug. The rest were content with their little corner of creation.

Eldrgap rose up like Mount Doom as I rode on. A thin smoke trail curled upward from its summit. I had passed the last tree a while ago. Now it was just dusty, rocky flats.

An hour later I was steering around long-cooled lava flows. By the time I reached the base of the mountain near where Sviarr said I would find the cave, the Ducati was low on gas. Fortunately, I had a spare gas can.

The terrain had become too rugged for the bike, so I left it and climbed the old lava flows, jumping from ridge to ridge. It wasn't too long before I spotted the lava tube I was looking for. Sviarr claimed it was no longer connected to the volcano's main lava dome, but it made me nervous nonetheless.

"I hate caves," Manny cawed.

"Then stay here."

"I still say this is a mistake."

"But you haven't said why."

We stared at each other. He backed down first, which is unusual. I shrugged my shoulders and entered the lava tube.

The lava tube did indeed look like it hadn't been active for ages. I followed the twists and turns of Sviarr's instructions with a nice military flashlight I had brought from Midgard. Sometimes I was in a natural cavern, sometimes a lava tube. I was always heading down. I tried to mark the way as best I could with stacked stones or scratches on the walls. After a while, I felt it getting warmer.

Finally a narrow fissure I crab-walked through showed an exit lit dull red. I turned off the flashlight and eased forward as quietly as I could. I peered into a decent sized room with smooth stone walls clearly built by dvergar hands. Against the far wall a lit forge glowed. Scattered around the edges of the room were dozens, maybe hundreds, of steel weapons, shields, and bits of armor.

I ducked back as a shadow passed between me and the forge, leaving me in the dark for a moment. I was surprised to see what looked like a nine-foot tall steampunk robot, with blocky arms and legs and large exposed ball joints. It was made of a few different metals, from silvery steel to reddish copper and golden bronze. The head was a simple sphere with lenses for eyes and a grill for a mouth. The right arm ended in a blacksmith's hammer, narrow on one end and wide on the other. The left ended in some sort of clamp.

There was something about its gait and posture that made me think it was female. It couldn't pin it down, but I couldn't shake it either. She bent and picked up a sword and trudged to the forge. Her spine was a rectangle maybe four feet long and six inches wide with nine distinct-looking locks all in a row. Son-of-a-bitch. This must be Sinmoera. Laegjarn's chest was built into her. Now I understood why Sviarr wanted her body.

She placed the sword in the fire, letting it heat. There was no getting around my having to destroy her. I doubted I could talk her into giving up her spine. I searched for a weakness I could exploit. No visible off switch. No power cord. No exhaust vent. So much for the easy ways. Maybe if I could knock her over she wouldn't be able to get back up. I really needed to stop watching bad TV. A dvergar smith wouldn't make such a simple design mistake.

No animal shape was going to give me an advantage here. But there was still galdr magic I could use. I backed down the crevasse and softly chanted some spells. It didn't take long and I was soon back looking into the forge room.

Returning to the edge of the crevasse I waited for her to turn in the right direction. Aiming carefully from the dark shadows of the fissure, I tossed a small stone as far as I could. It clattered somewhere off in the darkness. She turned her head to look that way.

I burst from the wide crack in the wall and swept up a battleaxe I had chosen from the many weapons on the floor. Sinmoera spun on her waist joint and grabbed the red hot sword from the forge fire. My distraction had bought me just enough time to get armed and ready.

"Sinmoera, I presume?" I asked.

Charging, I swung the battleaxe with everything I had at her knee joint. Given the spells I had cast, everything I had was quite a lot. I really hoped this would work. Metal rang on metal and the jarring vibrations caused me to release the axe, which embedded in her leg where the ball joint met her calf.

"That must have hurt."

Towering over me, she swung her heated sword, striking a glancing blow on my upper arm. I heard the sizzle of it hitting the icy armor I had formed over my body. There wasn't much moisture in the air here, so it was just a layer of hoarfrost, but it was enough to deflect that hit.

"Bet you didn't expect that," I taunted.

She kept spinning on her waist joint, the hammer following the sword. I stumbled back out of reach. Her top half did a full three-sixty rotation on her stationary legs. I grabbed the first weapon I found on the ground. A spear. Bad choice.

Sinmoera lunged with the glowing sword. I turned sideways and the edge creased my chest with another sizzle of melting ice. I swept the butt end of the spear at her ankle, hoping to send her to the ground. Instead, the spear shaft broke. I saw the hammer swinging at my head out of the corner of my eye and ducked.

"Almost got me there," I said. Why was I talking to her? She certainly wasn't talking back.

Staying low, I ran past her, angling toward a broadsword on the other side of the room. I heard her metal steps behind me. I grabbed the sword, lifted it, and spun to face her. She took an awkward step on the leg with the battleaxe sticking out of it. I heard metal snap, and my axe fell to the ground with a semi-circular bite out of the blade.

Her bad eye and bad leg were both on her left side, so I circled around that way. She was definitely favoring her leg. I wasn't prepared for her rush. You don't expect a machine to fool you with a fake injury. The hammer struck me in the gut with an underhand swing that lifted me off the ground and sent me flying across the room.

I landed half in the forge fire with what felt like a cracked rib. Magic ice armor, meet really hot fire. A fountain of steam erupted, which under other circumstances would have scalded me quite badly. Instead it just dimmed the forge fire.

Grimacing in pain, I rolled off the forge fire anticipating Sinmoera's charge. Peering through the steam, I saw her trudging toward me. Clutching at my rib, I scuttled off to the side and away from her. She pivoted slightly to keep me dead ahead. Fool me once, shame on you. Fool me twice, shame on me. This was another ploy, and I waited for the charge.

Except it didn't come. She kept marching forward, plodding really. If I hadn't had a pain in my ribs that made my vision blur with sudden movements, I could have run circles around her. Something had happened, and I didn't understand what.

I looked around the noticeably dimmer room for a clue. The steam was dissipating, but even so, I couldn't spot the cause. Except that the room was dimmer. The forge fire was clearly lower than when I had first entered the room. Somehow, Sinmoera was connected to that fire.

I struggle with divination magic, but I excel at fire magic. The problem was that seidr spells took time and concentration to cast. At least for me.

Still clutching at my side, I stumbled as quickly as I could to the far end of the room. The pain made the room swim in front of me and I collapsed against the far wall, miraculously not hurting myself as I fell among the discarded weapons and armor.

I chanted the spell I needed to control the fire.

Sinmoera marched forward.

There is a limit to how quickly you can chant without affecting the spell. Sinmoera kept coming.

She was maybe three steps from me when I took hold of

the flames. I felt the magic in the heat. The damn thing actually burned spirits.

Sinmoera was two steps away.

I pulled heat from the fire into myself.

Sinmoera was one step from me.

The fire banked and dimmed. The ice armor melted. Sinmoera stood before me; her red hot sword drew back for a killing blow. The fire died as I sucked the last of the heat and spirit energy out of it.

Sinmoera stood frozen in place, sword arm drawn back. I could just see parts of her from the dull glow of the sword. With effort and a few choice words of old Norse, I pushed myself to my feet, bringing a mace from the pile of weapons with me. I pushed the heat into the wooden handle, which burst into flames.

The room looked different in the flickering light of my makeshift torch. Sinmoera looked more menacing somehow. I dropped the mace and reached for a spear. I needed to get all the heat from the fire out of me before I burst into flames too.

It took five different wood-handled weapons to hold the rest of the forge fire. I placed them in a semi-circle behind Sinmoera so I could see her spine better. Simple latches held Laevateinn's lockbox in place. When I pulled the box out, I fell over backward with it in my lap. It was heavier than I had anticipated. The world went gray for a moment from the pain.

The makeshift torches were going out and I had no fire left to make new ones. I could have cast a spell with my own spirit energy to make a light, but that wasn't necessary. Instead, I shifted shape into a leopard. I'm really not a cat person. I'm much more of a dog person, but desperate times and all. Leopards have excellent night vision and are noted for their ability to drag heavy prey up into trees, which is just what I needed.

I really wish changing shape also healed me as it does in the werewolf stories, but no such luck. My rib still felt like shit. Still, I somehow managed to drag that stupid lock box all the way through the tunnels and back out to where Manny was waiting. I dressed in a spare change of leathers in my pack.

"Took you long enough," he cawed. He was wisely perched on a rock out of my reach. He looked delicious through my leopard eyes.

"I need to rest," I gasped. My broken rib hurt like hell.

I pulled out one of Idunn's fruit. Like an idiot I had left it with the bike, forcing me to haul that dam lockbox back with a cracked rib. I felt better after an hour or so and a slice of fruit.

"Time to hit the road, Manny."

29

THE LOCK BOX

O pen it," I said, tossing Laegjarn's chest on the floor at Sviarr's feet.

"Where is Sinmoera's body?"

"Right where I left it. You can go get it yourself."

"That wasn't our bargain."

"It is now," I said staring him down. "You left out a few important details about her."

Sviarr looked away. He crouched by the box and moved his hands over it without touching it. He peered into the lock at one end. He sniffed one in the middle.

"Engineering like this is a lost art," he said looking up at me. His eyes gleamed with anticipation. "Let me get some tools."

"This is a mistake," Manny said.

Sviarr scurried off. I found a distinctly dvergar chair and sat heavily. It was distinctly uncomfortable, but better than standing.

I must have dozed. My head jerked forward as I woke suddenly. I had new aches and pains from that damn chair. Sviarr was crouched over the box. Strange tools were scattered on the floor around him. He had a hammer and chisel in his hands. The sound of the hammer blow had woken me.

"Any luck?" I asked.

"Not yet," he said, looking irked. "I've formulated a theory though."

"Whatever. Just get it open."

I winced as I stood. I had only eaten enough of Idunn's fruit to start the mending process. It was a precious resource. I would heal the rest of the way like normal people. Slowly and painfully.

"Do you have anything to eat here?"

"Second door on the right," he said, pointing without looking.

The kitchen was simple. I found some unidentifiable smoked meat and a passable ale. I wandered through Sviarr's cave home as I ate. Some halls were square and straight, others natural caverns with fitted flagstone paths. It had few personal touches, but many strange devices and machines. I took the opportunity to move the smaller pieces around and hide a few others. I didn't find a bed or kitchen, but then the place was kind of maze-like.

Eventually, I got bored enough to head back. Sviarr was still crouched over the lockbox, but this time with a strange headpiece on. It looked like a welder's helmet with tubes and knobs added. He had a metal gauntlet on his left hand that connected to the helmet with a few flexible tubes.

"The great Sviarr is stumped?" I asked sarcastically.

"It took thirty-three years to build Sinmoera. I've only had a few hours to look at this box."

"Oh."

"Why do you want Laevateinn?"

"It's mine."

He flipped the visor up and looked at me. "That's not all of it, is it?"

"I need every weapon I can find to stop Thor. Laevateinn could be a great help."

"Or not," Manny cawed. Sviarr flipped the visor back down and returned his attention to the lockbox.

"What is your problem you old crow?" I asked, irritated.

"Laevateinn changes you," he said. "It brings out the worst of you."

"What are you talking about? It doesn't change me."

"All the great artifacts have a mood. Wielding one affects the wielder."

"That's true," Sviarr added without looking up from his work.

"So Mjolnir would make me stormy?" I raised an eyebrow.

"After a fashion," Manny said. "It has more effect on those most like it. Laevateinn makes you more you."

"So Mjolnir makes Thor more Thor?"

"Exactly," muttered Sviarr.

"And you think me being more like me is a problem, Manny?"

"Do you remember the forging of Mjolnir?"

I had the good sense not to answer that. It wasn't my proudest moment. Like a fool, I had bet my head that the famous dvergar smith Sindri couldn't make artifacts as wondrous as Sif's golden hair that the Sons of Ivaldi dvergar smiths had made. I'm pretty sure large quantities of mead were involved.

Since I liked my head exactly where it was, I snuck into their workshop and tried to spoil their efforts. I was partially successful with Mjolnir. It ended up with a short handle. When Sindri came for my head, I told him he could have my head, but none of my neck. Odin declared that I had to honor my deal. Sindri couldn't figure out how to do that, so he and his apprentice Brokkr held me down and sewed my mouth shut. I still remember Thor gleefully watching them do it.

"I think both of you are exaggerating," I said. "But regardless, if Laevateinn can help me stop Thor I'll take that chance."

"I still say this isn't a good idea," Manny cawed.

Sviarr directed me to a bed where I could sleep. Dvergar beds are much better than dvergar chairs. My ribs still ached, but somehow I was able to get some sleep. I'm not sure how long I slept, but I felt better when I woke. This underground home was messing with my sense of time.

I found Sviarr in a chair near the lockbox flipping through a large tome of some sort. He was dressed in a long robe covered in what looked like math equations. He wore a set of spectacles with one blue lens and one green lens.

"Any progress?" I asked.

"Yes."

"And?"

"I can't open it," he said cheerfully.

"That's progress?"

"Most certainly. I didn't know that before. Only you can open the locks. They are magically keyed to you."

"Okay, so what do I have to do?"

"I was able to puzzle out the first lock."

"Just the first one?" I asked, a little dismayed.

"The others won't respond until the first is opened. So I can't work on them until the first is sprung."

"So we're back to what do I have to do?"

"The first lock opens with a drop of your blood, one of your tears, and a little of your spit."

"You're kidding."

"No. That's your way, not mine."

The first lock had a little round hole. Muttering about gods damned dvergar and their gods damned machines, I pricked my finger and let a drop of blood fall into the hole. I put a little spit on my finger and pushed it into the hole too.

The tears were a little harder. I sat back and remembered my sons Narfi and Nari. After Baldr's death, I was hunted down and brought to "justice." My son Narfi was turned into a wolf by Odin, Skadi, and Frigg. He then attacked and killed his own brother, Nari, right in front of Sigyn and I. She wept and I raged against my bonds, swearing by all I held dear to make them pay. I guess tears aren't so hard after all.

I wiped a tear into the keyhole. I could hear gears rattling and other mechanical sounds, followed by a click. The lock slid off the lockbox as if pushed by an invisible hand. The space where it had been was unmarked. Sviarr swooped up the fallen lock, cradling it to his chest like a treasure.

"I can't wait around here for you to figure these out one at a time," I said.

"Leave it here. I'll work on it," Sviarr promised. I didn't like leaving it, but there wasn't much I could do with it.

"I'll be back to collect it," I said, turning to leave.

30

A STORY FOR ESME

The city of Utgard had visitors. Hundreds of giant, crude, hide tents were pitched haphazardly outside the walls. Jotnar of various sizes wandered among them doing whatever it is jotnar warriors do. It seemed Ymyd had called in the clans.

I garnered a few stares as I walked up the road to the city. I had left the bike on Yggdrasil; Jotunheim was too rocky for it. Unlike the previous time I had been to the city, there was actually a jotnar guard at the gates. He gave me a sour look but didn't try to stop me from entering. The guard at the castle was less slovenly and more formal. He didn't try to stop me either. His steward Hrim did though.

"Lord Loki," Hrim said. "We weren't expecting you."

"Well, there's a war to plan isn't there?"

"Indeed there is."

"I'm here to see Ymyd."

"He's not available right now, but you can join him tomorrow in the council room."

"I suppose that will have to do. Where can I find Ullr or Esme?"

I found them together in a garden courtyard that looked like it was in dire need of a gardener. Esme was drawing a small bow and aiming at a nearby tree. A couple of arrows were already stuck in it.

"Draw your breath with the bow," Ullr said. "Still your mind. Don't try to think. Just let yourself become one with the arrow."

Esme released the bowstring and the arrow flew just left of the tree. She stomped her foot and muttered something I couldn't make out.

Ullr put his hand on the small of her back. "It was a good shot. You just had your elbow out again."

"Don't let me interrupt," I said loudly.

Esme turned to look. "Low... Loki! You're back."

"How did you fare in Nidavellir?" Ullr asked.

"Not as well as I had hoped. How has your stay been, Esme?"

"They're treating me well," she said. "But it's weird being around giants all the time. It was frightening at first, like they might step on me."

"Have you found the answers you were seeking?" Ullr asked.

"Some of them. Apparently, these giants see you as a hero of some sort."

"Sometimes there is more than one side to a story."

"There are at least three sides to every tale," Manny said. "The teller's side, the listener's side, and the truth."

"No man is only a hero or only a villain," Ullr said.

"I feel like I stepped into a philosopher's convention," I said.

"I think I'm done with the bow for now," Esme said. "I'd like a drink. Ullr, would you mind if I talked to Loki by myself for a while?"

"Of course not." He stood there awkwardly for a moment before turning and leaving.

"So are you sleeping with him or is he just wooing you?"

"None of your fucking business."

"That was pretty fast. You've only known him for a few days."

"What part of 'none of your fucking business' didn't you understand?"

"You should be aware that fidelity is not a strong suit of the aesir."

"You're not going to drop this, are you?"

"I don't want to see you get hurt, Esme."

"Ullr won't hurt me. He's honest and kind and loyal."

"And ruggedly handsome too."

She punched me in the shoulder. Hard. Manny laughed, making us both shudder.

"I guess I have to get to know you all over again," Esme said, changing topics.

"The Lowell you knew is me. He's just not *all* of me. Being him wasn't pretending so much as just keep a part of myself under wraps."

"The part of yourself that is a killer?"

"That's one part. Many of the worlds beyond Midgard can be violent. You've always lived where there are laws that are enforced by police, and people generally follow them. It's more medieval out here. More like the Wild West. Sometimes you have to kill to survive or to protect people or things you care about."

We had found our way back to my chambers. I poured her some mead while we talked.

"I can see that, but I don't have to fucking like it."

"You know that Ullr has killed too, right? While I was rescuing you, he was shooting guards with a sniper rifle."

"Yes. He's told me. I'm not happy about that either."

"And you saved my life by driving a spear into the back of an alfar guard."

"I know, I know."

"You know that I would never hurt you?"

"I know you wouldn't, Lowell," she said, looking miserable.

I let the name thing slide. "But we are going to war to protect people. All the people of Jotunheim. You see them as giants, but they are people just like you and me."

"I'm still having a hard time seeing you as a regular person. Sorry."

"I don't ever want to be regular," I said with a laugh. "But I am a person."

"So if there are two sides to every story, tell me your side of one of the Norse myths about you."

"Are you familiar with Idunn?"

"Is she the one with the apples?"

"They aren't apples, but yes, she grows fruit and other things."

"In the story I read Loki kidnapped her. You kidnapped her."

"Let me tell you my side of that story."

Thor, Hoenir, and I were traveling through Jotunheim. We hunted aurochs, a type of wild ox. The ones in Jotunheim are larger than the cows you're familiar with and have a nasty temper.

"Hoenir had killed one the day before and we had finished butchering it. When I went to put some of the meat over the fire, it wouldn't cook. Thor blamed me, but when he tried to cook the meat, it remained untouched as well.

"A huge eagle perched high in a tree called down to us that it was keeping the meat from cooking. Eagles don't normally talk, so I knew there was magic involved. Thor took up his spear and threatened the bird. This was before Thor got his hammer.

"The eagle laughed and told us that if it was allowed to eat its fill of the meat first it would allow our fire to cook again. Thor and I agreed, knowing there was plenty of meat and that the eagle wouldn't be able to eat that much.

"The eagle glided down. It was so large that its head was level with mine. Picking the best pieces, it began to eat the raw meat. Thor wasn't happy about that. We watched as the eagle ate far more meat than a creature its size should be able to. I was sure magic was involved.

"With half the auroch gone, Thor raged. He did that a lot. He swung his spear like a staff, striking the bird on its breast. I assume he was just trying to drive it off or he would have used the tip.

"The shaft stuck to the eagle. Thor cried out that he was unable to let go of his spear. Whoever or whatever this eagle was, it had powerful magic. The eagle beat its wings and tried to take off. Hoenir and I grabbed Thor and tried to keep him on the ground, but the eagle was too strong and we had to let go or be borne aloft with him.

"I heard Thor threaten the eagle to let him go or he would kill him. The eagle laughed louder and flew Thor into tree-tops and against large boulders. After that, Hoenir and I could hear Thor begging for his life. Hoenir and I begged as well.

"The eagle said it would fly as high as it could and release Thor unless we did as it asked. It demanded that we deliver Idunn and her magic fruit to it. Reluctantly, Hoenir and I returned to Asgard without Thor.

"Hoenir feared Odin's wrath if he found out that we left

Thor in the clutches of the eagle. Paralyzed with indecision, he hid, leaving me to sort things out."

Her eyes widened and she nudged me to continue.

"I went to Idunn and tricked her into drinking ale that I had added a sleeping draught to. I took her and a basket of her fruit to the eagle. In exchange, the eagle dropped the unconscious Thor and then changed into its true form. The eagle was really Thjazi the jotunn. I knew him by reputation as a greedy, power-hungry jotnar wizard."

"What happened then, Low … Loki?"

"When I got Thor back to Asgard, he told a different version of events to Odin. In his telling, I struck the eagle with a stick and he and Hoenir tried to find me for days following the eagle's flight. He said that in a craven attempt to save my own life, I swore an oath to bring it Idunn and her fruit. With the coward Hoenir in hiding, there was nobody to contradict it.

"Odin, of course, believed his own son over me. I was ordered to bring Idunn back or be sentenced to death.

"Frigg was kind enough to lend me an enchanted feather cloak. I used it to fly to Thrymheim, Thjazi's home in Jotunheim. I snuck in and found Idunn. Frigg's feather cloak was strong enough to carry us both.

"Unfortunately, Thjazi discovered her missing and gave chase. In his guise as a giant eagle, he was faster than me. By the time I could see Asgard's walls, he was almost upon me.

"Heimdall had seen us approaching and told Odin. Just as Thjazi was about to snatch me from the air, Odin threw his spear and killed him. Hoenir never did admit to the true story. I think Thor threatened him. Idunn, of course, knew nothing except that I had indeed kidnapped her. It took her decades to forgive me."

Esme said, "That is a bit different than the story I read. Wasn't there something about a fire burning Thjazi?"

"I don't know where that came from. Probably some skald somewhere added it because it sounded more dramatic."

"Didn't the gods start to grow old without Idunn's apples?"

"Idunn's fruit aren't apples. Apples don't grow in Asgard, and they aren't native to Scandinavia either. It got changed later, probably to fit with the Christian idea of apples and Eden."

"But did the gods grow old without them?"

"If I hadn't gotten Idunn back, it would have happened eventually. Without Idunn, her orchard would die, but that would have taken years. And they aren't gods. They're just people."

"Can they do the things in the stories? Can Thor make lightning?"

"Unfortunately, yes," I said with a sour smile. "They may be people, but they're not human. They do have some specials gifts. Odin called them affinities."

"What's your affinity?"

"Odin says it's mischief. For many years I thought I didn't have one, but now I'm not so sure."

"You do find ways to get into trouble." Esme smiled.

We sat in silence for a while, sipping our mead.

"Thank you for rescuing me," Esme said.

"You're welcome. Besides, it was kind of my fault you were kidnapped."

"Don't remind me."

"So what are you going to do now? Do you want me to take you back to Midgard?"

"You mean Earth? No. I think I'll stay here for a while."

"Ullr is a cutie."

Esme punched me in the arm. Hard.

.

31

JOTNAR COUNSEL

I was just finishing my breakfast when Ymyd's adviser or seer or whatever she was, Solufn, knocked and entered my chambers.

"Ymyd is in the war room taking counsel from the clan chieftains. He would like us to join them."

"Then I suppose we should."

Hopefully the improvised glue I had used to stick the bottom of my over-sized bowl to the table would have a chance to dry before a servant tried to take it away.

Solufn led me through the over-sized halls of the castle to a heavy wooden door that must have been thirty feet high. She pushed it open and we entered a large chamber. Well, large for me. More modest for the six jotunn in it.

Ymyd sat on at high backed chair at the far end of the room. The legs and back posts were made of thick, round timbers a yard in diameter. Although it looked crude, Ymyd made it seem a throne, all two dozen feet of him draped in a fur cloak and lounging like he owned everything and everyone.

Five jotnar stood in a loose semi-circle in front of him, also draped in fur cloaks of varying colors and looking to be at least twenty feet tall, but none as tall as Ymyd. Surprisingly, one of them was a woman. Last I knew the idea of a female clan chief was unheard of. I suppose times change even in Jotunheim. Solufn waited by the door, so I did the same.

"The Stone Breakers can take care of themselves Ymyd," said a rather ugly jotunn with an undershot jaw.

"Gymir, the Stone Breakers are a mighty clan, but all of Jotunheim needs to face the einherjar," Ymyd said.

"Let the Stone Breakers hide in their caves," scoffed a heavily tattooed jotunn in mottled furs. "The Mountain Bear clan will take the field against Thor's rabble."

"How many warriors can you send, Midjung?" Ymyd asked.

"Two hundred and thirty."

"Loki, how many einherjar did you say Thor had in Valhalla?"

Obviously Ymyd had spotted me. All eyes spun to look for me. It took Gymir a little longer to think to look down. I strolled over to stand by Ymyd's seat.

"A hundred thousand, Lord Ymyd."

"A hundred and a thousand?" asked a clean-shaven jotunn with a giant nose ring. "That is far less than what they brought to Ragnarokkr."

"A thousand pardons," I said, bowing low. "I meant a hundred groups of a thousand each. Ten times what they brought to Ragnarokkr."

"Mother of Mountains!" the lone female chief said. The others shifted their feet uncomfortably.

"He speaks the truth, Skyr. This is not a time for the Stone Breakers or the Mountain Cloud clan or any of the clans to stand by themselves," Ymyd said, getting up from his crude throne. "We fight together, we live. We stand alone, we die."

Somehow I had envisioned myself making the grand speech to pull together the jotunn clans. Ymyd stole my thunder. Grudgingly, I had to admit he did a better job. Short and sweet. I'd have still been talking, probably putting them to sleep.

"The Ice Riders stand with Ymyd," said a heavyset jotunn in white furs. That was followed by a chorus of "ayes" even from Gymir, although grudgingly.

"So how many warriors do we have?" I asked.

"Aesir traitors don't question jotnar clan chiefs," Gymir growled.

"Not even ugly ones?" I asked innocently. A couple of the other chieftains chuckled, Ymyd loudest of all.

"I've fathered nine children with nine women," Gymir said with a glint in his eye.

"You must have disgusted each so much they refused to bear a second one and instead left you to find another."

Chuckles turned to guffaws. Ymyd outright laughed.

"The stories say Loki was a jotunn. You must have been the afterbirth from when your mother birthed a real jotunn."

Now the chuckles were at my expense. Even Manny laughed.

"Have you checked your children for udders? I heard your wives led cows into your bed rather than lay with you themselves."

Ymyd laughed at that one.

"And even the cows refused to do it more than once," I added.

Gymir was grinning and the others were laughing. "Those cows were so satisfied that they made nine times as much milk as normal for years."

The heavyset jotunn chief clapped Gymir on the back as he laughed. They were all laughing.

"You have the wit of Loki," Gymir said. "But wit won't win a battle. Do you have his magic?"

"A thousand years ago in these very halls I raced against Fire to see who could eat the most."

"That is a tale that grew well beyond the truth," Ymyd said.

"True," I conceded. "But I challenge Gymir to a drinking contest. Find the largest mugs you can. I'll drain mine faster than you."

"Done!" Gymir said.

"And if I do, you'll concede that I am indeed Loki, Lord of Mischief and entitled to parlay with jotnar clan chiefs."

"And if you don't I get to strike you once with my club," Gymir said with an unfriendly smile.

A death sentence for sure.

"Done."

Ymyd called for servants to scour the castle for the largest mugs they could find. While we waited I had a quiet word with one of the servants, who hurried off with a huge grin. It took a while, but eventually they arrived with two similar wooden mugs, each about the size of a cask of wine, filled to the brim. It looked like too much for even Gymir to drink. Mine was put on the floor, while Gymir's was on a table.

"On my command," Ymyd said. "Drink!"

I took a dainty sip of mine, putting my head down into the gaping mouth of the mug to reach the ale. Gymir picked his up and took a giant swig. He promptly put his mug down and spit out the amber fluid.

"That tastes like piss!" he roared.

"It does?" I asked innocently. "How did that happen? Mine tastes like Ymyd's finest ale."

"You cheating bastard!"

"We never specified what we had to drink. Just that it had to be in these mugs. So drink up Gymir. It took the horses a while to fill your mug."

He gave me an evil look and reluctantly hefted his mug again. I took another dainty sip."

"No half-breed jotunn is going to best me," he muttered.

"Gotta respect anyone willing to drink what's in that mug," I said cheerfully. "Tell you what. Because I admire your fortitude, I won't make you lick up what you spit out on the floor."

Gymir slammed down his mug, his face pale and sweaty. He looked like he was going to vomit. I looked him in the eye and took another dainty sip. He picked his mug up again. Obviously he wasn't going to let me win this way even if it made him violently ill.

I chanted a shape shifting spell and felt myself grow significantly larger. I heard my clothes ripping as I burst all the seams. I'd deal with that later.

"What kind of a boar is that?" Midjung asked. I'm sure none of them had ever seen a hippopotamus before.

Opening my huge mouth wide, I carefully picked up the entire mug. Tipping my head back I let the gallons of ale flow down my gullet. I bit down hard on the mug and felt it splinter in my mouth. I chewed while watching Gymir gape at me, his over-sized mug forgotten in his hand.

I really wanted to swallow the shattered mug, but there was no sense in risking what that would do to me. So I spit out the pieces and returned to my true self. I snagged a scrap of clothing from the floor to cover myself. The female clan chief looked at me with amusement.

"If you aren't Loki, you're as good as," Gymir said. He then promptly puked.

Ymyd had a servant get me some properly sized clothing,

and a stepbox to stand on. Other servants cleaned up Gymir's mess, although the stink still hung in the air.

"How many warriors do we have, Ymyd?" I asked, pulling a tunic over my head.

"Many of these clan chiefs speak for multiple clans. Not all could get here quickly. All told, maybe a couple of thousand."

"That's less than what fought at Ragnarokkr."

"The high peaks clans aren't here," Midjung said.

"Why not?"

"They are loyal to Thrasir," Ymyd replied. "He means to challenge me for the throne."

"So he's willing to let Thor's horde kill everyone?"

"He sees it like I did," Gymir said. "It's Ymyd's problem, not his. Let Thor and Ymyd fight it out and then he can come in and clean up after."

"Except that splits the jotnar, making it easy for Thor to beat both."

"I see that now, but he doesn't. He may even be willing to pay tribute if it means he gets the throne in Utgard."

"The only problem is that Thor isn't interested is conquering Jotunheim. He wants to wipe out the jotnar. There won't be any prisoners or peace treaty. He'll hunt down every man, woman, and child in Jotunheim and put them to the sword."

"I think you need to go to Thrasir, Loki," Ymyd said. "Persuade him. He's not going to listen to me."

"I'll go with him," Gymir said. I looked at him, surprised.

"Thrasir knows I'm not Ymyd's lackey. Together we might do what you can't do alone."

"A wise strategy," Solufn said. She had been so quiet I almost forgot she was there.

"I may be ugly, but I ain't stupid," Gymir said. His ugly face was split in a huge grin. Ymyd chuckled.

"Is this a private party, or can anyone join?"

I spun to see Brynhildr in the doorway. Behind her were eight more Valkyries. I rushed forward and hugged her armor clad body. She stood like a statue in my arms.

"I wasn't sure you would be able to persuade the others," I said.

"My host is loyal to me," she said, extricating herself from my embrace. "But I did give them leave to choose another to follow. None did."

"Any fresh news from Asgard?"

"None that will be welcome. Dvergar smiths have arrived. They are outfitting einherjar. I also saw a group of them bring several large wagons full of strange machinery."

"Any idea what it might be?"

"None. But it means that they intend to move soon. You don't have long to prepare."

"Welcome, Brynhildr," Ymyd said, interrupting. "Lord Loki is selfishly keeping you to himself."

"Lord Ymyd," Brynhildr said, warily.

"You and your host are welcome here. We will find you a place to rest. Food and drink is yours for the asking."

"You are a most gracious host."

"It's the least I can do for anyone willing to fight to save my people."

"And with that, I think Brynhildr and her host would like to freshen up," I said, pushing them out of the council chamber. Somehow I knew she was about to tell Ymyd and his clan chiefs that she held no love for jotnar or Jotunheim. Tact has never been her strong suit.

32

THRASIR

Gymir, Manny, and I set out the next day. Thrasir's hold was north in the mountains. I rode while Gymir walked, which is the only way I could keep up with his long strides.

There are those rare people that bond with you if you best them. Gymir was one of them. Having beaten him in a battle of wits, and then again in a drinking contest, he decided I was his lifelong friend. We traded friendly barbs and insults for the three days it took to get to the high peaks territory.

Thrasir's clans lived above the snow line deep in Jotunheim's soaring mountains. They considered themselves a breed apart from the larger jotnar population that lived in the greener valleys. The mountain clans saw them as softer, and having turned their backs on the old ways. At least that's how Gymir told it. We broke out the heavy furs when the cold started to bite.

We made no effort to hide ourselves, so it was no great surprise when we saw three jotnar waiting for us in a small pass. They were smaller than I expected, maybe only twice

271

my height, standing in snow knee deep to me but only half that to them. Bundled in thick furs that left only eye slits open, I couldn't see their features. Two carried heavy spears, and the third a club.

"Gymir," shouted one of them. "You are known to us. Who is your companion?"

"This is Lord Loki of Asgard. We've come to meet with Thrasir."

"We expected Ymyd to send a lackey, but not an aesir traitor."

"I am no traitor," I shouted. "I fought with Jotunheim against the aesir at Ragnarokkr."

"You betrayed your own kind, the aesir."

Gymir wisely ignored the lackey barb.

"My father was Farbauti, clan chief of the Vedrfell clan."

"Aye, and your mother was a half-breed bitch," the jotunn said. "Your father was so disgusted with you he traded you to the aesir to be rid of you."

"If you think to provoke me by insulting my family, you are a fool. Why, Gymir himself called me far worse and we never came to blows."

"Aye," Gymir said with a crooked grin.

Manny said nothing. Sometimes he's smart that way.

We stared at each other for a moment, then they turned and walked through the pass. We followed. I was a hero to much of Jotunheim, but not here apparently. This may have been a mistake.

The pass opened into a long, shallow valley filled with hundreds of caribou. A few jotnar were scattered around the herd, shepherding them. Over-sized log buildings stretched behind the herd. Dwarfing all of this was the carved face of the mountain.

Dozens of windows and balconies dotted the surface, each sized for jotnar occupants. Taken together, they formed a majestic jotunn face, like one of those pictures made from hundreds of different credit cards. It was an inspiring bit of artistic architecture.

"Thrasir's mountain palace," Gymir whispered.

"You should be honored," Manny cawed, tapping me on the head. "Few aesir have ever seen it."

We followed the jotnar greeting committee around the periphery of the herd. Massive stone doors became evident that had blended into the rock face from a distance. Still not saying anything, the trio pushed them opened and entered. We followed.

Every surface was carved and shaped stone. Even the floor was swirls of a snowstorm etched into the rock. The images varied from scenes of what I assumed were jotnar history to abstract shapes and patterns and everything in between. There was no logic or order to the flow that I could see.

Our guides opened a set of large timber doors that looked like all the other doors we'd passed. Standing aside, they ushered us in.

A large jotunn almost as tall as Ymyd stood on the balcony at the far end, facing away from us. His hands were clasped behind his back, feet shoulder width apart. The classic male dominance pose. I already didn't like him.

"Leave us," he said. Our honor guard left, closing the door behind them.

Turning to face us was a rough, serious visaged man with a heavily braided beard. He wore the same furs as the other jotnar we'd seen, although maybe a little better quality. It was freezing in this room with that wide open balcony.

"Lord Thrasir," Gymir said, stepping forward with an open hand.

"Gymir. It's been too long," Thrasir said, clasping his hand.

"I'm here with Lord Loki and Lord Muninn."

"Aesir royalty?" Thrasir raised an eyebrow.

"Hardly," I said.

"He meant me," Manny cawed.

"You prefer half-breed renegade?" Thrasir asked, ignoring my insolent crow.

"Aesir royalty it is," I said with a smile and a bow.

"So what brings the mighty Gymir and a half-breed aesir renegade to my home?"

Now I was sure I didn't like him. Manny laughed. All three of us flinched at the creepy sound.

"You know why we're here," I said, cutting in before Gymir could talk.

"Aye, I do."

"So, have you already decided not to join Ymyd in defending Jotunheim, or did you just want a personal invitation?"

I was betting on the personal invitation. That would be the dick move. Gymir was staring daggers at me.

"Ymyd is quite capable of fending off the aesir. He doesn't need my help."

"You mean, let Ymyd soften them up and then you can swoop in and save the day. Oh, and depose Ymyd at the same time."

"I had heard that Loki was a silver-tongued fox," Thrasir said coldly. "Gymir, are you sure this is he?"

"As sure as I love good ale."

I looked Thrasir in the eye and said, "I heard that Lord Thrasir is a straight talking jotunn who values honesty and candor over courtly manners and false praise."

"That is the jotnar way."

"Well, I'm tired of having to prove to everyone that I'm really Loki and that they should actually listen to me. If you want someone to fawn all over you and beg for your help, Gymir here is your man. But I'm going to tell it like it is."

Thrasir burst out laughing. Gymir stared at me, his mouth gaping open. I didn't think he could look any uglier, but that expression raised the bar a few notches.

"So, Gymir," Thrasir said, still chuckling but slowly regaining his composure, "they sent you to ply me with honeyed words?"

"By Odin's ass crack, no," Gymir said with a growl. "I'm here so that you don't throw this scrawny excuse for a jotnar half-breed off that balcony. Although I'm mighty tempted to do it myself right now."

"So tell me, Loki," Thrasir asked. "Why should I throw my lot in with Ymyd?"

"Have you ever heard the phrase 'divide and conquer?'"

"Aye. Wolves will split the herd to make it easier to take down the weak."

"Right now the aesir are the wolves and the jotnar are the herd. They will crush Ymyd and come for you next. But if you join Ymyd, you can defeat them."

"The jotnar are not caribou. If the aesir are wolves, we are bears."

"Let's not get lost in my metaphor. Or was that a simile? I can never keep those two straight."

"What?"

"Nevermind."

"You said it yourself," Thrasir said. "If Ymyd is too weak to defeat the aesir, he deserves to fall."

"And then you can step in and clean up what is left. Or maybe negotiate a peace with the aesir. Either way, you would claim the throne of Jotunheim."

"I would never plot against another clan chief," Thrasir said indignantly. Not that I believed him.

"Yeah. Right," I said, not bothering to hide my disdain.

"The only problem with your plan is that the aesir are bringing an army so large it will overrun Ymyd and then you."

"You are just a frightened little man, desperate to save his friend," Thrasir said, also not bothering to hide his disdain. "Your jotnar blood runs weak. Ymyd's runs weak. He has forgotten what it means to be jotnar. To embrace the mountains and the snow."

And there it is. Still a dick. But we needed him. So I swallowed my pride.

"If I can persuade you that the threat is real, will you join Ymyd against the aesir?"

"You cannot persuade me, but you are welcome to try."

"Manny, can you draw out my memories and give them to Thrasir?"

"Yes," he said. "Assuming Lord Thrasir is willing to accept them."

"Is this some sort of trick? The God of Mischief's pranks are well known."

"No, it's not a trick. And I'm not a god."

"I'll vouch for him," Gymir said.

"I will guarantee your safety," Manny cawed. "And the truth of his memories."

"Very well," Thrasir said reluctantly. "Do your magic."

"Manny, give him my memories of Thor and Valhalla."

"Very well." Then his beak touched my head.

I was back in Valhalla, bound and on my knees before Thor. The whole scene played out like a dream. Thor threatening me. Thor threatening to kill every jotunn in Jotunheim. Thor showing me the horde of einherjar. Then I was back with Gymir and Thrasir.

"Gods," I muttered, falling to my knees. It hadn't been any better the second time around.

Manny flapped up to Thrasir's shoulder. He peered

around his over-sized head. Thrasir nodded and Manny touched his beak to Thrasir's temple. Several long minutes went by. I began to wonder if Thrasir was reliving it in real time. Finally, Manny flapped away to perch on the back of a chair.

"By ice and sky." Thrasir's voice sounded raw. "He's mad! He truly means to kill us all. And his horde. So many!"

"Lord Loki spoke the truth," Gymir said.

Thrasir moved to the balcony looking out over the herd of caribou. He stood there a long while, leaning on the balustrade.

"Tell Ymyd I will bring every warrior from every clan loyal to me. I will join with him. Together we will save Jotunheim."

Ymyd summoned me to his council hall. The usual suspects were gathered there. Gymir gave me a curt nod.

"It's been nine days since you returned," Ymyd said, looking at Gymir and myself.

"I know, I know," I said with a sigh. "Thrasir hasn't shown."

"My lord," Solufn said. "I warned you he was not to be trusted."

"When we left him, I would have sworn he was persuaded."

"He may have been, Loki," Ymyd said. "But it doesn't matter. He isn't here."

In the distance we heard a horn sound. And then another, and another.

"The aesir!" Gymir said. I felt a chill down my spine. We so weren't ready.

Decorum was set aside as we all rushed out of the council chambers to the nearest balcony where we could see beyond the walls. Pushing and shoving got me nowhere in the forest of tree trunk-sized legs. But I managed to slip between them and peer between the struts of the balustrade.

A line of fur wrapped jotnar were filing into Utgard. Thrasir walked at the head of the column. It was hard to get a good count, but it looked like his numbers would add half again to our forces.

Thrasir spotted us above him. He stared down Ymyd. No nod, or salute or other greeting or acknowledgment. He was here strictly to defend Jotunheim and he meant Ymyd to know that.

33

SURTR AND IDUNN

A jotnar guard burst into my chambers, "Lord Loki, Ymyd is asking for you on the gate wall."

"What is it?"

"Something is happening. I couldn't see it, but Ymyd needs you."

"All right, all right, I'm coming."

People were rushing around in the halls chattering excitedly. By the time I made it to the courtyard the only thing I knew was that something strange was out there. I climbed the battlements where I found Brynhildr with Ymyd and his advisers. They were looking out over the wall, pointing and whispering. With the help of a crate that had been placed at the wall, I was just barely able to peek over the lowest part of the crenellation. A dvergar machine slowly rumbled toward the city walls.

"Sviarr!" I cried out. "I didn't expect him so soon."

I've never thought I'd be so happy to see that annoying, bloodthirsty dvergr again.

"What is a Sviarr?" Ymyd asked.

"He's a dvergar smith. That machine is Surtr. The new

and improved Surtr. If you look closely, you can see Sviarr inside it."

"That is the fabled Surtr?" Hrengr asked.

"It looks different from how it's described in the tales," Hrim said.

"The dvergar have been working on it for centuries. Like I said, new and improved."

I saw Esme and Ullr hurrying toward the gate as I made it back down to the courtyard.

I called out, "Surtr is here. Come on. Let's go see it."

A jotnar guard opened the sally port door set in the main gate. It was a big door for the three of us, but just wide enough for a modest sized jotunn to walk through. Ullr and Esme stopped in the doorway.

"What the fuck is that?" Esme asked.

"It's kind of hard to describe it exactly. Think of it as a huge tank that shoots fire. Or lasers maybe."

"That is Surtr?" Ullr asked. "It looks different."

"The dvergar have been tinkering with it for nine hundred years."

"In that case, I think I'll stay here," Ullr said. "You can go greet him."

"Suit yourself. Esme?"

"I'll stay here with Ullr," she said, clasping his hand.

Brynhildr pushed between them. "I'll come with you."

I wanted to say something snarky to Ullr about being a chicken, but I thought better of it. No point in getting on Esme's bad side.

The house-sized tank moved about as fast as I could walk. It was making a hell of a racket. Black smoke poured out of three different massive stovepipes. Centered on the front face above the massive barrel was a three panel glass enclosure. Sviarr was inside working some levers.

Surtr ground to a halt about fifty feet from us. The

rumble of the idling motor shook my bones. With a deafening cough, it stopped. Sviarr disappeared from the windows and moments later we heard metal clanging. Sviarr climbed out and stood proudly on top of it, his hands on his hips. Manny flew out from behind him and came to land on my shoulders.

"You owe me," he said.

"For what?"

"Sending me to fetch a that crazy dvergr."

"We all sacrifice for the greater good," I said piously.

Manny pecked my head. Brynhildr laughed.

"Ow!"

Truthfully it was rather gentle compared to when he's really upset.

"Sviarr," I called. "How did you get this monstrosity here so fast?"

"Speak kindly of my lovely Surtr," he said, tossing a rope ladder over the side and climbing down.

"Fine, how did you get this magnificent construction here so quickly?"

"I took the moon bridge."

"But the bridge won't manifest itself for another two weeks."

"The bridge doesn't stop existing when you can't see it. It's just out of phase. If you know how to find it, you can walk the underside during the new moon. Which is today."

"How do you walk the underside of a bridge?" Brynhildr asked. She was pacing and admiring Sviarr's siege engine of death.

"During the new moon the underside is on top."

"Why can't we see it?" I asked.

"You can't see the new moon in the sky unless you know where to look. I know where to look."

"So would I fall off during the other phases of the moon?"

"I don't think your quantum state could survive those phases."

"My what?" I asked. "You know what, nevermind. I probably wouldn't understand anyway."

"Also, now I can tell you where the bridge will touch down."

"That would be most useful, dvergr," Brynhildr said.

"It's maybe a league from these very walls. I hardly think that's a coincidence. Let me see to Surtr and some sustenance and I'll show you."

"I just had a thought, Sviarr," I said with a grin. "Why not use Surtr to burn the moon bridge itself? You said nothing can withstand it."

"Funny you should say that. Technically the moon bridge is made of nothing. It is substance as you know it turned sideways. Surtr can't harm it."

"I don't understand half of what you just said."

"Hardly surprising," he returned haughtily. "Although now that you mention it, with some changes... nevermind. It would take years to adjust the polarity of the beam to do it."

I just shook my head and turned to walk away.

"Hold up, Loki. I thought you might want this." Sviarr climbed back up into Sutr and dragged my lock box out. He dumped it unceremoniously over the side. It hit the dirt with thud. He climbed back down.

"Any progress?"

"I think you have to pick the second lock while singing to it."

"Singing?"

"Yes. Singing about how pretty it is and how much you love it."

"You've got to be kidding."

He shrugged his shoulders.

Sviarr went off in search of food and drink. Ullr and

Esme headed back to the palace, hand in hand, talking quietly to each other. I hefted the lock box and lugged it to my chambers. It seemed heavier, but that just may have been my imagination. Later that night I'm sure some of the palace residents heard singing coming from my chambers.

Thousands of jotnar had decided to seek the safety of Utgard's walls. Many were too young, or too old, or too infirm to fight, but the rest swelled Ymyd's army and the capacity of the city to handle them. Thrasir's ten thousand were garrisoned outside the walls. Ymyd had slightly more warriors inside them.

The worst part of war is the waiting. Two weeks with nothing to do but ponder impending doom wears on a person. Or a jotunn. Thrasir's jotnar were getting into more frequent scraps with Ymyd's. The two leaders were too busy planning Utgard's defenses to involve themselves in these petty squabbles. Hrim and I organized some arena competitions and stage shows, which seemed to help. Ymyd and Thrasir even showed up to one.

I was in my chambers when the jotunn guardian outside my door announced a visitor.

"Idunn! What are you doing here?" I asked.

Idunn looked the same as always. White gown, straight blonde hair, and those wrong-colored eyes. She carried what looked for all the world like a classic picnic basket.

"It seems everyone must choose sides these days."

"But you hate war. You don't even like people arguing around you."

"It's a senseless activity, but sometimes it's inevitable."

"Did Thor or Sif threaten you? Is that why you fled Asgard?" I asked.

"No, no. Nothing like that. I left of my own choice."

"You hardly ever leave your garden."

"I'm sure you remember the last time I left it."

I had the good grace to be embarrassed.

"I remember apologizing for years."

"Did you? I don't recall."

Idunn never forgot anything that I was aware of.

"You said you left on your own. Why?"

"I came to give you something," she said, rummaging around in the small basket she carried. "Here."

She handed me a strange looking fruit. It resembled a Midgard star fruit, but fuzzy like a kiwi. Its deep gray color did not make it look very appealing.

"Uh, what is it? I mean it looks like a fruit of some sort, but why do you want me to have it?"

"It's taken me a rather long time to grow that, so don't lose it. It's the only one of its kind."

"Okay, but you didn't answer my question."

"When you see Thor on the battlefield, eat it."

"What will it do?"

"What needs to be done. That's all you need to know for now. Just trust me."

"It's not going to poison me, is it?" It looked like it would poison me. That would be one way to stop the war between Thor and me. But I've never known Idunn to deal in poisons. I'd never seen her so much as kill an insect.

"No, no." she laughed. It had a strange echo built into it. "Far from it."

"You're really not going to tell me, are you?"

Idunn shook her head.

I sighed and wrapped the ugly fruit in a cloth and stuffed it in a pocket. I'd decide later what to do with it.

"I also brought some of my other fruit," she said, revealing a handful of her 'apples' from her orchard.

"You should give some to Ullr and Brynhildr. I'm still well-stocked."

As she turned to go, a thought occurred to me.

"Idunn, what would happen if someone from Midgard ate one of those?"

She looked at me curiously. Her violet eyes narrowed as she contemplated the question.

"Should we let your Esme have a taste and find out?"

"No! No. That's okay. I'm not going to let her be a guinea pig."

"A ginny pig?"

"It's an animal that Midgard people use to test new foods and medicines. If it's dangerous, only the guinea pig suffers and not a person."

"That's horrible," she said, her face withdrawn in shock.

"I suppose. But if you don't know what will happen if Esme eats one of your fruit, I'm not going to risk having her try it."

"Ah. I see."

She turned and left. I realized a minute later that she had never actually said she didn't know what would happen. Idunn would never risk a person's life, no matter where in the Nine Worlds they had been born. And I was supposed to be the tricky one.

34

THE MOON BRIDGE

The day had finally come. Tonight would be a full moon and the moon bridge would manifest itself. The tension in Utgard was as thick as congealed honey. Jotnar warriors stood nervously on the walls, shifting their spears from hand to hand. Every now and then one of them would shrink and then grow nervously.

I paced on top of the gatehouse above the main gate to the city as far from the front as I could get. I'm not good with waiting. No patience. I just want to do something or have something happen, anything. Despite being surrounded by warriors, and with Manny perched on my shoulder, I felt alone. I suspect they all did too.

Surtr was set up outside the walls, far to one side of the gate. Sviarr puttered with the massive war machine, making last minute tweaks I assumed. He seemed the least affected by the wait.

Ymyd and I lounged casually near him, the king's eyes never leaving the open fields beyond the gate. His family watched from one of the palace balconies. I spotted Ylva among them. She caught my eye and waved. She had spent a few more nights with me that I actually got to remember. I smiled to myself, hoping those memories wouldn't be the last.

"I hate waiting," I muttered.

"Patience is a virtue," Ymyd said.

"I've been told I'm short on virtue."

"Embrace your jotnar side. Long winters have taught my people patience. It's there inside you somewhere."

"Be the stone," Manny cawed.

"That's right," Ymyd said, surprised. "Oft repeated advice to jotnar children is to be the stone. It has many meanings. Be unyeilding. Be enduring. Be unnoticed. Be still and quiet."

"I'm sure jotnar mothers mostly want peace and quiet."

"Be the stone," Manny cawed pointedly.

"I hate waiting," I muttered.

The moon finally crested the horizon. Full and round it pushed up over the rim of the earth like an overripe melon. Jotnar warriors lit torches mounted on the walls, which flickered in the breeze. Only the occasional creak of leather or shuffle of feet broke the silence. The crowing of a rooster shattered the quiet. Fjalar, harbinger of Ragnarokkr, was sounding the start of the latest end of the world. The last time, I had not been in Jotunheim to hear it. Instead I heard Gullinkambi crow his warning from atop Valhalla. How either of those birds knew what was about to happen was beyond me. Manny screeched in response, almost as if he was joining in.

"Really?" I hissed at him.

He gave me a haughty stare and cawed, "Omens must be acknowledged."

We all watched as the moon bridge shimmered into

being. Thin and narrow in the center of the moon, its shallow arch touched down to earth, a hundred feet wide and pale as its namesake. It was exactly where Sviarr had predicted. I pulled out my binoculars and looked for Ullr on the hilltop a couple hundred yards to the side of the moon bridge. He crouched there, still and silent with the patience of the perfect hunter.

I had offered Ullr a pair of binoculars for himself. He'd looked through them, then squinted into the distance. Shrugging his shoulders, he'd handed them back. "They don't make much of a difference," he'd said. Shaking my head, I took them back.

I returned my attention to the moon bridge and waited. It began as a faint crowd noise. A thousand voices roaring out battle cries in the distance. The first few einherjar came into sight, charging down the moon bridge. They raced toward the city walls, screaming their wordless rage. The trickle became a stream. As the first reached the walls, they began to hack futilely at the enormous gates. The jotnar warriors on the walls stood their ground, not reacting. A spear flung from below struck a jotunn in the arm and he fell back cursing.

The einherjar were a motley crew. There were warriors from all over Midgard, from all points in the last millennium of history savagely screaming out their bloodlust. Mongols, Tutsis, Aztecs, Crusaders, Souix, and a hundred other cultures mingled on the battlefield. Each wearing ragtag armor and armed with spears, swords, axes and the like. It was a mob, not an army. All it lacked were the torches and pitchforks.

The word einherjar means "those who fight alone" or "one-man army." Each was alone on that battlefield, surrounded by thousands of other warriors equally alone in their own berserker fury. They were a primal force, meant to be released upon jotnar invaders, not commanded or led by anyone.

The stream of warriors widened, filling the full width of the bridge. I looked for Ullr in the binoculars again. He rose swiftly, bending his bow Einngr almost to breaking. The flaming arrow shot high and fast, almost extinguished itself. Arcing above the horde, it fell to ground just to the left of the bridge. Only Ullr could have hit those hay bales at that distance. The bales burst into flames, having been soaking in oil earlier in the day. The einherjar ignored them as I had hoped they would.

Thousands of howling warriors raced across the open ground toward the city. In no time they were at the wall, beating mindless on the stone. Those on the gates fared only slightly better against the massive wooden doors.

"Now," I shouted.

Ymyd sounded his battle cry and vats of boiling oil were dumped over the battlements. Where we had run out of oil, we used boiling water and honey. There were even a couple of cauldrons of heated pitch. The screams were horrific. Soon after the smells made you forget the sounds. The only saving grace was not being able to see the bodies well in the moonlight.

War has never been glorious or honorable. Odin had convinced the Vikings that death in combat was the most noble way to go. As far as I could tell, dying in battle was almost always painful, lonely, and useless.

Hundreds of einherjar died, boiled and burned at the base of the wall. A thousand more charged forward heedlessly to take their place. In the distance I could see that the fire from the bales had ignited the straw mats laid down in front of the moon bridge. My stomach turned as I saw einherjar charge thoughtless through it. I was shocked at how many of them came out the other side ablaze.

Brynhildr had arrived. Seven with spears and two with swords, they charged into the einherjar engaging the beleaguered jotnar flank.

"Yes!" I shouted to no one in particular.

Looking around I realized I was alone. Ymyd was gone, as was Manny. The walls were sparsely manned. Half the torches had gone out. I had been so intent on the battlefield I had missed something happening right next to me. I looked around frantically before spotting Ymyd and a hundred or so jotnar warriors running along the outskirts of the battle. He was heading right to where the three aesir were decimating the jotnar ranks.

Ullr. Where had he gotten to?

I scanned the towers, figuring he would go for higher ground. Sure enough, he was perched on one of the curtain towers. He was sighting down the barrel of the sniper rifle. I knew he would pick his targets carefully. I hadn't brought enough rounds for all the einherjar.

Watching the battle made me think of my sons. Fenrir and Jormungandr had wreaked havoc among the einherjar more than nine hundred years ago. Yet I would have surrendered myself to Thor and be bound to my rocks in a heartbeat to have them back again. Five hundred years past these thoughts would have had me tearing up. Now I just felt a familiar ache and emptiness in my heart.

I shoved away those morose memories and put my eyes to the binoculars again. I felt like I was forgetting something, but I couldn't put my finger on it. Setting aside that nagging feeling, I scanned for the Valkyries. They had driven back the einherjar enough to give the jotnar on that side some room. A few dozen of them surrounded Skirnir and Thor, pressing them hard. A brilliant bolt from the sky struck one of those warriors. He collapsed and fell over dead. A moment later the crack of thunder arrived.

Thor's mouth foamed as he roared silently, rain-slicked hair plastered to his face. He struck the giant axe from the hands of a nearby jotunn.

Skirnir had released Danzleikr and it was fighting on its own, a bright flame in the darkness. "Gods damned dvergar smiths," I said under my breath.

"Swords have two edges," Manny said, making me jump. "Would you give up Surtr to relieve Skirnir of Danzleikr? The dvergar work for whomever pays them."

"Shut up," I said. Not one of my best retorts.

Skirnir fought with an axe in one hand. His other pointed and slashed the air, directing the enchanted sword like an orchestra conductor. Gullinbursti, wet and glistening in the moonlight, darted between jotnar warriors, goring and tearing at anything he could reach.

Ymyd's reinforcements arrived at that moment, pushing back the aesir. Ymyd himself was scanning the battlefield, searching for something. I saw him charge toward a group of einherjar that had cut off a small group of jotnar warriors. Then I saw Meili, or rather a great brown bear, on its back feet, clawing at one of them.

Ymyd's axe hurled einherjar left and right as he drove toward Meili.

The Valkyries wheeled about in the sky, looking for easy targets. If a jotunn got separated from his group, the flight of nine descended on him in unison. Spears and swords made short work of such stragglers.

There was too much to watch. Too many places to focus. The battlefield had devolved into chaos with knots of jotnar surrounded by einherjar who died in droves beneath their axes and clubs.

Occasionally a giant warrior would stumble or fall and be dragged down by the masses. Then Surtr's sword would cut through the battle, incinerating everything it touched.

Lightning struck perilously close to the city walls. With a start I realized Surtr was hit. The thunder was still echoing when it was struck again, and again. Sviarr had drawn Thor's attention. The giant machine ceased it's grumbling and smoking.

"I bet that pissed off Sviarr something fierce," I said, grimly.

"Assuming he still lives," Manny cawed. I hadn't thought about that.

I found Skirnir again in the binoculars. Gullinbursti had cleared a small clear space around him. Danzliekr danced to and fro, jabbing and slicing at any jotunn foolish enough to get to close. Then one of Gullinbursti's eyes shattered.

Ullr's aim.

The metal hog reared and shook its head. Skirnir faltered for a moment and the jotnar surged forward. Two of them fell quickly to the dancing sword before the rest pressed him hard.

Unfortunately, Thor was faring better. He had left a swath of giant dead bodies behind him as he mowed down jotunn after jotunn. I couldn't count on Ullr to help with him. Thor was my problem, but I wasn't ready to face him just yet. There was something else too. What in the Nine Worlds was it?

Shaking my head, I found Ymyd before I found Meili. The two had come face to face in a small cleared space. The maddened bear paced from side to side. Ymyd waved off any jotunn who tried to engage him. He casually swatted any einherjar foolish enough to get close. I could see his mouth moving. His face was pleading with his adopted son.

Meili reared and charged Ymyd, who stood his ground. The bear swiped at the jotunn king, leaving a nasty four striped gash in his side before continuing on. Meili ran toward the edge of the battlefield, only engaging those who got in his way. Then he was past them and lumbering away.

Ymyd sank to one knee.

The einherjar saw their opening and swarmed him, clambering on his back and trying to push or pull him to the ground. With a silent roar he stood, shaking off the men clinging to him. He slammed his hands together and a dozen nearby einherjar were flung away. A moment later I heard a thunderclap. Apparently Ymyd also had neat tricks.

The jotnar king seemed to enter his own berserk rage. He charged recklessly into the einherjar, swinging his axe back and forth. Einherjar went flying in all directions, frequently cut in pieces. The jotnar he had brought to the battlefield moved to fill in behind him. Forming a wedge, they pushed toward the center of the einherjar mob.

I tore my gaze from Ymyd's suicidal charge and sought out Skirnir again. Gullinbursti was down. Both eyes were shattered. It looked like at least one knee was too. Skirnir stood with his back to the great golden beast. As I watched, his sword swung at an empty space, then jerked backward like it had been hit.

"What in the Nine Worlds—"

"The sword is deflecting Ullr's shots," Manny cawed.

"How do you know that?"

"I'm more observant than you," he said.

"Show off."

Looking back at Skirnir, I could see now that he was watching Ullr's tower intently. I watched Skirnir deflect three more bullets. I didn't know Danzleikr could do something like that.

It was time for me to do something. I had been holding back, hoarding my strength for when it would inevitably be needed. This was as good a time as any.

I had never cast a spell through binoculars before, but

there is a first time for everything, as the saying goes. I chanted a rhyme, focusing my intent, and a dense fog formed around Skirnir. Immediately I saw the dancing sword jerk as it deflected another bullet. Then the cloud swirled where a shot passed through it unblocked. Skirnir's body jerked and he crumbled. The cloud dissipated as I let it go. Half of Skirnir's head was gone.

Some people need to exact vengeance themselves. I'm not one of them. So long as it happens, that's enough for me. I had made good on my promise to Huld. I didn't need to be the one who pulled the trigger. Two down and just Thor to go.

That was it! I was forgetting Sif and Frigg.

I quickly panned back to the moon bridge. My head pounded with pain. My eyes slid right and left and refused to focus on the bridge. I muttered a spell and the pain receded. I could clearly see them now. Damn Frigg and her spells. Through the binoculars I saw her lips moving.

The two women were still on their mounts at the foot of the bridge, five aesir spread out behind them. I recognized Vali, Syn, Modi, and Magni, but not the last one. Vali is one of Odin's many bastard sons, and a right bastard of a man as well. Odin had a thing for jotnar women. Modi and Magni are Thor's sons with another jotnar woman, and famous for their raw strength. Like father like son I guess. Syn was a surprise. She wasn't at Ragnarokkr despite being skilled at arms.

Magni stood as tall as his father Thor, and brawnier. He reminded me of Thor in his prime. Modi stood taller but less heavily muscled. His leather armor was covered in steel studs. His long, unbound, red hair whipped about in the wind. He wore heavy furs instead of, or maybe over, armor. Where Magni and Modi sported thick beards, Vali was clean shaven and kept his pale hair in thick braids. Syn wore

Valkyrie armor and carried a spear and shield, her long
blonde hair braided for battle.

Behind those five were rows of mounted Valkyries.
Apparently not all the Valkyries wanted to participate in
today's festivities. Three flights had stayed behind. After
them, rank after rank of human warriors. An endless column
fading into the distance on the moon bridge. They were
armed and armored as haphazardly as the einherjar, but
appeared more disciplined. They shifted and wavered but
kept their loose ranks.

"Folkvangr," I said with dismay. "The army of the field."

"They've been gathering for a while," Manny cawed.

"Why in the names of the gods didn't you say something?"

"It's not my place to affect strategy."

I wanted to take a swing at him. I really did. But this
wasn't the first time I was reminded that Muninn was more
frequently an observer than a participant.

Folkvangr is Frigg's counterpart to Valhalla. In the old
days, before Ragnarokkr, the spirits of the dead were
picked over by Odin and Frigg. Odin took the heroes who
died in battle, which he defined as the most bloodthirsty.
Frigg took those who died a noble death, either on or off
the field of battle to live in the fields of Folkvangr. Hel got
the rest.

Hel. She still stood on that hill, watching. What in the
gods' names did she want? She had stayed out of the first
Ragnarokkr, preferring to accept the dead in her halls rather
than on the plains of Vigridr.

Baldr had told me that for every spirit that Odin claimed,
Frigg claimed one as well. However, unlike Odin, Frigg
accepted men and women. Valhalla and Folkvangr should
always have exactly the same number of dead. However,
Baldr also said that each of them constantly tried to cheat by
secretly claiming dead without telling the other.

If Frigg had another hundred thousand warriors ready to take the field, we were in serious trouble.

Ymyd and Thrasir's forces were winning on the battlefield, but were taking heavy losses. And Thor was still active, which could yet tip the scales. What in the Nine Worlds was Sif waiting for? Why not send her forces onto the field now?

Not feeling like I could trust Manny, I quickly stripped while focusing on the shape of a gyrfalcon. As soon as my transformation completed, I launched into the air, fighting the rain gusts. There is a joy to flying, especially as a bird of prey. I suppressed the urge to climb higher and sought out Ymyd. With the gyrfalcon's keen vision, I spotted his wedge of jotnar deep inside the ever dwindling mob of einhejar. A fair number of his guard had fallen. Ymyd himself looked near exhaustion, sustained only by his fading berserker rage.

The dive into their midst was exhilarating. I had to pull up short so I could land safely among the jotnar combatants. I changed back to myself, standing naked and proud in their midst. When you arrive somewhere naked, you might as well do it proudly. The nearest jotnar warrior almost took my head off, only pulling his swing at the last second.

"You need to pull back into the city," I shouted, pointing toward the walls.

"We follow Ymyd, not you," the jotunn said, kicking at an einherjar and sending him flying.

"If you value your lord's life, you'll find a way to get him back to Utgard, and soon."

I didn't wait to hear his response. Either they could get Ymyd to listen to reason or they couldn't. Returning to gyrfalcon shape I took a quick turn over the battlefield to assess the situation. I might as well take advantage of the aerial view.

The jotnar forces had decimated the einherjar, thanks in no small part to Surtr. The tight knot of them that remained was far smaller than I had realized. Yet Sif and Frigg still held their army at bay.

Thor was driving through his own einherjar toward Ymyd. I hoped the jotnar king could be turned around quickly.

Thrasir was nowhere to be seen.

Surtr stood silent. Gods knew whether Sviarr survived inside it or had fled.

Wheeling, I headed back to Utgard. Ullr waved to me. He had packed up the sniper rifle, which I took to mean he was out of ammo. I landed on a tower of the inner wall where a pair of jotunn stood waiting.

"Blow the retreat," I said as soon as I changed.

One of them looked me over in my altogether. The other fumbled with the large horn at his belt.

"Blow the retreat," I shouted.

The distracted jotunn jumped and grabbed his horn too. Together they blew a long, loud note. They kept blowing it over and over. I looked back at the field. Jotnar warriors on the battlefield looked around in confusion. They were winning. Why was the retreat being sounded? But the horn was insistent and eventually they began an orderly retreat.

36

FRIGG'S VISIT

G et down there and open the front gates," I shouted.
"The einherjar will get in," the jotnar captain
said.

"If you don't, your fellow warriors out there will be trapped. Open the gates!"

"Yes, milord Loki."

"Oh, and send out a few to push Surtr inside too."

I looked over the wall at the giant machine, briefly illuminated by a lightning strike.

"On second thought, send more than a few. That thing is heavy."

Not long after, the gates began to grind open. The jotnar in the field formed up loose ranks in front of it. The einherjar continued their relentless, mindless assault. I was shocked to see three warriors carrying the unconscious body of Ymyd. Hopefully he wasn't hurt too badly. A group of seven or eight jotnar jogged along the wall to where Surtr sat motionless. Fortunately the einherjar largely ignored them.

Then I saw Thor striding through the ranks of the einherjar toward the gates and the defensive line of jotnar warriors. He stood a full head taller than any of them. Long red hair was plastered to his head. His bedraggled beard made him look like a madman. He would reach the defenders long before Surtr or the retreating warriors could get inside.

Still naked from my previous shift, I turned into an eagle. I beat my wings hard to gain height, then I dive-bombed the god of the storm, ripping out some of his graying red hair in my talons. He turned and swung Mjolnir at me, just missing my tail feathers. I landed a good hundred yards from him and returned to my natural self. Enraged, Thor charged at me through the einherjar, knocking the slow ones out of the way.

"Come and get me you argr lover!" I shouted, waggling my naked hips at him.

In a foot race I had always been faster than Thor. Despite his longer stride he was more of a lumberer. I led him on a merry chase behind the einherjar mob. The trickiest part was not stumbling over the nearly endless corpses, both human and jotunn. Lightning struck all around me as I zigged and zagged.

When I finally saw the gates close behind Surtr and the retreating jotnar defenders, I turned back into an eagle and flew off to the city. I was nearly there when I was struck by lightning. That was the last thing I remembered.

I woke on the fields of Vigridr where more than nine hundred years ago I fought the aesir at Ragnarokkr and almost lost my life. The fresh corpses of the dead, einherjar, aesir and jotunn, littered the ground. Only the crows moved, hopping and flitting from meal to meal.

"You caused this, Loki."

I spun and saw Frigg just a few yards away. Her chestnut

hair and gold trimmed blue robes fluttered in a wind that I didn't feel. She would have been distractingly beautiful were it not for the haughty disdain in her face. Appropriate since she fashioned herself a goddess of love and beauty.

"It's not polite to enter a man's dreams," I said.

"We are well past polite, kinslayer."

"Are you here to gloat, Frigg? It's a bit early. The battle has only begun."

"You defeated the einherjar. Sif anticipated that. But now you are weak. Over half of your jotnar warriors lay dead on a field like this one. The rest are battle weary. We have fresh soldiers that number the same as the einherjar did."

"We still have a few tricks up our sleeves," I lied. Well, it wasn't a total lie, but it was close.

"They won't be enough."

"So you are here to gloat."

"It was clever of you to send Meili back to us," she said, switching topics. "It was a joyous moment to be reunited with my long, lost son. He and Thor bonded almost immediately."

"How touching."

"I rejoiced when Thor began to act like his old self once again. But that's also when the trouble started."

"Well, boys will be boys."

"He started ignoring Sif's advice. He quickly grew wild and uncontrollable. He and Meili drank and caroused late into the night."

"And by uncontrollable, you mean he ignored you and Sif. He became his own man again."

"He insisted on leading the einherjar himself. He squandered an army. All because Meili came home."

"You give me far too much credit, Lady Frigg," I said mockingly. "But you still haven't told me why you are here."

"I'm here to offer you a chance. A choice. Join us. Atone

for your wrongs. Open the gates and together we can rid the Nine Worlds of the jotnar scourge."

"And if I do that, all will be forgiven?"

"Sif has agreed to spare your life. You can live out the rest of your days in Asgard. You can have Sigyn by your side again."

Frigg was never a good liar. It's just not part of her nature. I, on the other hand, am a world-class liar. I can smell a lie a mile away and Frigg wasn't lying. But she wasn't being completely honest either.

"You keep saying Sif this and Sif that," I said, fishing for more information while I noodled out her offer. "What about Thor? Has he agreed to this bargain? Who is really in charge these days?"

"Thor sits on Hlidskjalf, but he listens to Sif. He'll do as she says."

"So Sif is calling the shots."

"He has the einherjar, or what's left of them. Sif has the folkvangr."

"And what about you?"

"I give her counsel and advice, but she has her own mind."

"And that's all?"

"I could give you counsel and advice too," she said with a purr. Only a blind idiot could have missed her insinuation.

"Just because I warmed your bed centuries ago, don't think you can tempt me again."

She frowned, clearly irritated that I hadn't reacted.

"Thor only listens to Sif so long as it suits his purposes," I said, switching topics. "He's the one I should be talking to."

"Sif is strong. She should be the one sitting on Hlidskjalf," Frigg said bitterly.

"But she's a woman," I said with a mock sad face. "And the aesir would never accept a woman's rule, at least not as long as someone like Thor is still available."

"If not Thor, then Magni, or Vali or any of Odin's other male progeny," Frigg said with a sour look. "But Sif will prove herself in battle. In this battle."

"Maybe the two of you should come to Midgard. Women have equal rights to men there," I said. At least on paper they do. Real gender equality is still a work in progress.

"I am the Goddess of Love, beauty, and fertility," she said, shaking her head. "Why would I choose to be a mortal?"

"There is that."

"You don't need to be mortal either. Join us. Leave these barbarians to their doom. It is inevitable."

"You know what else is inevitable? My fate if I join you. Oh, you'll spare my life and let me live out my days in Asgard. You knew I would know if you lied, so you wrapped it in truth. But it will be a life bound to the rocks with the slow drip of venom to keep me company. I'll live out the rest of my days in Asgard all right, but in agony. And Sigyn will once again be by my side. I just can't tell if she will be bound as well, or if she'll be allowed to catch the venom in a bowl again. Which is it Frigg?"

Her eyes flashed angrily as she hissed, "I look forward to Sif finding your corpse on the battlefield when she breaks Utgard."

Right before my eyes she became a flock of crows that burst apart and flew in all directions. Fittingly, the proper name for a flock of crows is a murder. Vigridr faded as I faded back into oblivion.

The pain woke me. It felt like someone had dipped me in some of that boiling oil. My skin was on fire and my side ached. I hope it was only a bruised rib. At least it was wrapped. I was in the infirmary.

My bed was oversized, like everything in Utgard. It took me a minute to recognize the heavily-bandaged man in the bed next to me. Sviarr. He wasn't moving, but he was breathing. We could have each spread our arms wide and not touched each other. Why give smaller folk their own beds when they can share one so easily?

"Finally awake," Manny cawed.

"Finally? How long have I been out?"

"About a day," Ylva said, walking into view. It was a nice view.

"You've been nursing me?"

"As best I could," she said, blushing.

"You are lucky to be alive," Manny cawed.

"If I had been on the ground, I doubt I would be."

"If the lightning hadn't killed you, the fall would have," Manny cawed.

"Hrengr caught you," Ylva said. "But it was still a hard fall."

"I'll thank him next time I see him," I said, gingerly getting out of the bed. I wore a loose pair of breeches. Someone had decided to protect my modesty.

I cursed inwardly at the long drop to the floor. My feet felt like pins and needles. Not the nice tingly kind, but real pins and real needles poking into my soles with each step. I pulled my tunic on and slipped my feet into my boots, which wasn't much of an improvement.

Neither Ylva nor Manny protested that I should remain in bed. They both knew we needed every man, no matter their condition.

"How is the siege going?" I asked, wincing. "Are we holding them off?"

"It hasn't started," Manny cawed. "Go see for yourself."

"Thrasir is dead," Ylva said somberly. "Many of his men died with him."

"He was a right bastard, but a good man,"

"He fought with honor. He fought for Jotunheim. He'll get a chieftain's funeral."

"He won't care. He's dead."

"No. Funerals are for the living. It's how we'll honor his sacrifice."

When had she gotten all wise and philosophical?

"I gotta go see what's going on."

"I'll check on you later," Ylva called out as I hobbled out the door. I blew her a kiss.

"Frigg visited me while I was out," I said to Manny as soon as Ylva was out of earshot.

"Dreamwalking?"

"Maybe. She wants me to betray Jotunheim."

I told him the whole story while we made our way to the walls.

The morning sun was bright as I stepped into the courtyard. I climbed to the parapets nursing my ribs. Ymyd was looking out over the battlefield with his advisers, including Hrengr, who had one arm in a sling. His head was bandaged, and he stood stiffly like it hurt just to breathe. Ullr and Esme stood off to one side, talking. Esme was looking through my binoculars.

I joined the jotnar peering over the wall.

"Hrengr," I said, looking over at him. "I hear I owe you a debt for catching me."

"I was right under you. It was either that or have your blood and bone ruin a good leather jerkin," he said, grinning.

"A good jerkin is hard to find," I said, nodding soberly. A few of the other jotnar chuckled. Dirty jokes are the same in all the Nine Worlds.

I saw our enemies had set up camp. It looked fairly organized, except for a large group off to the right. If I had to guess, that was what remained of the einherjar. The moon bridge was gone.

"You look better," Esme said as I joined her and Ullr.

"You didn't think a lightning bolt and fall from the sky could hurt me, did you?"

"I suppose not," she replied, looking confused.

"Hey, I was kidding. If Hrengr hadn't caught me, I'd be dead. The only reason the lightning bolt didn't fry me is that I wasn't grounded."

"Grounded?" Ullr asked.

"It's a science that the people of Midgard figured out. Esme can explain it to you."

Ullr shrugged.

"Can I use the binoculars, Esme?"

"I've never been in a war," Esme said, handing me the glasses. I promptly put them to use.

"This isn't war. This is genocide."

"Ullr told me that Thor wants to kill all the giants."

"Jotnar," Ullr said.

"Sorry. It's hard to keep up with all this."

"I'm sure it is," I said. "I'm sorry you got dragged into it."

"So are we all going to fucking die here?"

"Not if I can help it." I stared at the distant army through the binoculars.

"You shall not die here," Ullr said firmly.

"You can't promise that," she said, rounding on him. "Are you going to stop that whole army by yourself?"

"No, I cannot do that. But if it looks like all is lost I can get us away safely."

"Then let's leave. Right now."

"I can't"

"Yes, you can."

"No, he can't," I said interrupting. "A true warrior does not flee from battle."

"He just said he would if it got really bad."

"You have no idea what it means that he promised you that," I said archly, putting down the glasses to look at her. Ullr found one of the stone tiles suddenly fascinating.

"I... I don't—"

"No, you don't," I said vehemently. "He is willing to stain his honor. A thousand years ago he was teaching the humans of Midgard that the only way to get into Valhalla was to die in battle. Fleeing like a coward is unthinkable for him."

"Loki—" Ullr began.

"No. She needs to hear this. She needs to understand," I said before turning back to Esme. "His honor is at stake. He can live with himself, with the decision to flee, if it comes at the last second to save a woman he loves. But to leave now, before the battle? That is the mark of a coward. He might as well kill himself. His friends and family might do it for him if they caught him. So if you're going to be with him, you need to understand this. In your bones."

"Is all that true?" Esme said, turning pale and looking at Ullr.

The poor bastard just stood there stoically, glaring at me. He wasn't one to get all mushy with feelings and stuff. Heck, none of the aesir were.

"Now, you two lovebirds go figure this out while I try to find a way to keep us all alive a little while longer."

They left, Esme whispering urgently to Ullr, who just kept shaking his head. I turned back to the binoculars. I had found Sif's tent, so now it was stake-out time as I waited to learn something. Plus, it gave me time to think.

My eyes wandered to Hel, still standing on her hillock in the distance. What did she want? I turned my attention back to Sif's tent. Hel's intentions could wait.

Sif's engineers had been busy while I recovered. Two dozen trebuchets were in the final stages of construction.

While the bulk of the army was a half a mile away, the siege machines were closer. Unfortunately, there were a few thousand soldiers guarding the engineers.

"The stone throwers are almost ready," Ymyd said. Don't ask me how a jotunn four times my height could sneak up on me, but he did. I must have been distracted. Yeah, that's it.

"You know what those are?"

"It's not hard to figure out," he answered. "The design is somewhat ingenious."

"Just be glad they don't have cannons."

"Cannons?"

"Nevermind. Those stone throwers will take down your gate in short order once they get the range."

"That's what I thought too," he said with a laugh. He stiffly walked away, leaving me puzzled.

37

SIEGE

J ust after midday the bombardment began. The first stones fell well short of the walls. A slow trickle of horse-drawn sledges brought large stones from the far fields to the siege engines. I chuckled at the thought of how far afield they needed to go. Ymyd's men had scoured the area earlier for the stones they used to repel the einherjar.

A few hours later, all the trebuchets started picking up the pace. Stones were loaded and flung almost as fast as soldiers could deliver them. Yet all these stones were landing a good fifty feet short.

"It seems they still haven't found the range," Ymyd said, once again appearing behind me silently. His arm was still in a sling, but his head was no longer bandaged.

"They'll correct it shortly."

"Maybe. Maybe not."

I looked at the big smirk on his face. "What's going on, Ymyd?"

"It's possible they think they are hitting our walls," he said with a huge grin. That's when it hit me.

"You're using Skrymir's hoax!"

"It took you long enough," Manny cawed.

"You of all people should know that Utgard has defenses," Ymyd said.

"I remember when Thor and I were guests of Skrymir, back when I was still welcome in Asgard. Skrymir cast an illusion of a huge castle, of this city, Utgard."

"Not completely true. Utgard is real. You've been wandering its halls long enough now to know it's not an illusion. But it can be made to seem other than it is. Skrymir caused you and Thor to think the castle had vanished when it was still right there in front of you."

"So why haven't you just made Utgard vanish again?"

"The aesir know it's here. If it suddenly vanished, they would know it was just an illusion. Frigg would be able to reveal it. Fooling two young aesir is easier than fooling her."

"Let me guess. You've made the walls seem like they are fifty feet farther out than they really are. Sif's army thinks it's bombarding the walls when in fact all those stones are missing."

"It's not me. It's Utgard. Well, it's both of us, but yes. They see and hear stones striking Utgard's walls."

"It will only hold them off for a while."

"Maybe they'll run out of stones," Ymyd said, chuckling as he hobbled away. Manny laughed. Still creepy.

Hours later my watchful patience paid off. I spotted Thor storming through the tents of the folkvangr. The remnants of the einherjar were camped on one end of the field, as if they were ostracized. Unlike the orderly tents of the folkvangr, the einherjar were haphazardly clumped around randomly placed campfires.

Thor was clearly making his way toward Sif's command tent. I cast a spell I had prepared to let me hear him. Since it was galdr on myself, it was a pain to get my head oriented properly, but I managed.

Sif and Frigg came out to meet him, clearly having been warned of his approach. Sif was dressed for war in silver chain mail and a sword at her side.

"Why are we just sitting here?" Thor bellowed. "We should be attacking."

"Attacking what, dear husband?" Sif replied.

"The walls. Take some beams from those stupid contraptions and ram them into the gates until they break."

"You lost tens of thousands of einherjar charging those walls. I have no intention of wasting my army that way."

"Your army? *Your* army! *I* sit on the high seat! *I* rule in Asgard! This is *my* army and I will lead it into battle."

"Begging your pardon, Lord Thor," Frigg said. "But it's my army. The folkvangr belong to me and are mine to command."

"You?" Thor said with a sneer. "You can't command an army. Go back to Asgard and tend to the women huddled there."

"They are mine," Frigg said, standing just a bit taller and straighter. "I've given them to Sif for this war. They are hers to command. She has a vision of for a new Asgard, one you could never realize."

"And you," Thor said, rounding on his wife, rolling thunder in his voice. "As the obedient wife, I command you to give me that army. I know far better than you how to lead men into battle."

"Give them to you?" Sif asked with a sneer. "So you can throw them uselessly at the walls of Utgard? So you can lose another hundred thousand warriors?"

Faster than I thought possible, Thor stepped forward and

backhanded Sif. She flew a dozen feet, landing in the mud. I lost my focus for a moment and ended up listening to some soldiers complaining. But I saw Frigg step in front of Thor, preventing him from advancing on his fallen wife. Sif stood up quickly and laid her hand on her sword but didn't draw it. A few more quips or insults were exchanged and then Thor stormed off.

"It seems there's trouble in paradise," I said to no one in particular.

"Thor and Sif always did have a tempestuous union," Manny mused.

"You heard them?" I turned to look at him.

"Of course."

"'Tempestuous?' Really? You couldn't think of any other word to describe it?"

"It seemed fitting."

It's hard to tell when a raven is smug, but Manny sure looked it at that moment. I had seen everything I needed to see for a while. I took myself and my binoculars in to find something to eat.

<hr />

B y the time I had broken my fast the next day, stones from the trebuchets were hitting the actual walls. Skyrmir's hoax had been revealed. I hurried back to the wall. Ymyd wasn't at his usual post over the main gate; he was on a nearby tower.

"How long before they breach?" I asked, trying not to sound out of breath after climbing up that high.

"Those machines will clear the walls and the defenses over the gates."

I looked along the wall toward the gate. The crenellations were crumbled in one spot. As I watched, a large stone hurtled over the wall and smacked into the stone bulwark, destroying another.

"Then they'll bring in a battering ram for the gate," Ymyd continued. "Maybe fire. Fire would be faster."

"And without defenses on the walls, your men would be sitting ducks for archers."

"Ducks that sit?"

"Nevermind. It's a Midgard thing."

"Wait for the gate to come down," Ymyd said, shrugging. "Their numbers won't mean much in that narrow gap."

Another stone crashed into the main gate crenellations, shearing off a couple of them. At this rate it wasn't going to be long before the whole wall was stripped clean.

"On the bright side," Ymyd said grimly as he limped away. "We have a fresh supply of stones to drop on them."

I spent the rest of the day fretting about the siege. The sheer number of folkvangr warriors was daunting. No spell that I could cast would affect any reasonable number of them. I tried setting the trebuchets on fire, but they wouldn't catch. Pitting my magic against Frigg's was a losing cause.

Ullr was steadily picking off the warriors manning the siege engines, but he could only fire as fast as new arrows could be made for him. New siege engineers replaced dead ones almost before they hit the ground.

Ymyd ordered boulders to be dropped behind the main gate. I wish I had thought of that. A lucky shot from a trebuchet hit two of the jotnar workers, spraying blood, guts, and bone over the main gate roof. More came to help until the doors were blocked with rubble. It wouldn't stop the folkvangr, but it would slow them down.

After that, Ymyd ordered most of the warriors off the

walls. Only the towers were manned now. The trebuchets were ignoring the towers so far.

——————

"S omething's happening," Ylva said, waking me. She was dressed and tying her hair.

"What?" I mumbled fuzzily. "Where?"

"Ymyd is on the walls."

I dressed quickly and hurried to the battlements. Ymyd looked better than yesterday. His arm was still in a sling, but he was walking and breathing better. The sky was overcast, but no rain fell. Thunder rumbled occasionally.

"Over there," he said.

Three siege towers had sprung up while I slept. Long lines of warriors pulled them slowly with thick ropes, heading toward one of the nearby towers to the east of where we stood.

"What can Sif hope to gain?" I asked. "Your warriors will crush those men with boulders. Heck, I bet they could take down those siege towers too."

"She has the warriors to spare. What are the deaths of a few hundred?"

"The halls of Valhalla and Folkvangr fill themselves," Manny cawed.

I glanced over at the hill where my daughter Hel stood, still as a stone statue. I wondered if Sif or Frigg could see her. I couldn't see them just ignoring her presence. Clearly none of the einherjar or folkvangr were aware of her.

Ymyd turned to his aide, "Send warriors to defend that tower. Axes and clubs level with the wall, and rock throwers on the top. And send messengers to the other watchmen to keep a sharp look out and not get distracted by this maneuver."

We watched silently as the siege towers advanced. We could see now that there were thick poles extending behind the tower with men heaving and pushing it. Killing the men in front wouldn't stop it. Just to be sure, I tried a spell to set it on fire, but it failed.

"Sorry, Ymyd. Frigg's protections are too strong for me."

"It's to be expected, Loki. Only Odin was a match for her."

Soon the stones began to fly. Men died, crushed beneath stones scavenged from what the trebuchets had flung at us. I turned away from it until the screams died down. I may be used to death, but this senseless slaughter turned my stomach.

The ropes lay slack now, disappearing beneath the siege towers as they rolled forward. The towers moved noticeably slower, but still advanced. A few rocks had torn holes in the facing of the towers, but they hadn't stopped them. Then a lucky rock hit a corner support just right. The tower teetered before slowly crumpling over onto its side. A cheer arose from the defenders.

Then both remaining towers began to tip forward. Ymyd and I looked at each other confused. The siege towers were nearly at the walls, but they weren't going to make it. The first fell, its top brushing the base of Utgard's tower. The second fell a minute later, its top just shy of the stone tower.

"What the—"

Two large explosions, one right after the other, drowned out what was sure to have been a very witty expletive I was about to say. The tops of the siege towers had been filled with some sort of dvergar explosive. They never intended the siege towers to make it to the walls. They were meant as canons.

Thick smoke obscured the entire base of the stone tower. Then, in slow motion, the face of the tower slid off, crashing to the ground with a thunderous rumble. Dozens of jotnar warriors tumbled into the cloud of dust and smoke. Each of the interior floors of the tower was exposed.

"The walls are breeched!" Ymyd shouted.

38

BREECHED

I cursed myself for a fool as I ran down the steps to the courtyard. The siege towers hadn't made sense, but I had convinced myself that Sif was stupid enough to try them anyway. To make matters worse, we had loaded up the wall tower with extra jotnar. I felt partially responsible for the warriors who died when it collapsed.

I chanted a spell of protection similar to what I used in Vidrheim when I rescued Esme. Unfortunately, without the time to prepare it properly, it wouldn't be as effective. The leathers I wore were nowhere near as good as the riot gear either. I still had the military axes, but I hoped I wouldn't have to use them. Best to leave the fighting to the jotnar.

Jotnar streamed toward the fallen tower, and a line of giants waited to push through the door. That told me the fighting was inside the tower. The folkvangr would have the advantage in tighter quarters.

"Defend the doorway!" I shouted, stopping to catch my breath. "Don't go inside."

A few jotnar turned to look down at me, like who appointed you war chief?

An older, grizzled warrior nodded his head. "Loki is right. They can only get through the doorway three at a time. Inside they have the advantage. Encircle the doorway!"

"Fall back!" I shouted to the jotnar inside.

The jotnar shuffled into a loose semi-circle around the doorway, leaving a space for the folkvangr to get out and die. The grunts, clangs, and screams from inside told me the jotnar in there weren't taking my advice quickly enough.

I chanted, and in response the ground in the open space surrounded by the giants became a hip-deep mud pit. The folkvangr are not rabid berserkers like the einherjar, but they still charged forward. Those behind forced those in front on ahead.

Now it was butchery, not war. Giant, blood splattered axes and clubs rose and fell. Each blow was a folkvangr man dead before they could even get close enough to swing their weapons. They piled up quickly despite the mud. I stayed back, out of the way of axes and clubs longer than I was tall.

"Pull out the dead!" I shouted. "Make room for more."

A couple of the jotnar started reaching in and hauling out bodies. They flung them over their shoulders. I ducked a flying body that almost hit me. Despite that, men were dying faster than they could clear them. The metallic tang of blood mixed with the musk of sweat.

Just then there was a blinding flash and a loud crack of thunder. I turned to see a second lightning bolt strike the wooden gate. Momentarily blinded, I only heard the third hit. I smelled ozone and wood smoke. The main gate was burning. We were about to have two fronts to defend.

"Rams!" someone shouted. "They're bringing rams!"

As my vision cleared, I saw that the lightning had distracted the defending jotnar just enough to allow a wedge of folkvangr through. The jotnar still held the advantage, but now the folkvangr had opened up a small area to hold. They stood on the bodies of their comrades buried in the mud pit, pushing hard at the jotnar.

Ymyd shouted from above, directing jotnar to the gate. I needed to see. Ground level just wasn't doing it for me. I raced up the stairs to the battlements, leg muscles burning. Damn these jotnar and their long legs. Each step was waist high on me, but I had made them put narrow wooden crates along the wall so I could use them. Even so the wall was three times the height of a jotunn, making for a long climb.

Huffing and puffing I made the top of the thick wall. Stumbling forward, I leaned out to look at the gate. Thor's son, Magni, stood amid the pile of large rocks, hefting and flinging them away, his long red hair swirling around his head. From an early age Magni had been stronger than Thor, even when Thor wore Megingjord, his belt of strength. He was every bit as strong as the largest jotunn.

I prepared to cast a spell as the first arrow tinged off the stone wall near me. Looking up I saw a mass of folkvangr warriors waiting for the gate to be cleared. Several large logs were cradled in wheeled frames to be used as battering rams. Hundreds of archers were letting loose arrows.

All at me.

Two of them zipped past, narrowly missing me. I scrambled back and off the wall. Bravery in battle is for the stupid.

Scooting down the improvised steps, I saw Ymyd marshaling his warriors. He wore a thick chain shirt and a steel ram's horn helmet. The jotnar formed loose arcs around him, facing the burning gate. Each had an over-sized axe or club. Hundreds of jotnar focused on Ymyd who stood with his back to the gate, black smoke swirling around him, flames outlining him from behind. I spotted Ymyd's son, Hrengr, among them.

"Each of you is worth ten of them!" Ymyd bellowed,

pacing in front of his charges. The jotnar roared back in approval.

"We will show them the valor of Jotunheim. The mettle of its defenders!"

Another deep throated cheer arose as they lifted their weapons high, pumping them up and down.

"Your mothers, your wives and husbands, your children, are all at risk. Your homes, your homeland, everything you hold dear is in danger."

The jotnar chanted and stomped their feet rhythmically. I could feel the power swelling. They were casting some sort of primal spell together. I had never witnessed anything like it.

"One blood!" Ymyd thundered. They all raised their heads as one and a crooning groan filled with mighty rage rumbled across the courtyard. I stood there, just watching the spectacle. It hadn't escaped me that I kept running from place to place but not actually contributing to the defense of Utgard.

"One land!" He roared. The rhythmic groaning intensified. The stomping rattled my teeth.

"One Jotunheim!" Ymyd bellowed.

"One Jotunheim!" they called back.

"One jotunn!"

"One jotunn!" they roared, swaying to a beat only they heard.

They readied their weapons in unison. Ymyd turned and struck the gate with his huge axe, once, twice. The third blow broke the right side door which pivoted just on its bottom hinge before that twisted free and it fell. He pulled the other door open with his free hand.

Through the smoke and between the giant bodies, I saw Magni standing there, a large rock nearly as big as himself in both hands, clearly unprepared for the gate to be opened. Ymyd charged him, swinging his axe in a ferocious upper cut.

Magni shifted the rock to block the blow. The boulder cracked in half and Magni went flying.

The jotnar advanced through the gate, their movements lock-stepped. The jotnar in back walked in place waiting to squeeze through the bottle neck of the gate. All I could see now were giants' butts covered in furs or over-sized breeches blocking my view.

Frustrated, I yet again ran back to the steps leading to the top of the wall. I was pretty sure the archers wouldn't be bothering with a lone human-sized figure on the wall. I might be able to summon a useful spell if I could just see the battlefield better.

Ymyd and Magni were trading blows. The folkvangr swirled around them, rams forgotten, content to let the two principal figures duel it out. Ymyd's giant axe rang as it clashed with Magni's sword. Strikes that should have sent Magni reeling were stopped cold. Mangi's counter's rocked Ymyd back on his heels despite the king of Jotunheim being many times larger.

Half the jotnar warriors were out the gate and engaged with the folkvangr. They kept their lines, axes and clubs swung in lockstep unison, even if no foe presented itself. They advanced as one, all left feet moving, then all right feet. I don't know what Ymyd did to them, but they were one unit now. One jotunn.

Folkvangr fell left and right, pulped bloody by clubs or cleaved in half by axes. I watched a folkvangr drive his sword deep into the groin of a jotunn warrior who didn't notice or falter. Another hamstrung a jotunn, yet he kept marching on as if his leg still worked.

Not a jotunn had fallen yet.

I looked around for the aesir. If Magni was here, the rest couldn't be far behind. I spotted Modi on the left flank of the jotnar line; he was carving away at a jotnar warrior that just refused to fall. There was no sign of Vali or the unknown aesir. I caught Hel out of the corner of my eye, still motionless on her hillock.

The battle line of jotnar stopped moving forward.

The warriors had fled the city, but just barely. Facing down the front line was Syn, shield held forward and spear held high and crosswise. Sparks rose as the huge jotunn before her struck her shield and the length of her spear. She stood still as stone, unmoving and unmoved by the attacks. Syn, goddess of refusal. She who bars the way.

The folkvangr surged forward, pressing the jotnar line hard. The smaller human warriors darted between the massive legs to reach the jotnar deeper in the formation. I saw horrible wounds on many of the jotnar, wounds that should have killed them or left them crippled. Folkvangr died in droves, but more just kept filing forward.

I couldn't do anything to help the jotnar.

I sought Ymyd in the fray. Magni had driven him to one knee. Blood streamed from a dozen sword cuts. Magni was covered in blood, too, but I couldn't tell if it was his own or Ymyd's.

I quickly chanted a galdr spell, shifting into a white-tailed eagle. Immediately cursing my stupidity, I struggled to escape the clothes draped over me. Finally free, I lifted into the air. The battle below looked different with these eyes. The edges were blurry, lacking detail. But the center where I focused was sharp and clear as if I stood only a few feet away.

I banked toward Ymyd and Magni as they grappled each other, Ymyd still on his knees. Magni was clearly getting the upper hand. Folding my wings, I dove, pulling up at the last second. I raked my talons across Magni's face. He looked up, surprised and confused. Ymyd reared back and head butted the aesir warrior.

Ymyd's head was four times the size of Magni's. The son of Thor crumpled. Ymyd fell on his side next to him.

I wheeled about and landed next to them, changing back to human. Naked as the day I was born, I looked down at Ymyd. Magni had driven his sword into Ymyd's chest up to the hilt.

"Ymyd!" I cried, crouching down by his head.

"Loki," he said, coughing.

"Shh. Don't talk. I'm going to get help."

"There is no helping me now," he said weakly. "This wound is mortal. We both know that."

"No! There has to be something we can do."

"Yes," he said, coughing up blood. "Ylva—"

"What? What about Ylva?"

He didn't answer. He was gone. I turned my attention to Magni, intent on avenging Ymyd. Magni had silently risen and slipped away. I caught a glimpse of him stumbling through the surging mass of folkvangr trying to get to the jotnar lines. He was out of sight a moment later.

I grabbed a nearby hand axe and went after him. Not the best strategy for a buck naked man, but I wasn't thinking clearly. I just wanted to watch Magni's head roll in the mud at my feet.

A folkvangr warrior stepped in my path, eyes wild with battle fever. He swept a big sword at my head. I ducked and hacked at his arm as it passed over me. He howled and I left him behind.

I grabbed a shield from a fallen warrior and pushed forward, ignoring anyone who didn't actually swing at me. Block, hack... block, hack. I was losing my sense of direction in the swarm. Exhausted, my legs shook trying to hold me up. My arms felt leaden.

I stopped where I was and glanced around. The folkvangr were ignoring me. I probably looked like one of them. Magni was gone. I saw the jotnar formation to my left, weapons rising and falling in unison. All of them had what should have been mortal wounds. The nearest to me was disemboweled, feet tangled in his intestines. The jotunn next to him had a spear stuck through his chest with only a couple feet of haft showing.

Looking back at Utgard, I saw the gates stood open. Folkvangr streamed into it.

The battle was lost.

Sif had won.

39

TRUE SELF

I looked back at the jotnar in time to see them all fall at the same time. One jotunn. Unable to die until all of them died.

Hrengr with them.

A cheer rose up from the folkvangr.

I sank to me knees. Let them kill me. The first folkvangr to swing at me would earn the title of Loki-slayer. But none did, like I wasn't even worth the effort.

Manny landed on my shoulder. I looked at the bird, tears blurring my vision. He had something in his mouth, but I couldn't make it out. A great sob wracked my body and Manny shoved whatever it was into my mouth.

"Swallow you great fool of a god," he cawed.

Idunn's weird fruit. It had been in my pocket. The pocket in my clothes at the top of the wall. I wanted to laugh. I was sitting naked on a battlefield surrounded by my enemies. Those enemies were running rampant through Utgard as I sat here on my ass in the mud. An entire people, my people, were going to be slaughtered, and Manny wanted me to eat this stupid fruit.

"Ow!" I said around the fruit as he pecked my head. Hard.

"Swallow," he cawed.

I bit the fruit. Bitter juices with hints of strange flavors flowed across my tongue. I opened my mouth like a child showing his parent his food. It was petty, but I was feeling petty. I swallowed and showed him again. My mouth began to burn like I had eaten a jalapeno.

"Gods, that tastes awful."

"Medicine usually does," Manny cawed.

My stomach twisted. I felt like I was going to be sick.

My head spun.

She'd poisoned me. Idunn poisoned me!

Had that been her plan all along? Poison Loki to make things easier for the aesir to wipe out the jotnar? The laugh was on her. I hadn't really done much to save them so far.

I tried to laugh, but my chest tightened. A wave of heat crashed over me. I shook. Yep, definitely poisoned. Something fast-acting, but painful. Trust Idunn to find the ideal venom.

Then my head felt like it exploded.

Something was wrong inside me, like I fought myself. Two natures that refused to co-exist, jotunn and aesir. There was still a third part, small and quiet that tried to go unnoticed.

The struggle within grew, and I began to feel better.

Better than I could ever remember feeling.

I laughed at the joy of it. I looked around at the battlefield covered with the hacked up jotnar and folkvangr corpses. The two nearest me had their faces frozen in death agony. I moved their heads so that they looked like they were kissing.

"They look better this way, don't you think?" I giggled.

"Loki," Manny cawed. "What are you doing?"

"They looked lonely," I said with a pout.

I stood up. Then I really stood up. I didn't want to feel small anymore, so I didn't. Taller even than Ymyd, I stood and stretched. Looking down at my dead friend, I stuck my tongue out. Now he was the small one. That made me chuckle.

The nearby folkvangr noticed me. How could they not? Suddenly there was a giant jotunn dangling his naughty bits right in front of them. I was a giant even by jotnar standards.

Several moved to attack me, which really wasn't fair. The nearest tripped over a corpse and impaled himself. Another swung at me, but his friend got in the way and he lost his head. Blood spurted everywhere. The last one stepped in a gopher hole and snapped his leg in two. He screamed and screamed and screamed. There are no gophers in Jotunheim, which made me laugh louder.

More folkvangr turned toward me.

They fell, tripped, and cut each other. Bird poop dropped in the eye of one. Another choked on his own hair. Femoral arteries were cut by stray bits of torn armor. One man ran forward and didn't see the axe with the bent handle. He stepped on it and it flipped up just like the classic garden rake gag. He screamed as it cut into his balls.

So much screaming.

Manny landed on my shoulder. He was so small now. He could peck at my head all day and I wouldn't feel it.

"Loki," Manny cawed. "Utgard is under attack. Your friends are in there."

"And you want me to save them I suppose?"

"It's an idea."

I looked around. Then I *really* looked around. Beneath all this stuff, I could see the connections. I saw the random froth of chance and the inevitable free will it created.

Hot tangles of probability knotted in uncountable places.

One of the largest skeins was the figure on the hill. She held it all tight around her. She? Not really. Neither she nor he. Maybe at some distant time in the past, but no longer. But her knot was impressively large and complex. She wasn't the problem, so I turned to look elsewhere.

More folkvangr died or wounded themselves trying to reach me. I pushed out at them so I could slip forward. They flung themselves to their deaths and dismemberments, coiled in the random waves of misfortune that surrounded me. I danced a little jig while laughing at the absurdity.

I gazed across the battlefield toward the command tents. Auntie Frigg had her own bright tangle of power and strangely organized probability. My, my. She was quite the wonder. Sif stood next to her, all dark and cloudy with roiling folds of bleak randomness bleeding out of her. So different from the golden woman she had once been.

I edged toward them, folkvangr contorting themselves into devious death poses or awkward positions as more strange events beset them. This was the most fun I'd had in my long life.

I picked out Modi and Syn.

Magni sulked in a tent near Frigg.

Modi was berating his twin brother. All of them had ropes of strange quirkiness coiled, knotted and folded within them. Curious, I looked down at myself. A huge ball of tangled threads ran through me. Bigger even than Hel's. I plucked at one that looked familiar and followed the vibrating string as it sped toward Utgard.

When it reached Ullr's own knots and tangles, he spun to face me. Not that he could see me through the palace wall, but he felt my attention. He and Esme were racing toward a sally port. I saw that the door was rusted shut. They would never get it open. Then flakes of rust fell from the steel and oil welled up in the hinges.

"You're welcome," I said softly, knowing he couldn't hear me.

"What?" Manny cawed. "You're making no sense."

Manny. Glorious Manny. No knots at all. Strike that. Just very, very small knots. So small I could barely see them. But the lines. Oh, those lines, Going everywhere. More lines than all of us combined.

"Loki!" a small voice shouted.

I turned slowly and saw Esme a few hundred yards away. The sally port stood open behind them. Ullr was tugging on her arm, trying to get her to flee from the battle. Our connection was strong enough that I could hear her over the din of battle and the distance between us.

"Do something. Save them!"

Ullr finally succeeded in pulling her away. She glanced over her shoulder anxiously as he hustled her off to safety. I blinked and the folkvangr that noticed them suddenly became distracted with uncontrollable itching, boots stuck in mud, pants that fell down around their ankles, and other nuisances.

I suppose I really should do something. Friendship seemed like a distant concept. Certainly not as important as playing with all the little intertwined threads of probability, but not nothing either.

The earth trembled as I reached deep. The old stories associated Loki with earthquakes. Why not play to them? Fissures opened beneath the feet of the folkvangr. Thousands fell to their deaths. The shaking caused thousands more to fall, impaling themselves on whatever was handy. Those that kept their feet fled, trampling the wounded.

I stared at the wall of Utgard and it crumbled.

Large chunks fell inward, crushing the folkvangr inside the city. Somehow none of the jotnar were struck.

My laughter boomed across the battlefield.

So many of them turned to stare at me, and they did not notice the magma welling up through narrow fissures until the wave of heat struck them.

By then it was too late.

Poisonous volcanic gases shot from the earth, bringing the folkvangr to their knees. The lucky ones suffocated. The rest felt their lungs dissolving before they died.

Sif's army was decimated in minutes.

Maybe one man of ten still stood, but the bright skeins of power and chance of the aesir still stood. Their own natures conflicted with mine, granting them some measure of protection. The one I didn't know fled with Modi and Magni. The other two, Syn and Vali, raced toward me.

And Thor. He was farther than the others, but closing fast.

But the Valkyries got to me first. Flying in squads of nine each, they circled and attacked from all directions. A spear hurled fast and true dug into my shoulder. Another was driven into my thigh.

Strong upswells of wind pushed many of them off course and into each other. It was hard; wind and air are already so full of chaos that they are harder to influence. Plus, someone else was fighting me for control.

I swatted three Valkyries out of the air while turning toward my competitor. Thor. The wind and the storms were his. His tangles synced with the chaos of air far better than mine did. He stole the wind from me.

"Loki!" Thor shouted.

I waggled my hips at him. One of the only advantages of being naked on a battlefield.

Twin pains blossomed in my back. Valkyrie spears thrust deep, one into a lung, the other penetrating my kidney. I could see the knots inside myself unraveling. It was simple enough to fix; I may not be the master of air and water, but nobody was better at galdr. My tangle tightened back up to a nice, chaotic ball.

Vali and Syn stepped out from a curtain of volcanic smoke. He wore classic Viking armor and carried a huge two-handed sword. Syn looked more like a Valkyrie with shield and spear, her blonde hair bound in a thick braid.

"Shield maidens!" Vali bellowed. "Leave this one to us."

The Valkyries wheeled, circling me as they contemplated whether Vali had the right to wave them off. Then they turned toward Utgard and flew off. I waved goodbye to them.

Then I waved my arm at the pair of aesir, and the ground rocked and seized to the side of them, flinging a dozen bodies in their direction. Syn spun, lifting her shield. Her nexus flared, and like magic, the clot of corpses split and hurtled to either side. Syn the defender. She who guards the doors and shuts them to those who are not to enter.

I pouted.

With a roar, Vali charged through the scattered corpses between us, kicking through them like tissue paper. I winked and an arm got caught in his boot. Then a head, and some entrails, and another arm. Though his momentum was gone, he still got close enough to take a swing at my shin.

The blade cut deep, lodging in my bone, almost knocking me off my feet. I howled. Thoroughly peeved, I kicked at him while he tried to pull his blade free. I didn't so much connect with my kick as lift him because he was holding on to his still-stuck weapon. I shook my foot violently and he went flying a hundred feet, leaving behind his sword.

"Bad Vali. No biscuit!" I shouted, making sure his head hit a rock particularly hard. His own power resisted me and he only struck a glancing blow, but it was enough.

I plucked the blade from my bleeding leg while beginning to knit the muscle back together. The sword was as long as my forearm. I hurled it at Syn. She casually batted it aside with her shield. She stepped forward and put her foot into the hole of an animal den. A really deep one. Like up to her hip. She hadn't spotted it because it was filled with water. And mud. She wouldn't be going anywhere soon.

"Loki!" she shouted. "Fight me, you coward!"

Thor headed toward me, whipping his chariot pulled by those ludicrous goats. Goats! I laughed at the sight. I was so busy laughing, the lightning bolt that shot through me was a big surprise. It burned a path from my head down through my feet. It hurt like a son of a bitch.

"Well done, mighty Thor," I said, failing to suppress a giggle.

"Today you die!" he roared.

Single minded oaf. I began to heal the damage, but I felt another bolt building before I could finish. Thor was almost upon me. I didn't have time to finish mending my wounds. Worse yet, I didn't even have time for another bad pun. His chariot turned at the last second, affording him a clear shot at my kneecap. I pulled hard on his threads.

His bright nexus of chance resisted my influence, but not completely. Off balance, his hammer struck my shin just below the knee, close to where he likely aimed. Much to my embarrassment, I screamed. My shin had snapped in two. Thor's chariot struck an inclined shield, went airborne and flipped. Now the goats screamed, which made me laugh despite the pain. Thor went flying. I laughed harder.

Down on one knee, I was closer to Thor's height. Dragging himself to his feet, he stomped toward me, and I felt the ground quiver from his furious tread. I held up the dented shield in one hand. Man-sized, it looked tiny. I peeked over the top and batted my eyes at him.

"Die, you abomination!" Thor screamed as he drew back his hand.

Mjolnir was a blur as it hurtled down onto the shield that I managed to angle up at the last moment, deflecting the blow rather than taking the full brunt of it. The hammer continued its path and struck the ground with a thunderclap, shaking everything nearby. Three fingers on my hand were shattered.

"Hey!" I said. "No fair. Earthquakes are my thing."

I backhanded him, the hand axe protruding between my knuckles like a set of car keys. It was like hitting a tree. The hand axe fell from my nerveless fingers. Thor shook himself and took one step back, then lifted his hammer high over his head.

"Not even Sigyn will mourn your passing," he said.

The ground opened up beneath him and he fell. One meaty hand shot out and grasped the edge of the chasm. He dangled for a moment before starting to haul himself up. I willed the edge to crumble, but he hooked Mjolnir over the lip just in time. That gods-be-damned hammer had its own swirling knot of power. I tried to knit my fingers back together, but it wasn't going to be fast enough; I was running out of spell juice.

"Your tricks will not work, Loki!"

I hobbled forward on my knees and tried to push the hammer off the ledge, but it held. Thor's head appeared over the top. I struck at it with my broken shield hand, but it didn't budge him at all.

Another lightning bolt fried a jagged line through my body. I crumpled to the ground. My hands hurt too much to push myself back up. I could feel myself shrinking, losing control of my jotnar heritage.

Thor moved into my line of sight, standing over me. "You will die on your knees like the coward you are,"

"Technically I'm on my side—"

Ignoring my quip, he raised Mjolnir over his head in two hands. I didn't have enough left to stop him. Whatever Idunn's fruit had gifted me was fading fast.

The bullet hit him in the chest. The gunshot sounded faint, a mere whisper. I looked behind me to see Esme standing not far away, legs wide, pistol in both hands. Ullr stood behind her, bow at the ready, keeping away any stray folkvangr. She fired again. This shot struck him in the shoulder.

Thor was too tough and mean to go down from just two bullets, but I could tell they hurt. A lot. Healing wasn't his thing, so he had to just suck it up. Blood trickled down his chest, but he took a step toward her. The third shot went wide.

I reached out a broken hand, trying to hold or trip him. He stomped on my fingers, and I swallowed my scream. It's amazing how much foolish courage a man will show if a woman is watching. The next shot hit him in the forehead. He toppled over like a felled tree.

"Ullr!" Esme shouted. "Help me lift him."

Ullr sidled up to Thor, looking down at his stepfather. "He's alive," he said, clearly relieved.

"Ullr!" Esme said sharply.

"Finish him," I said weakly.

"No," Ullr said quickly.

"I… I'm not going to kill him in cold blood," Esme said. "That would be murder."

"You already shot him," I said. "In the head!"

"That was to defend you."

"Killing him would defend me."

"No," Esme said, clearly disturbed. "I can't do that. I just can't."

I stopped arguing. They hoisted me between them, most of my weight on Ullr. As they dragged me toward Utgard, the folkvangr who remained wandered back toward their camp. We left each other alone.

40

ULLR AND ESME

Utgard was a disaster. Before their retreat, the folkvangr had broken into more than a few buildings. Jotnar too old or young to fight back had been dragged into the streets and the surviving numb family members were gathering their mutilated bodies.

Ullr and Esme half carried me, an arm over each of their shoulders, toward the palace.

"I had hoped to never fight in another war," I said, my heart heavy.

"So long as men take breath, there will be wars," Ullr said.

"It's always been so," Manny cawed.

"Men," Esme said, bitterly. I could hear the break in her voice. She kept her eyes down, unable to look at the carnage.

"The folkvangr were gathered by a woman and led by another woman," I said.

"Ambition and hate are not exclusive to men," Ullr said. "Nor to humans, aesir, jotnar, or any of the other races of the Nine Worlds."

"Ullr has become a philosopher," Manny cawed. "Now I've seen everything."

"Well, this is my first war, and it fucking sucks," Esme said.

"Why did you come back?" I asked, changing the topic.

"It wasn't my idea," Ullr said, frowning at Esme.

"Thor was going to kill you," Esme said. "In all those stories, Thor always kills the giants. I couldn't let him kill you."

"So I'm the damsel in distress this time?" I asked, laughing. "Ow. That hurt."

"She repaid her life debt," Ullr said proudly. Trust him to turn it into some Viking-era thing.

"I didn't do it because I fucking owed him," Esme said sharply. "I did it because it was the right thing to do. Because he's my friend and he was in trouble."

"You were as brave and fierce as any Valkyrie," Ullr said. "That's why I love you."

"Wait… what?" Esme said, stopping dead in her tracks. Ullr took another step, stretching me out across their shoulders.

"Ow."

"Uh—" Ullr said, suddenly uncomfortable.

"Say it again," Esme demanded.

"Hey," I said, "Ullr, could you maybe crouch down a bit? This whole height difference thing kinda hurts."

"Fucking say it again!" Esme said, louder.

"Uh, that's my arm you're bending the wrong way," I said.

Ullr squared his shoulders and looked her in the eye, "I love you, Esme."

"Ow! Bend down! Bend down!"

"I love you too," Esme said, dropping her half of me. She wrapped him in her arms, tilting her face up. He bent down and kissed her, lowering me to the ground with one hand so he could enfold her in his arms.

"Hey, wounded guy here. Ow! Shit, this hurts."

"Don't be a wimp," Manny cawed.

They released each other after a lengthy kiss while I lay on the ground nursing my wounds. I was happy for them, I really was. But couldn't they have waited to do this until after I got to the infirmary?

"I pledge my troth to you, Esme. Will you pledge yours to me?"

"What? You're asking me to marry you? Whoa. Slow down there a minute."

"Still lying here," I said. "Still bleeding."

"Quiet, Loki," Manny said softly. "This is getting good."

"I love you too, Ullr, but I'm not ready to marry anyone just yet."

"But I confessed my love for you," Ullr said, confused.

"And that means a lot to me. Really. But I'm not ready to marry anyone yet."

"Esme," I said. "They are one and the same for him. To declare his love means he wants you to be his wife. He's old school that way. And could you help me sit up?"

"Well, I'm not," she said. "Ullr. I love you, I really do. But I'm not from your world. We don't do things that way where I come from."

"I thought you were a good Catholic girl." I said.

"Shut up," they said in unison.

"Look," Esme said. "There are a lot of things we need to figure out before we talk about marriage. That's a big step. Where would we live? Do I have to leave my family? My world? Is it even safe to be with you? What about children?"

"We would live in Ydalir, my home in the yew dales of Asgard. I want many children, and I will always keep you safe. I will hunt and provide for us. You will keep our home."

"Well, that settles that," I said. "Now if you could pick me up again—"

"So that's it? I don't have any fucking say in it?"

"I'm giving you my home, my possessions, and my name. I've professed my love for you," he said, looking perplexed.

"Ullr," I said. "Let me stop you right there. You see—"

"Shut up, Loki. I've got this," Esme said, without looking down at me. "No, Ullr. No, I will not marry you. Where I come from men and women are equals, especially in marriage. We decide things together. The man doesn't make all the decisions while the wife cooks, cleans, and raises the children. When you're ready to talk *with* me instead of *to* me, come find me."

And with that, Esme marched off. Ullr stood there, dumbstruck.

"An aesir lord brought low by a Midgard maiden." Manny laughed. Still creepy.

"Could you give me a hand?" I asked.

Silently, Ullr reached down and hoisted me up. I slung my arm over his shoulders again. It was awkward without the second person supporting my other side, but Ullr had born most of my weight anyway.

"She loves you, you know. You still have a chance to work this out."

"How can you know that?"

"That she loves you? Well, for starters she said so. But the real tell that you'll be able to work it out was she didn't curse once in that speech at the end."

Ullr grunted. We were at the palace steps. I stopped talking and started cursing as he lifted me up the giant steps one at a time. We stopped at the top so I could catch my breath.

"If you want her, you're going to have to meet her halfway. Ever since Ragnarokkr, you've refused to leave Asgard. Midgard has changed. They call it progress. They have technologies that would seem like magic to you. Like that rifle."

"What are you saying?"

345

"You offered Esme Ydalir. What she heard is that you are forcing her to live in a log cabin without electricity and running water or any other modern Midgard comforts, away from her family and friends and everything she knows and understands."

"They can all come with her. Ydalir has enough room for all of them."

"And their children and children's children," Manny said.

"And the electricity? The running water? And don't even get me started on TV and the internet."

"It used to be that a husband was enough for a woman."

"That was never really true. It's just the way it was. We didn't give women any other choice. Well, they have choices now. Lots of them. If you want her, you're going to have to give her more. You're going to have to give up as much as you offer. Maybe more."

Right then a half-dozen jotnar warriors rounded the corner bearing the body of Ymyd on an improvised bier. We watched as they carried him past us into the palace. Manny let loose a screech of sorrow. Ullr silently hoisted me up again. Between the soft sobs for my friend and the wincing cries of pain, I wasn't so quiet. Ullr half carried me to the infirmary. Without a word he found an over-sized bed and put me in it.

You've been summoned," the jotnar messenger said. I was in my old room. Between the talents of the jotnar healers and my own galdr skills, I was mostly recovered from my wounds only two days after the battle. Manny was nowhere to be found.

Ylva was seated in Ymyd's old chair. Four clan chiefs stood respectfully to either side. The Ice Riders had been virtually wiped out by the folkvangr. The remains of the clan were being adopted by other clans.

A nervous looking jotunn I had never seen before stood in for Midjung, whose funeral would be tomorrow. Gymir's left side was heavily bandaged.

"A woman on the throne of Jotunheim," I said. "I never thought I would see the day."

Skyr, the lone female clan chief glared at me. To be honest, she kind of scared me. Ylva smiled wryly.

"Ylva has the support of the Stone Breakers," Gymir said.

"And the Mountain Cloud clan," Skyr said.

The other two shifted uncomfortably. Ylva's support looked razor thin.

"And mine," I said. "For what it's worth."

"I'm honored," Ylva said.

"What about Thrasir's clans? He made no secret of his ambitions."

"What's left of them retreated to their lands. Even after Thrasir's death they don't recognize Utgard's right to rule. I doubt we'll see them for a while."

Grudgingly, the other two clan chieftains muttered their support for Ylva. She wasn't going to have an easy time on the throne.

"How can I help Utgard, my queen?" I asked.

"We need someone to carry our offer of peace to Asgard. We thought you would be the obvious choice."

"Offer or ultimatum?"

"Offer. Far too many jotnar grace the funeral pyres. Even if we wanted to carry the fight to them, we could only field a token force."

"A token force is all it would take," said the clean-shaven clan chief with the giant nose ring. I never had learned his name.

"Enough, Gridungr. The debate is over," Ylva said, firmly. Now I knew his name.

"Okay. When do we ride?"

"You'll be going alone," Ylva said, unable to look at me.

"Alone?"

"Are you afraid, mighty Loki, God of Mischief?" Gymir asked slyly. "You defeated the folkvangr almost single-handedly, and Thor himself."

My reputation has always been a problem for me. Now it seems I had a new reputation. I could defeat armies and wrestle the god of thunder himself. Nevermind that Esme has saved my bacon.

"No, of course not," I said. "I just thought the honor of Jotunheim would be better served with a larger force, one with representatives from all the clans."

Gymir chuckled, "You are a slippery one, Lord Loki."

"It's been decided," Ylva said. "You will go alone."

I could have said no. "As you wish."

"Walk with me a moment, Loki."

I offered her my arm in answer. She had graciously adjusted her size to be only half a head taller than me. We strolled out of the throne room and toward a tower that overlooked the battlefield. I could hear the sounds of hammers and blocks of stone being maneuvered as the jotnar worked to rebuild their city.

"Why you and not Sydro?" I asked. "I know Hrengr is... that he passed. Ymyd's wife has a stronger claim to the throne than his granddaughter."

"She turned it down. She watched the folkvangr cut down her son Uglr right in front of her. She wants nothing to do with ruling."

"I heard she made them pay though. They found her cradling Uglr's body surrounded by a dozen or more folkvangr corpses."

"The surest way to enrage a mother is to harm her cub."

We stood looking out over the walls in silence. It was her meeting. If she had something to say, she would say it.

"Where will you go after Asgard?" Ylva asked.

"Ah," I said, shaking my head. "I assume you mean anywhere other than Utgard or you wouldn't be asking."

"Your presence here does present some problems."

"The clan chiefs would think you are too soft on Asgard."

"That, and I have to choose a husband."

"Oh," I said, "I'm not sure how I feel about that."

"Gymir and Gridungr have both offered."

"A fate worse than death to be sure."

"Fear not." She laughed. "I'm going to offer myself to one of the chieftains of Thrasir's clans. Jotunheim cannot be divided anymore. An alliance there would unite us."

We reached the tower and gazed down over the battle-field. Asgard's forces had decamped. Without the moon bridge, I wondered if they had found a way out of Jotunheim. A spider web of narrow cracks in the earth crisscrossed the open field. A handful of black puddles of cooling lava dotted the landscape; they would take months to cool.

Jotnar were busy pushing folkvangr corpses into the chasms. I had conveniently created an easy way to bury tens of thousands of corpses. Not something I was about to put on my resume. Others were hauling jotnar corpses off the field for a proper funeral pyre.

I saw Hel still standing on her hill, still as death. The battle was over. She had reaped a mighty harvest of souls. What was she still doing here?

"You didn't consider an alliance with Asgard?" I asked, bringing the conversation back to her impending betrothal.

"Marry you? That's your pride talking, Loki. We don't love each other, despite the nights we spent together. Please tell me you didn't fool yourself into believing that."

"No, I didn't," I said, sighing. "But a guy does like to be asked."

"I would turn down Odin himself if he lived. Any aesir groom would divide the tribes worse than they already are."

"Also true," I said. "I think I'll go back to Midgard. After a thousand years of living there, it's the realm that most feels like home."

"Actually, it's just more than nine hundred years," she said with a grin.

I flipped her off and went down to talk to my daughter. I was pretty sure she was specifically waiting for me.

L ater I found Esme in a small tower room. It had a great view and they had furnished it with furniture people our size could actually use. She was drinking tea and offered me a cup.

"What are you going to do?" I asked.

"Go back to Earth," she said.

"Chicago? Do you think you can pick up where you left off?"

"I'm going to try."

"You know things about the worlds that you didn't before. That can be hard on people. Trust me, I know."

"What else would I do?" she asked with a frown. "Live here? Don't be ridiculous. And I'm certainly not going to live in a log cabin in the middle of fucking nowhere."

"Don't be too hard on Ullr. Of all of us, he lives the most apart from others. He's a simple man who leads a simple life. Other than inventing cross country skis, he's never had any use for progress."

"He invented skiing?"

"Go figure, huh?"

"I don't want to leave him," she said quietly.

"I know."

"I love that idiot."

"I know."

"It hurts, Lowell. It hurts so fucking bad. But I can't. I just can't."

"I know."

I hugged her for a long time while she cried on my shoulder.

I was getting ready to leave when Ullr found me. He helped me saddle the horse and stow my gear without saying a word. Manny fluttered up onto the pommel. I held my hand out and Ullr clasped my forearm.

"You can ride with me to Asgard if you like," I said. "I wouldn't mind the company."

"As much as I would like to see Ydalir again, that will have to wait."

"Oh?"

"I'm taking Esme back to Midgard. To this Chick-a-go where she lives."

"Chicago. You're in for a bit of shock. Midgard has changed a lot since you were last there. Especially the modern cities like Chicago."

"Maybe it's time I caught up with those changes."

"You're going to stay a while, aren't you? For her."

"Ydalir will still be there in thirty or forty years."

"A blink of the eye for you, but a lifetime for her," Manny cawed.

"You're serious," I said, trying not to let my jaw hit the ground. "It's going to be harder than you think to adapt. A lot harder."

"Esme will help me," he said.

"You're going to let a woman help you?"

"Esme. I'm going to let Esme help me," he said. "If that's the price to win her heart, I'll do it. I once tracked a winter wolf for nine months, and through a blizzard. I can do this."

"You have her heart, you idiot," I said. "It's her mind you need to win over."

"Then that is what I'll do," he said, shrugging.

"Midgard lifespans are longer than they were a thousand years ago. You might have to live there for fifty or sixty years."

"Maybe I can persuade her to spend the summers in Ydalir."

"She might go for that."

Once he was around the corner, I sought out the threads that bound us. Threads that I hadn't ever been able to see before. I could barely see them now. Idunn's gift had left a small crack open inside me and I had the urge to explore it. I tugged and twisted. Then I heard him cursing. I didn't know what exactly I had caused to happen, but it was probably something like his pants falling down. As I guided my horse out of the stable, my saddle slowly slid around the horse, dumping me on the ground. That son of a bitch.

41

PEACE

I rode into Asgard alone. Just me. Nobody else. Well, other than my horse. And my crow. Well, he was his own crow, but he hung out with me. On the inside I was chanting "I ain't afraid of anything. Not nobody, not no how." On the outside I was the picture of haughty confidence. That was me. The Cowardly Lion of Asgard.

I got all the way to Valhalla before I was confronted. Magni and Modi stood on the steps of Odin's massive hall. I guess it was Thor's hall now. Now as in for the past nine hundred plus years. Assuming he lived. Maybe it was Sif's hall now. That would be interesting.

With an effort I pulled my mind back to matters at hand. Neither of Thor's sons looked to be worse for wear after the battle. Magic has its benefits. That and Idunn's fruit. Of course, Modi had fled like a coward, so he likely hadn't been wounded at all. Both were in chain mail, geared up for a fight. Magni held a large maul set head down on the ground. Modi carried a large battleaxe in both hands.

"What do you want, traitor?" Magni asked.

"I'm here to negotiate terms," I said as imperiously as I could.

"Terms?" Modi asked, surprised. "You've come to surrender?"

"Jotunheim won the battle of Utgard."

"Asgard will never surrender to the giants!" Magni said fiercely.

"Peace talks, you idiots. I'm here to negotiate the terms of a truce."

"I don't trust him," Modi said. "This is just a trick to let the jotnar into Asgard. We should kill him."

"No," Magni said firmly. "That's for Sif to decide."

"We are Thor's sons," Modi said, hotly. "We don't bow to a woman. Not even Sif. We should be the ones on the throne, not her."

"Thor sits on the throne. Sif is just his regent until he recovers. When he recovers, do you want to tell him we didn't obey her?"

I interrupted their back and forth, "While it's really swell of you guys to greet me and share your misogynist views, I really do need to get these negotiations started."

I swung off the horse and strode past them. I pushed and twisted at the ghostly curled probabilities around them. It was so much harder now, especially against aesir. Behind me they fell with a clatter into a tangled heap, apparently having tripped over each other trying to stop me. I hoped they wouldn't take it out on my horse.

My arms were shaky from that bit of mischief as I pushed open the doors. The hall was the same as before, but emptier. The courtiers were out and about doing courtier things, like hiding. Sif sat on Hlidskjalf talking softly with Frigg. Those two were still thick as thieves.

"My lady Sif," I said loudly as I approached.

They stopped talking and glared at me, neither particu-

larly surprised. Sif wore a simple silver crown, very under-
stated. Her golden hair was piled high inside it in an elegant
bun of sorts, and fine battle leathers dyed pure white. She
looked very chic.

I went down on one knee and bowed my head, "I've come
to discuss terms of peace between Jotunheim and Asgard."

"You mean terms of surrender," Frigg said bitterly.

"Why does everyone assume that?" I said with sigh,
getting to my feet.

"There can never be peace between Jotunheim and
Asgard," Frigg said. "You saw to that."

"Never is a big word, even for the aesir."

"I'll hear you out," Sif said.

"My lady!" Frigg cried.

"A good general knows when the war is over," Sif said,
looking down at her.

"Loki brought the giants to our front door. He's responsible for the death of Odin, my husband and your liege. He
almost killed Thor, your husband. Twice! The jotnar are our
enemies. It has always been that way."

"Maybe so, but always is also a big word."

"There is no peace with them," Frigg said vehemently.
"The only way we can have peace is if we kill them all. Every
last one of them."

"Lady Frigg, I think you should leave us for a while," Sif
said.

"But... with him? It's not safe."

"Nevertheless."

"But—"

"Now."

Fuming, Frigg turned and stomped away. I tried to tweak
her lines, but her power and fury shrugged me off. Can't win
them all.

It didn't take long for Sif and I to come to terms. Ylva's offer was generous. Too generous, if you ask me. Sif would have been a fool to turn it down.

Both sides stick to their own worlds. No incursions of any kind. Jotnar guards would be posted on the Asgard side of the moon bridge and aesir guards would be posted on the Jotunheim side. Since it only appears once a month, a surprise invasion was almost impossible.

Every summer solstice Ylva and Sif would meet to discuss any issues. Figuring out how to make each side feel safe for that meeting consumed most of our time. The first meeting would be to discuss what to do about Thor. Sif had lost no sleep over his condition, but she knew the aesir only accepted her rule while he still lived. At least for now.

Afterward, I sought out Frigg in Sessrumnir, her large, beautiful hall. I wandered from room to room, constantly observed by a seemingly endless herd of cats. I finally found her on a broad balcony overlooking the now empty field of Folkvangr, with her handmaidens in attendance.

"Lady Frigg."

"Loki," she said bitterly. "Come to gloat?"

"Maybe a little."

"Leave us," Frigg said to her ladies. As they filed out, Fulla gave me an appraising look.

"Crow while you can, Loki. Eventually Folkvangr and Valhalla will fill up again. Midgard warriors die faster than filthy jotnar can breed."

"True," I admitted. "But you will never again see that many at your disposal."

"It will take some time, but we have time."

"You mistake me, Lady. You see, I made a bargain with my daughter before I came to Asgard."

"Hel? What do you mean?"

"The spirits that fill your halls do so by her bidding. She alone has the ear of Yggdrasil."

"The Valkyries gathered warriors for Valhalla and Folkvangr long before you and Angrboda spawned that monster. Buri and Bor laid out the magic for them after the aesir first arrived."

"I don't know the early history of the aesir, although that statement is intriguing. But I do know that it has been Hel's purview for well over a millennia."

"What are you driving at, Loki?"

"Hel has agreed to limit Valhalla and Folkvangr to nine hundred and ninety-nine warriors each. Yggdrasil has consented."

"What!"

"Yes. We believe it to be enough to defend Asgard from outside threats. Yet it will be too small to use to invade any of the other worlds."

"You can't do that!"

"Well, technically I didn't. Hel did. But she still has a fondness for her father and his people."

"This is outrageous!"

"I'll tell you what is outrageous. Outrageous is sending assassins to kill me in Midgard. Outrageous is holding Queen Alfhildr's granddaughter hostage. Outrageous is drugging Thor to keep him weak."

Frigg turned white. "Don't tell Sif. You can't let her know."

That last part had been a guess on my part. With more than nine hundred years to work on him, Frigg and Idunn should have been able to cure anything. The fact that Thor still hadn't fully recovered after all that time was just inconceivable.

"Sif has already agreed to release Alfhildr's heir," I said.

"But I think you'd sooner have me tell her all that than tell her what you did to her."

"Wha... what do you mean?" Frigg stammered. She was looking even paler, if that were possible.

"I never really believed the aesir to be gods. I still don't. We're people with special powers. Powers that those of the other worlds don't have. Powers somehow tied to the natural world. I've come to have a better appreciation for what we are."

"We were worshiped by the humans of Midgard," Frigg said nervously, but with a touch of haughty pride. "We were their gods. They bowed down to us and gave us tribute, as they should."

"True. But the primitive Vikings didn't know any better. Midgard has come a long way since then. Still, you've distracted me from what I was saying. You found a way to change an aesir's power. To change someone's fundamental nature. To change Sif. She used to care about family, hearth, and home. Her powers used to revolve around those things."

"We didn't need another goddess of fertility and family," she spat. "There must be half a dozen aesir gods for that. With Tyr dead, we needed a goddess of war."

"So you made her over. I cannot even imagine the spell it took to do that. Obviously she didn't know what you did to her. It must have taken decades to accomplish. Only the greatest sorceress of all time could have done it."

"Centuries," Frigg said proudly. "It took centuries."

"And doing so changed you as well," I said. "Were you even aware of that?"

She turned pale again.

"It was probably an unspoken price for the magic you cast on Sif. You yourself were once a goddess of fertility, as well as love and beauty. Now you just have affinities for beauty, death, and vengeance. Especially vengeance."

"No," she whispered. I could see the wheels turning as she saw her inner self in the internal mirror I held up to her.

"Oh, yes," I said with an unsympathetic chuckle. "You paid a heavy price to get vengeance on your enemies. On Jotunheim. On me. And you lost."

"I suppose you're going to kill me now."

"No. Don't get me wrong, I want to. I really want to. But I promised Ullr I wouldn't. And it would break my newly-forged treaty with Sif. Oh, and by the way, I already let her know what you did to her. She isn't likely to take your counsel any time soon. So you'll just have to live with the stink of your own failure. And the constant reminder of your loss every time you look over these mostly empty fields. And if you try anything remotely like this again, I'll finish your son Thor for good. He isn't part of the treaty."

EPILOGUE

The crow left Loki back on Midgard, puttering around on his houseboat. His world was restored to its new normal. Or so he thought.

Muninn didn't understand how Loki could leave behind his heritage for a life among mortals.

The wind lifted his black wings as they caught a thermal and rose above the water. All around the shore the houses and docks of the short-lived humans clustered like endless sores on the buttocks of Midgard. Muninn wondered how Loki could cherish these short lived, ignorant masses.

It didn't matter. The bird's purpose was memory. He remembered. He remembered it all. Aesir, jotnar, the people of Midgard, they can all lose track of a memory. Not Muninn. The concept of forgetting was baffling to him.

A memory is there and then it's not. Where did it go? Incomprehensible.

His trip would be quick. He knew of ways and paths long forgotten. Ways that fewer souls than the number of talons on his claws knew. But he remembered. How could he not?

Hel was already with him.

The long dead one-eyed king sat in his rustic home looking weary and threadbare. She sat at his feet, wearing her child's form.

"It's time, Valfodr," she said.

"Do not call me that name."

She canted her head to look up at him curiously. "You lost the right to Alfodr centuries ago. I only call you by your rightful title."

"So now you insult me by calling me Father of the Slain? After I have given you so much?"

"You gave me nothing. We bargained. You entered into the pact fairly and with full knowledge."

"I was dead. I was desperate. The bargain is nullified. You cannot claim me."

"Father of lies to the end," Hel said with a deep sigh. "Muninn, I call upon you as witness to remind the Valfodr of his debt."

"I, Muninn, eldest of the Thegnratad, vouchsafed the bargain between the Alfodr and Hel, sealed in spirits. The Alfodr shall reveal all his secrets, pass on all his knowledge, and train the supplicant Hel in all his sorceries. In exchange she shall let him keep the full measure of his spirit while within her halls, and when he has no more to teach, she shall assist him in bringing about one last epic battle the likes of which shall rival Ragnarokkr."

Odin looked at the crow venomously. He saw a traitor. But Muninn could only be what he was. No more, no less. There was no room for falsehood in the house of memory.

"I kept your spirit fully aware. I put you into the dreams of your wife, Frigg. I nudged and jostled fate to fall in your favor. And finally, I gave you your battle. You have nothing left to teach me. It's time."

"No."

"Silly man, I wasn't asking," Hel said, standing.

She didn't gesture. There were no eldritch lights, no thunderclap. The bird just watched the light fade from his eyes as his spirit diminished. Not completely. Just to the same lost-soul state of the other spirits of her domain. After all, he was still remembered by millions across all the Nine Worlds.

Hel put her hand on his cheek fondly. He briefly looked at her, confused. With a sad but satisfied little smile, she skipped out of the house singing a child's ditty lost to the memory of almost all living creatures.

Muninn waited, watching Odin stare at nothing.

Time went by. Less time than it takes the sun to traverse the sky.

With a flutter of wings the bird's twin landed on the sill of the open window.

"Huginn," Muninn cawed. "It's time for us to fulfill our bargain."

"Indeed. I thought so."

Muninn hopped onto one of Odin's sagging shoulders. Huginn hopped onto the other. In unison they touched his temples with their beaks. Muninn poured Odin's memories back into him. Huginn refilled his empty thoughts.

Time went by. Less time than it takes the moon to traverse the sky.

Finally, they were done.

"It's good to be me again," Odin said with a crafty smile.

The End of *Mischief Maker*

Please leave a review – they buoy my spirits and keep me motivated while writing the next book.

Follow me on Amazon to be notified of my next book.

APPENDIX: NORSE MYTHOLOGY AND LANGUAGE

This story draws on Norse mythology and culture. Throughout, I have attempted to explain terms and concepts as I introduce them without interfering too much in the storytelling.

I'm including this primer. While I have tried my best to be historically accurate, I don't pretend to be an expert on such things. Consider any errors to be literary license. I certainly took great license in the writing of this tale and put my spin on many of the things below.

The Nine Worlds

Norse cosmology centers on the world tree, Yggdrasil. This mighty ash connects the Nine Worlds that formed the universe. A modern reader could think of each world as a separate dimension.

1. **Asgard** is the world of the gods, where Odin, Thor, Loki, and all the others lived.
2. **Vanaheim** is the world of the old gods, presumably a pantheon that was usurped and

replaced by the Norse gods we know now. Very little is known about Vanaheim.

3. **Jotunheim** is the realm of the giants, sworn enemies of the gods. The giants were usually depicted as clever but barbaric. Interestingly they were often more clever than the Norse gods.

4. **Alfheim** is home to the light elves, the alfar, creatures of nature and magic.

5. **Nidavellir** is the world of the dark elves, the dvergar, master craftsmen and smiths. Over time Germanic mythology changed them into dwarves.

6. **Midgard** is the world of men.

7. **Hel**, or Helheim, is the place of the dead, and is ruled by Hel, one of Loki's three monstrous children. Not to be confused with the Christian hell.

8. **Niflheim** is the world of primordial ice and cold. Nothing lives there, but it is part of the creation myth.

9. **Muspelheim** is the land of primordial fire and heat where the fire giants are said to live. It is also part of the creation myth.

The Norse Gods

The Vikings didn't worship gods in the way modern people do. There were no churches or temples to them, and no priests or holy men. The Norse people venerated their gods and dedicated deeds and places to them, in exchange seeking their blessings. They were seen as supernatural protectors, although not wholly trustworthy ones.

The genealogy of the gods is complicated; many have giants in their family trees, including Odin, while others had children by multiple women. It is impractical to list all the gods and goddesses, however what follows are some of import.

- **Baldr** is the son of Odin and Frigg, the most beautiful and beloved of all the gods. Loki tricked Baldr's blind brother Hodr into killing him.
- **Freyr**, also known as Yngvi, is the twin brother of Freya, also known as Frigg. He is the god of wealth, harvests, and virility. As a child, he is gifted with all of Alfheim. Freyr is killed by Surtur at Ragnarokkr.
- **Frigg** is the wife of Odin and most likely the same as the goddess Freya. She is a Vanir master of magic and associated with foresight, and she had several children, including Thor and Baldr.
- **Heimdall** watches over the Bifrost Bridge, which connects Asgard to the other worlds. When Loki leads the giants over the bridge to attack Asgard, Heimdall warns them by blowing his horn. Loki and Heimdall kill each other at Ragnarokkr.
- **Hel** is one of Loki's three monstrous children; the others are the wolf Fenrir and the Midgard serpent Jormungandr. She rules over the world of Hel where most of dead end up.
- **Idunn** is the goddess of youth and rejuvenation who grows the golden apples that give the gods their immortality. Apples weren't known to the Vikings, so the type of fruit was likely altered to apples by Christian historians.
- **Loki** is not actually aesir, being half giant by birth. He is a trickster god accepted by the aesir until he goes a step too far by insulting all the gods at once and getting chained to a rock. Eventually he

escapes and starts Ragnarokkr, where he and Heimdall kill each other.

- **Magni** and **Modi** are two of Thor's sons. Magni is famed for his strength.
- **Odin** is the foremost of the gods, also known as the All Father, or Alfodr in Norse. Together with his brothers Vili and Ve, he created the world from the corpse of the frost giant Ymir. Odin is a god with many spheres of influence, including knowledge, magic, battle, and the gallows. Odin died at Ragnarokkr, swallowed by the great wolf Fenrir.
- **Thor** is the god of storms and strength, the son of Odin and Frigg and the protector of humanity. He only had one child by his wife Sif, Thrudr the Valkyrie. Thor died at Ragnarokkr, poisoned by the Midgard serpent Jormungandr.
- **Sif** is the wife of Thor and is associated with the earth and agriculture. Not much is said about her in the stories beyond a tale where she lost her hair and gained a wig made of gold.
- **Sigyn** is the wife of Loki, and mother to two of his children, Narfi and Nari, who are killed cruelly to imprison Loki.
- **Tyr** is the god of war, and son of Odin by an unknown mother. He lost his hand to Fenrir when the gods chained that giant wolf. Tyr is killed at Ragnarokkr.
- **Ullr** is the god of archery and skiing. Sif was his mother, but Thor was not his father.

Races in the Norse Language

The grammar of old Norse has some oddities. I've used a few of them for flavor.

- **Alfr vs. Alfar**: Alfr refers to an individual light elf, whereas alfar is for multiple light elves or as an adjective for things that are elvish.
- **Dvergr vs. Dvergar**: Dvergr refers to an individual dark elf, and dvergar refrences multiple dark elves or is an adjective for things that are dark elvish.
- **Jotunn vs. Jotnar**: Jotunn is an individual giant, while jotnar refers to multiple giants or is an adjective for things that are giantish.

ACKNOWLEDGEMENTS

The Mischief Maker team Includes Beta Readers and Proofreaders - with my deepest gratitude!
Micky Cocker
James Caplan
Kelly O'Donnell
John Ashmore

NOTES FROM THE PUBLISHER

If you liked this book, we ask that you leave a review. Kind words are good words and help keep us motivated while slogging through the next book.

If you liked this book, you may like some of the other books published by Craig Martelle, Inc. Stop by https://craigmartelle.com and take a look. We appreciate the time you took to read this book. Even if you don't read one of ours, keep reading. It helps us all to be better.

AUTHOR'S NOTES

If you are reading this, you are a special person to me. You've read my book and thought enough of it to bother to read these author's notes. Thank you! If I could, I would have a personal conversation with everyone who finished it. But since that is not possible, I've written these notes. Hopefully, you'll get some insight into what went into the making of *Mischief Maker*.

This story got its genesis with the saying, "history is written by the victors." What if that applied to the stories in Norse mythology? What if Loki wasn't the villain he's been made out to be? That rabbit hole yawned wide and dark before me, and I gleefully dived in.

I'm an avid background researcher when I'm writing. I already knew a lot about Norse mythology. But I wanted to get into the details. I read several books. I reread all the myths. I devoured everything Wikipedia had to say. I wanted the story to have solid foundation in what we understand about Viking culture and Norse mythology. I even started a D&D campaign based on Norse mythology. Unbeknownst to my players, I used it to try out some of my ideas. I owe Bastion, Ivar, Raelyn, Trevale, and Ulf a big thank you.

As is frequently the case when I create stories, I knew the beginning and I knew the end. Linking the two was going to be the hard work. I started by creating a list of moments, memorable scenes, and events that I knew I wanted to include. From there I made a chapter-by-chapter outline. Yes, I'm one of those authors.

I've spent decades creating worlds and making stories. I worked at TSR, Inc. as a game designer. I authored several game worlds and many adventures for them. Later I joined Bethesda Softworks where I worked as a designer in their storied Elder Scrolls and Fallout games. I learned a lot about how to build worlds and write stories.

The character of Loki came easily. He's such an iconic personality. But he needed to be softer and more vulnerable than the Loki of the myths. Most mythological characters are very two dimensional. The heroes are always heroic, and the villains are always villainous. But that's not real life, and I wanted my characters to feel like real people.

To survive over nine hundred years of human history, Loki would have to change and adapt as times changed. He would have to become a modern man over and over again. His attitudes about things like religion, race, gender, and sexuality would have to adapt. I used these as themes in the story. But the primary theme is about divinity and what it means to be a god.

At one time, Loki accepted the idea that the aesir were gods. It is only with a modern perspective that he would be able to see them as people too. People with hopes and fears and desires. People with flaws. But still people with other worldly powers. But not himself, of course. No, never him. That would mean looking a little too hard into the mirror. However, we can only avoid looking in the mirror for so long. In Loki's case, Odin helped him see that being a god isn't necessarily what he had always assumed it was.

For more information on this and other books by Bruce Nesmith, you can find him at his Amazon Author Page - https://www.amazon.com/Bruce-Nesmith/e/B08YKG3DM4/ Or on Facebook - https://www.facebook.com/Bruce-Nesmith-Author-103769655138160